LARRY BOND'S
FIRST TEAM

ANGELS
OF WRATH

**Forge Books by
Larry Bond and Jim DeFelice**

Larry Bond's First Team
Larry Bond's First Team: Angels of Wrath

LARRY BOND'S FIRST TEAM

ANGELS OF WRATH

LARRY BOND AND JIM DEFELICE

A TOM DOHERTY ASSOCIATES BOOK

NEW YORK

LARRY BOND'S FIRST TEAM: ANGELS OF WRATH

A Forge Book
Published by Tom Doherty Associates, LLC
175 Fifth Avenue
New York, NY 10010

www.tor.com

Forge® is a registered trademark of Tom Doherty Associates, LLC.

ISBN 0-765-30712-X
EAN 978-0-765-30712-5

First Edition: January 2006

Printed in the United States of America

0 9 8 7 6 5 4 3 2 1

For the world's real Father Tim Caseys, of all faiths and beliefs

PROLOGUE

And I heard a great voice out of the temple saying to the seven angels,
Go your ways, and pour out the vials of the wrath of God upon the earth.

—Revelation 16:1 (King James Version)

SUBURBAN VIRGINIA

"Bless me, Father, for I have sinned. It has been about ten years since my last confession."

Father Tim Casey jerked upright in the confessional and turned toward the plastic window shielding the penitent's face. The shadow was as recognizable as the voice. "Ah, faith, and it's a wonder the good Lord himself doesn't come down from the cross right now and strike you dead for yer sins, Ferg," he said. "A true wonder."

"Aren't you supposed to be making the sign of the cross right about now?"

"Don't be jokin' about a thing like this. You're a good Catholic lad now, or were, upon a time."

"Never," said Bob Ferguson, shifting his weight on the kneeler in the confessional. "But I did go to Catholic school. One of the priests there taught me a confession has to be heard."

"Oh, all right then. Tell me your sins. Leave out the venial ones; I expect they're legion."

"Alphabetical order?"

"Here you have me believing you're serious," said the priest, "and then you're committing sacrilege. There'll be no mercy for you at St. Peter's gate. He'll be adding ten years to your stay in purgatory for riding me today."

"I'm serious. What order do you want?"

"Any order will do." The door on the other side of the confessional opened, and Father Casey recognized the faithful sighs of Mrs. DeGarmo, an eighty-two-year-old widow who came every Saturday to confess the misdeeds of her youth. The wooden walls of the confessional were thin, and Ferguson's voice carried a good distance; Father Casey decided he would have to seek a change of venue. "I'll tell you what now, Ferg, it might be better for you to hold your peace and wait for me until regular hours end. Then we can speak at our leisure, as seriously as you want."

"How about Murph's?"

"I was thinking about the side altar, lad."

"I'm buyin'."

"Faith, if temptation isn't everywhere, even in the confessional," said Father Casey.

"Not up to it?"

"I've the five o'clock this evening."

"It's only two."

"All right then," said the priest. "Given that I haven't had lunch and you were a decent student once. A half hour."

Casey started to close the window.

"Hang on," said Ferguson. "What's my penance?"

"I haven't heard your confession yet. Surely I taught you there's no advance credit."

"What if I die before you hear my confession?"

"Your time isn't that short," said the priest. "Ah, all right. Say three Our Fathers and Two Glory-Be's, and we'll consider it a down payment. May the Good Lord have mercy on your soul—and on mine."

NEW MEXICO

When the phone rang, the man sitting on the couch waited until the seventh ring to answer, even though he had been waiting for the call all day.

"Yes," he said, his tone flat, neither asking nor answering.

"When?" said the caller.

"Three days."

"Too soon."

"We cannot control the timing," said the man, struggling to keep his tone neutral.

"Next week is not good."

The man closed his eyes, conjuring the vision that reassured him: angels with golden trumpets raced above the clouds, light raining down on the earth. Fire burned in the sky, and from each corner of the earth came an angel.

"It is already in motion," he said calmly.

"Very well."

"Very well," echoed the man, hanging up the phone.

CORSICA

There was no God.

Aaron Ravid stared at the folded photo of his wife and son, dead nearly eighteen months. They'd been on a bus in a Jerusalem suburb when an Islamic suicide bomber from the West Bank detonated herself, killing five and wounding eight others. Ironically, three of the dead had been Muslims, including Ravid's wife.

For Ravid, the attack was the final sign that the faith he'd been born into was empty at its core, a tradition rather than a religion. God did not exist, for if He did, He would not take the lives of innocents. God could only be an invention of man: a way to justify murder, and wrath, and unspeakable crimes.

Ravid lay the photograph on the table and turned his attention back to the reason he had pulled it out from his wallet. At the lower right-hand corner of the page in the Sunday newspaper sat a small advertisement, boxed with a double rule. It asked an outrageous price for an old clunker of a car, and gave a number Ravid knew to be disconnected. Few people on the island would have use for the old VW featured in the ad, and most likely no one would bother to try the number. But that was all right; the ad's real purpose was to summon Ravid to Tel Aviv, to meet with his Mossad control.

It had been more than a year since he had been in Israel, and longer than that since he had spoken to his superiors. Immediately after the attack, his supervisor had told him to rest, and until today he did not believe that he would ever be called back. A small but decent sum appeared in a bank account each month, providing for his simple needs.

Ravid reconsidered the meeting. He had not been told to rest. He had been told he was not needed and would not be needed.

"You will not be called upon," Tischler said when they met in the secure room. He said it quietly and quickly, without even offering condolences as a prelude. No agent, especially one groomed to walk among the enemy as Ravid had been, could be relied on once his emotions were "exposed."

A curious way to put it, Ravid thought then, especially as his cover as a Palestinian intellectual had been maintained. But it proved apt. The deaths of his family had torn the skin from his face, leaving his blood vessels and bones open to the air. The Mossad would not take chances unnecessarily, and a man who had suffered as Aaron Ravid had suffered was an unnecessary risk.

Ravid had been planted at great effort and expense in Syria, where at the time of his family's murder he had a job as a university professor occasionally used by the Syrian government and the Palestinian Authority as a low-level diplomat. Ravid regularly met with members of the Syrian intelligence service and the so-called political arm of Hamas. (They were all murderers at heart, but Ravid brushed shoulders primarily with men who used their brains and mouths rather than their hands to kill.)

More to protect the people who had helped him than to maintain his cover, Ravid had returned to Syria after the meeting with his Mossad supervisors. There he finished out the semester, lecturing for several weeks on Islamic history, before applying for an unpaid sabbatical. This was readily granted; his colleagues at the school knew that he was a "committed Muslim" and would spend the time furthering the cause.

Such a man might have good reason to disappear for a year or even more, but the day Ravid left Syria he expected never to return. He believed his days as an undercover agent for Israel were over. The nerve that had once been a taut steel wire binding his chest had melted under the fire of his grief. His courage turned to liquid and evaporated.

He fled to Corsica, an island where he knew no one and no one knew him. For many months, he drank to survive. Now he simply drank: vodka in the morning, vodka in the afternoon, vodka in the evening.

Ravid stared at the advertisement. If they were calling him this way rather than simply dispatching a low-level messenger to Corsica, there could only be one reason: they needed him in Syria again. The message implicit in the ad was that he must assume the identity of Fazel al-Qiam once more.

Ravid began to laugh. The sound bounced off the stones of the eighteenth-century house, strange and foreign; it seemed to belong to someone else.

Yes, it must. Aaron Ravid was no longer capable of laughter.

If they wanted him back as Fazel al-Qiam, it would only be for something critically important. An assassination, perhaps, or something even greater.

Revenge?

Not for him. To avenge his wife's death alone would take something colossal. And to avenge his son's . . . there was no possibility. It could not be measured. Wipe out Mecca, destroy Medina, wipe Islam off the face of the earth. Would that suffice?

If he still believed in God, perhaps it would. But the belief now was as foreign as the sound of his laughter, still ringing in his ears.

Ravid reached for the vodka bottle on the table. As he did, the newspaper caught against his arm and pushed against the bottle, knocking it over. Vodka lapped out onto the floor. As he reached to right it, anger seized him and he took the bottle and threw it against the wall. The stench of alcohol stung the air.

"I will leave today," Ravid said, rising, his mind already sorting through the arrangements he would need to make.

SUBURBAN VIRGINIA

Ferguson waved from his chair at the far end of the bar as Father Casey came in through the side door. The priest was not unknown here, especially on Saturday afternoon during the college football season, and it took him a few minutes to make it over to Ferg, who was about half way through a Guinness. Casey's collar, bald head, and priestly demeanor made him seem like sixty or older, but the priest was barely in his forties. He had been fresh from Ireland and the seminary when he met Ferguson at the Catholic prep school twelve years before. Casey had taught Ferguson about Plato and Aristotle, coached him in lacrosse, and shared a thought or two about the lamentable degradation of penmanship since the introduction of the computer; the most important lessons were of a deeper nature and were ongoing.

"Notre Dame is getting squashed," Ferguson said, pointing at the television as the priest sat down. "Quarterback can't throw to save his life."

"Aye, and didn't I tell you to go to the school? You would've had all the records. You'd be in the NFL by now."

"And you'd be on the sideline, right?" Ferguson had sprouted a few more inches from the seventy he'd stood as the prep school's quarterback, but his frame remained on the trim side, and he would have been small even for a college quarterback. More important, he would have been bored most of the week. "I ordered some chicken wings," he told the priest. "Extra hot."

"Ah, you know I can't eat them, Ferg, much as I'd like."

"Yeah, I know. I got you some bread and a beer."

"Well, thank you for that." Father Casey turned and nodded at the barmaid, who was pouring a Guinness for him.

"And a filler-upper for me," said Ferguson.

The priest said a quick prayer when the beer arrived, blessing himself before drinking.

"One of life's small pleasures God gave man," said Father Casey, sipping at the light head that topped the dark beer. He'd made the excuse before. "So how are you, Ferg?"

"Not bad today. Yourself?"

"Better than to be expected, thank the Lord."

"Your hair's growing back," said Ferguson, gesturing at the priest's head.

"Not so you'd notice." Father Casey ran his hand over his bald pate. "I'm used to it now. I've been thinking on it. It's not bad for a priest to lose his hair. It makes him look distinguished."

"You were always distinguished."

"Ah, as if it would've helped me with the likes of you and your friends. A hard crew you were, Ferguson. A hard crew: good boys all of you and pistol fast. Too much for me."

"You were a good teacher. The students were the problem," said Ferguson. But Casey was right about his teaching abilities, at least those required in high school. He'd seen the light after a few years and found a berth as a parish priest. Still, Ferguson and the other young men had found the young priest a relief from the Sisters of Charity and the ancient Jesuit priests who held most of the positions at the school.

"It's the ladies I feel sorry for," said Casey. "You see them with their kerchiefs. A hard thing, I think. Especially with the wee ones gaping at you all day. But we get through it. The good Lord tests us, but we get through it. You know how it goes."

Ferguson did know. Both men had cancer, thyroid cancer in Ferguson's case, which had metastasized beyond his thyroid and spread to his lymph nodes before being detected. The treatment of choice in his case was removal and radiation. He'd already done both, and in fact had reached the point where further radiation would have doubtful effect; the prognosis was hopeful or not, depending on which doctor was comparing his case history to which set of statistics.

Casey's disease, pancreatic cancer, was much more virulent than Ferguson's, and, unlike his, a death sentence without potential for remission. The priest would not be hearing earthly confessions six months from now.

"Before I forget—the Youth Soccer League," said Ferguson, pulling a folded envelope from his pocket. "Covers the shortfall. You can end the season."

"You are a saint, Ferg, a true saint."

"I thought you said I was a sinner."

"A man can be both, and sure as I'm sitting here, you're proof of that."

Ferguson laughed. Lunch arrived. Casey ate less than a quarter of his plain piece of bread.

"Do you remember Ryan Dabson?" said Father Casey after the plates were cleared.

"Sure."

"Working for IBM now."

"Oh, there's a surprise," said Ferg, mocking his old classmate.

"I still remember pulling him off of you one practice."

"I'm sure it was the other way around," said Ferguson.

"It might have been," said the priest, "but you wouldn't want to fight him now. You'd be giving away a hundred pounds," warned Casey, who had no idea what Ferguson did, except that he worked for the government. Casey began talking about Dabson, now married and with a little one on the way. The priest had the tone of a proud father, and in Dabson's case, he had every right; he'd surely influenced Dabson more than his biological father, who'd left his mother when Ryan was three. Dabson had attended school with the help of a well-off aunt; when her funds ran low, Casey had arranged a scholarship.

"He's planning a trip to Dublin in a few months. Tried to get me to go," added Casey.

"You ought to," said Ferguson.

"What? To Ireland? I left the country for good when I came here, Ferg. I'll not go back there now, not even to die." He fell silent but only for a moment. "I'll tell ya the place I'd look to go, if I had the chance: Jerusalem."

"Jerusalem?"

"Aye. The Holy Land. Before I shake the mortal coil, to trod where Christ did. Aye, that I would give half my soul to the devil for."

"So go."

"Priests aren't rolling in dough, Ferguson. Not at all."

"Your order won't send you?"

"It's not the sort of thing I'd ask them to do," said Casey. "It would be an abuse of privilege."

"Take that money," said Ferg, pointing at the envelope.

The priest's face blanched. "Jesus, Mary, and Joseph, Ferguson."

"I didn't mean it like that. I meant a rich parishioner might find a way to contribute."

"If it's the present company you're speaking of, you're not a parishioner."

"Relax."

"And you claim not to be rich. If I thought you were, son, I would have been asking you to support the basketball team as well. Now there you would do so much good for some boys who didn't have the choices you had yourself in life."

"Not lacrosse?"

"Can't trust the kids with sticks these days."

Ferguson sipped his beer. Today was his last day off, and his last in the States. It was likely that the CIA agent wouldn't be back for a long time, which meant it could well be the last time he saw Case, as the kids used to call him. "Why would you want to go to Jerusalem?"

" 'Tis the Holy City, Ferg. The place of our good Lord's passion. A special place."

"Sure, if you're a fanatic. The whole Middle East is wall-to-wall with crazies."

"Religion is not fanaticism, Ferguson. We've had this discussion before. I thought you'd have been paying attention. *Belief* is not the fault of God; you can't be blaming God for man's sins. No, sir. Your terrorism is not God's fault. It's blasphemy to say that. A great sin."

"I was just saying it's an interesting place."

"It's a place I'd like to go. Better there than Ireland, of that I'm sure." As a young man, he had seen bad times in Ireland—mother murdered and his father convicted of it—but even he couldn't say why that had turned him toward God. The Lord hadn't appeared to him on a cloud or spoken to him in a darkened room, but he had just as surely been called.

"Jerusalem, huh?" said Ferg, checking his watch.

"Don't get any funny ideas into your head now, son."

"That's all that's in there, funny ideas." Ferguson rose, then pointed at the pocket the priest had put the envelope into. "Make sure there's no name in the bulletin connected with that."

"Your secret's safe with me," said the priest. "You're a blackguard as far as I'm concerned, no truer blackguard in all Christendom." He smiled and gave Ferguson his hand. "Thanks, lad. A lot of kids will be better for it."

"I doubt it. But you don't." Ferguson took a pair of twenties from his pocket and dropped them on the table. "So do you want the mortal sins by category, or can I just hop around?"

ACT I

And the first went, and poured out his vial upon the earth;
and there fell a noisome and grievous sore upon the men
which had the mark of the beast . . .

—Revelation 16:2 (King James Version)

1

"Coming at you, Ferg."

Ferguson made a show of looking at his watch as their subject, a well-dressed man in his early forties walked out of the small cafe on Ben Yedhuda Street, heading southward in the direction of Nakhalat Shiva. Ferguson began walking before the man quite caught up with him, letting him catch up and then pass him. Their subject continued past a row of restored nineteenth century residential buildings before crossing the street and going inside a jewelry store.

"All right, I give up," said Ferguson into the microphone at the sleeve of his shirt. "What the hell is he doing?"

"Got me," said Menacham Stein, the Mossad agent who'd trailed the man out of the cafe. "He's your guy; you tell me."

Ferguson heard Stephen Rankin snicker in the background. He pulled out his tourist guide, leafing through it as if lost. Inside the store, their subject went to one of the side counters and bent over a display: completely innocuous, but then everything he'd done since arriving seemed completely innocuous.

"Hey, Skippy, you in the market for a watch?" said Ferguson, speaking to Rankin.

"Screw yourself, Ferg," said Rankin. He'd been called Skip since he was a kid, but absolutely hated being called *Skippy*. The fact that Ferguson found this amusing irked him even more.

"Make it an expensive one," added Ferg.

Rankin pushed out of the side street where he'd been waiting. Ferguson took a step back on the sidewalk as Rankin approached, watching their subject inside. As far as Ferg could see, he hadn't spoken to the proprietor yet.

Though two inches shorter than Ferguson at five-eleven, Rankin weighed close to forty pounds more. Bulky at the shoulders and with a face that looked as if it belonged to a middle linebacker, he appeared naturally menacing; the owner drew back apprehensively as he entered the shop.

"So, Menacham, this jewelry store a cover for something?" Ferguson asked as he played up his lost-tourist act, fumbling with a map and moving to the side of the street.

"Few jewelers are known for their radical beliefs," replied the Mossad agent. "Maybe he's looking for a good deal on a ring."

Ferguson examined his map. He and two other members of the First Team had trailed Benjamin Thatch to Jerusalem the day before as part of an operation to break up an American group that called itself Seven Angels. The title was a reference to a passage in The Revelation of Saint John the Divine in the Bible concerning the Apocalypse. Based loosely around a church in Santa Fe, New Mexico, the group was dedicated to facilitating the Apocalypse's early arrival and had apparently amassed more than a million dollars to do so. The FBI, which had initiated the case, believed the money would be handed over to radical terrorist groups willing to cause mayhem in the Holy Land.

Some of the briefing papers on the group erroneously identified them as "fanatical Christians." In fact, the members viewed Christianity, as well as Judaism and Islam, as having run its course. Only a few of the group's active members had even been born Christian; the rest came from Jewish, Buddhist, and agnostic backgrounds. They interpreted various scriptures, especially John the Divine's Revelation, to predict a new two-thousand-year millennium of peace . . . built on incredible bloodshed, of course.

Among the many various groups of crazies the FBI kept tabs on, the church had caught their attention not because they looked toward the destruction of holy sites in the Middle East but because an eccentric millionaire had apparently bequeathed them money to encourage it. Failing to penetrate the church's membership, the Bureau had put several of its leaders under surveillance over the past few months. The church's leader had recently declared that the time for the new age to dawn was rapidly approaching. With the exception of some minor currency and tax violations, the Bureau lacked evidence that the group had committed any actual crimes. Then one of the members had made plane reservations to Israel using an assumed name. The man was Benjamin Thatch.

The CIA and the Office of Special Demands had been brought in to help only a week before. In Ferguson's opinion, it was one of the only things the Bureau had done right. They didn't know who Thatch was meeting or exactly where he was going; they didn't even know that much about him, except that he was an accountant.

As the agent in charge of the First Team, Ferguson had high standards. Officially known as the Joint Services Special Demands Project Office, the

First Team was a CIA–Special Forces unit that could call on a wide range of resources, including a combined Ranger/Special Forces task group that had its own specially modified MC-130s. The Team had been created to address unconventional threats in an unconventional way, without interference from the bureaucracy of either the intelligence or military establishments. The arrangement made Ferguson and the men and women who worked with him essentially free agents, and Ferg was a free agent par excellence.

The Mossad had been called in on the Seven Angels project not only because they had a handle on all the radicals in the region but also because it was nearly impossible to run an operation in the Middle East without their knowledge and at least tacit approval. As usual, Ferguson found the Mossad operatives assigned to assist incredibly efficient and utterly dedicated. They were also, he knew, potentially ruthless and ultimately loyal to Israel, *not* the United States.

"Coming out," said Rankin.

Ferg pulled a pair of sunglasses out of his pocket.

"What was he doing?" asked Stein.

"Don't know. Didn't talk to anyone that I saw."

Ferguson bent down, pretending to admire the display in the store he'd stopped in front of. He watched Thatch's reflection as he passed, counted to three, then started to follow.

"Where we heading?" Ferguson asked Stein.

"Not a clue," said the Israeli. His accent had a decidedly Brooklyn flavor to it, a legacy of several years as a case officer in New York City. "You're moving parallel to the Old City, which would be his most likely destination if he were a tourist."

"Maybe he's lost," said Ferg. "It's his first time overseas, let alone here. I was just about born here, and I'm confused."

Ferguson slowed his pace to let Thatch get farther ahead as he crossed the street. He followed at about ten yards as the subject continued to the next intersection and then turned right. A block later, the distance had widened to fifteen yards. Ferguson decided to close it up as Thatch turned right down a side street; he trotted forward, then stopped abruptly at the intersection, momentarily unsure where Thatch was. Cursing silently he started to trot again, then stopped as Thatch appeared in the crowd a few paces ahead. Ferguson followed as the traffic cleared. Thatch waited a moment at the curb for the traffic and crossed, all alone on the block. Ferguson crossed behind him.

A short, frumpy-looking woman wearing a raincoat turned the corner and walked in Thatch's direction.

Someone at the other end of the block shouted. As Ferguson turned to see why, the woman exploded.

JERUSALEM

Ferguson woke up in the ambulance, the siren piercing the sides of his skull.

"I'm OK," he groaned, trying to get up. The attendants had belted him in, and he didn't get very far.

"Just take it easy," said Stein.

Ferguson didn't recognize the voice at first. He tried again to get up. "There some sort of force field holding me down or what?"

"You're strapped in," said Stein.

"Don't want me leaving without paying the bill, huh?"

Stein leaned over Ferguson. "You're going to be all right. You have a concussion and some cuts."

"Yeah, and my leg's missing right?"

"Your sense of humor's intact."

"Already on the road to recovery." Ferguson worked his arms out from under the restraints and undid the belt.

"You think you should do that?" asked Stein as he sat up.

"Probably not." His head pounded like a jackhammer. "Where's Thatch?"

"Gone," said Stein.

"Convenient."

Stein didn't say anything.

"Who was the woman?" Ferguson asked.

"We're working on it. She tried to get on a bus at the corner around the block, but someone saw that she had a raincoat and the sun was out."

So probably, thought Ferguson through the pounding, it was just incredibly bad luck for Thatch. And for them. Maybe the FBI wasn't incompetent; maybe the case was just cursed.

Ferguson brought his legs down to the floor. "All right, let's go."

"Where?"

"Check out his hotel room."

"I'll call your people. You're going to the hospital."

Rankin watched from the end of the block as the Israelis continued to work. Barely an hour had passed since the suicide bomber had blown herself up, and already the cleanup had begun. A truck with two large panes of glass pulled up nearby; after a brief conversation with the driver, the police waved it through the barricade. The area would soon be reopened to traffic, and within a few hours it would be difficult to tell that anything had happened here. This was all part of the Israeli coping mechanism: you dealt with the horror brusquely and moved on quickly.

Besides Thatch and herself, the woman had killed two elderly men walking behind her. About a dozen people had been injured, including Ferguson. As the police continued to interview potential eyewitnesses, Rankin took another walk around the block, trying to decide whether someone could have been acting with the suicide bomber as a lookout. The answer was yes, but even Rankin thought it was unlikely that Thatch had been assassinated in some sort of elaborate plot.

Manson, the FBI agent who'd been in the control van, walked up to Rankin when he returned. He was the ranking FBI agent on the detail to Jerusalem, though the surveillance operation was under Ferguson's direct command. "What do you think?" asked Manson.

Rankin shrugged. "You tell me."

"Crappy luck."

"Yeah."

"Ferguson called from the hospital. He wants us to check out the hotel room. Our forensics people are on the way."

"Yeah. OK, let's do it," said Rankin. "I'll call Guns."

Guns was Marine Gunnery Sergeant Jack "Guns" Young, another First Team member, who had been tasked to stay at Thatch's hotel and see if anyone went into his room.

"You want to stop at the hospital, check on Ferguson?" asked Manson.

"Why?"

Surprised by the sharp, almost bitter tone of Rankin's answer, Manson said nothing.

Rankin's sat phone rang as they drove over. He took it out of his pocket and slowly swung up the antenna. "Rankin."

"What's going on?" asked Jack Corrigan. Corrigan worked back in the States, supporting the First Team from a specially equipped communications bunker known as the Cube. It was located outside of Washington in a Virginia industrial park. The Cube sat below an innocuous-looking building owned by the CIA, officially known as CIA Building 24-442.

"Same as ten minutes ago."

"Thirty," said Corrigan.

"Whatever."

"How's Ferguson?"

"Doc said he'd live. He's already giving orders."

"The Israelis know not to release his name, right?"

"It's their show," Rankin told Corrigan.

"What's that mean, Sergeant?"

Before coming to work for First Team and the CIA, Corrigan had been an officer in special operations, in PsyOp. As far as Rankin was concerned, PsyOp wasn't real fighting; it was trick fighting, lighting, bullshitting. Sissy crap, even if you did get away with it. And of course, Corrigan had been an officer, which meant he didn't do any real work anyway.

"Corrine Alston wants to talk to you," said Corrigan when Rankin didn't answer. "She's worried about Ferg."

"She doesn't have to worry," said Rankin. But he waited for her to come on the line.

"Stephen, what's going on?"

"Looks like some Palestinian whack job blew herself and our subject up. I don't think he was a specific target."

"How's Ferg?"

"OK."

"Corrigan said he was in the hospital."

"He's all right. They're checking him out."

"The embassy will send someone to the morgue to handle Thatch," said Corrine. "Can you get over there with them to see if someone else turns up?"

"Not a problem," Rankin said. She was right; he should have thought of that himself. "I'll get back to you."

Ferguson held his hand up as the nurse approached with the needle. "I don't need it, thanks."

"It's just a painkiller."

"Doesn't look like Scotch." He smiled at her, and, keeping his hand out to ward her off, pushed off the gurney. "You're frowning at me," he said, reaching for the curtains. "Don't do that."

"Of course I'm frowning. You need treatment."

"I've had worse hangovers," said Ferguson. He glanced toward the wall and saw that it was past two o'clock. "Can I have a glass of water? I have to take a pill."

Ferguson reached into his pocket for a small metal case he used to carry his medicine—he took two different types of thyroid hormone replacement drugs every day—and pulled out a small pill.

"Should I ask you what that is?" said the nurse when she returned with a cup.

"I misplaced my thyroid one day," he told her. "Left it with my car keys and couldn't find either. The car was easier to replace."

Stein had just finished talking to some of the other victims who'd been taken here when Ferguson found him.

"Get anything?" Ferguson asked.

"No. Looks pretty random. Fanatics." He shook his head. "They kill their women and children. Life means nothing."

Ferguson had locked eyes with the woman perhaps a half-second before the bomb ignited, maybe at the moment that she had pushed the trigger. He saw them now, blank, questioning—doubt, he thought, not faith.

Am I going to paradise?

Will the bomb go off?

Or maybe he saw none of that. Maybe that was his concussion reinterpreting what had happened. Because, damn, his head hurt.

"Let's go over to the hotel," he told Stein.

G uns watched as the FBI people worked the room. Thatch had left early this morning, and it had been cleaned; still, the three men moved through, meticulously lifting prints from the surfaces and using chemical sniffers to check for traces of explosives and other items. Thatch's suitcase sat on a folding stand near the bed. It contained two pairs of pants, two shirts, three pairs of underwear, one change of socks.

Not enough socks, in Guns's opinion. As a Marine, he'd learned in boot camp to think of his feet before anything else.

"Find it yet?" asked Ferguson, walking into the room. Stein trailed behind him.

"What the hell are you doing here, Ferg?" said Guns. "You're supposed to be checked out."

"The nurses weren't pretty enough to stay."

"Are you all right?" said Manson. The FBI supervisor sounded like a concerned parent.

"I've been better." Ferguson sat in the chair opposite the bed, slowly scanning the room. "No money in the mattress? No microdots?"

"What's a microdot?" said Manson.

"You don't know what a microdot is?"

The FBI agent shook his head.

"Rent some old James Bond movies sometime," Ferguson said. "See how it's supposed to be done."

"This might be something," said one of the forensics people. He brought over a piece of paper containing an image lifted from a pad of hotel paper. By placing the pad in a device similar to a flatbed scanner, they had found an impression left from writing on an upper sheet. The expert gave it to Manson, who passed it to Ferg. It had an address on it.

"So, he was supposed to go to Cairo?" Ferg handed the paper to Stein.

"Cairo wasn't mentioned in the wiretap."

"Maybe he didn't have to."

"You sure that's a Cairo address?"

"Yeah." Ferguson had spent several years off and on in Egypt when his father was based there with the CIA.

"That's not necessarily his handwriting," said the FBI expert.

Stein stared at the address. "It's near the Old City, the Islamic quarter."

"Isn't every quarter in Cairo Islamic?" asked Ferguson.

The Mossad agent smiled wryly, handing back the paper.

EVANSTON, ILLINOIS
LATER IN THE DAY . . .

As Thera Majed got out of the car in front of the suburban Chicago home, she noticed the basketball hoop and backboard over the garage. It reminded her of the hoop on her parents' home in Houston, and she thought of what her parents would feel if someone were coming to tell them she'd been blown up by a fanatic in Jerusalem.

The situation here wasn't precisely parallel. The driveway Thera was walking up belonged to Benjamin Thatch's sister, Judy Coldwell. And Thatch might justifiably be called a fanatic himself.

Thera straightened her skirt, letting the State Department official and the Cook County sheriff's deputy take the lead. The men thought she was with the FBI, a mistake she had encouraged. In actual fact, Thera was a CIA First Team operative working with the FBI on the Seven Angels case. She'd come up from New Mexico primarily because she was the one member of the task force easily spared. The others, all FBI agents, were trailing church members and preparing search warrants to shut down the group. While the Chicago-area FBI agent with her knew she wasn't with the Bureau, he'd been briefed on the sensitivity of the operation and let the misconception stand as well.

Judy Coldwell opened the door as they reached the stoop. "I know why you're here," she announced. "Come in."

Coldwell led them inside to a dining room off the living room. Even if Thera hadn't known from the backgrounder that Coldwell and her husband didn't have any children, she could have read it in the house's pristine order and the ceramic vases that sat on low tables near the side of the room. Coldwell, thirty-six, looked maybe ten years younger. Unlike her older brother, who'd been overweight, she was extremely thin; her five-eight frame might have been suited for modeling had her face been prettier. It had a harshness to it, a bleached asceticism maybe. Thera thought it might come from dieting fanatically, though it could just as easily have been a symptom of suppressed grief.

"My brother and I really weren't that close," said the woman, looking at Thera. "I didn't even know he was overseas. Not until you called."

"That would have been Mary Burns," said the State Department rep. He took charge, telling Coldwell what she already knew: her brother had been killed by a suicide bomber; the Israelis would release the body in a few days, and he would be flown home at their expense.

Coldwell nodded once or twice. Her face remained almost entirely blank, cheeks pinched ever so slightly, as if she smelled a faint odor of vinegar. Only when the sheriff's deputy told her that police protection would be provided if she wanted did she speak.

"I don't believe that would be necessary. Do you?"

"Probably not," agreed the deputy.

Thera watched Coldwell. She was an accountant with a small local practice. Thera thought it a cliché that accountants were more comfortable with numbers than people, but Coldwell seemed to be living proof of it.

Distant rather than uncomfortable, Thera thought. People reacted in different ways to grief; it was difficult to judge them from the exterior.

"I wonder, Mrs. Coldwell," said Thera when the last of the mundane but necessary details of the death and its aftermath had been squared away, "if you'd be willing to help us with an aspect of the situation that may seem a little unusual."

Coldwell blinked at her. "I'm sorry. I've forgotten your name."

"Thera Majed. I'm with a task force. The FBI, as you could imagine, is interested in examining the circumstances as they occurred in Jerusalem." Thera made her answer seem improvised and almost haphazard, though it was anything but.

"The FBI is investigating?" asked Coldwell.

"Our interest is routine. It wouldn't be an official investigation, unless the Israelis made a request."

"Did they?"

"They've asked for some help on our part." Even if they were necessary, Thera disliked having to use weasel words. She wasn't lying exactly, but she was leaving a lot out. "Primarily, in a case like this, the agencies have to make sure that what seems to have happened, did happen."

"Can there be any doubt?"

"It's not really my job to say that." She smiled, as if agreeing with Coldwell that, of course, there could be no doubt at all. "In cooperating with the Israeli government, we would like a few more days before this became public."

"I don't understand what you mean."

"The government of Israel is withholding public confirmation of your brother's identity for forty-eight hours," said Thera. "Just so that everything can be checked out. Our government is prepared to acquiesce."

"Why?"

"As I said, a few days to look into this quietly would be most useful."

"Are you saying my brother wasn't a random victim?"

"I'm not saying that, no. It looks as if he was, but there are questions. The Israelis would like to be sure, and so would we." The Israelis *were* withholding Thatch's name, though at the FBI and CIA's request.

"Was my brother doing something illegal?"

"Do you think he was?" asked Thera.

"I don't. But it sounds to me as if you do."

Thera had reached the point in her script where she had to make a judgment call: what exactly to tell the sister. She could just shrug and pass this off as routine. Or she could gamble that Coldwell might know something that might be useful to the FBI.

Which way to go?

"Have you ever heard of the Church of Seven Angels?" asked Thera.

"What is it? A church? A born-again church?"

"It is a church, but it's not Christian," said Thera, studying the emotionless face across from her. "They're not Christian at all. They consider themselves . . . apart."

Thera struggled for the right word. The church members believed that they were part of a "post-Christian vanguard" in the same position to Christians as Christians were to Jews.

"Your brother flew several times a year to New Mexico to attend services," said Thera. "It seems that he may have gone to Jerusalem on their behalf."

"On some sort of tour?"

"No. Business."

"For a church? Were they his clients?"

Thera sidestepped the question. "You wouldn't happen to know why he decided to go to Jerusalem, would you?"

"No."

"Did he talk about going?"

"We really haven't been that close."

"Did Benjamin know anyone in Jerusalem? Or Cairo?"

"I couldn't tell you. Maybe from the Rotary Club. He's an accountant."

"Like yourself?" said Thera.

Coldwell smiled ever so slightly. "Maybe it's in the genes."

Outside, Thera walked past the local FBI agent's Crown Victoria and pulled out her satellite phone to talk to Corrigan.

"I think we're good," she told him. "She's not going to talk to the media."

"You sure?"

"I didn't ask her to sign a contract, Jack. It's a gut call. The FBI tapped her phone; they'll let us know if something is up."

"Tapped the phone? Is that necessary?"

"Not my call, Jack. This is the FBI's case. They want to make the arrests as soon as they can."

"What are you doing now?" Corrigan asked.

"I'll go back to New Mexico. I might as well be there for the arrests."

"I thought they didn't have much of a case."

"They don't. But that's never stopped the FBI before."

When the intruders were gone, Judy Coldwell went back to the dining room and cleaned off the table. She took the cups and saucers inside to the kitchen, placing them carefully in the dishwasher. She did the same with the silverware. She measured the detergent carefully as she always did, using a spoon. As the prewash cycle began, she went to the dining room and removed the cloth from the table, taking them down the hall to the laundry room. Life required a certain meticulous order; tasks great and small were best performed immediately.

Only when that was done did she open the drawer to retrieve the tiny medallion, the lone token of her brother she possessed in the world. It looked like a twelve-sided dime nestled amid the silver corn cob holders. Coldwell took it out and pressed it into the palm of her hand, hard enough to make an impression, hard enough to sear her soul.

Benjamin's death hadn't seemed real until the intruders arrived. But now it was very real.

The intruders had tripped over themselves trying to describe the church. They were so wedded to the old age, the ways that had dominated for the past two thousand years that the coming age was beyond their vocabulary. Calling the Seven Angels Christian was like calling Christians Jews. Yes, there were intersections, but the Seven Angels were no closer to Christians—or Jews or Muslims—than they were to Buddhists. They recognized the old age had ended and were dedicated to the new.

The words of the Christian Bible *did* predict the changes to come, for in the old there are always the seeds of the new. But the Christians in their blindness did not know how to interpret the words they themselves held dear.

The Book of the Apocalypse mentioned seven vials: seven wars. These would begin in the Holy Land, where the other ages had begun. Before the wars had run their course, all of the old holy places—Jerusalem, Nazareth, Mecca, Medina—would be destroyed just as Jerusalem had been torn asunder to signal the birth of Christianity. All that was required was a spark.

Benjamin was to have provided that spark. But the old resisted the new, clinging selfishly to its ways.

Coldwell knew that the intruders were lying about her brother's death being an accident. They might blame a suicide bomber, but surely that was part of a plot to obscure what had happened. The Jews controlled Jerusalem, and it was only natural for them to blame the Muslims. One did not like to jump to conclusions without evidence, but surely some sort of deliberate act had taken her brother's life.

Coldwell despised mendacity, but it strengthened her in a way and even provided some comfort. These people were her enemy. They were powerful, but they were not so strong as they pretended. Nor as knowledgeable. They seemed to have no idea that she, too, was a member of the church. But then that was by design. Judy Coldwell had done much for the church soon after the angels visited the Reverend Tallis and instructed him to start the movement. Her job as an overseas accountant with an energy firm and then an exporter had been based in the Middle East, and her contacts helped lay the groundwork for Seven Angels' early missions. These were primitive and paltry, greatly limited by the group's lack of funds.

That changed when Kevin Durkest became interested in the group. A real estate developer in the Washington, D.C., area, he had been convinced to sell off some of his minimalls and leave the money in various accounts for the group's use. Coldwell did not know all of the details. There were rumors that some of these transactions had occurred after the reclusive Durkest had died, and scandalous talk that Durkest's demise had not been the accident the coroner claimed. But death was of little significance to those who believed, as they would be reborn as high priests in the new age, and so these details were not important to Judy Coldwell. And, in any event, by the time he died, she was no longer close to Tallis and the others, nor did she play a visible role in the church.

Which was not to say that she was no longer a member. Soon after Durkest became involved, the Reverend Tallis had asked her to break her active association with the group and become, in his words, "a sleeper." Such an agent, he predicted, might become necessary in the future as the new age dawned. The old religions might fight back, just as the Jews and Romans had persecuted the followers of Christ.

At first, Coldwell was skeptical. Tallis had never been comfortable with strong women, and she wondered if this was just a ploy to strip her of influence. But her brother convinced her that what Tallis said was true, and after contemplation she agreed that the old religions would surely try to stop the new. And so she stopped associating with the group. She quit her job and took what amounted to an entirely new identity, working for herself in middle America until she was needed. All record of her involvement in the church had been wiped out. She even went as far as to stop communicating directly with her brother, a great sacrifice, as they had been extremely close as children and adults, certainly much closer in her case than her spouse, a boob who fortunately spent much of his time away from home on business. But the sacrifice was of temporal time only; the Reverend Tallis promised that they would be reunited in the new age, and Coldwell knew this to be true.

It would arrive soon, perhaps within the year. The stage was already set for the first war; it would take only a small spark.

Coldwell took the medal with her to the bedroom, where she retrieved a thin silver chain from the bottom of her jewelry box. Slipping the chain through the small hole at the top of the medallion, she placed the medal around her neck, under her shirt. Tears began to slip down her cheek, grief for her brother.

She had a sudden impulse to fly to the Middle East to fulfill Benjamin's mission. But she couldn't, or rather she shouldn't, not without hearing from Tallis. And in any event she didn't know what Benjamin would have been asked to do. She could guess: money or weapons were to be provided to groups eager to make a catastrophic attack on a holy site, be it Jewish, Christian, or Islamic. There were many such groups, ready fools fired by wrath they did not understand.

Wrath was the hallmark of the old age; hatred was its sign: hatred toward other religions, subjugation of other races. In the new age, all would be different.

CAIRO
A DAY LATER . . .

Ferguson walked along the long street that paralleled the Cairo meat market, slipping through the knots of tourists and locals. A variety of sharp odors filled the air: cooking spices mixing with diesel fuel and dung. He took a left, then a quick right, turning suddenly to make sure he wasn't being followed.

Ferg's father was a career CIA man, an officer with a long and varied history. By the time Ferguson had come along, most of his real adventures were over and his service in the Middle East was fairly routine. Still, there had been some harrowing times: the alley where he'd been shot in the head was a few blocks away.

He'd been shot, hit, wounded, but lived to tell about it. That was the point of his dad's story, one of the few he told. Anyone could get themselves shot in the head. Living to talk about it was the trick.

Ferguson crossed the street and kept walking, catching a glimpse of Al-Azhar, the grand mosque and university, before following a zigzag to the address on Radwan.

The address belonged to a *kahwa*, or coffee shop, a gathering place that didn't figure prominently in any of the Mossad dossiers about Cairo activity. Though the CIA regularly cooperated with Egyptian intelligence, Ferguson—with approval from CIA Deputy Director, Daniel Slott—had decided not to contact them in this case. The Egyptians were not necessarily the most tight-lipped group in the world and tended to get especially antsy if they thought the Mossad was involved.

For its part, the Mossad had agreed to provide only "distant support": fake IDs and some equipment. Which was fine with Ferguson; it was safer to keep them at arm's length here. He'd drawn on two CIA officers in Cairo for additional support, one of whom could liaise with the Egyptians if necessary.

Ferguson walked past the building, glancing down the alleyway next to it. The area was popular with tourists; an American such as Ferguson—or Thatch, whose ID Ferg had doctored and was carrying—fit right in. He stopped at a small stand where a man was selling scarves. His Arabic was a little rusty, but the Egyptian inflections he'd heard as a kid came back as he pulled out a long "*laa,*" or "no," to an offer, falling into a rhythm as he negotiated. The seller finally broke the back and forth to launch into a long harangue about the quality of the material, unsurpassed in Egypt and certainly worthy of an American who had shown himself educated enough to speak the language like a native. Ferguson bowed his head gratefully, listening to the lecture without interruption so he could surreptitiously glance around and see if he was being watched.

If so, it wasn't obvious. Ferguson held up three fingers for a price, got another frown, and started to walk away. This resulted in a quick agreement; the merchant solemnized the deal with a tirade of praise for the tourist's negotiating skills, to which Ferguson responded by praising the great artistry of the man's wares. The vendor wished him a thousand lifetimes of pleasure and handed over his purchase.

Ferguson continued ambling around the bazaar. He spotted Rankin and one of the CIA station people buying some food from a man with a small charcoal burner and decided to walk over. He heard their accents, or so it seemed, and introduced himself as a fellow tourist, new in the city, just a tourist, happy to say hello, his name was Benjamin Thatch, and if they were ever in New Mexico and needed an accountant, they should look him up.

Now that he had announced his name for the benefit of any nearby lookouts, Ferguson went into the café. Tourists mixed with locals in the main room. Though it was early in the afternoon, the place was crowded, and Ferguson had to wait for a table, which suited his purpose perfectly. He pulled out a hundred-dollar traveler's check and his passport, asking if it was possible to get the check changed. The cashier obliged, and he managed to say "Thatch" loudly enough that the waiter at the end of the counter waiting for a coffee looked up. Ferguson looked at the money he lost on the exchange rate as an investment.

Shown to a postage stamp of a table at the side of the room, Ferguson ordered *kahwamazboot*, a Turkish coffee with medium sugar. The idea of "medium" was relative; the brew tasted as if it had been made from jelly beans. Ferg leaned back in the chair, watching as a quartet of British tourists shared a hookah pipe, clearly not sure what to make of the experience. An Egyptian soap opera played on the television above the barlike counter; more than half of the patrons were watching it, though they were all male.

The lone exception—an Egyptian woman in western dress—approached Ferguson and asked if he was a tourist.

"Yup. Seeing the sights," he told her.

"Many sights here."

"Beautiful ones. Name's Ben, Benjamin Thatch." He shook her hand, the sort of faux pas an American tourist would be likely to make. She smiled at him but then turned and walked to another table.

Ferg concentrated on his coffee, sipping slowly. He had a second but declined a third, not sure his teeth would survive another infusion of sugar. He got up slowly and made his way out, walking lazily back to the street. He got to the end of the block before he was sure he was being followed.

Guns pulled the earphones down, figuring that the wireless bugging system they'd planted inside the café was no longer of much use. He pulled his shirt collar up, repositioning the small microphone that was clipped to the inside of his front collar.

"Two guys following him," he told Rankin and the others.

"Yeah," said Rankin, watching a video feed on a small handheld device about the size of a PDA. "With our luck they'll turn out to be pickpockets."

Ferguson was supposed to walk back in the general direction of the hotel after making contact, and they had set up their plans accordingly. Guns feigned interest in a stand selling cloth wallets as he waited for Ferg and the others to pass. The two CIA people they'd borrowed for the operation—Phil Thalid, a resident officer who worked with the Egyptian security forces, and Abu Yeklid, an agent who was technically a free-lancer—were waiting just up the street. Thalid and Yeklid would pick up the trail at close range.

Ferguson walked twenty yards past Guns then promptly turned around, ambling diagonally through the different bazaar stalls.

"What the hell is he doing?" grumbled Rankin. "He's supposed to go back to the hotel. He's heading back toward the café."

"Maybe he forgot something."

"I wish he'd stick to the game plan just once."

Ferguson continued down the block, trying to judge whether anyone besides the two men he'd spotted were following him. They had the stiff necks and stooped shoulders he associated with Jihaz Amn al Daoula, the State Security Service, which was part of Mukhabath el-Dawla, the interior ministry's General Directorate of State Security Investigations.

Though to be honest, the fact that he remembered one of the men from an assignment a year before was a surer giveaway. The men had either decided to trail him because he was acting suspicious or because they were bored. More likely the latter.

Ferguson passed near the empty alley next to the café and then found a watch repairman's window, where he stopped to admire the man's small display. Discovering that his own watch was several minutes behind those in the window, he reset it slowly, debating whether he should talk to the Egyptian agents. He had just decided to do that next when the woman who'd approached him in the café came out of the door and walked hurriedly past. Ferg smiled at her; she stared ahead as she passed.

"Excuse me," said a man walking a few paces behind, nearly bumping into him.

"Sorry," said Ferguson.

"Qasim's Tailor Shop in an hour," said the man. "Give your name."

They're Egyptian intelligence," Thalid told Rankin as Ferguson entered a carpet shop near the edge of the Islamic quarter. "Ferguson must have figured it out."

"Maybe we should tell them who we are," Guns suggested.

"I wouldn't trust them to keep their mouths shut," answered Thalid. "Besides, then they'll have to ask all sorts of questions."

"Ferg'll shake them," predicted Guns. "That's why he's going into the carpet shop."

"Yeah. You're right." Rankin leaned out from the corner where they'd stopped. The two Egyptian agents were standing about half a block away, just lighting up a pair of cigarettes. "Guns, go around the back. You other guys, get the cars."

If the Egyptian agents had been trying even a little, they would have seen Ferguson going out the back of the carpet place. That told him they didn't know who he was, and so with his trail shorn he made his way over to the tailor's.

The front door opened into a room packed with jackets and trousers in every conceivable stage of construction. Bolts of fabric lined the walls, and the place smelled of exotic tobacco and hashish. Two Egyptians, one fat, one skinny, stood on separate pieces of carpet nearby, submitting to the ministrations of young tailor assistants who poked and prodded their pinned suits into shape. A short, harried-looking man emerged from the back, a roll of measuring tape partially wrapped around the thumb of one hand and a swatch of fabric in the other. Speaking in rapid-fire Arabic, he berated one of the helpers, then turned to the skinny customer and displayed the sample, which the man reached for but was not allowed to take. At this point he turned to Ferguson and asked in Arabic who he was and what he wanted. Ferguson pretended not to understand, and the man repeated the question in English.

"Ben Thatch," Ferguson said. "I was told this was the best tailor in Cairo, which must mean it is the best in the world."

The man called him a jackass and easy mark in Arabic, then said in English that he must have an appointment in order to get a suit.

"Well, then I'll make one," Ferguson said.

"Yes, yes," said the man, who turned to the customer at his left and began a harangue about the importance of choosing the proper shade of gray.

"Can I use your phone?" Ferg asked. "I want to check my itinerary."

The man waved at him dismissively.

Ferguson stepped over to the desk, which was partly obscured by fabric and a pile of large, yellowing papers that proved to be customer invoices. He picked up the phone and punched the numbers rapidly, connecting with a local line that had been set up for the First Team. The line was being moni-tored by Corrigan.

"Jack, how are ya?" he said brightly. "I'm standing here in Qasim's Tai-lor Shop and looking to know—"

Something prodded him in the ribs. Ferg turned and saw one of the as-sistants holding a Beretta.

"It's just a local call," he said, but when the boy poked him again he thought it best to replace the receiver on the cradle.

Rankin felt the phone vibrating in his pocket. He reached down and hit the "OK" switch. The unit was similar to stock iridium phones though smaller and with several customized features: besides the silent alert it had 128k encryption and plugs that would let him use his radio's mike and ear set.

"Ferg just called from a tailor," said Corrigan. "Something's up."

"Yeah, he needs a new pair of pants."

"You're starting to sound just like him."

"I'm standing across the street from it. We got it covered."

Why are you here?" the fat customer asked in the back room of the shop.

"Best suits in Cairo," said Ferguson. The man didn't quite understand his English. "I got a message that said to come here. I follow directions."

The customer turned to the younger man who had pulled the gun. They spoke in Arabic so quickly that Ferguson couldn't catch it all, but what he did catch wasn't particularly encouraging: the fat man called him an "un-necessary nuisance" and berated someone named Ali for originally making contact with the "American idiots."

"In the car," the fat man told Ferg.

"Which car?"

"In the back. Go."

"This is just business. We don't need a gun. We're friends."

"In the car."

"It would make me less nervous if he put that away," Ferguson said, gesturing with his head toward the pistol. The fat man frowned but then told the younger man that Ferguson, being an American idiot, was harmless.

Out in the alley, Ferguson stopped to tie his shoe. As he did, he acti-vated the homing device in his heel and turned his radio on. The fat man grabbed him by the shirt and pulled him upward, pushing him in the direction of a white Mercedes S a few yards up the alley.

"Nice," said Ferg cheerfully. "This is the executive version, right? Got the bulletproof glass, armor on the side; must've cost you a fortune."

"Just get in." The fat man opened the door with a key fob device.

"Want me to drive?"

"The back, idiot," said the man, adding a string of curses in Arabic.

Ferguson slid into the backseat and pushed over. He gave Fatman a goofy smile as he got in and slammed the door. The kid got into the driver's seat.

"What is your interest in Palestine?" asked Fatman as the car reached the street.

"Does it matter?" said Ferg.

The man made a snorting sound that reminded Ferguson of a choking walrus. He supposed it was meant to be dismissive.

"You think the Prophet Jesus will come on a cloud," said Fatman.

"Well, I don't know if it would be a cloud." Ferguson looked out the window, trying not only to get a rough idea of where they were going but also to watch Fatman in the reflection at the same time. The nearby buildings were covered with large, colorful billboards featuring popular entertainers, each proclaimed as the spirit of his or her generation.

I don't like this," Guns told Rankin over the radio as they followed northward in the direction of Shubra, a working-class suburb. "Maybe we should call in the Egyptians."

"Ferguson knows what he's doing."

"What do you think?" Guns asked Yeklid, who was driving the car.

"I have no idea. This is your gig, man."

"How long will it take to get help out here?"

The officer shrugged. "Ten minutes or never. Nothing in between."

How did you know to contact us?" said Fatman as they turned off the main street toward a row of closely packed buildings dressed in white tiles and yellow bricks.

"It was all done for me," said Ferguson. "I just follow directions."

The car drove up a hill, then turned abruptly down a narrow street that wound down toward an area of small factory and warehouse buildings. They took another turn and then another, finally driving up a tight alleyway.

Four men were waiting near the back door of a brown brick building. The men were fairly nondescript; their AK-47s were not.

"So this is where we get out?" Ferguson said.

"You're an amateur, Mr. Thatch. And a meddler. We don't like you, and we don't need your money," said Fatman. He turned to the driver.

Under ideal circumstances, Ferguson might have noted how ironic it was that someone who hadn't bothered to frisk him was calling him an amateur. But these weren't ideal circumstances, and besides, he was too busy sliding his hand down to the back of his pants to grab the small Glock 23 pistol hidden there. He put one bullet into the head of the driver, then turned to Fatman, who made the incredibly bad decision of reaching for his own weapon. Ferguson put two slugs into his head, then dove forward over the car seat as the men with the AK-47s began to fire at the bulletproofed car. Ferguson pulled the driver's body to the side—like most Egyptians he didn't wear a seat belt—and flung himself behind the wheel as the first bullets cracked but did not pierce the windshield. He jammed the car into reverse, turning to see where he was going. As he did, one of the guards fired point-blank at the rear window's shatterproof glass.

Which, to Ferguson's great surprise, shattered.

The range finder on the tracking device showed they were a half block away when Rankin heard the stutter of automatic rifle fire.

"Damn it," he yelled, reaching down to the floor where he'd stashed his Uzi. "There! Stop!"

Yeklid jerked the wheel of the car and hit the brakes just in time to miss the Mercedes as it shot out of the alley and rammed into a car parked across the street. Rankin threw his door open in time to empty his submachine gun at the men running from the alley with AK-47s. Guns ran up behind him with a grenade launcher and pumped a tear gas canister into the alleyway, not realizing it was too late now to do any good.

The crash had deployed the Mercedes air bags. Ferguson pitched himself down as the guns erupted, reaching to his sock for his other hideaway. He rolled out of the car onto the ground, a gun in each fist.

"Ferguson, get the hell out of there!" screamed Rankin.

"Yo, Skippy! Don't hit me," yelled Ferguson.

"Come on, get the hell out of there," said Rankin.

Guns pumped another tear gas grenade into the alley. The acrid smoke drifted back toward the car.

"Get out of here, come on!" yelled Yeklid.

Ferguson got up and trotted to the car. Two men with assault rifles came from down the block; Ferguson spun around and cut them down.

"Trail car! Trail car!" he yelled, seeing their way blocked.

They clung to the second as Yeklid backed out into the main street, barely missing a truck.

"I called the Egyptians, but I think it's better if we lay low for an hour," Yeklid told Ferguson when they collected themselves several blocks away. "I'm going to call one of the senior people I know. This may end up being a real pain."

"You're good with understatement," said Ferguson. "I like that."

ACT II

And the second angel poured out his vial upon the sea; and it became as the
blood of a dead man.

—Revelation 16:3 (King James Version)

1

CIA BUILDING 24-442, VIRGINIA

Corrine Alston stood as patiently as possible in the small booth in the basement of CIA Building 24-442, waiting as the equipment behind the stainless-steel walls scanned her for high-tech bugs. Security here was so meticulous that no one—not Corrine, not CIA Director Thomas Parnelles, not even the president himself—could bypass the bug scan, let alone the weapons and identity checks. But the ritual only heightened her anger.

The small green light in the center of the ceiling lit. Corrine stared at the door, willing it to open. When it did, she walked down the hall to an elevator that opened as she approached. She didn't have to press any buttons once inside, which was fortunate; she would have broken either the panel or her fingers with the jabs.

The elevator opened a few seconds later fifty feet below the level where she had started. Corrine walked to a stairwell at the far end, ignoring the two plainclothes CIA officers flanking the entrance. Downstairs, her heels echoed loudly on the cement floor as she strode to the small conference room next to the secure communications suite used to support First Team operations. The door to the conference room was ajar. Corrine pushed it open and found Jack Corrigan sitting alone at the far end of the conference table.

"Why wasn't I told?" she demanded.

"I did tell you."

"You waited three hours. I heard about it from the State Department first, for cryin' out loud."

"I know, uh, that was a mistake. My mistake. I called your office and Teri said you were with the president. So I waited."

"You should have used the personal phone. That's why I have it."

Corrigan tried not to act intimidated, but Corrine Alston's fury was not easily withstood. Though only twenty-six, she was one of the most powerful women in the administration, serving as the president's counsel and his personal representative to the First Team, in effect, Corrigan's boss.

Complicating matters was the fact that she was pretty good looking, too: touch up her nose, add a little makeup, maybe hire a hair stylist, and she could pass as a model or at least a B actress.

"The Egyptian reaction was better than expected," offered Corrigan, trying to salvage what he could of the situation. "The tailor turned out to be Ahmed Abu Saahlid. They wanted him for terrorist activities, so—"

"Why was Ferguson in Cairo in the first place? He didn't clear that with me. He exceeded his authority. He was told to proceed with caution on the entire operation."

"I think getting Bob Ferguson to proceed with caution, Ms. Alston, would be well beyond even your considerable abilities," said CIA Director Thomas Parnelles, striding into the room behind her. "And I think you would be doing the country a great disservice besides."

Corrigan's military training kicked in, and he jumped to his feet. "Mr. Parnelles."

Corrine felt her face burn. "Special Demands will not be a rogue organization," she told Parnelles.

"I quite agree," said the CIA director softly. He pulled a chair out and sat down.

Corrine took a moment to gather herself, putting on what she thought of as her lawyer face: neutral, reserved, calm. She wasn't exactly sure where she stood with Parnelles. The president had appointed him CIA director partly based on her recommendation; she had known Parnelles from her work as counsel to the Intelligence Committee, when as a retired CIA official he had acted as an informal and valuable consultant to some of the committee members. But they had had a few disagreements after his appointment, when as counsel to the president she recommended against some of his suggestions as a matter of legal principle. And now that the president had appointed her as his representative overseeing Special Demands, she wouldn't blame Parnelles if he saw her as an interloper. The appointment effectively usurped the deputy director for operation's authority over the First Team, and since the DDO worked for Parnelles, it tended to cut him out as well.

She had heard from others that Parnelles implied he had himself suggested that she take the position, acting as the president's eyes, ears, and conscience on sensitive covert missions. It hadn't happened that way; the president had had the idea himself. Or so she believed.

"I called over to your office to find out what was going on," Parnelles told Corrine, answering her unasked question about why he was there. "When I heard you were on your way, I thought it would be wise to join you in person for an update. Unless, of course, you have an objection."

"I have no objection at all," Corrine told him. "You're CIA director."

Parnelles smiled. He pressed his finger to his lip in a thoughtful pose, inadvertently emphasizing the scar on his cheek that was a souvenir of a nasty incident during his salad days as a CIA officer.

"Mr. Corrigan was just giving me a briefing," said Corrine. "And I would be pleased for you to hear and offer your insights."

Corrigan recounted the events in Jerusalem and Cairo, adding very little to what Corrine and Parnelles already knew. With the First Team operation over, the FBI had made a dozen arrests in the Seven Angels case earlier in the day; Corrine had been with the president when the attorney general personally briefed him. Among the charges were conspiracy to fund terrorism and several counts of tax evasion. From what she had seen, Corrine thought the terrorist case would be hard to prove, but the tax evasion and related currency violations were slam dunks. She kept that opinion to herself.

She also didn't share her opinion that the group was a collection of schizoid crazies who would have been ignored if they hadn't had access to a few million dollars and if the FBI didn't need a political score to shore up its standing with the administration.

"The FBI felt it had to go ahead with the arrests," said Corrine. "With Thatch dead, there was little prospect of gathering more information about the groups that Seven Angels may have been trying to contact."

"Good timing with the president's visit to the Middle East coming up," said Parnelles.

That was the sort of comment from the CIA director that threw Corrine. She knew—and she suspected that Parnelles did as well—that the president thought just the opposite. Anything involving the Middle East had the potential to throw off the delicate negotiations he was trying to foster between the Palestinians and the Israelis. The arrests were preferable to terrorist activity, certainly, but only just.

"So Seven Angels is wrapped up?" Parnelles asked.

"From the FBI's point of view, yes. But there are a few things Ferg wanted to look at," said Corrigan. "He thinks he may be able to get more information about the group's contacts, maybe leverage that into information about terror groups that we have poor intelligence on. There were some phone calls preceding Thatch's visit to a dentist's office in Tel Aviv. It may be a wild goose chase, but you know Ferguson."

"He does love wild goose chases," said Parnelles.

Parnelles didn't say anything else. Corrine sensed he had come not about this—the briefing could have been done over the phone—but because he wanted to talk about something else.

"I think we're in a wrap-up stage on Seven Angels. The action in Cairo was unfortunate," she said.

"Unavoidable, I would say," said Parnelles.

"The Egyptians used that word," said Corrigan, sensing he might escape without further roasting.

"Is there anything else at the moment, Jack?" asked Corrine.

"No, ma'am."

"I think the director and I might spend a few minutes reviewing some budgetary matters," she said.

Corrigan was only too happy to be relieved.

"You dealt with Senator Sondborn masterfully," said Parnelles when they were alone.

"I simply told the senator that executive privilege is an important principle that must be maintained," said Corrine, aware that she was being buttered up for something else. The head of the Intelligence Committee had asked for a public session on the recent attempt by terrorists to explode a dirty bomb above Honolulu; his inquiry would have undoubtedly revealed enough about the First Team that its efficiency would have been threatened. Turning him back was a no-brainer and one of the easier tasks Corrine had accomplished the week before.

"Ferguson exceeded his authority by going into Egypt without clearing the operation first," said Corrine. She knew Parnelles and Ferguson had a long-standing personal relationship, and guessed that was his concern. "I don't think there's a question about that. This was an FBI operation, and he went overboard. It was just Ferg being Ferg."

"That may be." Parnelles smiled wryly. He had known Ferguson for a long time, and would have been surprised if Ferguson *hadn't* gone off in his own direction. Getting the First Team involved in the Seven Angels operation had been overkill, but it precluded the possibility of a mess if the FBI, as usual, bungled. More important for Parnelles, it positioned the First Team for a more serious task.

"I wouldn't want to micromanage Ferguson," Parnelles said. "Sometimes a horse has to be given his head."

"Or a man enough rope?" suggested Corrine.

"If we have the proper people in place, we learn to trust their judgments," said Parnelles. "I'm not here to second-guess you or to stick up for Bobby."

"Okay." Corrine folded her arms. Talking to Parnelles was like playing three-dimensional chess blindfolded: sometimes it was a struggle simply to know where the pieces were, let alone dissect his strategy.

"Mossad has developed information that a member of the Iraqi resistance will be en route to Syria for a meeting within the next few days," said Parnelles. "Nisieen Khazaal."

"Khazaal would leave Iraq?"

"Mossad's information is almost always correct, especially if they're passing it along. Nonetheless, we haven't been able to confirm it. Not through the ordinary channels. Our dedicated resources in Syria are skimpy. The NSA is sifting through intercepts, and the staff in Damascus and down at the farm are sifting the wheat, but we have no verification."

Nisieen Khazaal had been a member of the Iraqi army before the war. He had been identified by the new government's intelligence service as well as the CIA as the leader of "New Iraq," a resistance movement responsible for more than two dozen strikes against various American and Iraqi targets in the last twelve months. Capturing him and putting him on trial would be a major coup. Especially now, with the Iraqi government just starting to gain legitimacy.

"We have to get him if we can," said Corrine. "Even if it's a long shot."

"I quite agree."

S everal hours later, back in D.C., the president poked his head into Alston's office.

"Well, now, Miss Alston, I am glad to see you here so late," he told her in his gentlemanly Georgian voice. "The taxpayers are getting their money's worth."

"We have to talk, Mr. President," Corrine said.

"So your note said, my *deah*. And here I am." He slid into the chair across from her desk. "So what do you want to tell me?"

President Jonathan McCarthy came by his twang honestly: he traced his ancestry to an indentured servant who'd come over before the Revolution. The accent could range from a very light note to a thick brogue, depending on political requirements—and how tired he was. Since it was going on eleven p.m., she supposed fatigue was responsible for its thickness . . . though she was never one hundred percent sure.

After Corrine relayed what Parnelles had told her about Khazaal, the president's smile turned to a frozen frown.

"Why would he be going to Syria?" he asked.

"We're not sure. Our theory is that there is some sort of summit planned, with outside groups meeting to coordinate strategy and possibly pass money. Khazaal's organization needs funds. The new government has had some success clamping down on the money that was coming from out-side religious groups."

"I find the timing curious."

"It may have nothing to do with your trip to Iraq," she told him. "Or it may have everything to do with it."

The president had decided to visit Baghdad to help dedicate the new Parliament building there a week and a half from now. It was a critical sym-bol of democracy in the struggling country, and McCarthy was convinced that his presence would demonstrate how far Iraq had come. At the same time, it would allow him to make what would seem like a spontaneous visit to Jerusalem as well, with the idea of helping the peace process along. The side trip was a closely guarded secret since it was supposed to seem like a spur-of-the-moment idea, but the visit to Baghdad was not. As McCarthy put it, the president of the United States was not some skunk who snuck into town at midnight to sniff around the garbage cans. Iraq was a struggling democracy; his visit would help convince others that the outcome of the struggle was not in doubt. Or at least that was what he hoped.

"I'd like to use Special Demands to investigate this," said Corrine. "The First Team and the supporting Special Operations elements are al-ready in the Middle East for the Seven Angels case. That's just about wrapped up. It would be quite a coup to capture Khazaal. And who knows what it would avoid? The possibilities are immense."

"Do you know what the old farmer thought of possibilities, Miss Al-ston?"

"I couldn't begin to guess."

McCarthy didn't bother telling her the punch line. "Use the Team. Find this man and arrest him. He should be brought to justice. Just remem-ber, Miss Alston, that my trip to Baghdad is very important. I would not like anything to disrupt it."

"We'll make sure that doesn't happen," she said.

"I know you will, *deah*. I know you will." He rose. "There is one other item I'd like you to possibly attend to, if you have the time and inclination."

A request from the president was more than a mere request, and they both knew it. But McCarthy hewed to his well-taught manners, asking rather than demanding. It was one of the reasons his staff worked so hard for him.

"Of course I'll do it. What do you need?"

"Our ambassador to Iraq, Mr. Bellows. I believe you know him fairly well."

"My father does."

McCarthy smiled. Peter Bellows had been a business partner of Corrine's father two decades before. McCarthy, who had known Corrine's family since before she was born, knew that. Ten years before, Bellows had left
business to become an ambassador. While his first appointments were made
mostly as political paybacks, the previous administration had found him very
useful, and he was now seen as a very capable man, though McCarthy himself had not had an opportunity to test his mettle.

"I am thinking that with the initiative to the Middle East, I will need a
special envoy, someone the Palestinians especially would be comfortable
with. And Bellows would be a prime candidate," said the president.

"I'm sure he'd be fine."

"How do you know?"

The truth was, she didn't. Corrine had had no dealings with him, not
even when she was working in the senate for the Intelligence Committee.
Special envoy was not only an important position, it was also the sort of post
that might lead to a Nobel Prize, certainly if the president's initiative
brought the two sides closer together.

"I have only one outstanding requirement for the job," continued the
president, "but it's critical. I need a man, or a woman, who will tell me the
truth, even if it is something I do not want to hear."

"That sounds like my job description," said Corrine.

"I'm sorry, *deah*, but you would not be qualified for this job."

"I don't want it."

"Well, good. Then I won't have to worry that you might be prejudiced." McCarthy's lips turned up in a half smile. "I'd like you to go on to
Baghdad ahead of me and make an assessment. I know Mr. Bellows's résumé
is impressive. And I know he's personable. He and I even get along, for
which there is something to be said. But that's not what I truly need to
know."

"Jonathan . . . Mr. President—"

"Jonathan is fine when we are alone. Go ahead, tell me what I don't
want to hear but must hear."

"You're putting me in a difficult position."

"Now I thought *that* was your job description." McCarthy smiled
again, and this time traces of it lingered on his face as he continued to speak.
"You might find an excuse to visit Tel Aviv and Palestine and the other countries in the region as well, ahead of my visit. Take their pulse, as it were. I
suspect that you should be in the area as this Special Demands project runs
its course."

"Yes, sir, of course," said Corrine, who hadn't been thinking that at all;

she had plenty of work to do in Washington, and her role was to supervise the First Team's operations, not take part in them. Then again, she was looking for an opportunity to talk to Ferguson in person. He could blow her off too easily on the phone and made a regular habit of it.

"I'll leave as soon as I can," said Corrine.

"Now, now. No need to rush," said McCarthy. "Give yourself twenty-four hours to wrap things up. And make sure that your secretary knows how to get in touch with you."

"I will."

McCarthy started to leave but then turned back. "Now you remember one thing. If you get hurt, I'm going to have to be the one to tell your daddy. And neither one of us wants that. So you be careful, *heah?*"

CAIRO

THE NEXT AFTERNOON . . .

"Before you blow your top," Corrigan told Ferguson, "listen to the whole deal. This is a good one, Ferg. A real good one."

"Corrigan, I don't blow my top. Your top, maybe." The old wooden chair creaked as Ferguson leaned back. It felt so rickety, he thought it was going to send him in a tumble to the floor at any minute. Ferguson, Rankin, and Guns were sitting in a secure communications facility in the Cairo embassy, a room within a room with an encrypted communications link back to Washington. They had the option of using video and seeing Corrigan as they spoke, but the vote not to do so had been unanimous.

"So tell me what the story is," said Ferguson. "Why are we being jerked off one wild goose chase and put on another?"

"How'd you know there was a new assignment?"

Ferguson rolled his eyes for the others. "Spill it, Jack," he told Corrigan.

"Khazaal. Nisieen Khazaal."

"That's it?"

"The name doesn't mean anything to you? Jesus, Ferg, where have you been? This is only the most infamous Iraqi scumbag going. I bet Rankin knows who he is."

"Yeah, he's at the top of the Who's Who of World Scumbags," said Rankin.

"Where did we get this?" asked Ferguson.

"Mossad. Came from the top. I think Parnelles huddled with Ms. Alston, and here we are."

Corrigan gave them everything he knew about Khazaal, which wasn't all that much. The Israelis either didn't know or wouldn't say where exactly he was going. The Agency had several indications that he had moved west from the Tikrit area—a favorite of Rankin's—and theorized that he was near the border, though not yet across. Several groups tied to his organization had transferred funds into bank accounts used by smugglers, and Iraqi intelligence had several leads about where he was in the western desert.

"Yeah, Iraqi intelligence," said Rankin. "Hajjis with IQs equal to their shoe sizes."

"The assignment is to locate and apprehend," said Corrigan, ignoring him. "Apprehend as in arrest, as in bring him back alive."

"And what do I do when he tells me to get bent?" said Ferguson. "Rhetorical question, Jack," he added quickly. "Mossad involved?"

"No. They're tied up."

"Where's Thera?"

"I put her on a plane to Athens. We've asked for a liaison from the Iraqi security service. Where do you want him?"

"Paradise," said Rankin.

"I don't know yet," said Ferguson. Mossad's posture struck him as odd; if they bothered to pass something along, they almost always provided a complete dossier and at least a liaison to feed back notes. "Listen, I want to talk to Parnelles."

"Why?"

"I'm having some trouble with my 401K."

"We don't have a 401K plan."

Guns and Rankin both started to laugh. Ferguson grinned, relaxing a little. "Get him for me, will you?"

"I can't just snap my fingers and get him on the line."

"Use the bat phone, Robin."

"Come on Ferg. Parnelles is traveling. I don't know where he is. I can leave a message."

"Tell him *I* want to talk to him, not you. Say it's important."

"OK. Listen, Corrine wants you to meet her in Tel Aviv. She wants to talk to you. She's pretty upset about Cairo."

"What about it?"

"You didn't run the operation by her. She wants you in Tel Aviv—"

"I'm not going to Tel Aviv."

"Hey, Ferg, you can't blow her off. She's the boss."

"All right. Let me talk to her."

"She's not here, Ferg. It's the middle of the night over here. Like four a.m."

"The way you're calling her Corrine and everything, I thought you were at her apartment."

"Ferg."

"Go wake her up."

"Come on."

"Look, I'm not going to Tel Aviv. Why should we go to Tel Aviv from Cairo?" He looked at his watch. "Thera's going to Athens?"

"Yeah."

"Hold her there. Tell her I'll be in tonight or maybe tomorrow."

"What should I tell Cor— Ms. Alston?"

"Tell her I'll be in Athens. Actually, probably Incirlik, with Van and the Ranger boys."

"She really wants to talk to you."

"My phone is on twenty-four/seven."

"What about Rankin and Guns?"

"They can get their own girl."

"Ferg, listen. Alston is going to be pissed."

Ferguson tossed the phone on the table. The others looked at him. Ferguson folded his arms across his chest but then reached across and picked it up.

"You OK, Ferg?" asked Corrigan. "Maybe you need a rest."

"Yeah, a nice long rest," Ferguson said. "So Alston wants to chew my butt in person, huh?"

"Well, I don't know that she wants to chew you out."

"Oh, come on, Jack. But hey, who knows? Maybe some hot-looking blonde who graduated magna cum laude at daddy's law school can run covert ops better than I can."

"Listen, you don't have to like it," said Corrigan. "You just have to do your job."

"You know what, Jack? I'm going to take your advice," said Ferguson. "Tell *Corrine* she can look me up in Syria if she wants, because I don't have to like it, but I have a job to do."

This time when he tossed the phone, he got up and left the room.

OVER SYRIA
THREE NIGHTS LATER . . .

A cold hand grabbed Thera Majed as she fell from the aircraft, wrapping itself around her throat and squeezing tightly. Her heart jumped in her chest, and she felt her eyeballs freeze over. She was breathing oxygen from a small bottle strapped to her side—a necessity when parachuting from 35,000 feet—but even her lungs felt as if they had turned to ice.

"Looking good," yelled Ferguson over the short-range radio they were using to communicate.

Guns and Rankin had gone out first. Thera's unfamiliarity with the procedure had cost the second pair a few extra seconds, which at four hundred knots translated into nearly two miles.

And counting.

Between the wind howling around her and the tight helmet, Ferguson's words sounded more like "luck of gold," and it took a few seconds for Thera to decipher what he was talking about. By the time she figured it out, the Douglas DC-9 she'd jumped out of had disappeared.

Thera struggled to get her body into the "frog" position she'd learned nearly two years before at the Army Airborne school. Since that time, she'd made no more than two dozen jumps, only three of which had been high-altitude, high-opening forays like this one, and none had been at night. Everybody said it would be easy—her body would remember how to do it once she stepped out of the plane—but the only thing her body remembered was how cold it had been . . . not half as cold as this time.

Ferguson, arms spread and legs raised as if he were a miniature aircraft, zoomed toward her. On his left wrist he wore a large altimeter, which had a sound alert wired into his helmet's earset. On his right he had a GPS device that looked like a large compass. An arrow dominated the dial, showing the direction to their destination and a countdown of the mileage. A pair of lightweight night-vision glasses were strapped beneath his helmet like goggles. The aircraft had been going nearly four hundred knots when they jumped out, which meant they were, too. Their trajectory to the landing zone had been calculated before takeoff, then tweaked ever so slightly a few minutes before the jump to account for the wind.

"Let her rip," he told her, the altimeter buzzing in his ear as they fell through 30,000 feet.

Thera's first tug on the handle was too tentative, and the parachute failed to release. But her interpretation of the problem was that she wasn't in the proper position—true enough, as it happened, though this had nothing to do with the chute deploying—and she struggled to push her head downward and get her arms out before trying again. As she did, something whipped by and tapped her on the head.

It was Ferguson. Worried that she was having problems, he shaped his body into a delta to gain speed in her direction, then flared out to slow down. He misjudged his speed slightly in the dark as he pulled close and rather than paralleling, flew past. He recovered, sailing to the left and then back around, inching forward.

It felt like inching. In fact he was moving at over a hundred miles an hour.

"We have to pull now," he yelled into the radio. "We're getting off course. Hey! Hey! You ready? Ready?"

Thera thought Ferguson was the one having trouble, and she started to maneuver toward him.

"Pull!" said Ferguson, motioning at her.

She reached to the handle and yanked, feeling the gentle tug of her harness as the chute unfolded above her. And now it really was like they said it would be: her arms moved up as she took stock of the chute and herself, making sure the cells had inflated properly and orienting herself with the aid of a GPS device wrapped around her right wrist. She was back in control or at least as much in control as anyone being held up in space by engineered nylon could be.

R ankin reached the bluff overlooking the Iraqi border ahead of Guns. He put down the bike and increased the amplification on his night-optical glasses, which looked like a pair of very thick sunglasses. The wrap-around glasses combined generation-four infrared and starlight enhancement technology with electronic magnification to a factor of ten. While not as powerful as the new gen-four devices being tested by Army Special Forces units, the glasses' light weight was more than fair compensation; they were more than powerful enough to illuminate the rocky desert terrain below.

Rankin could see a warren of "rabbit" holes and days-old tracks through the gritty soil. The holes were the entrances to tunnels used by smugglers, who used them to avoid the new Iraqi government's surveillance aircraft and patrols.

"What'd you do, tune the bike?" Guns asked, walking up next to Rankin.

"Less wind resistance." Rankin rested his right hand on his Uzi as he surveyed the desert. While the fewer than ten thousand American troops still stationed in Iraq were concentrated near Baghdad and the northern oil fields, Rankin figured the Iraqis and certainly the Syrians could stop the smugglers if they really cared to. But smuggling goods was a lucrative business, especially for the local commanders who averted their eyes.

"We can put the main post down in the those caves. Watch the border from here," Rankin told Guns. "Let's go mark a landing spot for the Rangers."

"Shouldn't we wait for Ferg?"

"He knows where we are."

Thera stepped forward as the ground finally came up to her legs. She twisted slightly and crumpled to the ground as she landed, falling on her side. It wasn't pretty, but at least she was down. She got up, expecting Ferguson to fall on top of her any second. Gathering in her parachute, she looked around for a convenient place to hide it. Ten yards away a small collection of boulders huddled together on the ground. That would do.

With the chute stuffed between the rocks, she took stock of her situation, checking her position with a GPS device. Their rendezvous point was about five miles away, on a ridge overlooking the nearby valley.

She was supposed to hit no farther than a mile away. It was an inauspicious start to her first real mission with the team. She knew Ferguson only by reputation. Depending on whom you talked to, he was either easy to get along with or the biggest SOB in the world, but everybody agreed he was driven; he'd probably be mad that she had fallen so far away.

Thera checked her radio, then decided it would be better not to call in until she was a little closer. Trudging in the direction of the rendezvous area, she'd gone about a quarter of a mile when a rich baritone echoed in her headset.

"*Oh come tell me, Sean O'Connell, tell me why you hurry so.*"

"Ferg?" she said.

"*I've got orders from the captain,*" sang Ferguson, "*for the pipes must be together, by the rising of the moon.*"

Thera dropped to one knee, scanning three hundred and sixty degrees around her. The only thing nearby were rocks.

"Where are you?" she said. "Ferg?"

The sound of a motor in the distance made her freeze. She brought her submachine gun up.

"Ferg?"

"Yee-hah!" he shouted over the radio.

Thera whirled in time to see the shadow of a motorbike fly over the rise behind her. The bike had two very large mufflers at its side to dampen its engine sound.

"Ferguson," she said.

"You're expecting someone else?" he asked, skidding down the hill.

"How did you get down so fast?"

"Hop on. The bikes landed back on the other side of the hill. I just about tripped over them when I came down. Good thing you took your time going out; we would have been all night finding them."

Two hours later, Ferguson watched as a large Pave Low helicopter skimmed across the desert terrain toward the chemical glow light Rankin had placed to guide it. The chopper shook the desert as it rumbled a few feet over the terrain, flying low to avoid the Syrian radars to the west. The Pave Low's immense blades kicked a sandstorm around it as it flew. Ferguson shielded his night glasses as the bird settled in. A company's worth of Rangers augmented by two Delta veterans and an Iraqi intelligence officer began emerging from the rear. The men and their equipment had been detailed to support the First Team, providing on-ground security and extra eyes at their base of operations in the desert wilderness. Additional troops were on call to be used for the actual "snatch," assuming conditions allowed.

Ferguson watched for the Iraqi intelligence officer accompanying them. He wasn't particularly hard to spot; more than twice the age of most of the soldiers, he walked with a nervous hop away from the helicopter, ducking even though it was unnecessary.

"Fouad Mohammed?" yelled Ferguson when the man reached him.

"Yes," said the Iraqi.

"Bob Ferguson. Call me Ferg. Step into my office." He motioned back to a run of rocks twenty yards away where he'd parked his bike. The landing area was about a quarter mile from the small caves and overhangs where they'd located their base camp.

"You know Khazaal?" Ferguson asked the Iraqi.

"I met him some years ago," said Fouad, whose ears and bones still reverberated from the helicopter ride. He greatly preferred quieter modes of transportation, though he knew better than to mention this to the American; in his experience Americans never found machines quite noisy enough.

Fifty-three years old, Fouad had dealt with a number of Americans over the years, beginning with his very early service as a glorified gofer and eavesdropper for the Iraqi foreign intelligence service. Stationed in Cairo at the age of twenty-two, he had kept tabs on various expatriate movements and Jews: easy work, though the detailed weekly reports often took two or three days simply to write. By the Iran-Iraq War he had progressed to a liaison officer working with the CIA. Out of favor for a while, he had been sent north into exile in the Kurdistan area until just before the start of the Gulf War, when he worked on a group assigned to prepare for the defense of Baghdad. After the war he found his way to the great sanctions shell game. For the first few months he helped hide evidence of banned weapons from weapons inspectors but soon turned to the more critical task of trumping up evidence of continuing programs to impress the fading dictator and keep external enemies at bay. Fouad lay low in the northern Kurdish region after the second Gulf War until friends in the government convinced him to come to work with them. A brief job with an American security contractor had renewed some of his CIA ties; eventually Fouad found himself back in service with the interior ministry's security apparatus, serving as a liaison to "external services," the latest euphemism for the CIA.

"You think Khazaal would go through one of the tunnels?" asked Ferguson, sitting on a rock near his motorcycle. "I thought he liked to travel in style."

"We all adapt," said Fouad. Something about the American was very familiar.

"All right." Ferguson wasn't sure if Fouad was parroting the intelligence report he'd seen or if he was its author. In his experience, the Iraqi intelligence people demonstrated a wide range of abilities, from extreme competence to extreme ineptitude. As a rule, the more confident they made themselves sound the less able they were. "So we watch for a car that meets him?"

"Possible. It may be a wild goose chase."

"Not what I want to hear."

"You want the truth or what you want to hear?" said Fouad, who knew that the latter was almost always preferred, especially by Americans. Putting the question bluntly sometimes saved problems and sometimes not.

"Truth. Always." Ferguson smiled at him. "But all truth is relative."

Fouad shrugged, though he did not agree; God's truth was absolute, after all.

"What we think will happen is that he'll come across the border on foot, get picked up and driven to one of the abandoned military camps northwest of here, where a plane will meet him," said Ferguson. "We're going to stake out the camps so we can hit them when he's there. On the other hand, he may just take a car all the way across the desert. If that happens, we take the car."

"What if you miss?"

"Then we punt. We find out where he's going, and we try to get him there. Problem is, we're not sure where he's going. Unless you are."

"There are so many rumors about Khazaal you can make something up, and it is just as likely to be true."

"We think tomorrow night," said Ferguson. "What do you think?"

Fouad could only shrug.

"Can you ride a motorcycle?"

"Not well."

"You're my passenger then. Come on." Ferguson picked up the motorcycle.

Fouad hesitated. He did not like motorcycles and had had several bad experiences with them. "I knew a Ferguson once," he said.

"Yeah?"

"In Cairo. And during the war with Iran."

Ferguson realized that Fouad was talking about his father. But he only started the bike and waited for Fouad to get on.

"That was my dad in Cairo," he said after they reached the base camp. "He had a bunch of jobs over here during the Cold War."

"Yes, I can see him in your face." A very solid officer, thought Fouad, not a liar, like many. Good with Arabic. How much like the father was the son?

"*Anaa saäiid jiddan bimuqaabalatak,*" he said in Arabic. "I am very glad to meet you. Your father was a very dependable fellow."

"*Anaa afham tamaaman,*" replied Ferguson, using the rudimentary phrase a visitor to an Arabian country would use to show hc understood what was being said. But then he continued in Arabic: "I understand perfectly: you're trying to butter me up because you think I'm just another CIA jerk who's easily turned by a compliment."

"No. Your father was a brave man. And you speak Arabic well, though with an Egyptian accent."

"Grammar school in Cairo. Before the nuns got a hold of me." Ferguson laughed.

The son was like the father in many ways, thought Fouad. A thing both good and bad.

SYRIA, ON THE BORDER WITH IRAQ
THE NEXT NIGHT . . .

Rankin turned to the Iraqi and gestured at the car that had turned off from the highway. It rode across the open desert, approaching the foothill two miles away. "Is that for him?"

"Who can tell? But the car is like the one that left from Thar in the afternoon, an old Mercedes."

Just like a *hajji*, thought Rankin: never a straight yes or no.

Thar was a small town on the other side of the border. Iraqi intelligence officers there had prepared a list of half a dozen suspicious vehicles, all with single drivers. The theory was that the vehicle would go over alone and wait for Khazaal to slip through, a practice often employed by criminals and others trying to escape the country without documentation. The Mercedes would have been thoroughly searched before being allowed over the border.

Two shadows came from the rocks. "You see a face?" asked Rankin.

Fouad shook his head.

Rankin looked over at Guns, who was using his satellite radio system to talk to Corrigan back in the Cube. The radio had a "local" discrete-burst mode for short-range communications with other team members on the ground and a longer-range mode that used satellites to communicate. The latter was easier to detect; though the transmissions were encrypted and virtually unbreakable, the presence of the radio waves could lead someone to the user.

"Where are we, Guns?" asked Rankin.

"I just uploaded the video. They're looking at it."

"What's the UAV see?" Rankin asked. A Predator robot aircraft, or "unmanned aerial vehicle," was orbiting overhead, helping with the surveillance. It would follow the vehicle to a spot where it could be ambushed.

"Nothing so far."

"Tell Ferg what's going on."

"Already have," said Guns.

"Hold on," said Rankin. "There's another car coming."

The trick was to let the Mercedes get far enough from the border area so that any of the local smugglers and Syrian spies nearby wouldn't be tipped off but to not let it get so far away that they couldn't stop it. With two cars, the task became more complicated, especially once the two vehicles got on the nearby road and headed in different directions. Ferguson and Thera staked out the first car, which was moving northwestward; Rankin and Guns followed the second, traveling two miles to the south.

Just to make things even more interesting, a third one appeared soon after the second made its pickup. Two Rangers were detailed to follow that one, staying close enough to trail them but not take them unless ordered to do so by Ferguson.

The first car took a turn off the highway onto a packed dirt road in the direction of an abandoned military outpost a few miles west of the border. The road wound around a series of dry streams, or *wadis*, and loose sand traps. Since they were on motorcycles, Ferguson, Thera, and the two Rangers traveling with them were able to sprint ahead and check out the site. Ferguson sent the Rangers down the road to watch, in case his hunch about where the Mercedes was going proved wrong. As he and Thera approached the camp, Fouad warned that a Land Rover was parked in front of one of the buildings. The Iraqi had taken over for Guns and was watching the Predator's video feed. The vehicle had not been there in the afternoon's satellite snapshot. Ferguson and Thera got off their bikes and went to scout the base. A low ridge sat to the south about a quarter mile from the fence. Standing at the top, Ferguson could see most of the base area.

"There," Ferguson told Thera, pointing to the second building in the row. "You can just barely make out the shadow inside."

"How many people?"

"At least two." He pointed to the road beyond the complex. "Maybe they're forming a caravan here. Or maybe waiting for a plane. You could land our MC-130 on that road at the back there."

Ferguson dropped down, sliding to the bottom of the hill. They were no more than fifteen minutes ahead of the Mercedes; if they were going to take it here, they had to get a move on.

"What we have to do is take out the guard by the gate, then the person or persons in the building," Ferguson told Thera. He took the M203 grenade launcher from his pack and stuffed a dozen plastic shells in his pants pockets, which were already bulging with magazines for the MP5N submachine gun. His vest had concussion and smoke grenades, along with ammo for his pistol and slugs for his shotgun, which he had over his right shoulder.

"Are we taking these guys prisoner or what?" asked Thera.

"Khazaal's the only one we have to apprehend alive," said Ferguson. "But, yeah, we dunk these guys if we can. Have your gas mask ready. Crossbow?"

Thera held up the weapon, which was very similar to the type used by deer and other game hunters in the States. A marriage between a miniature rifle and high-tech bow, the weapon fired a titanium arrow over fifty yards, was as accurate as a rifle at that range, and would send its missilelike arrow through the side of a skull. It could also fire two different types of nonlethal ammunition: a syringelike dart with a fast-working anesthetic and a lollypop-shaped hard plastic arrow that was supposed to stun someone struck with it. The anesthetic was related chemically to sodium thiopental, the barbiturate commonly known as truth serum. It worked even quicker though it left the subject feeling as if he or she had a full-body hangover. Thera didn't trust the lollypops and had left them back at the base camp.

"Wait until I'm outside of the buildings if at all possible," Ferg told her. "But if you have to shoot, shoot. He doesn't have a vest. Shoot at the chest."

Ferguson jogged to the west side of the base, taking advantage of the *wadi* near the fence, which obscured the view. He found a hole under the fence and crawled into the compound between the two warehouse buildings at the southern end of the compound.

Thera used a drainage ditch to cover her as she closed in on the guard. She found a brace of weeds thirty yards from the entrance and got into firing position. The guard, clearly bored, stood with his gun down against his leg. She took a grenade out just in case—no sense fooling around if she missed—and put her MP5N within easy reach.

"Thera, where are you?" hissed Ferguson in her ear.

"Here," she whispered. *"Just tell me when."*

Ferguson hunkered on his haunches. There was no sign that there were more people than the guard and the one whose shadow he'd seen in the large building to his right. The building had a window at the back; he was tempted to try and get in that way but decided it was too risky. Nor did he have anything to use to booby-trap the exit.

"Thera?"

"Yeah?"

"After you take out the guard, I want you to get to the west side of the southern-most building, all right? There's a window there. You think you can cover it?"

"Yeah, but—"

"No but. Wait until I'm ready if you can."

Thera steadied the crossbow, zeroed in on the guard. She'd first used a bow when she was twelve years old, hunting with her father at his cabin in the Catskills. He was a New York City detective back then, two years divorced from her mother, a much heavier drinker than now. She could feel his hand on her shoulder, gripping gently, his thumb pressing as the buck walked toward them in the field.

The guard turned toward her. Suddenly he started to bring up his rifle. Thera pulled the trigger on her crossbow. The weapon made a whispery *thwang* as it shot. She watched through the scope as the arrow struck the guard flat in the chest. He shook, stunned, not quite comprehending what had happened. Then he started to grab at the arrow, stopped, raised his gun again, then fell off to the side, knocked unconscious by the massive dose of synthetic narcotic in the warhead.

Ferguson heard Thera's heavy breathing over the radio and realized she'd shot the guard. He moved up the side of the building, reached the corner, and glanced toward the front. He saw no one. He checked the grenade launcher—he figured he would hit anyone coming out in the chest with the tear-gas round, which would knock them down at very close range—then knelt on one knee to wait for Thera.

Thera ran to the stricken guard, made sure he was down, then grabbed

the dart and his rifle and went to the back of the building. Ferguson caught a glimpse of her as she ran.

"Ready?" he asked.

"Let me catch my breath."

"Not enough time. Use the gun if you have to. Get your mask on."

Without knowing exactly how the building was configured, Ferguson decided on a simple, two-step plan: tear-gas grenade in window, then duck. Standard grenades needed about fourteen meters to arm; this was a precaution against the grenade going off too close to friendly troops. The arming mechanism in these rounds allowed them to explode as soon as they struck something.

Ferguson rammed the metal butt end of the grenade launcher through the window, breaking the glass. Then he pumped the round inside and grabbed his shotgun. A man emerged from the building; Ferguson fired point-blank at the man, striking him in the chest, neck, and face with the plastic pellets in the shell.

"Ferg?" asked Thera.

"Watch the back, watch the back," he yelled, reloading the M203 and pumping another round inside the building before running over to the man he'd shot, who was writhing on the ground. Though the shotgun pellets were plastic, he'd been so close to Ferguson that the round cut as well as bruised his face, and he wailed in pain, temporarily blinded. Ferguson put him temporarily out of his misery with a shot of Demerol.

As he rose, he heard Thera scream.

EVANSTON, ILLINOIS

Judy Coldwell waited for the bank clerk to leave the safety-deposit area before opening the box. Her fingers trembled as she picked up the passport and the envelope filled with hundred-dollar bills.

As she had hoped but also feared, she had been called on to fulfill her brother's mission. It would not be easy. The church was under attack. The Reverend Tallis had been arrested. So had other elders, perhaps all of them. The bank accounts in the United States and Cayman Islands had been frozen, according to the FBI press release she read on the Internet.

Tallis had managed to send her a one-word message: *Latakia*.

Coldwell knew that meant Latakia, Syria, and that she should go there. Beyond that, however, she was unsure exactly how to proceed. She knew that her brother's mission would have been to contact groups interested in attacking holy sites. She knew where to get the necessary authorizations (and find willing bank officers) to enable her to access the group's hidden overseas funds. But she did not know what groups Benjamin had been dealing with.

Latakia had been a favorite spot of arms dealers and other smugglers when she last visited roughly three years before, and she guessed that whomever Benjamin had been dealing with had arranged to meet him there. Whether they would accept her as a replacement or not remained to be seen. Traveling to Syria was not easy for an American, but that at least would not be a problem; the passport in her hand indicated she was a Moroccan of French and Italian descent.

Whatever must be done would be done. Generations were counting on her to bring forward the next age.

Coldwell glanced at the passport. She would have to get her hair cut so that it matched the photo, but by tomorrow afternoon, Judy Coldwell would no longer exist. Agnes Perpetua would have taken her place. The tickets for the first leg of her journey were already waiting at the airport to be claimed.

Coldwell put the passport and money into her purse, then closed the box.

"I'm done here," she told the clerk outside. "Done."

EASTERN SYRIA

Thera's scream was followed by a steady rattle of gunfire from an AK-47, followed by an MP5's sturdier whistle. Ferg ran around the north side of the building, aiming to flank who'd ever come out.

"Thera," he said as he ran. "Where are you? Yo."

She didn't answer. When he reached the back corner of the building he threw himself down, moving forward slowly on the ground.

Something moved near the doorway. Thera.

She bent down, reaching for the doorknob.

"What are you doing?" said Ferguson.

"Duck!" she told him, flipping a grenade in through the crack and then running back toward the berm ten yards away. She made it just as the grenade went off.

Ferguson rose and walked toward the doorway. Two men lay sprawled in the dirt nearby; a third had been killed inside the building by Thera's grenade. None of the men was Khazaal.

"Run up and cover the front of the building," Ferguson told her.

"You're not going in, are you?" she asked.

"Just get up there and make sure no one came out while we were playing back here."

The interior of the building had been divided in half by a wall that ran only partway to the high ceiling. Except for the dead man and a few scattered cartons, the room at the back was empty. Ferguson moved inside as quietly as he could, then raised his grenade launcher and pumped a shell of tear gas over the wall. He pulled up his shotgun, aiming it at the open doorway, then ran forward to the wall. Though he had a pretty strong suspicion that the front half of the building was empty, he rolled on the floor and crawled his way inside.

A hundred boxes or more lined the wall on his left. The rest of the place was empty. The boxes were filled with infant formula, according to the writing on the side.

"Is this where Khazaal is going?" asked Thera when he came out.

"I don't know yet," he told her. "Let's go put down markers for the airborne guys and then hide."

"I'm sorry I had to shoot," said Thera.

"Forget about it now. Come on. Their Mercedes should be about ninety seconds away."

Nearly ten miles to the south, Rankin stopped his bike in the desert and pulled out his paper map, correlating his position against the handheld GPS device. He flipped the radio into satellite mode. "Fouad, is he still coming this way?"

"Yes," said the Iraqi.

"Where's he going?" asked Guns. The two Rangers they'd taken with them pulled up behind them.

"Maybe for that airfield at the corner there," said Rankin. "Let's move up the road to the intersection with the airport."

Ferguson hid behind the Land Rover, and Thera crouched at the edge of the building as the battered Mercedes rounded the turnoff and headed for the complex.

"You have the first guy out. I have the second," said Ferguson. "Make sure the mask covers your glasses. This gas is worse than CS by a factor of ten."

"No way."

"Try it and see," said Ferguson, readying the grenades.

The Mercedes stopped alongside the Land Rover. The two men inside made things easy by getting out at the same time.

Thwack!

Thera's crossbow landed in the driver's left shoulder, where the plunger tip injected enough anesthetic to knock him senseless within three seconds. By then, Ferguson had knocked the second man to the ground with a plastic round to the head. He soft-tossed a tear gas grenade into the car as he ran to the man, kicking away a fallen pistol. Though the man had been knocked unconscious by the blow, Ferg injected a heavy dose of the sodium pentothal to keep him out. A fog of tear gas enveloped the area; Ferguson and Thera had to pull the two men all the way to the fence before they were clear.

Ferguson cursed when he took off his mask. Neither of the men in the Mercedes was Khazaal. He took out a small digital camera to transmit the pictures back to Fouad.

"I don't know who they are," Fouad said. "They may be with the resistance, but most likely they are smugglers."

"Smugglers sell baby food?" asked Ferguson.

"Maybe. It might have been stolen inside Iraq and stored there, to be sold elsewhere. The relief agencies bring in supplies, and the scum steal it away."

"All right. We'll get them picked up anyway. Where's the third vehicle and what was it?"

"A Ford. I do not think it belongs to the resistance."

"Which would be why they would use it, no?"

"I don't think they are that clever."

"But I do," said Ferguson. He pulled out his map and spread it on the hood of the Land Rover to orient himself. As he did, Rankin told him over the radio that the second Mercedes had just passed the airstrip.

"We're going to be too far behind now to catch him if he stays on the highway," said Rankin.

Ferguson looked at the map. The highway headed southwestward for over a hundred miles before approaching civilization; there were few places on that stretch where it could turn off. The MC-130 with the special operations forces aboard could make it across the border within a few minutes and get ahead of the car, but if they missed the ambush they wouldn't get another shot. And Ferguson and Thera would have to take the other car out by themselves.

"I'll have Van Buren's Rangers set up an ambush down the road," Ferg told Rankin. "Just keep following."

OVER SYRIA

Colonel Van Buren moved from the command area at the front of the First Team's specially equipped MC-130 into the assault bay, where Captain Ricardo Melfi and a team of hand-picked Rangers and Special Forces soldiers were waiting to jump.

"Godspeed," said Van Buren, holding up his thumb. Melfi, about twenty feet away, signaled back. Van Buren found a handhold and watched his people crowding toward the cargo ramp, eager to get into action. They were shadows in the unlit bay, and he tried to keep them that way, anonymous warriors; it made it more difficult to deal with problems if he thought of them as individuals with families and loved ones.

Designed to fly through hostile territory at very low altitude to avoid radar, the MC-130 used a satellite system to show its flight crew precisely where they were. The airplane banked and began to rise over the target area, a desolate curve in the highway the second Mercedes was taking. The men went out quickly, executing an extremely dangerous low-level drop as if they were stepping off an amusement park ride back in the States. By the time the airplane banked north, the troops were on the ground, squaring away their chutes.

Van Buren went back to his post. Modified from a stretched version of the Hercules (officially, the C-130J/J-30), the forward area of the First

Team's MC-130 was equipped with radio surveillance and communication gear similar to those used in the Commando Solo and ABCCC airborne battlefield controller versions of the Hercules, with a few of the links used by JSTARS thrown in for good measure. Van Buren got on the radio to the two Chinooks that had been tasked for the pickup. The aircraft were now airborne over Iraq and were about twenty minutes from the border.

"We can hear a vehicle coming north," said Melfi when he checked in.

Van Buren checked the image from the Predator.

"That'll be them. Get ready."

Melfi crouched a few yards from the road as the Mercedes approached the curve. The trick wasn't stopping the car; it was stopping the car without killing the people inside. The fact that his men had been on the ground for less than ten minutes made things even more interesting.

Two Special Forces sergeants took positions on the right flank of the road, aiming SRAW weapons at the car. SRAW stood for Short Range Assault Weapon. The missile—known as a "Predator" before the Air Force hogged the nickname for its UAV—was designed to disable tanks as well as light-armor vehicles and built-up positions, replacing the LAW and AT-4. Essentially a modern version of the World War II–era bazooka, the stock weapon typically struck an armored target from the top rather than the side, guided by a laser range finder and a magnetic detector. The warhead normally consisted of two parts, an explosive penetrator and a fragmentation grenade: the warhead would penetrate the outer shell of whatever was being attacked, and the grenade would kill whoever was inside.

Melfi's men were using a special version of the missile. Its titanium and steel warhead did not contain explosives. The idea was that the slug would destroy the front of the car and its engine, stopping it without killing the people inside.

"Now," said Melfi, ducking down.

The missile made an unearthly hiss as it leapt from the shoulder of the weapons man. The car veered to the right under the blow, plowing to a halt across the road. As it skidded, a Ranger jumped up with what looked like a mortar in his hands. He sighted a red laser dot on the top of the car and squeezed the wide trigger at the base of the weapon. A large, blimp-shaped missile flew from the throat of the gun. The shell disintegrated in midair; by the time it hit the vehicle it had spread into a wide net. Two dozen miniature flash-bang grenades exploded as it hit, the effect not unlike the finale of a massive Fourth of July fireworks display. As the air ripped with the explosions, two pairs of soldiers ran to the car. One man in each pair wielded a pointed sledgehammer, the other carried CS grenades. The back window and one of the side windows were walloped and the grenades inserted.

"Team up! Team up!" yelled Melfi as smoke began pouring from the car. Six men in heavy body armor and gas masks came forward, armed with crowbars and chain saws; they were covered at close range by four others with more conventional weapons of war. One of the occupants of the vehicle had managed to open his door before being overcome by the gas. He was pulled down, secured under the netting. The team tore off the roof of the vehicle, cutting through the nylon mesh as well as the metal.

"Go, let's go!" said Melfi. He pulled up and snugged his gas mask as the fumes surged from the car. "Do it! Get every one of them out."

By the time Rankin got there, all of the men had been taken out and trussed. Two were unconscious, leaning against each other. One lay on the ground moaning. The last sat a few feet away from the others, staring sullenly into the night.

None of the men looked remotely like Khazaal.

"Any papers?" Rankin asked Melfi.

"Nothing. Nothing in the car."

"Take their pictures. Let the Iraqi look at them."

Melfi squinted at him. It was the cross-eyed squint captains reserve for NCOs, even those on special assignments, who give them orders. Nonetheless, he told one of his men to do it.

"How far off are the choppers?" Melfi asked.

"Eighteen minutes," said Rankin. "We'll hear them a good way out."

EASTERN SYRIA

Ferguson decided the motorcycles were too far away to walk to, so he hotwired the Land Rover instead. Telling the two Rangers he'd posted on the road to come in and watch the prisoners, he took off with Thera to a spot where he thought he could intercept the third vehicle.

Driving across the open terrain would have been difficult enough in the daytime, since it was pockmarked with boulders and sandpits, but at night without headlamps it was treacherous, which only made it more interesting. Ferguson had Thera pull the satellite photos from his pack as he drove, trying to dodge the worst of the obstructions. They had more than two miles of hardscrabble to get through before reaching a road to the northwest.

"Let me see that sat photo with this grid in it."

"It's two satellite photos," Thera told him, reaching down to get them from the pack on the Land Rover's floor.

"Point to where we are and where that other road is," said Ferguson.

"Here and here," said Thera.

He took the photos and held them on the wheel for a second, then tossed them back.

"All right. Let's try this," he said, pulling sharply off the road.

"Jesus, Mary, and Joseph!"

"Friend of mine says that," Ferg told her. "You Catholic?"

"What are you doing?"

"Shortcut. You Catholic?"

"Greek Orthodox, but I went to parochial school."

"Good thing that didn't come up in the job interview," said Ferguson. "Would've disqualified you as a fanatic."

"I heard you went to Catholic school yourself."

"That's what I mean."

When he finally spotted the highway, Ferguson misjudged the depth of the ditch along the side of the road and nearly rolled the Land Rover trying to veer onto the pavement. Thera flew forward, barely keeping herself from slamming into the dashboard. Belatedly, she began fishing for the seat belts.

The Ford was behind them now, but with the road and terrain fairly open, Ferguson needed a strategic place to lay a trap. He'd spotted an intersection about three miles ahead on the map. He told Thera they would put the truck in the middle of it as if it had broken down, then shoot out the Ford's tires when it stopped to see what was going on. After that they'd use the crossbow and tear gas routine again.

They were still about two miles from the intersection when a shadow loomed over the empty field to his right. Ferguson jammed on the brakes.

An airplane flying at very low altitude, no more than a few feet off the ground, passed over the roadway ahead.

Ferguson jumped out of the car. "Son of a bitch."

"What?"

"Look." He pointed in the distance.

"What?"

"You see that?"

"The airplane? Is it ours?"

"Nah. It's a little Cessna thing. Or some Russian plane like a Cessna." The plane continued on a straight line to the west, twelve or so feet above the ground.

"Back in the car," said Ferguson, deciding they'd take the Ford anyway.

"You really think that was Khazaal?" asked Thera.

"Who else would be flying a plane at low altitude across the Syrian frontier?"

"Dozens of people," she told him. "Smugglers, drug dealers, some other terrorist scumbags we don't know about."

"Nice try, but you're not going to cheer me up," said Ferguson. He stepped on the gas, going up over a hill and then down so fast that they went airborne for a moment. That gave him an idea. He hit the brakes and backed up, putting the car off one side of the road.

"All right. Out," he told her. "Take off your shirt."

"What?"

"Just to rip the sleeve," he said, pulling open his pocketknife. "The left sleeve. Driver's side. You can leave it on if you trust me."

"I'll do it myself, thanks," said Thera, holding out her hand for the knife.

"Come on. We probably have less than two minutes," Ferguson told her. "Open the door and lean out. When they stop and come over, drop the tear gas canister. I'll be over there with the shotgun."

"What if they don't stop?"

"I'll take out a tire with your crossbow. If they don't hear a gun they'll stop," he told her. "And if they don't we can always catch up to them in the Land Rover. But if you rip enough of that shirt off, they'll stop."

"Ha, ha."

"Who's joking?"

Ferguson trotted down the road. He had one shell with netting and flash-bangs, a large projectile with a very short range. It was tempting, very tempting, to load the grenade launcher with a high-explosive grenade and use it on the car; the Ford wouldn't be armored. If anyone asked any questions, it would be easy to claim that the vehicle tried to run him down. No one would know any different. But *he* would know, and that was enough.

Ferguson barely had time to get his weapons laid out and set himself before the Ford came over the hill. It moved much slower than the Land Rover had. Ferguson steadied the crossbow then put it down as the vehicle skidded to a stop. Four men, all with small weapons, got out of the car.

Ferguson aimed the grenade launcher point-blank at the tallest of the men and fired. The launcher kicked up as the grenade shot off. He missed the man and hit the side of the truck, igniting the stun grenade and the micromesh net. Ferguson dropped the launcher and thumped two slugs from his shotgun into the men who were still standing, the thick plastic bullets pounding the back of their heads. He had to hit one of the lugs a second time before he fell. By then, tear gas had begun curling out of the Land Rover.

Thera scrambled back through the front of the truck, kicking out of the open passenger-side door. As she reached the ground, one of the men began firing an AK-47 in her direction. She huddled low, grabbing for her own gun. Whirling around, she saw one of the men crawling through the truck. He had a pistol; she fired her own gun point-blank into his forehead.

Ferguson ran to the far side of the Land Rover, grabbing Thera as she staggered backward, coughing from the gas. He pulled her away and gave her a water bottle to irrigate her eyes, then trotted back to the truck. Two of the men were writhing on the ground, one still holding his gun. Ferguson blasted each one in the skull and got the other man for good measure. Then he hit them with the syringes.

"You weren't kidding about the gas," said Thera when he got back to her. Tears were streaming from her beet-red face.

"I meant for you to put the mask on before you pulled the grenade," said Ferguson.

"How?"

He pulled his off, then held it to his face. "You could have run back to the side. It's all right. Men find it hard to resist a woman's tears."

"You're on a roll tonight," she told him sarcastically.

"Tell me about it." Ferguson walked over to the car. Besides a half-dozen guns on the floor of the rear seat, he found a duffle bag filled with hundred-dollar bills.

None of the men were Khazaal. The night had been a total wipeout.

ACT III

They have shed the blood of saints and prophets, and thou hast given them
blood to drink . . .

—Revelation 16:6 (King James Version)

1

Menacham Stein, the Mossad officer who had worked with the First Team on Seven Angels, met Corrine at the airport in Tel Aviv. He looked more like a businessman on vacation than a spy: six feet tall, with slicked-back hair and a light scent of aftershave, he walked up to her as she came out of the tunnel off the plane and led her away from the others. He slid a magnetic card into a reader on a door, showing her into a stairwell that led to an empty corridor. After several more twists and turns they emerged in an area of offices before exiting in the main terminal section. Here he slowed his pace to an easy nonchalance, guiding her with a gentle tap on the shoulder to the doors. As they walked to the car she realized that there were at least two other men watching them.

"Your people, I assume," she said.

He smiled but said nothing, leading the way to a blue Ford in the middle of the lot. Corrine noticed another pair of men sitting in a car nearby.

"More?" she said.

"We don't like to take chances with important visitors," said the officer, popping the trunk for her bag.

While it looked ordinary from the outside, the vehicle had been heavily modified: the sides, roof, and floor had been armored and the glass reinforced. A phone sat on the console between driver and passenger. The Mossad officer reached under the dash and put his finger on a small device that read his fingerprint. This gave him five seconds to insert his key in the ignition and start the car.

"First time in Tel Aviv?" asked Stein.

"It's my third or fourth, but it's been ten years. You sound like you've spent a great deal of time in the U.S.," she added. "Do you come from New York?"

"I lived in Brooklyn for a few years," said Stein, but he didn't elaborate.

Inside the Mossad building, Corrine was searched politely but not perfunctorily. Stein took her to an elevator that led to an isolated part of the building, where a special room was set up for top-secret conversations. To secure the room against possible eavesdropping, it had been sheathed in a layer of copper and its supports isolated from vibrations, so that it literally floated within the space. More conventionally, radio and microwave detection devices hunted for transmissions emanating not only from the room but from any of the nearby areas, and white noise generators provided a sonic barrier around the facility.

To get into the secure area, they had to walk down a tunnellike hall made of polished cement. As they started down it, another man came up from the other side. Corrine thought it was David Tischler, the Mossad supervisor she was meeting with, coming out to greet her. But after holding her glance for a brief moment, the man abruptly turned his head toward the wall and then put his hand up, shielding the other side of his face.

Stein touched her elbow, leading her through a small anteroom to the chamber where Tischler sat waiting.

"I hope your flight was a good one," said the Israeli, rising. Unlike Stein, he was short and a little overweight; it might not have been fair to say he had a potbelly, but he certainly didn't look like an athlete.

"We appreciate your help with the Seven Angels case," she told him as she sat down.

"Of course."

"I want to be assured that his death was random," said Corrine.

"God does not call us randomly. But in the sense you mean it, yes. It was an accident. Whether it was fortunate or unfortunate, I suppose we can't tell."

"It was unfortunate for our investigation," said Corrine. "He would have been apprehended, and you would have had more information about the people he wanted to contact."

Tischler's narrow brown eyes held no expression; his mouth was the mouth of a man staring into space, revealing nothing.

"Ferg was there," said Stein, who unlike his boss seemed agitated at the question. "What did he think?"

"Mr. Ferguson was a little too close to be objective," said Corrine.

"He thought it was random, too," suggested Stein. "As did I."

"Mr. Ferguson wasn't prepared to say it wasn't random. But he lacked proof, one way or the other."

"Spoken like an American lawyer," said Stein.

The faintest of grins appeared on Tischler's face.

"We've made arrests in the case," said Corrine, loosening her tone slightly. "The FBI will share what's appropriate as it becomes available. If you require specific items to assist you, I can certainly facilitate sharing that. As I said, we appreciate your assistance. I'm wondering if you've developed any additional information that might be useful to us."

"We've shared everything we know," said Stein.

"There was a jeweler?"

"A blind, as far as we can tell."

Corrine looked at Tischler, whose face was once more a blank wall. "Do you see a connection between Seven Angels and Nisieen Khazaal?"

Tischler's eyes widened ever so slightly. "Is there one?"

"Thatch was on his way to Egypt. We believe the people he was to see in Cairo may have been on their way to the meeting that Khazaal is going to."

Tischler's eyes went dull again. "I guess."

"It would be difficult to believe," said Stein. "The Seven Angels would be more aptly named Seven Wanna-bes. They're really amateurs. Thatch would have been killed by them, just as Ferguson almost was."

The connection between Seven Angels and Khazaal was every bit as far-fetched as Stein said. Egyptian intelligence indicated that the tailor, Ahmed Abu Saahlid, commanded a network of terrorists and had plans to travel to Lebanon or Syria—typically for the Egyptians, they couldn't be specific. The tailor opposed the Egyptian government and was "of interest," something that might be said of at least a third of the Egyptian population. Nothing in his dossier, however, showed that he had any connection with Khazaal or any Iraqi for that matter. The Egyptian report made it seem unlikely that he would have been willing to act as a go-between with Seven Angels even if he did have access to Khazaal. Several of his recorded statements showed he despised Americans in general, and Ferguson's experience with him demonstrated a willingness to act on those beliefs.

But something in Stein's answer interested Corrine a great deal: the line about wanna-bes. It had been in an FBI report she'd read on the way over, one that was *not* among the documents shared with the Israelis.

Coincidence? It was a common phrase.

"I suppose it's unlikely there's a connection," said Corrine, moving on to the real reason she'd come to see Tischler in person. "What else can you tell us about Khazaal?"

"Very little," said Tischler.

"You know his travel plans?"

"Only that he is due to see others in Syria. Two men we have interest in over in Damascus transferred some money into an account used by one of the exile groups friendly to the so-called resistance. And a room there was rented for the weekend."

One of the men was being followed by Iraqi intelligence, and the bank account was being monitored by the CIA. But it was possible that the exiles had already been tipped off; the second man had disappeared.

"Do you expect the meeting in Damascus?" asked Corrine.

"Not necessarily," said Tischler. "Damascus would not be ideal, because of the Syrian government's presence. Somewhere in the east, perhaps."

While that would sound logical to someone uninitiated in the intrigues of Iraq, the sparsely populated desert areas of Syria were much worse than the capital of Syria. Strangers there tended to stick out, and there were many competing interests—Kurds, informants, smugglers, drug dealers—who would have much to gain by supplying information to the Syrians or to the Iraqi spies and operatives in the area. A meeting outside of a city would be visible to spy planes or satellites. Though in reality the coverage over the area was spotty at best, the resistance people tended to think American coverage was twenty-four/seven.

So why had Tischler even suggested it, Corrine wondered. "Could you make an educated guess?"

"Syria is a place where educated guesses can often get one in trouble," said Tischler. "I wouldn't try."

Corrine let the matter drop temporarily, asking if the Mossad required assistance on any other projects and receiving the bland answers she expected. Finally she glanced at her watch.

"I'm afraid I'm running a little late," she said, rising. "I'm due at the embassy."

"Of course." Tischler rose. "If we can be of further assistance while you're in Tel Aviv, please tell us."

"Thank you. The Khazaal meeting—"

The Mossad officer looked at her expectantly as she paused. He was well practiced at keeping his face expressionless, and Corrine simply couldn't tell now whether he knew more about it than he had shared.

"You would suppose that would be more likely in the west than in the east," she suggested.

"I've learned not to suppose."

An answer there could be no arguing with, Corrine thought. "If we get any additional information," she said, extending her hand. "We'll share it."

"As we will with you," said Tischler, walking out with them.

CIA BUILDING 24-442, VIRGINIA

Thomas Ciello could not believe his good fortune. The CIA analyst had stopped at the post office on his way to work and found, completely unexpectedly, a new manuscript on UFOs by Carmine P. Ragguzi. Professor Ragguzi, a true genius who had devoted nearly forty years of his life to the problem of extraterrestrial communication, had sent a select group of devotees an advanced copy of a mammoth work on UFO sightings he hoped to publish next year. A letter that accompanied the book urged Ciello to "make whatever suggestions you feel are warranted." Of course, given that Ragguzi was a genius, Ciello doubted that he could do much more than cheer. Nonetheless, the opportunity to read a Ragguzi work before it was released to the rest of the world was truly an honor. He took it inside with him, hoping to steal a glance at lunch or on his morning break.

The security person at the entrance to the CIA building didn't bother hiding her skepticism when Thomas told her what it was. He was used to that sort of reaction and waited patiently while she applied a blacklight stamp to several of the pages and made random photocopies of a few more so the work could be checked on the way out. Security at the CIA in general was tight, but Building 24-442 had even more elaborate precautions. Even though it had been logged and inspected, it was possible that the manuscript would be confiscated when he tried to take it home and held until it had been thoroughly checked for classified information. The process could take days—there were no preset limits—but Thomas was so eager to start reading the book inside that he didn't mind the hassle. Besides, he'd spent just about every waking hour here since joining the First Team as what Corrigan called its resident "geek freak." If he was going to find any spare time at all, it would be here.

Thomas thought "geek freak" was a compliment, though sometimes the people on the action side of the agency were too eccentric to decipher.

Cleared down to his office, Thomas immediately went to work, signing into his network and "checking the traps" as he called it: reviewing overnight alerts, briefs, and regular news developments. Thomas's position at the Agency was unique: he was assigned to facilitate intelligence gathering for a specific group and had access to nearly every area of the Agency to do so. Still, it mostly came down to reading. Making sense of what you read was important, surely, but you had to read it first.

Three days before, he had asked the National Security Agency to "harvest" possible communications in Syria related to Nisieen Khazaal. The request had yielded two phone conversations which included an alias Khazaal was believed to use: Snake. Translated by computer from Arabic, the conversations were both brief and frustrating:

1.
MAN'S VOICE 1: The Snake is not here.
MAN'S VOICE 2: Yes.
MAN'S VOICE 1: Yes.

[Disconnect]

2.
MAN'S VOICE 1: When?
MAN'S VOICE 2: The day after tomorrow.
MAN'S VOICE 1: Difficult.
MAN'S VOICE 2: The snake will be in the East. It must be then.

[Disconnect]

Did they pertain to Khazaal? The NSA didn't pretend to know. That wasn't their job; they just gathered conversations and passed them on.

Thomas set the intercepts aside in one of his note files on the secure computer and continued trolling through the information and notes that had accumulated while he slept. He had a memo from the desk—from Corrigan, actually, who usually personally supported the First Team during a critical mission—about the desert snatch operation, and a brief on the preliminary interrogation of the men they'd stopped in Syria. Two of the men who'd been in the last car stopped, a Ford, had been positively identified, and Thomas recognized one of the names right away, Sadeghi Saed, a Palestinian who had helped fund a Shiite resistance group in Iraq. Thomas set that aside as well.

Were there a lot of Fords in Syria? He hadn't thought so. He punched into a database, trying to see if it was significant.

There were in fact many thousands. But perhaps some additional information about it would allow him to trace it. He accessed another database compiling foreign registrations and found that VIN or vehicle identification numbers were sometimes used to show where sales were; different series indicated different regions. It was a tenuous link, but he could at least differentiate between vehicles brought into Syria and Iraq; and, after he looked through some customs records poached by an NSA computer program from Lebanon, that country as well.

Thomas wrote a quick "action note" for Corrigan, asking for the VIN attached to the various components; the brief on the vehicle had already indicated there was no visible registration.

Two hours and many notes later, the UFO manuscript beckoned at the corner of his desk. Deciding he was ready for a break, Thomas dragged it over and opened to a page at random.

The 1950s Turkey sightings and landings were the most phenomenal event in the history of mankind, and a key extraterrestrial moment.

Thomas gasped. That was a serious error. The sighting he was referring to had actually been U.S. Air Force spy flights, with the UFO story floated out as a cover when the Soviets became suspicious.

"Ah, there you are," said Debra Wu, peeking in the doorway. Wu was Corrigan's assistant.

Thomas practically jumped out of his chair, grabbing the manuscript and holding it to his chest. Unfortunately, the papers weren't bound, and they flew all over the office.

Wu rolled her eyes. Ciello was eccentric, even for an analyst.

"Corrigan wants to see you. He's downstairs."

"I'm going." Thomas grabbed the papers and took them to one of the lockable file cabinets at the side of his room. Technically, the cabinet was only supposed to be used to temporarily store classified information. But he had no other place to put the manuscript, and besides, his cabinets were all empty.

He leaned to the side so she couldn't see his combination, then stuffed the pages of Professor Ragguzi's book inside. He gave the lock a spin, then another and another.

"I'm not going to break in," Wu told him disgustedly as she walked away.

Corrigan was in the middle of a call with Corrine Alston when Thomas cleared security to get into the Cube's situation room. Unlike in the movies, the facility was extremely simple: no large-screen video panels, no wall of constantly updated radar plots and infrared views. Corrigan sat at a simple metal desk with a single computer and a large telephone set. If the situation called for it, several more very plain desks and computers could be set up in the open area to the left. The chairs that were used were terribly uncomfortable and the computer screens among the cheapest available. Corrigan's main equipment consisted of a telephone headset. The lines it connected to were scrambled, and some actually tied into radio frequencies, but the operation of the phones themselves was no more difficult than the setup for a typical corporate office cubicle. It was what you did with the phones that mattered.

Corrigan raised his finger as Thomas came in, signaling for him to take a seat.

"The interrogation is ongoing," Corrigan told the person on the other end of the phone line. "I don't know why Ferg couldn't make it to Tel Aviv, but I assume that had something to do with it."

Thomas couldn't hear the other side of the conversation, though he could tell from Corrigan's expression that it wasn't pleasant. That led Thomas to conclude, correctly, that Corrigan was speaking to the president's counsel, Corrine Alston. Thomas had never met her, but he'd heard that she was difficult to satisfy and expected prompt and perfect results.

Thomas tapped his feet impatiently as he continued to wait. He wondered if he should ask Corrigan about the Turkey UFOs, perhaps even share Professor Ragguzi's manuscript with him. They'd never actually discussed UFOs, at least not in depth, but he was fairly certain Corrigan was a fellow believer, one of the very few he'd encountered at the Agency. Working for the CIA had the unfortunate effect of dulling most people's capacity for imagination.

Corrigan held up a piece of paper for Thomas, sliding it toward him.

It was the VIN numbers he had asked for. He recognized the sequence at the start of the long number: it was one of the Lebanese vehicles. It was also two years old.

"Thomas," said Corrigan, finally off the phone. "We need to find out where Khazaal is going. Absolutely need to find out."

"The Ford came from Lebanon originally," said Thomas.

"It's a start. What else do you know?"

Thomas told him about the snake intercept and a few other things.

"So the bottom line is, you know nothing," said Corrigan. "What would you say about western Lebanon? Could the meeting be there? It could be there, couldn't it?"

"It could be anywhere. I think the car—"

"Yes, yes. The car came from there."

"No," said Thomas. "The car originally was shipped into Lebanon two years ago."

"We have a map showing Tripoli circled, the Tripoli in Lebanon on the coast, not the one in Libya. You think it could be there?"

Thomas was not an expert on the Middle East (he'd been brought into the job primarily because he was more a generalist, though he had a great deal of experience tracking terrorist groups), and so he could only shrug.

Not that he would have had a different answer if he had been an expert.

"Ferg says there's an Iraqi community there," Corrigan told him. "Got to get everything you can get and tell me what you think. You have one hour."

ISRAEL, NEAR GAZA

Ravid folded the newspaper under his arm as the line began to move forward again. The corrugated steel roof of the Israeli checkpoint shut away some of the sun but not the heat nor the dust and certainly not the languid boredom and anxiety that mixed together as the crowd waited to pass into the Gaza Strip. It had become nearly as difficult to get out of Israel as it was to get in, at least if you were a Palestinian, as Ravid's papers claimed he was. Weapons gates and ID checks were routine, and it was not unusual for Israeli intelligence officers to choose someone at random for interrogation. Palestinian guards waited on the other side of the border, and while they rarely stopped anyone, they could make one's life thoroughly miserable, with less chance of appeal than one would have in Israel.

In Ravid's case, life could be very miserable indeed; his Palestinian papers were forgeries, part of the elaborate shell game of covers he played, his true identity hidden like the heart of an onion under many skins. As an Arab intellectual and activist, it was natural for him to use a cover to travel into Israel. If he got caught by the Israelis, well, that would be inconvenient but would at least shore up his phony identity.

If he got caught on the Palestinian side, however, his fate was less sure. Eighteen months ago, he had known many people who could clear up a "misunderstanding." Now there was no telling if they were even still alive.

Tischler had told Ravid relatively little of his mission. This was Tischler's way, for his own protection as well as the mission's: information became available as it was necessary, never before. But Ravid got the definite impression that Tischler no longer trusted him. The Mossad supervisor had asked about the drinking, trying to make it seem offhanded: "Still enjoying the vodka?"

"No," said Ravid. "No."

The truth, though of course it was not quite that simple.

Up ahead, one of the guards began giving a woman a hard time. Her documents were due to expire tonight. He decided that meant she had to be searched; the machine and the wand were not good enough. A pair of female guards walked over and began talking to the woman, who balked for a moment before conceding to the inevitable and following them to a small building nearby.

Ravid glanced at the young man behind him. He had a dull, dazed look on his face. The man just wanted to return home with a minimum of hassle. He would endure whatever he had to, as long as he achieved his goal.

Two years ago, the look of resignation would have roused pity in Ravid. Now it kindled anger, incredible anger. He wanted to kill the man, to kill all the Muslims here, every one of the them, stomp them from the earth.

He clenched his fist against his rage. Wrath was useless here. Stomping a few men, even a few hundred, wouldn't satisfy him.

Coming back might offer him a chance for revenge on the scale he wanted, but never with Mossad's blessing. He was not so foolish to think that he would have it. And to even hint at simmering animosity, let alone the deeper emotions he felt, would have been the end of the interview with Tischler. There was a line that he could not cross no matter how badly he was needed. Simply to deny emotion was the safest course.

Mossad would be watching him very carefully. There were other agents, men and women, not quite as good, not as experienced or adept, but able nonetheless. They would be watching for him to slip, hoping (perhaps) that he wouldn't, but ready if he did. This would make it difficult for him to find a way for revenge but not impossible. Not if a big enough opportunity came.

To a man of his abilities, to a man of his wrath, nothing was impossible.

Ravid's throat felt so dry it cracked. He wanted a drink. Vodka, gin even.

A drink!

With all the will he could muster, Ravid pushed his tongue around his lips, wetting them. If he could master this thirst, he could master anything.

The line began to move. One of the guards pointed to him, gesturing him toward a metal detector. Ravid hesitated, his thirst overwhelming. The young man with downtrodden eyes nudged him gently, anxious that he wouldn't lose his own place in line.

"Wait," said the Israeli, pointing toward his arm.

Ravid did not understand at first, and by the time he realized what the soldier was after, the man had pulled the paper out from under his arm. *Sawt Al-Haqq Wal-Hurriya* (Voice of Truth and Freedom) was considered anti-Israeli.

"Why do you have this?" demanded the guard.

Ravid stared at the soldier rather than answering. Silence was always safest.

The man took the paper and threw it into a nearby trash bag. "Go," said the soldier, gesturing dismissively.

INCIRLIK, TURKEY

Van Buren tried hard not to glance at his watch. If he wanted to catch his son before he left for the weekend tournament, he had to call him before ten o'clock Eastern Time. It was now ten minutes to the hour. But the planning session was too important to interrupt, not the kind of thing you stopped for a personal matter.

"I don't know whether the Israeli information is wrong or not," said Ferguson. Ferguson got up and went over to the side of the large conference room to try some of the coffee. They'd been given the use of several rooms at the U.S. Air Force facility in western Turkey, where the First Team MC-130 and other support units were temporarily based. The location made it easier to fly near Syria and was less vulnerable to Iraqi resistance spies and possible attacks than a base in western Iraq would have been. Ferg, Fouad and the prisoners had transferred from the Chinooks to the MC-130 at a small airfield and come directly here the night before.

"The map we found with the money shows a route to Tripoli, Lebanon," said Ferguson.

"Doesn't mean Khazaal's going there," said Van Buren. "Or that he got past us."

"The airplane was headed toward Beirut when the Israelis lost track of it. And the car that grabbed our friend came from Lebanon."

There were holes in the intelligence supporting Ferguson's theory, and he knew it. The vehicle had been stolen from northern Lebanon, not from Beirut or the western coast. And the Israeli surveillance plane that had managed to spot the plane had lost sight of it near Beirut. They weren't even sure it was the same plane, only that it had come from the right direction, was the right size, and did not correlate with any known or filed flights.

But there was also circumstantial evidence to support the theory. Tarabulus esh Sham, more commonly known as Tripoli, sat on the Lebanese coast at the end of a long oil pipeline back to Iraq. There were many Iraqis in the city and region. Drug dealers liked the spot because of the port.

"What do you say, Fouad?" asked Van Buren.

"As Mr. Ferguson would have it, the fact that I don't expect it makes it likely."

"Not everybody's thinking two steps ahead," said Van.

"Khazaal does," said Ferguson. "I know it's a long shot, but at the moment it's our best guess."

"Assuming we missed him."

"Even if we didn't miss him. I can't search all of Syria and all of Lebanon. I have to start making some guesses."

"We can't run an operation there," said Van Buren. "It's too urban."

"I don't expect you to," said Ferguson. "Best bet is to go in by sea. This way I don't advertise to the local security types that I'm in."

"They know you?"

"I was there last year, briefly," said Ferg. "One or two might have reason to remember."

Van Buren liked the CIA officer a lot, though he tended to cut things a little too close to the bone. The First Team was a cooperative venture between the CIA and the Special Operations Command; the two men headed their respective halves, cooperating better with each other than anyone would have predicted before the program began. The arrival of Corrine Alston as the president's direct representative—and, in effect, their boss—bothered Ferguson a great deal, because he saw it as political interference. Van Buren didn't know it as fact, but he gathered that Ferguson believed his father's career at the Agency had been sabotaged by similar second-guessing.

Van Buren's take on Alston was different. As a colonel and career military man, he was used to dealing with bureaucratic politics, and Alston had been nothing but supportive. She had her own set of questions and priorities, but considering that the latter probably came directly from the president, she had been relatively easy to work with.

"We leave the scout mission at the border intact," said Ferguson. "But we'll start looking around in the cities nearby in case we've missed him already. Fouad can help Rankin and Thera handle that. Your guys stay on the border with Guns, ready to run a replay of last night. Hopefully with better results."

"You're just going into Lebanon by yourself?" asked Fouad.

Van Buren had the same question, though it was typical of Ferg. He had a knack for slipping in and out of places he didn't belong.

"It's a scouting mission. I'll be in and out. If the meeting is going to be held there, I'm going to want as many clean faces as I can get, including yours. And maybe Van's."

"Thanks, but my job is with the troops."

Ferguson laughed, then became more serious. "Once I see if anything's up I'll fall back and regroup. We just don't have enough time to sit out in the desert and wait. This meeting's supposed to take place in a matter of days."

"Well, I agree we must try a chance," said Fouad. "If this is the best of your information, it makes sense."

"It's the best at the moment." One of the earliest lessons Ferguson had learned was to be prejudiced toward action; you didn't accomplish anything by hanging out and drinking coffee.

Well, you might, but only if that was part of the plan.

"I know some people around town," Ferguson told them. "Maybe if nothing's happening, I'll head down to Beirut. It's not as bad as you think. Really."

"How friendly are these people to Americans?" asked Van Buren.

"To Americans, so-so. But I'm going as an Irishman." Ferg winked. "Everyone loves Irishmen."

"You have to talk to Alston about this, you know. She's still worked up about the fact that you went to Cairo without briefing her. Even I heard about it."

"I'll take care of her."

"She's only trying to do her job."

"Go make your phone call. I'll deal with Alston," Ferg told Van Buren. "But first I have to rustle up a milk truck."

EASTERN SYRIA
JUST BEFORE DAWN . . .

Rankin listened to the heavy crush of the Chinook's propellers as the massive chopper approached from the east. The desert reverberated with the big bird's distinctive sound, and though they'd scoured the area for insurgents with the UAV and even sent a pair of patrols toward the road, Rankin worried that a *hajji* would pop out of a spider hole they'd missed and slam the chopper with a shoulder-launched surface-to-air missile. He'd been on two helicopters that had barely escaped SAM attacks, and while he knew that the men and aircraft chosen for the mission here would be well equipped and trained to deal with the danger, he couldn't push aside his concern.

He'd noticed that a lot lately. He didn't fear for himself, but he worried about others getting hurt, almost like a father worried about his kids; or so he imagined. He personally had no experience of being a father, and his time with his own had been extremely limited, his parents divorcing when he was three.

"Two choppers?" said Guns, coming up next to him.

"Sounds like it."

"There's one of them." The Marine Corps sergeant pointed to the shadow of the first helicopter as it approached. The chopper had rotors fore and aft. The dual power plants made the Chinook among the most powerful helicopters in the world, capable not only of transporting forty-four fully armed soldiers but also of carrying upward of 26,000 pounds beneath her belly. This one had been chosen for just that reason: dangling in a massive sling beneath the chopper was the rear section of a tank truck.

Rankin and Guns watched as the Chinook squatted over the landing area. Several Rangers trotted over to help unhook the truck.

"Hate to be down there," said Guns.

"How's that?" asked Rankin. He was still thinking about the possibility of some scumbag popping up with a missile.

"Dirt and crap flying all over the place," said Guns. "You never get the grit out of your skin."

Rankin remembered the powdery sand that had clung to his body when he'd been in Iraq during the search for Scuds. Ancient history now.

Relieved of its load, the helicopter seemed to step back in the air before circling off to the right and landing a hundred yards or so down the road and disgorging its passengers. Meanwhile, the second chopper moved into position, the truck's cab dangling beneath its fuselage.

"That'll be Ferg," said Guns, gesturing toward the men coming off the helicopter ramp. "Maybe we ought to go check it out."

"I guess."

"Why don't you like him?" Guns asked.

"What's it to you?"

"Ain't nothin' to me," said Guns.

"Good."

Ferguson watched as the mechanics fiddled with the engine, trying to get it to start. With the way his luck was running, the stinking thing wouldn't work, and they'd lose the entire day. Fouad folded his arms next to him, his long face even longer.

"How was Turkey?" asked Thera, who'd come down from the base.

"Dark. How are these guys treating you?" asked Ferg.

"Not bad."

"Like being the only woman in the desert?"

"I'm used to it," said Thera. "What I'd like to try some time is being the only woman in a palace."

The engine coughed. A mass of black smoke emerged from the exhaust.

"Getting there," said one of the soldiers.

Ferguson wasn't so sure. He saw Guns coming down the path from the rocks, trailed by Captain Melfi, who'd come east to the base camp with most of his men after the snatch operation the night before.

"Hey, Houston, why don't we grab the rest of the team and have a little planning session?" Ferguson suggested, taking his rucksack.

"You going to keep up that Houston business instead of using my real
name?"

"It's better than some of the alternatives, don't you think?"

"I think Thera is fine."

"You don't get a vote." Ferguson smirked at her frown.

Melfi gave Ferguson an update on the traffic, or rather the lack of
traffic, as they walked back up to the command tent. They found Rankin
sitting at the table that dominated the room, staring at the large map. Ferg
helped himself to a cup of coffee, then leaned over the table, orienting himself.

"Couple of things might have happened," Ferguson told the others.
"One is that we missed him. In that case he may be waiting for the folks we
grabbed to show up in one of the cities around here. So we check them out."

"How did he get past us?" asked Rankin.

"Disguised, scooted right through with the rest of the traffic near Aby
Kamal," said Ferguson, pointing at the border city on the Euphrates.
"Bribed the guards, tricked the Americans."

"I don't see how they could have," said Melfi.

"Which of course would be how they did it," said Ferguson. "Or he
used one of the tunnels we don't know about. Or he came over a few days
ago. Or our information is completely bad."

Ferguson outlined the general game plan, telling Melfi that he and his
people would continue to watch the border area.

"In the meantime, Fouad, Rankin, and Thera are going to go over to
Sukna and then Deir Ex Zur and see if they can catch a whiff of the trail."
Ferguson reached into his rucksack and pulled out a large padded envelope,
which contained travel and identity documents, along with a bundle of
money. "You go as Egyptians with the milk truck. Everybody knows you're
smugglers looking for business."

"I don't look very Egyptian," said Rankin.

"No one will question it if you don't talk too much," said Fouad. "You
smear more red tone on your face and keep growing your beard, you look
fine."

"Maybe I ought to dress like a Bedouin," suggested Rankin.

"That's overdoing it," said Ferguson. "Anyone who studies your face is
going to know you haven't spent your life in the desert. You'll be all right.
Just the normal pajamas will do."

Rankin had a customized *salwar kameez,* an oversized shirt and baggy pants, which in his case were bulky enough to hide a lightweight bulletproof vest along with his weapons. He could obscure his face when necessary with a head scarf or *shimagh.*

Despite its poor relations with the U.S., in many ways Syria was much more liberal than many Middle Eastern countries, and Western-style clothing would be the norm in the larger towns and cities. Fouad was dressed little differently than a man would dress in America.

"The milk truck has a series of fake compartments," Ferguson told them. "I got it off a genuine smuggler. Actually, the First Airborne got it off a smuggler, and they said I could borrow it."

He explained how the compartments worked. There was one toward the cab area large enough to fit weapons and a series of smaller ones. "You can chain two of the motorcycles on the back, and another at the side. They may come in handy."

"Where are you going to be?" Thera asked Ferguson.

"The map those clowns were working with suggest they were going to Tarabulus esh Sham, Tripoli. Long shot but worth checking. It's north of Beirut."

"What happened to Syria?" asked Thera.

"Still in the running. It may be that they were going here first, maybe to pick up someone or sell something or even buy something, then heading north. I don't know." He shrugged. "Won't know until I get there and maybe not even then."

"What am I doing, Ferg?" asked Guns.

"For the time being, big guy, winning Melfi's poker money. Your Arabic isn't good enough to ride with those guys, and I don't want to burn you in Lebanon with me in case I need you to come in as a Russian drug dealer or something like that. If you're seen with me it'll kill your cover. Just remember, I get half your winnings here."

Guns smirked. Melfi didn't.

"Questions? Complaints?" asked Ferguson.

"There's five thousand Euros here," said Thera, flipping through the money.

"That's all they'd let me sign for."

She stared at him.

Ferguson realized she was thinking about the cash they'd found in the smuggler's car and laughed. "Don't forget your sunblock," he told them.

6

Sukna was a very small town, and it was clear as they approached that they were not going to get any information there, even it was to be had. A small patrol of Syrian soldiers met them outside of town and quizzed them. Fouad handled it somewhat nervously, and Thera worried that the man was going to make the mistake of offering the Syrians a bribe. Close to the border that might be expected, but here it would be regarded as an insult and perhaps worse.

Rankin pressed his elbow into the Iraqi's side, hoping to shut him up. Fouad blubbered on, talking inanely about the swarm of bugs that followed the truck, worrying that they were attracted by the souring milk in the back. Finally even the guards grew tired of him and waved them past the checkpoint.

"Why did you tell them that the milk was sour?" said Thera, leaning across Rankin.

The Iraqi shrugged.

"Talk less," said Rankin.

"I have been in this business longer than you have been alive," answered Fouad, though it had been many years since he had traveled undercover. The weather didn't help his mood, and the flies were atrocious. He thought to himself that he should have insisted on going to Tripoli, where at least he might have been able to find a pool to cool off in.

"This doesn't look like a good place to stop," said Thera as they came to a cluster of buildings that marked the start of the town center. Soldiers stood on both sides of the road.

Rankin agreed. They drove through slowly but saw no hint of what was going on. There was a second checkpoint at the northern outskirts; this time the soldiers wanted to check their truck. The interior had been dummied up against just such a possibility with a mixture of brackish water and milk. One of the soldiers made the mistake of tasting some of the liquid as it poured from the back and spit it into the sand; his companions laughed at him.

"Obviously a new recruit," said Rankin as they drove away.

"You think Khazaal's in the town and that's why they're here?" asked Thera.

"Nothing can be completely ruled out," said Fouad. "But the Syrian government would not want to be seen actively cooperating with the resistance at this time. If anything, the soldiers would be looking for him and others. You see how our truck was searched? They were looking for a person, not merchandise. They probably heard the helicopters yesterday or rumors of the gunfights. That is why they are here."

Rankin waited until they were a few miles out of town, then used the sat phone to call Corrigan and tell him about the Syrians. "They didn't look like a search party exactly," he told him. "But I don't know. Better tell Guns and the rest of them to be careful tonight."

They made decent time on the highway, stopping once for diesel. Thera found herself nodding off as they continued north, fatigue and the heat lulling her to sleep. Green appeared on the horizon; the wind suddenly felt humid. Then she drifted, sliding somewhere near Houston, where she'd grown up.

Rankin let Thera's weight shift against him. She had a compact body, not quite buxom enough on top to be a knockout but trim under the loose Arab clothes she wore. Her nose had the slightest hook to it, the sort of blemish that made a woman seem ugly at first but kept your eyes returning to her face until you realized that she was actually very beautiful. A curly strand of hair fell over her ear, drawing a line between the two post earrings.

He reached over and moved her against the side of the truck, not wanting his gun obstructed. He had a small Glock in his pants pocket; his Uzi was strapped beneath the dashboard.

"The woman is sleeping?" asked Fouad.

"Yeah."

"Women can always sleep."

"I guess."

"I have not been to Deir Ex Zur in many years."

"Makes two of us," said Rankin, though in fact he had never been there.

"It is the most likely place in the area that he would come," continued Fouad. "Everyone goes through it, and you can buy many things."

"Yeah. You're probably right."

Deir Ex Zur sat on an important trade route that dated well into prehistory. During the French domination of Syria, it had been an important French outpost, albeit a small one. Like so many other places in the Middle East, the discovery of oil here had changed the city's fortunes dramatically. It was now a relatively large city, by far the biggest in eastern Syria, with Western-style hotels and a smattering of Europeans on the streets. The Euphrates sat on the northern side of the city, less a boundary than a wide, rich vein of green and blue—and a gathering place for the squadrons of swarming bugs. They made their way to 8th Azar Street, one of the main thoroughfares. Rankin woke Thera when they found a lot to park in. They were a few blocks from the microbus station, which itself was several from the river and the heart of town.

"Time to go to work," he told her.

The area around the river had changed considerably since the last time Fouad had been here. While it had always had its share of tourist traps catering to Western visitors as well as Arabs, they had multiplied tenfold in the last two years. The forest of English signs crowding out Arabic pained Fouad as well as disoriented him.

Their first stop was a café frequented by Iraqi exiles on the south side of the river.

"It looks exactly as it did when I first saw it twenty years ago," said Fouad, surprised as well as relieved. "Wait for me."

"You sure you're all right?" asked Rankin.

Fouad, annoyed, put up his hand but said nothing.

When he had been gone five minutes, Rankin told Thera to come along.

"I thought you told him we'd stay out here."

"I don't trust him."

"Ferg does."

"I ain't Ferg."

Thera followed him inside. The influence of tourism had loosened local customs to the point that women were a sizable minority inside the café. If anything, Thera's rust-colored *jiba* and lace-up *hijab* and scarf were on the conservative side here. She followed Rankin to a seat several tables from Fouad, whose back was turned to them at a table in the corner. He was sitting alone.

They ordered tea, Thera doing the talking. She had a pistol strapped to the inside of each thigh as well as her left ankle; on her right were three small pin grenades, miniature flash-bangs that could be used to divert attention if she needed to escape. A knife, spare ammo, and two more pin grenades, these with smoke, were strapped below her breasts. The weapons

felt uncomfortable under the long dress, but it was something she'd have to get used to.

"Didn't even talk to anyone," grumbled Rankin as Fouad got up to leave. They met Fouad outside after she finished her tea.

"We have to find a taxi," the Iraqi told them. "I have an address."

TRIPOLI (TARABULUS ESH SHAM), LEBANON
THAT AFTERNOON . . .

Ferguson had found that, as a general rule in life, it was best to simply show up at the place where you wished to be. Less questions were asked, more things assumed, if one simply walked out from the crowd. And so it was that Bob Ferguson made his appearance in Tripoli, striding out of the surf at the Palace, a recently built luxury resort that featured the self-proclaimed biggest and best sand beach in all Lebanon—not much of a boast in a country not known for sandy beaches but a slogan nonetheless.

Ferguson wiped the seawater from his eyes and looked around, peering left and right as if looking for friends amid the throng. He scanned up and down for a few moments, getting a feel for the crowd. Though it was past high season, there was a good number of people here. Finally he found what he was looking for: an unattended towel. As he scooped it up, a hotel employee approached. Ferguson smiled and, before it was possible for the man to say anything, asked if he could possibly have a martini. The man was flustered; Ferg repeated the question in French. He was a little rusty and the grammar came out wrong, but the employee was hardly in a position to correct it. The man asked him in Arabic if he was with the Ugari party. Unsure what the right answer would be, Ferguson replied in French that he wasn't sure what time it was, as he had left his watch upstairs. After two more tries the man turned around and headed back toward the building.

Wrapping the large towel around his shoulders as a gesture to modesty, Ferguson set out in the direction of the catamaran concession, where ten slightly damp one-hundred Euro notes procured him the last boat on the dock, a craft that had been promised to a man who'd gone to gather his family just a moment before. Ferg hopped aboard as the man returned, running up his sail and pulling away as the concessionaire explained over the man's loud protests that there had been a mistake.

Steering northward, Ferguson passed a second beach—from the water it looked just as big as the first one, but he wasn't checking slogans for authenticity—and then a stretch of jagged rocks. Sail furled and anchor set in the shallow rocks, he slipped into the water, diving down and retrieving the pair of plastic torpedoes he had tied to one of the rocks below. Back in the boat, he opened one of the containers and slipped on a shirt and a pair of cargo hiking shorts. Then he took one of the small Glocks from the torpedo and stuffed it into his belt line, letting his shirt cover it. He took three magazines of 9mm bullets and put them into one of his pockets; a pair of pin grenades went into his other. The weapons, which looked more like oversized fancy metal pens than pins (or grenades for that matter), were downsized flash-bangs, useful for diversions and skipping out on bar bills. He debated taking out another gun but decided against it. Carrying one could always be defended as a matter of personal protection, but two bordered on ostentation. Ferguson got out his Irish passport and put it into his shirt pocket, along with a ticket stub indicating that he had arrived two days before in Damascus from Germany.

From the second torpedo-shaped container, Ferguson daubed a layer of cold cream to his nose and cheek, old-fashioned protection against sunburn. Wraparound sun glasses in place, he donned a pair of rubber gloves and applied a thick layer of gel to his hair.

The wind began to kick up, and by the time Ferguson was ready to go back onshore he had floated several hundred yards northward. That was fine with him; he didn't want to go back to the hotel beach in case the waiter brought back more than a martini. He went where the wind took him, sailing until he found a familiar-looking dock jutting from one of the vacation villages that dotted the area. Tying the torpedoes together, he slung them over his shoulders and sauntered onto the dock, wandering up the pebbled path and around to the road.

The way, unfortunately, was barred by a security guard. The man demanded in Arabic to know who Ferguson was. Ferguson answered in Arabic that he was a guest of Muhammad Lassi, whom he was just going up to see.

Lassi was, in fact, a resident here, a fact Ferguson knew because he had visited Lassi the year before. Unfortunately, the guard had seen Mr. Lassi not too long ago: a week ago, in fact, at his funeral. He informed Ferguson of this as he pulled out his pistol.

Corrine spent a good portion of the morning meeting with the American ambassador, who wanted to talk about some of the nuances of the president's upcoming trip. As part of her cover—she was supposedly working for the Commerce Department on a special assignment—she met with Israeli officials to discuss a proposed protocol for loan paybacks. In between she got an update on the Khazaal situation to the effect that there was no update. Ferguson had managed to call while she was in one of the meetings, leaving only a message that they should "catch up" when she got a chance. It was his only acknowledgment of her request that he meet her here.

Corrine had lunch with the Commerce Department negotiator, a pleasant enough middle-aged woman who missed her five- and six-year-old children dearly and spent the entire lunch talking about them. As they waited for the coffee to arrive, Corrine excused herself and went to call Corrigan and try Ferguson again. One of the Delta bodyguards assigned to her by the embassy followed her to the restroom.

"You're not coming in with me," she said to him.

The man looked embarrassed. "No, ma'am."

Corrine felt compelled to tell him she was joking, but he didn't noticeably relax. The restroom was a coed affair and not terribly clean, but it did have a lock on the door. She scanned the room and turned on the white noise box, then pulled out the sat phone. Corrigan was off-duty; Lauren Di Capri, his relief, told her there was nothing new.

"All right. Can you connect me to Ferguson?"

"He's off the air right now. His phone's off. When he checks in—"

"Where is he?"

"On his way to Lebanon. He should be there now."

"Why?"

"He had a hunch on where Khazaal might be going."

"Why the hell didn't he check in with me first?"

Lauren didn't answer.

"You tell him to call me. No excuses."

"All right."

Corrine slapped the phone off. Was it a coincidence that he had called when she was unavailable? The people at the Cube had access to her schedule. It wouldn't take much to weasel out the best—or, rather, worst—time to call her.

The incident in Cairo had been explained away by the Egyptian police, largely because they were grateful that an enemy of the regime had been taken care of. But an incident in Lebanon would be something else again.

And, really, who did he think he was, blowing her off? She'd sent word for him to meet her in Tel Aviv; he hadn't even acknowledged her.

Corrine had to straighten this out. She could give him some leeway—she'd given him plenty already—but major operations were supposed to be approved by her first. Especially now, with the president due in the region next week.

Ferguson was a walking time bomb: he was exactly what the president had appointed her to head off. She had to confront him directly. Waiting for him to call her wasn't going to work.

TRIPOLI, LEBANON

"I didn't realize you knew Lassi," Ferguson told the guard holding the pistol on him. If ever there was a situation where the truth was called for, Ferg reasoned, this was it. "He was an uncle to us all," continued Ferguson in Arabic. "Of course, now that his cousin owns the apartment, that is whom I am staying with."

"Where is your identification?" demanded the man. He held the pistol in one hand and used his other to reach for the radio.

"Right here," said Ferg. He took the Irish passport from his pocket, tapped it on his nose, and then swiped it across his hair as he nervously scratched an itch. The officer took the passport, frowning as his fingers smeared across the gooey mixture from Ferguson's hair. He held it against his radio, squinted at it, then crumpled to the ground.

The gel was an enzyme that activated the synthetic opiate in the cold cream. Ferguson reached into his pocket for a handkerchief and picked up the passport gingerly, wiping off the residue on the man's shirt. He pulled the man to the side, ejected the bullet from the chamber of his gun—it was very dangerous to carry it that way, when you thought about it—and for good measure took the magazine with him as well. Then he went to find the microbus, which would take him into town.

10

EASTERN SYRIA
THAT EVENING . . .

The taxi driver refused to take Fouad and the others anywhere near the address Fouad had given him, dropping them on an empty street three blocks away despite the offer to triple his tip if he drove past the building.

The scent of raw oil hung heavy in the air. Rankin held his Beretta in his hand, hiding it in the crook of his arm as they passed row after row of dilapidated steel buildings. The structures looked like warehouses that might still have been in use, though they saw no one nearby. Night had begun to fall, shading the buildings with a dimness that made them seem even more ominous.

"What do you think?" asked Thera when they stopped at a wide though empty cross street.

"Don't know," said Rankin.

Fouad said nothing. His stomach had started to gnaw at him: nerves mostly, though he realized he must also be hungry by now. Some men claimed that they became immune to danger, even comfortable with it, but Fouad would not tell such a lie or even attempt it.

They crossed the street. An odor of sewage replaced the petroleum scent; they were close to the river.

Two dusty Lexus SUVs sat across the road as they walked up. Rankin and Thera realized they were being watched from the roof, though both pretended not to notice. Fouad understood where he was now and saw a script to follow, a path that he had trod before. He picked up his pace, walking to the middle of the block, where two masked men with AK-47s met them.

The masks were a good sign. They did not want to be identified later on. This wasn't an ambush.

The men would not search Thera. She handed over her small Glock as a sign of her integrity, keeping the knife and the other Glock as well as her grenades. Rankin gave up the pistol in his hand as well as the Colt at his back. Fouad surrendered a revolver. As a weapon it was not much, but he had had it long enough now that it had emotional value, and he told the men not to lose it.

They were shown through a narrow door into a reception area at the center of one of the steel buildings. The floor had been tiled with an elaborate black-and-white mosaic, but the walls were plain panels covered with thick white paint. A window similar to those manned by a receptionist at doctors' offices in the States sat at one side; there was a steel door next to it. A bare forty-watt bulb in the ceiling supplied the only light.

The steel door opened, and a man with an AK-47 appeared in the doorway.

"What do you want?" he demanded in Arabic.

"Business," replied Fouad.

"What business?"

"We transport items. We seek work. We are here to speak to Ali."

The man made a face and disappeared back through the door. He returned less than a minute later, far too quickly to have actually consulted with anyone.

"Come back tomorrow," he said.

Fouad knew that this was a test, but he wasn't sure what the proper response was. He waited a moment, then began to step back.

Thera reached across Rankin and took his sleeve. "Tomorrow we should be at the border. If there is no business, we can't afford to wait," she told him in Arabic. "Making good customers angry to please one we don't have makes no sense."

"But if there is no business, there is no business," said Fouad, falling into the act. "We cannot be too greedy."

He looked to Rankin, as if giving the other partner the final say. Rankin shrugged.

"Then we'll leave," said Thera.

They started to, but the man called them back.

"I have been a poor host, forgive me," he said. "Perhaps we can find some work for honest people."

He came around to the door and waved them inside the warehouse proper. It was large and dimly lit, and almost entirely empty.

"What business do you have here?" said a woman's voice as they approached a pair of trucks at the back near the garage-style doors. The trucks were Russian military transport models, nearly as old as Fouad.

"We are open for anything," said Fouad.

A woman in Western jeans and a flowing top came out from behind one of the trucks, flanked by two young men with M16s.

"You're just petty smugglers," said the woman dismissively.

"Honest carriers," said Thera. "Trying to make a living in a difficult era."

"Don't lie, sister." The woman walked to her, pointing. "You're simple thieves."

"Carriers."

"You must be a whore to be with such men."

Thera stared at the woman, whose eyes were focused on her in fury. When Thera did not rise to the provocation, the woman turned back to Fouad. "Talk to Oda," she said, walking back to the trucks. Oda was the man who had led them inside.

"We have our own trucks," he told them. He brought them to a corner at the far end of the warehouse, where several chairs sat around a table. "But sometimes we have material that needs other shippers."

"Our forte," said Fouad. "What part of Iraq do you come from, my friend?"

"Why do you ask?"

"Your accent. Did you leave before or after the war?"

It was a delicate question but worth the risk; Fouad thought overcoming Oda's discomfort would provide a basis for the questions he had actually come to ask. Oda told him that he had come only within the last few months—a neutral answer and clearly a lie, though one Fouad could easily go along with. The two men traded a few more lies before Fouad managed to mention Baghdad, saying that he had not been that far east in many years. He mentioned a street that any recent native would have recognized as the home area of one of the insurgent groups, but if this had an effect on Oda it neither registered in his face nor his questions. They turned to the sort of notice required for transport. Thera took over briefly to say that they could stay in the city for two days in the future, as it was a pleasant place, but only on their way back from Damascus.

Fouad began talking of others they did business with, carefully slipping in the names of Syrians who smuggled arms to rebel groups. Again, there was no reaction. Finally, Fouad looked at his watch.

"We must go," he said, rising.

"Be on Ben Whalid Street at nine tonight," said Oda in a low hush, before moving quickly to the door. "A third at pickup, the rest at delivery. One thousand, American."

"Done."

Why make such a big deal out of it like that?" said Rankin when they finally reached the more populated part of the city.

"They watch how we react; we watch how they react," said Fouad. "Smuggling is a matter of trust."

"He was definitely setting us up," said Thera. "A thousand is too much for a first-time job."

"No, not necessarily," said Fouad.

"We being followed?" Rankin asked.

"I don't think so, but maybe they have a nightscope in one of the buildings or someone watching us from up there," said Thera.

"They wouldn't bother," said Fouad. "We're not worth it. We're small beans."

"Potatoes," said Rankin.

"Whatever we are, we aren't important enough for them to follow. They don't have that many people."

"You don't think the meeting is a trap?" said Thera.

"A trap it may be. Or not." Fouad wasn't sure. He wanted to know what they were shipping, and the only way to find out would be to show up. "There is a Kurd in this city who might be of help," said Fouad. "If we can find him before nine, then we need not keep the appointment."

"We're not going to keep it, not all of us," said Rankin. "You go. Thera and I will take the bikes and trail you."

"A reasonable plan," said Fouad.

They didn't find the Kurd, and so Fouad drove the truck down Ben Whalid at exactly nine p.m. The street ran through the downtown area, and as he approached each intersection Fouad slowed, expecting to be signaled. But there were no men, no signs, no signals. He reached the western end of the street; unsure whether to go left or right, he turned right toward the river. As he did, something thumped against the left side of the truck. He turned to see what it was. In that brief moment Oda leapt from a hiding place between two cars along the road, hopped onto the running board of the passenger side, and opened the door. It happened so quickly that Fouad did not have time to feel fear.

"I thought I had gotten something wrong," said Fouad.

"Nothing wrong," said Oda, pulling himself inside the truck. "Drive on."

Fouad wondered what would have happened if he had gone the other way, but the answer soon occurred to him: there was another man posted along the other street; they would have simply changed places. The other man would now be trailing, probably wondering where his companions were.

Y ou see him?" asked Rankin. He was riding on the motorcycle a few hundred yards behind the milk truck.

"Not yet," answered Thera. She'd gone ahead, turning down a side street, and was now doubling back.

"All right. Looks like we're heading up along the river."

"That's not the river. The tributary."

"Whatever."

"I see him now. He's got a guy in the cab with him."

Thera passed the tanker, saw the car that Rankin said was trailing it, then passed Rankin. She rode a little farther then turned around. She'd changed from her long dress and put on coveralls and a helmet so she looked like a man, albeit a highly suspicious one.

"Turning," said Rankin. "Going toward the river or tributary or whatever that is. Stopping."

He killed the bike's motor, coasting off the road near a thicket of grass and brush. The truck and car had stopped about thirty yards ahead. He let the bike down as quietly as he could, then slid the Uzi from his backpack, extended the stock, and walked in the direction of the truck.

Fouad was still in the cab.

"So where is my cargo?" he asked Oda.

"Where are the others?"

"They wanted to get dinner. And other things. You know how it is when you are young," he said.

Oda wasn't much for innuendo and responded by taking out his pistol. "Where are the others?"

It had been a long time since anyone had pointed a gun at Fouad's chest, and the first thing that he thought of was: I do not want to die for the Americans.

"I'm not sure of the restaurant," he told Oda. "Why do we need them?"

"You are cheating them?"

"No," said Fouad. "I am an honest man."

"For a criminal."

"I merely make a living. If I am cheating the regime, who is the loser? The Americans who want our oil and manhood? If that is who I am hurting, you should congratulate me as a patriot."

Fouad wanted to sound brave but even to his ears the note was too forced, too off-key to impress. Oda lifted his gun.

"Where are they?" he asked again.

"We can look for them, I suppose."

"Out of the truck."

"The cargo?"

"You are a genuine fool."

"I am getting out of the truck," said Fouad. As he reached for the door, he made a judgment. There was a gun tucked against the seat within easy reach, but he calculated that he could not swing it up and around before Oda could blow his brains out. And so he left it there, and started to pull open the door—which was promptly yanked from his grip. A pair of hands grabbed him, and he felt himself flying down from the truck.

As he landed, something flashed above him and the world reverberated with the sharp, loud crack of a grenade exploding.

11

Corrine's plane was met by a staffer from the U.S. embassy, who arrived with four marines as bodyguards and a separate police detail. Two members of the Lebanese government's trade committee also turned up, having heard that the Commerce Department fact finder was especially interested in how agricultural trade might be facilitated.

The trade issue was particularly difficult for President McCarthy; oranges were Lebanon's major exportable crop, and he had narrowly carried Florida in the recent election. But the issue gave her more than ample reason to tour the country and to get over to Tripoli. The men were invited to come with her on the ride to the embassy to make their case.

Corrine nodded several times and even managed to praise the quality of the country's fruit, mentioning that she hoped to further acquaint herself with different exportable items in preparation for a full report to the commerce secretary "at the most opportune time." The men interpreted this as a positive sign, immediately offering to assist her. Corrine lamented that her schedule was not her own but that official help would be welcome.

Considerable dancing and a feint or two later led her to say that she planned to see the Mediterranean coast, mentioning that she was interested in tourism and the potential impact of the industry on "full" trade and relations. The men, of course, praised her decision and began working on an itinerary by cell phone. Corrine had a full slate of tours for the next day and a half by the time they reached the embassy.

Inside, she used the secure communications center to call Lauren, who was on duty in the Cube. "Where is Ferguson?"

"Tripoli, as far as I know. He should be checking in any second. Should I have him call you at the embassy?"

"No. I'll be in Tripoli in the morning," she said. "Tell Mr. Ferguson to find me."

"What?"

"I'll be at the Medici. Tell him if he doesn't find me, I'll find him. I assume he'll find it much more expedient if he picks the time and place, but I am quite prepared to take matters into my own hands."

EASTERN SYRIA

Rankin managed to get Fouad out of the cab just as the flash-bang he'd thrown into the truck exploded. But before he could fire at Oda, the car that had followed the truck off the road pulled to a stop. Rankin sprayed the windshield with his Uzi, killing one of the two men inside. The other jumped out and began returning fire, hitting Rankin in the chest, where the bulletproof vest he wore beneath the coverall stopped the slug, leaving him with only a minor bruise. Rankin fired at the top of the gunman's skull. The man's head exploded like a pumpkin, gore spraying everywhere; even Rankin winced involuntarily at the sight.

Fouad lay on the ground nearby, trying to push himself toward some nearby bushes for cover while staying as flat as possible at the same time. He crawled forward, chin scraping the hard-packed dirt. He feared that the American would mistake him for one of the attackers or, worse, would throw a grenade or indiscriminately blanket the area with gunfire, not trying to kill him but not particularly caring one way or another.

Rankin hadn't warned Thera before he tossed the grenade, and its explosion off the road surprised her. She hunkered low on the bike and passed the turnoff the others had taken. When she realized this she throttled down and braked until she could drop the bike. The motorcycle flew from her hands, but she managed not only to stay on her feet but also to pull her

M4 carbine up and ready, crouching as automatic weapons fire erupted off the road.

A car approached from the north with its lights off. Thera hunkered on the shoulder. She had her night glasses on and could see all three of the men as they got out of the vehicle. She didn't fire until she saw a weapon in one of the men's hands. The delay allowed one man to dive to the ground and roll or crawl into the thicket; the others fell where they stood.

Thera crouched, looking for the man who'd gotten away. For a moment she thought he had run off, but a stream of bullets dancing on the nearby macadam told her that was wishful thinking. She jumped over to the side of the shoulder, looking for cover. As she did she saw another car coming from the north, also with its lights off. Thera drew her gun to take aim, but she came under fire again, bullets ricocheting less than a foot away. She squeezed right and got off a few rounds, sending the gunman farther into the weeds. By that time, the car had stopped. She turned to see someone running from it toward the turnoff.

Fifty yards away, Rankin moved warily toward the front of the truck, trying to see what had become of the man who'd been in the cab with Fouad.

Something moved on the other side of the truck. Rankin couldn't get a target and held his fire.

"Rankin?" whispered Thera in the radio. "Where are you?"

"I'm near the truck."

"Someone's coming down from the north end of the road. I'm pinned down up here."

"I'll come for you when I take care of this."

"I'm just warning you, asshole," said Thera. "I'll take care of this."

Rankin continued around to the passenger side of the vehicle and eased toward the cab. When he saw that it was clear he swung up into the interior and was crossing over to the driver's side when he snagged himself on the large shifter at the center of the cab. He forced a slow, deep breath from his lungs, twisting back and then spreading himself along the seat, moving forward again. When he reached the side he slid down into the well beneath the dashboard. He couldn't quite see all the way down the side of the truck to the back. Pushing out to get a better angle, he spotted someone and goosed the Uzi, striking him in the head with the second burst.

Not sure now how many other gunmen there were nearby, Rankin leaned out from the side of the truck, hesitated a second, then dove forward about a half second before Oda began firing into the cab from the passenger side.

As Rankin rolled into the dirt, bullets followed him to the ground. Oda dropped to his knees and fired under the truck, his bullets spraying wildly. Several struck the oil pan and one the feed from the gas tank to the engine. Oil and diesel fuel began seeping and then pouring downward. Rankin, fearing that the liquid or at least its vapors would ignite, rolled backward and got into the brush.

Fouad in the brush smelled the diesel, too. He didn't think the diesel was volatile enough to easily ignite, but the smell gave him an idea.

"Set the truck on fire," he yelled aloud in Arabic, speaking quickly. This brought an immediate response from Oda who began firing in his direction. Rankin clambered to his feet and hunched by the wheel, waiting for a chance to fire.

Thera took out a pin grenade and threw it into the area between the two cars. As it exploded she ran along the road to her left, waiting until the gunman began firing again. When she saw that he was firing at her old position, she crossed to his side. She dove down as the bullets began firing in her direction. For ten or twenty seconds she didn't breathe, her mouth in the dirt. Then she sidled to the left, down a slight incline that ran along this side of the road. She expected to find the gunman in the ditch but didn't. Confused, she stared in the direction of the car, then glanced over her shoulder, worried that he had managed to outflank her after she crossed.

If that was the case, her best bet was to take his old position. She began working toward it. When she was about ten feet away, Thera finally saw the gunman up on the road, pressed against the side of the vehicle. She moved her M4 to the right and squeezed the trigger. The first two slugs caught her enemy in the ankle. He howled and fell backward, managing to roll away behind the car. Thera jumped to her feet, raising her weapon high and firing, more to keep him pinned down than in hopes of hitting him, since she was off balance and firing blind. She leapt up the embankment, spun left, and fired a long burst into the body sprawled on the ground. A tracer spit from her barrel, a cue that she was near the end of the box. She pulled her finger off the trigger, heart thumping, knowing that she had hit her target several times but not yet convinced he was dead.

Back by the truck, Fouad moved to his left, eyes scanning the darkness as he looked for Oda. The fuel continued to run from the truck; he could hear it splashing when the gunfire on the roadway faded away. Something moved before him and he fired, two, three, four shots, the bullets whizzing into the brush.

Rankin leapt up as Fouad began to fire, running to the back of the tanker. Oda, hiding behind the fender at the front, raised his gun to fire at Fouad, but Rankin pulled his trigger first. Oda curled backward, dead.

Rankin slid to one knee, scanning quickly to make sure there were no others.

"Thera. Hey!" he yelled.

"Hey, yourself," said Thera over the radio. "You all right?"

"I'm fine."

"You got the man who came down?"

"Yeah. I got 'em all."

"Where's Fouad?" she asked.

"He's over on the other side of the cab. Fouad!" Rankin yelled.

Fouad, arms trembling, lowered his weapon. "Rankin?"

"Stay where you are until we have this sorted out. I'm on the other side of the truck, opposite you."

Rankin ran to Oda's prostrate body. The bullets had caught him across the neck, nearly severing it. Blood gurgled down over his shirt, pooling around his shoulders.

"Thieves," said Fouad, walking over.

Rankin looked up. "I told you to stay by the side of the road."

The Iraqi stared at him, but he said nothing.

"They wanted the truck and figured we were easy pickings," said Fouad. "Fortunately, they thought we were amateurs and didn't take us seriously. We were lucky."

"Luck had nothing to do with it," said Rankin. "Let's make sure they're all dead, then let's go see your Kurd."

Fouad rode with Thera back to town, clinging to her as she worked the bike around the narrow streets before they got to the café where he believed he would find the Kurd. The bulletproof vest under her coveralls exaggerated the firmness of her body, but even without it he thought he would find her flesh stiff and hard, not so much the product of exercise or deprivation but an expression of will, as if to be a warrior she had shed everything soft from her.

She had beautifully curly hair, just long enough to peek out of the back of her helmet. She would be quite a pretty wife.

Fouad poked her side as the last turn came up, afraid she would miss it. When she stopped, he felt his legs wobble, his equilibrium shaken by the ride.

"You look like you could use a drink," said Thera, pulling off her helmet.

"A devout Muslim does not drink."

"Are you devout?"

Fouad stared as she unzipped the front of her coveralls, forgetting for a second that she had clothes on beneath it.

"I didn't mean to insult you," she said, pulling the coveralls down. She left her bulletproof vest on, dropping her oversized *jibab* over it and the matching baggy pants.

"I wasn't insulted," he said.

The image of her undressing stayed with him as he led them inside. Fouad had not seen the Kurd, Abu Nassad, in four or five years. But he recognized the man the instant he saw him across the room, and as their eyes locked he felt the other man's fear.

There was no reason for Nassad to fear him any longer, but the emotion was reflexive. Fouad approached him across the room, standing over the table and leaning toward him menacingly, though his voice was mild. "I hope you are well, Abu Nassad."

The Kurd blinked. "Yes."

Fouad sat in one of the empty chairs. The man sitting next to Nassad looked first to Fouad and then to Nassad before rising and walking over to the other side of the room. The two other men remained sitting, looking at their coffee impassively. There was a pipe on the table; Nassad offered Fouad a smoke, but he shook his head.

Thera and Rankin sat at a table nearby, Thera watching the room and Rankin watching Fouad and the Kurds.

"I'm looking for information about someone," said Fouad.

"I don't sell information."

"I do not buy." Fouad wished he had a cigarette, not because he felt the need to smoke—he had never been much of a smoker—but because it was a useful prop. There was so much that could be done with it. "Khazaal was here, and I would like to know where he is now."

Nassad's face turned pale.

"He's here still?" asked Fouad.

"No." Nassad shook his head. "The devil has gone."

"Very well. Where?"

"It seems to me, Fouad, you owe me a great deal. When last we met you extorted a bribe from me. I would like my money back."

Fouad turned his anger into a trite frown, as if he weren't insulted, as if he weren't angry at being held up by a man whom he could have had executed, whom he could have executed himself. "Where did he go?"

"The old ways do not work anymore," said Nassad, the effort in his voice obvious. "You cannot intimidate me."

Oh, but I can, Fouad thought. He leaned across the table. "Where?"

"How much do you want?" said Rankin behind him.

Nassad, who had started to slide back in his seat, sat upright immediately. "Five hundred American."

"Fifty Euros," said Rankin.

"Nothing," said Fouad.

Rankin reached into his pocket and threw a fifty-Euro bill on the table. "Everything you know. Or the Iraqi will show you how angry he is."

Nassad reached for the bill, but Fouad threw his hand over it.

"Khazaal, the pig, was here," said the Kurd. "He left in the morning. He paid for a car with a jewel. He's traveling with jewels, not cash. He has necklaces and gold. Many of them. In a case his bodyguard keeps. Ask his hotel."

"Which hotel?"

"The Palmyra."

"Where did he go when he left?" said Rankin.

Nassad shrugged and reached for the money. Fouad let his fingers touch the edge of the bill.

"How many jewels?" said Fouad.

"Khazaal and I are not on speaking terms."

"What was he trying to buy?"

"Here? What would you buy here?"

"Which direction did he go in?"

Nassad stared at Fouad. Was it fear that he saw in his eyes or defiance? Both maybe.

Rankin, meanwhile, slipped around the back of the Kurd. He had slipped the palm-sized Glock 22 into his hand and pressed it now against the man's skull. "Answer my friend's question," he said, his voice hoarse.

"I think west. Mansura, maybe. He asked about a car and flights out of the airport. I believe he was going to the coast because he said something about the sea."

"Lebanon? Or Syria?"

Nassad shook his head.

Rankin studied Fouad's venomous look. It was the hardest expression he'd seen on his face since they had come. Fouad wanted to kill the Kurd. The emotion reassured Rankin; until now the Iraqi had been a blank to him, with no visible emotion, a dangerous mask that could not be trusted, especially in an Iraqi.

"Let him have the money," Rankin told him. "Whether he deserves it or not."

Fouad lifted his hand. As the Kurd reached for the money, one of his companions at the table sprang at Fouad, only to find himself spinning and then wrestled to his knees by Thera, who pressed the sharp edge of her knife against the soft part of his neck near his Adam's apple.

"I'm not holding this very well," she told him in Arabic. "So you will bleed to death slowly if I kill you. I'm sure you would prefer a painless end."

The man croaked as he dropped his knife. Thera threw him down, and as someone else moved forward she raised her other hand, revealing a grenade.

A conventional one, not one of the miniature flash-bangs on her vest.

"No pin," she said.

Fouad rose from the table. He too had drawn a knife. Had Thera not intervened, the man who sprang, would be dead now. The thought made him shudder slightly. He returned the blade to its scabbard beneath his jacket and walked slowly to the door. The others followed.

"The bikes!" said Thera as soon as they were outside. "Go!"

She waited until she could hear the footsteps approaching the door to drop the primed bomb in her hand—it was a smoke grenade—and tossed a pin flash-bang on the ground before running to catch up with the others.

As the name suggested, Il Medici had an Italian motif, with buff marble statues and a massive fountain that greeted visitors as they entered the hotel's main hall. The hotel had been built only the year before on land that had once been a dumping ground for cars and trucks. The city fathers hoped Il

Medici would encourage a new era in tourism, drawing visitors from Europe as well as northern Lebanon and southern Syria. Perhaps it would someday; for now, though, only a quarter of its rooms were occupied and its spacious casino and clubs were at best half full.

The casino had, however, become the locus of choice for entrepreneurs in the import-export trade or, more precisely, the specific subset of that trade dealing with hashish and similar items. This made it a convenient place for Ferguson to stay, and after buying some cheap luggage and clothes in the bazaar in town, he went over to the hotel and checked in. Room secured, bugs located—one in the bedroom beneath the desk where the phone was and another in the bathroom—he sauntered down to the casino, wandering past the roulette wheel and casting an eye toward the card tables. There were several bars. The one he found at the back of the casino clearly catered to the intended clientele; bored Europeans attracted by the cut rate prices, high payoff rates on the machines, and vaguely dangerous atmosphere. There were Greeks and Turks, along with a number of Frenchmen, a few of whom looked to have been here since the occupation. Attractive women in tight-fitting two-piece rayon dresses that exposed their midriffs hovered nearby, smiling fitfully.

Ferg circled the bar, then sidled up near the waiter station and ordered a German beer, Einbecker. He started to pay with a Lebanese note but caught the frown of the bartender. Smiling, Ferg slid a ten-Euro note on the bar and ignored the change. He walked to a table near the side, sipping the beer and watching the crowd.

"You are alone?" asked one of the young women, leaning toward him.

"Sit," he invited her.

"You buy drink?"

"Sit," said Ferguson, gesturing.

The woman glanced over her shoulder, though Ferg knew that her employer would not be in the casino. The glance was meant to imply that she had protection if he didn't play by the rules. Unfortunately for her sake, this wasn't true; if he took advantage of her services without paying, there was a fifty-fifty chance her boss would come for him. But there was a hundred-percent chance she would be punished and that a beating would be only the beginning. The woman would not be in a position to complain; she was likely to be Palestinian, not Lebanese, and had less standing with police than even a foreign spy.

Ferguson reached into his pocket and pulled out a wad of bills, American this time. He peeled off two hundreds and a fifty, understanding that the woman would be able to give her boss the fifty and keep the rest. He folded them individually between his fingers and laid his fist on the table, poking the fifty up with his thumb.

"What are you drinking?" he asked.

"Ginger ale," said the woman.

Watered-down ginger ale was the most expensive item on the menu here, one reason the hovering women in rayon were tolerated.

"Get one," he told her.

The woman looked over toward the bar and nodded.

"I'm looking for where the Russian hangs out," said Ferguson, letting the fifty-dollar bill fall to the table.

The woman shook her head as if she didn't understand. Ferguson repeated the question in Arabic, and this time added that he was looking for men "who buy and sell," the euphemism of choice the year before, though he wasn't sure now if he was out of date, as it tended to change. "The Russian is the one I want."

The woman looked over her shoulder, then reached for the bill. He let her take it.

"He's not here," she said.

"Downstairs?"

Ferg slid one of the hundred-dollar bills out so that it appeared between the fingers of his fist. "Where can I find him?"

"I—"

He slid the bill out a little farther. Another of the women who had been standing nearby saw it and stepped over to see what was going on. This convinced the woman already at the table to become more cooperative.

"I hear at the Krehml," she said, reaching for the money. "Krehml" meant "Kremlin," a very nice club at the other end of town. It wasn't the right answer, but her willingness to guess was all Ferguson wanted for now.

"Show me where it is," he told her.

The woman blanched. The other stepped forward.

"Both of you can show me," said Ferguson, rising. He pushed his thumb into his fist, demonstrating that there were two bills there, then put the money into his pocket. He dropped another fifty Euros on the table to cover the ginger ale. The women were trading glares behind him, following. When he reached the roulette table he stopped and turned to them.

"Red or black?" he asked.

They looked at each other. He gestured at the game. "Red or black?"

One said red; the other, black.

"Decide. Agree on one," said Ferguson. He stepped over to the cashier and exchanged the two thousand Euros for chips. When he returned, they had agreed on black.

"Black?"

The women nodded.

Black came up.

"Dresses," he said, dropping the chips into their hands. "Go exchange those. Then we get a car."

The women looked at him incredulously.

"You have to look a little stylish around town, no?"

Despite the fact that it was now past nine p.m., the concierge had no trouble accommodating him. A Mercedes appeared outside the hotel within a few minutes of Ferguson's request. Had he bothered to scan for a bug, he was sure he would find at least one, and it was a good bet that the driver was on the police payroll. But this was a necessary part of doing business, and something that could be worked to his advantage if required.

The port area of the city had a small row of boutiques on the road from the hotel; one happened to belong to a friend of a friend of the concierge, who knew he would be open late. (He also knew he would receive a cut of the profit if the rich foreign customer was as indulgent toward women as he seemed.)

For nearly two hours, the women tried on clothes while Ferguson passed judgment on their choices—no fool, he claimed to like everything— and sipped the complimentary champagne brought over by the owner. One of the women called herself Kel and the other, Aress. Not even Ferg could have guessed how close these were to their real names. Their winnings didn't cover what they selected, but Ferg made up the difference, with a generous tip on the side for the salesclerk's patience and the owner's champagne, not to mention the lateness of the hour.

He checked his watch. Seeing that it was not yet midnight, he told the driver to go over to the Simon, a restaurant at the top of one of the residential towers near the water. They had dinner—Ferg offered to include the driver, which was expected, but the man turned him down, also expected— and by the time the Mercedes pulled up at the Krehml it was after two.

"You know what? Let's hop down the street to La Citadelle," he said. "Just for the hell of it."

The driver, who probably was expecting this, nodded. Kel pulled back. She'd been the second one to join him at the casino.

"I thought you wanted fun," she said.

"There's fun there."

"Very dangerous there," she said in English.

"Some people like danger. It's good for the heart."

She made a face, but she was too comfortable in the dress to back out now.

La Citadelle had a weapons detector at the front door; knowing this, Ferguson had taken only the big Glock with him. He surrendered it with the proper amount of decorum and was admitted with a nod. A swing band with a slight Middle Eastern accent played inside to a rather noisy crowd. Ferguson guided the women down to the floor that overlooked the terrace. Aress picked up the beat as they walked, but Kel remained apprehensive, glancing around at the crowd, which included a fair amount of the world's seamier characters. Ferguson smiled at the faces that turned to meet his, then slid into a chair near the window, ordering a bottle of champagne to keep with the theme of the evening. He let the two women drink and leaned back, gazing pensively at the ceiling as if contemplating the cost of the gold-and-jewel–encrusted border. In reality, he was examining the reflections of the people in the dark glass. He didn't see who he was looking for, but that didn't matter; he would eventually come to him.

First, though, there were diversions: a short, portly Lebanese man with a buzz cut and several gold chains approached the table, took a few steps past, then pretended to suddenly remember that he had seen Ferguson's face before.

"Not my Irish friend," said the man.

"Sarkis! How are you?" said Ferguson, getting up, his English suddenly rich with the sound of Dublin. They exchanged kisses, each feigning happiness at seeing each other. "Sit and have a drink."

"No, no, no, thank you anyway."

"Come on now. An Irish whiskey with an Irishman."

Sarkis glanced at the girls but resisted temptation.

"What brings you to town?"

"Why does anyone come to town?"

Sarkis nodded grimly. He was not a dealer—on the contrary, his job was to stop trafficking—but he received several times more money each month from the local dealers than he did from the government.

"I am interested in finding Romanski," said Ferguson.

Sarkis made a face. "Romanski finds you, if he wants to."

"I'll mention you sent your regards when I see him," said Ferguson.

————

Ferguson stopped at two more clubs, flashing money and making himself generally visible, without finding Romanski or even anyone as interesting as Sarkis. The scene here was still pretty much as it had been a year before: an easy place to buy drugs wholesale if you knew whom you were dealing with, an even easier place to get killed if you didn't.

Ferguson called the Cube from the men's room of a jazz lounge called Blu Note. The place, owned by a French couple, was a relatively quiet bar rarely frequented by dealers or government officials.

"Where have you been, Ferg? Boss lady wants to talk to you. She's freaking."

"Corrine? Don't worry about her. What's up with Rankin and Thera?"

Lauren told him that they hadn't had anything interesting when they last checked in, then went back to berating him about Corrine. "She's on her way to see you."

"What?"

"She's really mad that you blew her off. She's flying into Tripoli tomorrow. She says either you find her or she finds you. She's going to be at the Medici."

"Aw, come on."

"She's pissed, Ferg. I keep telling you. You can't just blow her off."

"Tell her that I'll contact her. Remind her I'm a member of the IRA, right?"

"She knows you're undercover."

"And tell her this isn't the Yale Drama Club."

"I don't think you're being fair."

"You're right. She wouldn't have passed the auditions."

Ferg snapped off the phone. When he got back, Kel and Aress were slumped in the booth. Aress had fallen asleep; Kel looked at him through slit eyes.

"Who are you?" she said, speaking in Arabic. "What are you doing here?"

"Just a traveler."

"Who do you work for?"

"Time for bed. Come on."

He slid his arm under Aress and got her to her feet. A woman played a piano nearby, working the keys slowly as she moved through a bluesy version of a Cole Porter song. She glanced at Ferg and he smiled at her, admiring the way she flipped her shoulder-length hair as she turned back to her keyboard.

Ferg found the driver napping in the car. He woke him up, and they started back to the hotel.

"Where are we going now?" Kel asked.

"I'm going to my hotel and sleep," he told her cheerfully. "You can go anywhere you want."

"And her?"

"She can have my couch." Aress was too far gone to leave anywhere.

"You don't want both of us?"

"I don't even want one of you. Nothing personal."

"What do you want?"

"Usually what I can't have."

14

EASTERN SYRIA

"They didn't like you in there," Thera said to Fouad when they stopped outside of town.

"No. They were Kurds."

"Iraqi Kurds?"

"Kurds believe they belong to their own country. They were our enemy. They are our enemy now."

"They're part of your government."

"I don't expect Americans to understand," he told her.

Rankin, who'd doubled back to see if they'd been followed, finally caught up.

"We're clear," he told them. "What was the business about the jewels?" he asked Fouad.

"He cannot carry money, so he carries jewelry, probably things stolen or hidden during the regime."

Fouad explained to Rankin about the airplane. As in most places in Syria, even scheduled flights tended to be sporadic there, but it might be possible for Khazaal to rent a plane, especially if he had enough jewels.

"If he wanted to take an airplane, where would he be going?" asked Thera.

Fouad shrugged. "Somewhere in Syria, but from there, who knows?

There is a plane every week to Damascus, but it is suspended every so often for different reasons. Sometimes security, sometimes one of the dictators has a notion of something. It is hard to say where he would go."

"But he's out of here?" said Rankin.

"That much I would believe. Nassad would not lie about that."

"Right," said Rankin.

Fouad stared at him but said nothing.

"Push on or call for pickup?" asked Thera.

"We should go to the airport," said Fouad.

"How far is Mansura?" Rankin asked.

"A little more than a hundred kilometers up this highway. Two hours. We can rest outside of town and go in during the afternoon."

"Yeah, he's right. Let's go. We can always get picked up." He kick-started the bike, revved the motor, then started down the road.

Kel decided she would stay in his room as well. Ferguson ended up giving the women the bed and sleeping in the bathtub, not because he was chivalrous by nature but because it was the only room in the suite that he could lock. He woke around ten in the morning to the sound of furious banging, punctuated by a teary whimper.

"I have to pee," said Aress outside the door.

"Can't you find a cup or something?" he asked.

"Please?"

He got up out of the tub and unlocked the door. Aress glanced at his pistol but was in too dire shape to say anything or even pause. Kel lay sprawled on the bed, one of her breasts exposed. She opened her eyes and blinked at him.

"One of your boobs is showing," he said, gesturing with his Glock.

She pulled the sheet up. He went to the telephone and ordered two pots of coffee from room service. Kel watched him as he looked around the room. He had scanned it before turning in, wanting to know if anyone—Romanski he hoped—had gone to the trouble of adding their own bugs. They hadn't, and no one had come in during the night. (He'd attached small detectors near the door and window, which would have sounded an alert if they had.)

"There's aspirin in the medicine cabinet," he told Aress in Arabic.

She looked at him, nodded, then went back and got it.

"What are you going to do with us?" Kel asked in English.

"Get you some breakfast. Show you the sights."

"That's all?"

Someone kicked at the door, much harder than a room-service waiter would have dared. Ferguson reached into his pocket and tossed Kel a hand grenade. Her eyes nearly bolted from her head.

"Hold on to that."

"Where's the pin?"

"Lost it. Peel off the tape and hold down the trigger, preferably not in that order. Once you let go, you have about four seconds. Maybe three. Throw it and duck. By the way, in here wouldn't be a good place to throw it."

Whoever was outside kicked again, the door shaking.

"Open the door, would you?" Ferguson told Aress.

She went and unlocked it. As soon as she turned the handle, it flew open. Two men in Western business suits pushed her aside, standing in the doorway with Steyr AUG/HBARs, light machine-gun versions of the Steyr AUG assault rifle, packed with forty-two–shot boxes. Behind them came a tall, mustachioed man in Arab dress. His squared-off jaw, bald head, and regal gait made him look like Caesar of Arabia, a description he would have encouraged.

"You're up early, Romanski," said Ferguson, who had zeroed the big Glock at his face. "Then again, you took your time getting to me. I was starting to think I might actually have to pay for the room."

"Ferguson. Always with a joke." Romanski's English was perfect; he had spent nearly a decade in New York as a young KGB man before going to the Middle East. "But you point a pistol at me? My men could cut you in half with their guns."

"Not before you got a third eye."

"They are very fast."

Romanski glanced toward the bed, where he saw Kel holding the grenade. "What is this?"

"An assistant," said Ferguson.

"A common whore."

"It's not smart to insult people who are holding grenades," said Ferguson. "Especially when they don't have pins in them."

"So what do you want?"

"My coffee, for starters. Then you probably want to close the door."

Corrine and her bodyguards left before dawn and drove north from the capital to Tripoli in a pair of Mercedes, escorted by an unmarked Renault police car. The hotel was located south of the city proper, not far from the Olympic Stadium, but protocol required Corrine to first pay a visit to the local mayor. This meant going into the city, a gray-looking place that still showed signs of the occupation by Israel that had ended many years before. A faceless apartment building gaped at a small fruit stand not far from the center of town; closer to the sea, a brand-new mansion muscled its way into a quarter of battered old brick buildings that had stood since the time of the Crusades.

The mayor and the dozen other city officials who met her were so gracious that Corrine found herself feeling guilty for using them as a cover to come here. She listened as they made a short and almost subtle pitch about the importance of better trade with the U.S. and all countries. When she told them that she would take their message back to the president, she meant it.

Walking back to the car, she saw a wall pasted with posters of Bashir al-Assad, the dictator of Syria. The image was a popular one here, though it was difficult to tell if it was a sincere appreciation or something simply meant to curry favor from the muscular and dominant neighbor, which had also occupied Lebanon in the past.

Corrine and her small entourage headed back south, passing the Olympic Stadium and catching a grand view of the Mediterranean as they pulled into the hotel lot. The embassy had detailed two marines and two Delta Force bodyguards, all dressed in civilian clothes, as escorts. The men fanned out around Corrine as she walked into the hotel. One of the Delta ops and a marine went upstairs to check her room out while she waited below.

The hotel's display cases showed off eleventh- and twelfth-century Italian manuscripts, pages that had originally been part of prayer books brought to the Holy Land by crusaders. Though the works were exquisite, Corrine thought it odd that the hotel would feature a display devoted to the art of the country's ancient invaders. She wondered at the disconnect between war and art, between the reality of what the crusaders had experienced and done, and the beauty of the artists' work.

Her brief moment of distraction was interrupted by one of the marines, who tapped her on the shoulder.

"We have a problem, ma'am," he said. "Men with guns in your hall."

Ferguson made sure Romanski took two full sips from his coffee before he drank his. The Russian saw this and nodded.

"A lesson from your father?"

"Common sense," Ferg told him.

Romanski claimed to have known his father from service in Germany as well as the Middle East, though Ferguson had never bothered to check. He was the right age, pushing sixty, and he had been in the KGB's Foreign Intelligence Service, or Sluzhba Vneshney Razvedki (SVR), which was succeeded more or less intact (as far as his area was concerned) by the Central Intelligence Service, or Centralnaya Sluzhbza Razvedkyin (CSR), in the early 1990s. He had retired in 1995 to set up shop as a businessman; as long as he did not sell drugs to Russians, his former employers left him alone. Romanski knew everything that was going on in Tripoli and northern Lebanon, indeed, in the rest of the country and much of Syria as well. He had better sources now than when he had worked as an intelligence officer.

Which wasn't the same thing as sharing information or even sharing the truth.

"Can the women be trusted?" Romanski said, pointing toward the women. Aress had joined Kel on the bed.

"As much as any women," said Ferg.

Romanski frowned. "You are here why?"

"Nisieen Khazaal."

"Khazaal? The Iraqi lunatic? You're looking in the wrong country. He's in Iraq."

"I heard he was on his way here."

"Why would he come here?"

"Big meeting of lunatics."

"I doubt it."

"You wouldn't be doing business with him, would you?"

"Terrorists do not buy drugs."

"I was thinking Khazaal might be a seller, looking for money."

"The only thing the Iraqis can sell are weapons. And most of those are toys that stopped working long ago. Why do you waste your time, Ferguson?"

"Is he hiding over at Oil City?"

"Bah. The Iraqis there all work for the government now. They are fat and lazy; why would they have him in their midst?"

"You tell me."

"Bah. You have CIA agents in Iraq," Romanski told Ferguson, refilling his coffee cup. "What do they say?"

"They ask who Khazaal is."

"I would not be surprised. What do the Israelis say?"

"They say he's going to Syria."

"Then look there. Mossad is very good."

"Big country."

"There are only a few places to look."

"How about you ask the Syrians for me?"

"A favor? You have the nerve to ask for a favor?"

"I have nothing but nerve."

Romanski gave him a crooked smile. "Why are they meeting?"

"Not sure."

"The Iraqis sell weapons and beg for money. For either of those things I would go to Latakia."

Romanski took another sip of his coffee. Before Ferguson could decide whether that was an educated or uneducated guess, the phone at Romanski's belt began to ring.

"Do you mind if I answer that?" asked the Russian.

"I wish you would."

He took it out and held it up. His face flushed. "You set a trap for me?" he thundered at Ferguson.

"Let's not do anything rash." Ferg gestured with his pistol toward Kel and the grenade. "I didn't set a trap. What's going on?"

"Armed men coming upstairs. Americans."

Great timing, Ferguson thought to himself.

"It's just my boss. She's here to chew me out." Ferguson got up and walked to the terrace. They were on the third floor; jumping down would not have been a problem except for Romanski.

"I have a rope," said Ferguson. "I'll get you out."

"This is a trap."

"Aw, come on Romanski. Why would I bother?"

Ferguson got the rope from his bag and tied it to one of the bed legs.

"You, down," Romanski said to one of his men. "See if the way is clear. Give me your gun first."

He took the Steyr AUG/HBAR. The bodyguard hung off the terrace, then dropped down.

"How many of your men are outside?" Ferguson asked.

The Russian scowled. "I can handle the situation, thank you."

"I thought you had all the police in town bribed."

"You owe me, Ferguson. I will get a repayment."

"I'll double it for real information about Khazaal."

Romanski slung the gun over his shoulder and climbed out the window. He got down to about the middle of the first floor, then let go, rolling on the ground. His last bodyguard bolted over the terrace and paid for his haste with a sprained ankle.

Ferguson went to Kel and took the grenade. It was wet with her sweat. He let the spring trigger snap open, setting the grenade to fire. He held it for a moment, then dropped it out the window, where it began spewing smoke.

"Don't think I didn't trust you with a real grenade," he told Kel when she stopped screaming. "It was all I had handy."

Someone pounded on the door before he could answer. A voice claiming to be the police told them to open up.

"Just a second," said Ferguson in English. He took the large Glock and dropped it out the window into the billowing smoke.

"Aress, open the door, would you?"

Before she could reach the knob, the police broke it down.

Rankin, Thera, and Fouad stopped outside of Mansura a few hours before dawn and slept in a field until nearly noon. Several hours of rummaging in town turned up no trace of Khazaal. All of Fouad's old contacts were gone, and Thera had trouble with the accents in the small restaurant when they bought lunch. Their bikes stood out, but Rankin didn't want to leave them outside of town. Parking them in a lot near a bank didn't help much. He had his Uzi stuffed into his pack on his back, but the pack probably made them look almost as suspicious as the gun would. Rankin felt uncomfortably out of his element, exposed and obvious. This was the sort of situation that Ferguson made look easy, the sort of place where a glib bullshit artist could parlay some vague lie into a plan of attack, wheedling information out of stones. But Rankin wasn't a bullshitter. Never had been, never would be.

You had to be, maybe.

"Best thing is to go down the road a bit," he whispered to Fouad when he noticed the stares as they walked through the old part of town. The Iraqi agreed. They went back to their bikes and got onto the highway, riding until they found a turnoff with a view of the river. It was postcard perfect. Thera oohed, and even Fouad was impressed. Rankin stared at the blue shimmer.

"Let's see if we can turn up anything at the airport," he said finally.

Fouad nodded.

"They're probably not going to tell us anything," said Thera.

"Then we'll just have to figure out a way to bullshit them into it," Rankin said, walking back to the bike.

TRIPOLI

The police were incredibly understanding, thanks partly to a suggestion to the sergeant in charge that a processing fee for the incredible amount of paperwork sure to be involved would probably be most appropriate if paid in advance. Kel's timely rearrangement of the bedclothes didn't hurt either. Aress swore she had seen one of the men going into a room down the hall; the police mustered after the fresh lead.

Corrine was not so easily dealt with. She and two of her guards appeared in the hallway, glancing through the open doorway as the police finished their interrogation. She gave Ferguson an evil glare.

"You look Irish," he said loudly, giving his English a Dublin twist. "Tourist?"

"I beg your pardon," said Corrine.

"Oh, excuse me," he said, as if realizing he was wearing only his shirt and shorts. (He'd scooped off his pants and shoes under the cover of the blanket as the policemen entered.) "Can I buy you a drink?"

"I hardly think so."

"In the bar. Right now. Come on. Soon as I get m'pants."

"Thank you, no."

"You have a big appetite," he said, gesturing toward the men.

Corrine flushed. Even though she knew it was an act, she was furious with him, so mad that the emotion clouded her judgment.

"Drinks?" suggested Ferguson. "Lunch?"

"No, thank you," she said stiffly. The police were now breaking into another room down the hall.

"Well, I'll be there if you change your mind," said Ferguson.

H e wasn't in the restaurant or the casino when Corrine went down to look for him a half hour later.

"Where the hell is he?" she demanded when she called the Cube from her room.

"Go swimming," said Corrigan, who'd come back on duty.

"What?"

"Go swimming. Ferguson will meet you in the water."

"We'll be seen."

"He'll figure it out. Go swimming."

Corrine didn't have a bathing suit with her. "Tell him it will take a while. I don't have a bathing suit. I'll have to go buy one."

Wait until the General Accounting Office saw *that* voucher, she thought to herself.

"He's pissed, just to warn you," said Corrigan. "He says you almost blew his cover."

"Screw him."

She snapped the phone off. Corrine leaned back in her chair and picked up the small white noise machine; she'd found two bugs with the scanner and used the screener just in case.

Ferguson *was* being difficult, but from his perspective, it might in fact look as if she had screwed up. It was just a coincidence that they'd chosen the same hotel. Actually, Corrigan should have told her he was at the Medici, and she could have made other arrangements. Although maybe that would have seemed suspicious.

It had been a bad decision to come here, that was the problem. But she couldn't let Ferguson do what he wanted. She had to bring him to heel.

Parnelles had a point about giving a good officer room to do his job, but how much room was that? *Her* job was to make sure that the First Team didn't just run amok. And if you considered the number of bodies that were falling . . .

That might not be a fair measure, but the Intelligence Committee and Congress weren't necessarily known for being fair.

Corrine continued to wrestle with notions of what to do until she arrived at the dress shop from the hotel. There she turned her attention to an even knottier problem: finding a bathing suit that fit. The European-style suits came in two sizes: incredibly tiny and ridiculously infinitesimal. Finally she found a one-piece suit that didn't make her look like a bimbo or an idiot. She got a modest wrap and some sandals, and took out her personal charge card to pay, wincing as she mentally worked out the exchange rate.

"I need at least two people on the detail with me on the beach," Corrine told her escorts as they walked back to the car. "Volunteers?"

"Uh, we don't have suits, ma'am," said the sergeant in charge of the detail.

"That's my point. There's a men's store right over there. Put it on this," she said, tossing him her card. "And go easy. That's my personal card."

Corrine walked to the far end of the sand near the kids' pool but didn't see Ferguson. She spread one of the towels she'd rented—those she charged to the room—and waited for a while. Finally, she decided to go for a swim in the ocean.

The water relaxed her. Corrine had been on the swim team in high school, and she fell into an easy pace now, her muscles remembering the early morning routines. That had always been the way back then: dread for the first lap, then contentment as she fell into the exercise.

"Whoa," said one of the marines, swimming near her. He stopped paddling and stared at the beach.

A bevy of rather attractive young women had come down from the hotel in ultra-skimpy two-piece suits and were fussing over their blankets. There were more than a dozen women between whom the material of their suits wouldn't have filled a square foot.

She was a bit far to know for sure, but Corrine assumed among them were the two girls she'd seen in Ferguson's room. She spun in the water, just in time to see one of the marines darting downward.

"It's all right," she hissed. "He's with me. Let him go."

Corrine had meant the warning for the Marine, but when Ferguson bobbed upward, it was the bodyguard who was in his grip, not the other way around. The second Marine made another lunge, but the CIA officer was too quick, releasing the other man and paddling backward.

"It's Ferguson," hissed Corrine. "Relax, Bob. They're with me."

"Nice work if you can get it," said Ferguson. "Step into my office." He paddled backward, using the marines to help screen them, though it was difficult to think anyone would look out to sea while the girls continued to preen on the beach.

"You're lucky I was on the swim team," said Corrine.

"So that's why you're in the shallow water. What was your event?"

"Butterfly."

"I'm freestyle."

"I never would have guessed."

"So what the hell are you doing here?" asked Ferguson in his most cheerful voice. "Besides trying to get me killed."

"The president is going to Baghdad next week."

"Everybody and his brother knows that."

"He's also going to make a side trip, to Jerusalem to announce a new peace accord between Israel and Palestine. They've agreed on a shared security arrangement to keep the holy sites of Jerusalem safe for all faiths. The trip hasn't been announced, and it won't be until it happens."

"It'll be hard to keep that a secret."

"You didn't know it," said Corrine. "How hard can it be?"

"Touché." Ferguson took a few strokes, glancing back toward the beach to make sure his diversion was still in force. "So, are you going to answer my question or not? Why are you here?"

"Bob—"

"You can call me Ferg."

"If Special Demands does anything to mess that up, the president will not be happy."

Ferguson didn't respond.

"Why did you go to Cairo without clearing it with me first?" said Corrine.

"My job is to make the operational decisions," said Ferguson. "That hasn't changed. Once we were on Seven Angels, it was my show."

"The original plan called for you to follow Thatch in Jerusalem. You weren't following Thatch, and you weren't in Jerusalem."

"What if he had gone to Tel Aviv?"

"He didn't. He died."

"See, the problem is, Corrine, we're not arguing a legal case here.

We're doing a covert action that you can't define beforehand. I went to Cairo because I thought I might have a chance at finding out who Seven Angels was connecting with, and from that getting more information about them and their plans, which would help us close them down. That's my job. It's a real pain to have to explain step by step what I'm doing."

"You can't just go off on your own. There are other considerations. Like the president's peace plan and visit."

"You want my opinion on that?"

"No."

Ferguson smiled and took a few strokes away, checking on the beach show.

"Is Khazaal a threat to disrupt the visit to Baghdad?" Corrine asked.

"I don't know. I'm not even sure where he is at the moment. Probably not here. But I'd stay the hell out of Baghdad on general principle, don't you think?"

"I haven't been there."

"Take my word for it."

"This is an historic moment," said Corrine.

Ferguson stopped in the water, trying to knock some water out of his ear. Every moment was historic. The problem was, the really important ones were never obvious until a hundred years later on.

"Maybe Khazaal is running away from Iraq because the heat is on," suggested Corrine. "Maybe the insurgency is dead."

"You're listening to Corrigan too much," said Ferguson. "He got that idea from Slott. And with all due respect to our esteemed deputy director of operations, he doesn't know diddly about Iraq or the Middle East. He was an Asia hand. People are much more logical there. As for Corrigan, he thinks he won the war against Saddam by putting McDonald's ads on Iraqi television."

"So what's Khazaal up to then?"

"First I find him, then I psychoanalyze him."

"The Israelis said he might be going to Syria."

"Yeah, but we missed him on the border. Maybe they gave us the information too late. Or maybe we're just slow. Or maybe they're wrong. What are they holding back?"

"I don't know. I agree that they are."

Well, at least she figured *that* out, thought Ferguson. He kicked back in a circle behind her.

"So you only came here because you wanted to spit at me in person?"

"You work for me, Bob. Not the other way around. You have to show some respect," said Corrine.

"You have to earn respect."

"No, I represent the president. I don't have to earn anything. First of all, when I say I want to talk to you, I *want* to talk to you. I am supervising Special Demands. Not Parnelles, not Slott, not you. Me. I didn't want the job. The president stuck me with it. If you disagree with him, fine. Tell him. But until he changes his mind, I'm in charge. I'm not trying to be an asshole," she added, softening the strident note in her voice. "I don't want to micromanage you. I just want to do my job. And that means that we have to communicate. To head off problems."

"Yeah."

"Yeah?"

"Yeah," said Ferguson, more neutral. "You would have told me about the visit to Palestine and the peace plan?"

"I don't know."

"Well you shouldn't have. If I got dropped, it wouldn't have been secret."

"That's true now."

"I rest my case."

"Well don't get dropped."

Ferguson laughed. "Good advice."

"I'm trying to balance what you need to know with enough information so you trust me," said Corrine.

"I could say the same thing about Cairo," said Ferguson.

"You're right," she said.

Ferguson was mildly surprised by the admission. He started swimming parallel to her, matching her pace.

"Do you think Khazaal has enough money to buy an airliner?" asked Corrine. "That was one of the theories on the threat matrix."

"Ah, that matrix crap is bullshit. They just throw that together for the briefing," said Ferguson. "We don't know how much he has. Rankin and Thera found out last night he's traveling with jewels, so he could have a lot, but buying an airliner, or renting one? It'd be shot down halfway to Baghdad. That's not it." Ferguson stopped. "Do you want my opinion?"

"Yes."

"Our best bet is just to kill the son of a bitch when we see him."

Profanity aside, Corrine, as a citizen of the U.S. and an admirer of the president and what he stood for, didn't disagree. But as counsel to the president, as someone whose job called for her to uphold the Constitution and its principles, she had to disagree. Khazaal should be tried in an Iraqi court. Only after he was convicted should he be stomped to death.

"The president has specifically directed his apprehension, not his assassination," she said.

"He didn't have his fingers crossed behind his back?"

"They were in clear view on his desk at all times."

"I'm not being a smart aleck. I don't know if I can take him alive," said Ferguson. "Especially in Syria. It's pretty easy to get away with things in Lebanon, but Syria: the police don't like Westerners, Americans especially, and the upper ranks of the intelligence service are pretty competent. Some of the lower-ranking guys can get bought off but not dependably. Once we're out of the desert, things can get very complicated . . ." He shook his head. "If I start something, he may make me finish it."

"If you have a high probability of success, go for it."

"That's kind of mealymouthed."

"If you have to protect yourself, do it. Then it'll be different."

"Why?"

Corrine resisted trotting out the textbook distinctions between justifiable homicide and murder, knowing that Ferguson was getting at a much larger question, an issue that, frankly, she herself could not completely decide. If an individual was allowed to defend him- or herself against an attack, wasn't a nation? And given that the answer had to be yes, how far could it go? Would pulling a gun on a robber in a dark alley be more acceptable than pulling it in your own home? What if you left the window open and invited the robber in to rob you?

"The law says it's different," she said. "I didn't draw the distinction, but I can uphold it."

"If I come up with a plan that's so bad it puts me in danger, I get to kill him. That doesn't make sense, does it?"

"You wouldn't do that."

"How do you know?"

"I know your record. I know what you did in Chechnya and over the Pacific," Corrine added. "I was there. You wouldn't come up with a crappy plan."

"Everybody has a bad day," said Ferg. "Listen, since we're up close and personal here, why did you yank us off Seven Angels without even talking to me and explaining the situation?"

"I didn't take you off. That operation ended."

"No, it didn't," said Ferg. "Thatch got himself blown up, but that wasn't the end of the operation."

"The FBI made arrests. Come on, Ferguson. You don't think those crazies were a legitimate threat, do you?"

"They might have led to people who are. I had a few more leads to check out in Tel Aviv. There were phone calls made from a dentist's office there that haven't been explained. And even if I didn't have anything else to look into, even if they are just whackos, you talk about courtesy: you should have called me yourself and told me, not had Corrigan do it."

"Fair enough," said Corrine. "My mistake."

Two instances of acting decent within five minutes of each other, thought Ferguson; maybe there was hope for her.

Nah.

"Nice suit," he told her. "I have to go. I'm not sure what our next move is, but I should know by tonight. I'll call. Better yet, if you're still in town, I'll tell you in person."

"I have to take a tour this evening and one tomorrow morning. I'm here as a liaison to the Commerce Department, representing the president."

"Yeah, I heard. Your escorts will include government security people, secret police. Syrians pull a lot of the strings behind the curtains. They have two people on the beach watching you."

"Syrians?"

"Half of Lebanon is on Assad's payroll. You see his pictures everywhere? There's a jazz club we can meet at tonight to go over notes," he told her. "I'll leave a message with the time."

"*You* like jazz?"

Ferguson started swimming again. She followed.

"Don't notice me in the club," he told her. "I'll only come close if it's safe."

He gave a strong kick. Corrine realized he *was* a good swimmer; she could keep up but just barely.

"Ferg?"

"Yeah?"

"What's with the bimbos?"

Ferguson laughed and stopped swimming. "Good diversion, huh? The two Syrians who are watching you have their eyes pasted on them."

"I meant in the room."

"The cute one, Kel, is a Mossad agent. She claims she didn't know who I was when she picked me up, but I'm not sure. She also claimed she knew I figured out who she was before my Russian friend appeared, but I think that's bull."

"She's Mossad?"

"The Israelis move people in and out all over Syria. Most of them are contract people they bring up for a few weeks, then get out."

"Is the other one an agent, too?"

"Nah. She can't hold her liquor." Ferguson glanced at the beach and saw that the girls were preparing to leave. "Diversion's over. You should stay out here for a while before you go back. Glad we had this talk."

"I never know whether you're being sarcastic or not."

"I'd think it was pretty much a given."

18

EASTERN SYRIA

Thera came up with the idea, and it was a good one: "worthy of Ferguson," said Rankin. Only Ferguson couldn't have carried it off.

Primarily a military facility, the airport was patrolled by two companies' worth of soldiers and two armored personnel carriers, vehicles that dated from the days when Syria was a client of the Soviet Union. Most of the force was concentrated on the military side of the airport, and the two soldiers at the gate to the civilian terminal building didn't seem to even notice Fouad and Thera as they approached.

Fouad took care of that.

"An outrage!" he yelled in Arabic. "An outrage and dishonor on my family for generations! Shame and the curse of Allah be upon the dog." He gestured at Thera, who bent her veiled head down over a freshly curved belly. Fouad continued to rant, sketching out the outlines of the story: his daughter's fiancé had left the city by plane the day before, and he demanded justice.

One of the soldiers looked away, hiding a smirk, but the other, about the age to have children of his own, Fouad thought, nodded with concern. Fouad continued his tirade as they walked along toward the building, complaining about how few people devoted themselves properly to the Koran or common decency.

"You're going a bit over the top," whispered Thera as they came up the concrete walk to the main door of the terminal. "Take it down a notch."

He didn't understand the slang.

"You're overacting," Thera said. "Too much."

Fouad didn't think so. If he'd had a daughter who'd been dishonored, surely he would be this angry, angrier. He was entitled to exact revenge on the miscreant, by custom if not by law, and few judges would dispute that right.

Fouad had never had children—his wife had died of cholera two years after they married—but he thought of her now as he refined his rant inside the terminal, acting as if her blessed memory had been besmirched. It took several minutes before they managed to find a charter office where Fouad could lay out an explanation, in rambling style, of what he wanted: information on where the fiancé had gone. Persistent complaints and pleading led them to the office of the airport manager, where the secretary, a thoroughly modern Syrian, proved entirely unsympathetic. He was on the verge of calling the military people up when Thera grew violently ill. They helped her to the restroom together, where a female worker took over and led her inside.

"Surely you have your own daughter," Fouad said to the man, who was in his late twenties. "You understand and can help."

"No, by the grace of God," said the man. "Only a boy so far."

"You are ten times luckier than I, a thousand times, by the mercy and grace of God you are highly blessed. I am a poor man, wretched," moaned Fouad, "to be terribly disgraced like this. I shall kill her and then myself when she comes out of the restroom. I will wait until you return to your office so you are not disturbed."

"The plane that day left for Latakia," said the man. "That was the only plane. But the passenger . . . I doubt it was your son-in-law."

"Why not?"

The man shook his head.

"Women?" suggested Fouad. He knew, or thought he knew, the answer, but guessing it would raise too many suspicions.

"No."

Fouad gave his best puzzled stare.

"Foreigners," said the man finally.

"Americans?"

The man turned pale. "What would an American be doing here?"

"You said foreigners, not *Jews!*"

"Iraqi criminals," whispered the man. "A smuggler, I think, with bodyguards. Not Syrians. The man paid with gold chains."

Rankin could see the civilian terminal building from a small rise on the road about a half mile from the fence. He stopped there, pretending to work on his bike as he eyed the two soldiers in front of the building. They were older men, career guys who probably viewed the posting as semiretirement.

One cupped his hands to light a cigarette. It wouldn't be hard to take them, Rankin realized; the trick would be dealing with the other twenty guys who would come after them.

Unnecessary planning, he hoped.

Thera and Fouad had taken only their phones with them, reasoning that the radios would be hard to explain if they were searched. Rankin had suggested hiding them in Thera's "package," but she pointed out that they would set off a metal detector. It was an obvious mistake, and he wished he hadn't made the suggestion; it made him look like a fool.

Worse would have been her not questioning it.

Thera came out of the terminal door, followed by Fouad and another man. One of the guards came over.

Were they under arrest?

Rankin reached around to his pack, then saw that the other man who'd come out had gone to the soldier to bum a cigarette. He swung the pack back and gunned the bike to life. He rode down to the gate, passed by, and turned down a street across from the airport fence, riding up a short distance to a cluster of buildings where they had left the other bike. He parked next to it, debating whether to go into the store and get something to drink. He could see from the street that it had a Western-style beverage case, the sort of help-yourself arrangement that would minimize the amount of Arabic he would have to speak.

His Arabic wasn't *that* bad.

He went in and bought an Arab cola, a precise knockoff of Coke except for the Arabic script. He paid with a ten-pound note that brought some change. He pointed to his mouth and groaned "toothache" when the proprietor tried to start a conversation. The man nodded sympathetically and advised him on a number of cures, all available at the store. Rankin simply shook his head patted his pocket, as if he had aspirin there. It was an old trick but an easy one, and when he left, the store owner had the impression they had had a long conversation.

Outside, he sipped the soda, the best thing he'd tasted in days.

After two gulps, a soldier appeared on the road. The man stared at the bikes as he approached; Rankin watched the man from the corner of his eyes.

"What business do you have here?" asked the soldier, walking up to him.

"Me?" asked Rankin in Arabic.

The soldier thought he was being disrespectful and asked again, this time in an even more demanding tone.

"No business," said Rankin. The words were right and even the accent was fine, but he didn't say it quickly enough, and the soldier's suspicions had already been aroused. The Syrian began to swing his gun up to challenge him; Rankin flew forward, throwing his forearm into the soldier's chin so hard that the man's teeth nearly severed his tongue as his head snapped back. Rankin rode him to the ground and knocked him unconscious with two hard snaps to the head.

As quick as he was, Rankin hadn't been quite fast enough; two of the man's companions turned the corner of the fence nearby. They were talking to each other, arguing over soccer; it took them a second or more to see the two men sprawled on the road nearby.

It was too late for them by then. Rankin grabbed the soldier's gun, leveling it against his stomach and thumbing down the selector to automatic fire without conscious thought. As he pulled the trigger he realized he might have chosen to run instead. If they'd been a little farther away or if he'd had another moment or two to think, he might have made that choice, but you didn't survive in wartime by second-guessing your instincts. By the time he dismissed the idea the men were already dead.

Rankin jumped on his motorcycle, pulling it backward away from the curb before starting it. He started down the road toward the airport. Thera turned the corner, running toward him.

"On! Get on!" he said, pulling up.

"What's going on?"

"Come on."

"We can't leave Fouad."

"I'm not. Get on."

Thera had to hike her long dress to her waist before she could do so; they lost a few more seconds before Rankin could spin back toward the other motorcycle. Rankin let her off, retrieved his Uzi from the top of his pack, then sped back toward Fouad, just turning the corner, face flush and chest heaving. Rankin pushed him down as if swatting a fly, then emptied the Uzi at the two soldiers who'd come out from the gate to see what the gunfire was about. Both men hit the dirt, but from this distance, a little better than a hundred yards, it was impossible to tell if he'd put them down or they'd simply taken cover.

"Up! Up!" he yelled to Fouad, reaching down for him. "Up! Let's go! Come on!"

Fouad got his hands beneath his chest and pushed forward, more a beached whale looking for the water than an intelligence agent trying to escape. Rankin grabbed him and pulled him onboard, nearly losing his gun as he started moving again. Shots whizzed by before he turned the corner.

"Come on!" yelled Thera, who was waiting. "Let's go!"

"That way," said Rankin, pointing ahead. "Head for the highway!"

TRIPOLI

"Hey, beautiful. This towel taken?"

Kel looked up from her blanket on the beach below the Hotel Cairo, which was next to the Medici. Ferguson had left her there before swimming out to meet with Corrine.

"Bob, back already?"

"I told you, everybody calls me Ferg." He grabbed his towel, giving the beach a quick glance while drying his hair.

"Still no one watching us," said Kel.

"Syrians must be busy." Ferguson plopped down next to her. "Thanks for hiring the girls. They did a good job. All locals?"

"All locals." She leaned her arms back, stretched in the sand. "Now it's time for you to pay up."

"A hundred Euros apiece wasn't enough?"

"I was talking about me," she said, craning her head back for a kiss.

20

Rankin and Thera stopped their bikes in a grove of trees overlooking the river about fifty miles from the airport. As far as Rankin could tell, they hadn't been followed, but he was sure they would be.

Corrigan cursed when he heard what had happened. For once, Rankin didn't snap back and tell him to screw himself.

"We're going to get back on Route 4 and ride up near Aj'aber," Rankin told him. "At that point we'll cut south into the desert. Fouad knows a couple of good places for pickups. We should be OK until nightfall."

"The Syrians are going to go ape."

Rankin said nothing. He was about to kill the connection when Corrigan told him that Ferguson wanted to talk to him.

"When?"

"I think he can talk now. Hold on. I'll find out."

Rankin's shoulders sagged as he waited, partly from fatigue and partly because he knew he hadn't had a particularly good run the last few days.

"Hey, Skippy," said Ferguson. "How do you like the bikes?"

"They're all right."

"Tell me about the jewels Khazaal had."

Rankin told him the little that he knew, then gave him the information that Thera and Fouad had found out at the airport.

"It's a logical place," said Ferguson. "How are you doing?"

Rankin told Ferguson what had happened.

"Yeah, Corrigan mentioned something along those lines. Sucks," said Ferguson. "I'm going to have Corrigan figure out how to get you guys over here after you bug out. Take Guns, too. In the meantime, let me talk to Fouad."

Rankin passed the phone over to the Iraqi. Fouad blinked into the sun, which had fallen halfway down the sky.

"Khazaal went west," Fouad told him.

"So I heard. Why would he do that?"

"I have no answer for you."

"Why would he go to Latakia you think? Buy weapons?"

"It would be logical."

"It's either that or gamble. I don't figure him for that. If he was going to sell the jewels, he would have gone to Cairo, don't you think?"

"A good bet."

"Who would he know up there in Latakia?"

"We have people in Damascus," said Fouad. "Perhaps you could speak to them."

"There's a waste of time. Why would the resistance need to buy weapons?"

"Perhaps they aren't buying weapons but services. Or maybe he is escaping: from Latakia he could go to Turkey." The more Fouad thought about this, the more he thought it must be the answer. The insurgency was doomed, and Khazaal, not being a stupid man, would try to get out while it was still possible.

"If he was going to Turkey, it would have been easier to get out through the Kurdish area," said Ferguson.

"Not for him."

"Point taken."

Fouad didn't understand the expression, but he assumed it meant that Ferguson agreed with him.

"How's Rankin treating you?" asked Ferg.

"Very well." When Thera had begun running at the first crack of gunfire, Fouad had assumed the worst: that the Americans were abandoning him. He was ashamed now.

"He can be tough on Iraqis."

"Yes," said Fouad. "But I am tough on Americans as well."

"Fair enough. See you guys when you get here."

21

Corrine went through the motions of the tour, admiring the equipment she was shown, nodding appropriately, and twice taking notes. Her hosts were very cordial and accommodating, traditional Arabs who did not let political or even religious differences disturb the mandate to be gracious hosts. They staged an elaborate dinner with enough food for an army; Corrine thought to herself that she would not fit into the bathing suit she had bought earlier in the day without considerable exercise. As the dinner wound down, she managed to ask her hosts for their opinion about a new peace plan for a Palestinian homeland without offending them. They were vaguely hopeful, but perhaps that too was due to politeness.

Her car was escorted back to the hotel by four police vehicles. It presented the illusion of safety while creating an obvious target for anyone who hated the regime as well as the U.S. Still, by the time she got into the hotel Corrine could almost believe that the media had overhyped the hatred Arabs felt toward Americans; her experience here had been as pleasant as any she had had in Europe or Asia.

Once again she waited in the reception area as her room was checked; once again she examined the illustrated manuscript pages. Gazing at them through the glass, she noticed a man approaching the reservations desk who looked vaguely familiar. She stared for a moment, unable to place him, and then, as he turned and met her gaze, she realized it was the man she had seen in the Mossad building.

She turned her head away, pretending not to notice, feigning absorption in the art.

The man came over to her.

"Ms. Alston?"

Corrine hesitated for a split second before turning around. Her escorts were right at his side bristling, ready to intervene. A few feet behind them, the Lebanese police too were ready.

"Yes?" she said.

"You don't remember me, do you?" said the man, bowing his head slightly in greeting.

"I'm afraid not." It was the safest thing to say.

"I was with the delegation to the UN two years ago. I had the great privilege of presenting the Pan-Arab view on the injustices faced by the Palestinian people."

"Yes, I'm sure," she said, emphasizing the noncommittal tone.

"You did not treat us well." The man wagged his finger at her. "You personally, of course, were very gracious, but your *employers*—" He stumbled over the word, as if choosing one that would be neutral. "I was glad to see a new president elected, with better ideas toward the Arab view, I trust."

The Lebanese security people, who had begun by looking suspiciously at the man, now turned those same glares toward Corrine.

"I'm afraid I've totally forgotten your name," she said.

"I am Fazel al-Qiam. I no longer have my government post," said Aaron Ravid. He'd come to Lebanon en route to Syria, renewing his contacts and gathering information.

The American had clearly recognized him from Tel Aviv and wasn't practiced enough to hide her expression, which was sure to be seen by the Syrian and Lebanese agents watching the lobby. So he'd done the only thing he could do, approach her and try to cover it.

Was it a coincidence that she was here, an accident of luck? Or was the Mossad somehow using her?

It must be an accident, but he would put nothing past Tischler.

Corrine, not thinking, extended her hand to shake. Ravid reacted as a conservative Arab might, frowning and smiling nervously but hesitating to shake. Realizing the faux pas, she quickly dropped her hand.

"Excuse me. I beg your pardon," she said.

"Apologies are not necessary for such a gracious and beautiful woman. I am in private life now, a simple man."

"Well, it was nice to see you again." Corrine started to turn away.

"You didn't answer my question. Does the new president understand the needs of the Palestinian people?"

"I think the president wishes to understand all of the complicated needs of the people in the Middle East," she said. "I would hope, strongly hope, that better arrangements can be made to our mutual benefit. I am here to help report on a trade agreement. I have found my hosts gracious and wonderful. Candidly, I don't think there are friendlier people in the world."

"We could do much trade with America if our rights are respected. Of course, that is tantamount. For too long the Arab people have not been accorded the proper respect. You are happy to take our oil, but do you treat us with the consideration equal partners are due? Sadly, you do not. Our civilization is many times older than yours, but we are treated like the little brother." Ravid smiled, as if stopping himself from the rest of the rant. "I apologize. You, Ms. Alston, are certainly not personally responsible for this. You have been honorable and respectful, even though I see you disagree with me."

"I don't disagree. I—" She stopped herself midsentence. "I may disagree on some points but not on the whole. Some day, at your leisure, I hope, we may discuss them."

"With the grace of God, we shall."

U pstairs in her suite, one of the marines found a brochure of tourist spots stuck under the door as they entered. Corrine took it from him before he could toss it in the garbage.

Convinced it was Ferguson's message on what time to meet, she thumbed through the English section several times without finding any clue, much less a note or directions. Out of desperation she looked in the directory for jazz clubs. There was only one: the Blu Note, in an older part of town. She didn't see a clue there either, until she realized that the digits for the acts had been carefully erased or changed, until the only ones that were legible were all the same: 1.

22

Pleasant though it was, Ferguson's personal-information sharing with Kel yielded no useful knowledge about any Islamic militant meeting in Tripoli and nothing but generic warnings about cells that were operating in the city. As a courtesy, he waited until she was out of sight to scan his room and suitcase, removing not one, not two, but three bugs and a tracking device. You couldn't blame a girl for trying.

The rest of the day and evening were equally unproductive. The majority of the local Iraqi community were employed with the Iraqi Petroleum Company at its massive processing and distribution facility a few kilometers north of town. Fouad had directed him toward the local intelligence contact, who as he predicted was useless; the nonofficial contacts were more thoughtful but had not heard that Khazaal was in the area. Ferguson left bugs in the café they frequented, arranging for an uplink just in case. But if the meeting was taking place here, it remained a well-kept secret. Ferguson wandered through the clubs where the drug dealers hung out; he could have bought huge portions of dope and smaller quantities of weapons, but information was much harder to come by.

Several hours of wandering the bars and casinos of Latakia had given Ferguson a splitting headache but not appreciably more information. He walked into the Blu Note a little after one a.m. and headed for the restroom, where he tried fighting off the headache with a small dose of Cytomel as well as aspirin. The thyroid hormone sometimes gave his system a jump start, but it didn't tonight, and he didn't have to put on much of an act to look like one of the disaffected Europeans as he sauntered into the bar area.

The jazz singer he'd seen the night before was back. Ferguson stared at her, looking at Corrine from the corner of his eye. She had a table with her marines and Delta troopers. Two members of the Lebanese police force sat across from her but seemed to be undercover.

Two other people were watching her from across the room. Ferguson decided they were probably Syrians, though it was difficult to tell. He sipped a seltzer, working out how to approach Corrine without blowing his cover; even though he was leaving town, he didn't want the Syrians to pick up on him, if possible.

Easiest thing to do would be to wait until she went to the restroom.

Or just bag the in-face meeting. It was unnecessary.

He leaned back against the bar, turning to the right in time to see a possible diversion come through the door in tight jeans and an equally snug red camisole top. She smiled at Ferguson and walked toward him.

He reached for his bankroll when a man ran into the room behind her. Clearly out of place, he wore a long raincoat, his eyes wide. Someone behind him shouted. Ferguson cursed, reaching to his back for the big Glock. He steadied, fired, and suddenly his headache felt ten times worse.

ACT IV

And the fourth angel poured out his vial upon the sun; and power was given unto him to scorch men with fire.

—Revelation 16:8 (King James Version)

1

From the inside, it felt like a slow-motion kaleidoscope, a cut and jumble of color and action and sounds, none of which made any sense to Corrine.

On the outside, she saw a man enter the club, heard someone shout behind him.

He's going to kill us, she thought to herself.

The man's head exploded, but his body didn't. A bullet had caught him. Ferguson's.

Ferguson!

The CIA officer jumped over the rail from the bar, gun in hand. The bodyguards leapt to their feet. One ran up toward the suicide bomber Ferguson had just killed, double-checking to make sure the man was dead. The other three were pulling her toward the door. Someone nearby jumped up, and just before any one could blast him waved a Lebanese police ID.

Ferguson saw the room as people: the blues singer, frozen at her piano; the two Syrians trying to get out the door; two young men, teenagers really, running for the back.

And then he realized what the hell was going on.

"No!" he yelled, shooting both of the young men. As they fell, the small submachine guns they'd had beneath their clothes, Mac-11s, fell to the floor.

Ferg bolted out the door behind the marines. Two cars were pulling up.

"No!" he shouted. "Out of here! It's a trap! It's a kidnapping! These guys are terrorists. Back through the front!"

One of the car doors opened. Ferguson fired once, then pirouetted in time to get a gunman coming down the ally. The marines started to fire at the gunmen appearing from the cars. Corinne ducked and began running back into the building.

"Yeah, that way," said Ferguson. "Go! Go!"

He grabbed her and threw her through the doorway. As the bodyguards followed, he grabbed the small smoke grenade he had inside his belt, yanked the pin with his teeth, and whipped it behind him. Then he took another and threw it into the room ahead of them.

"Go! Front door! Go!" he yelled as the bomb exploded.

Ferg grabbed Corrine by the back of the shirt and pulled her with him through the pandemonium. One of the bodyguards took hold of Corrine by the right arm and Ferg let go, swooping down to grab the hideaway gun near his ankle. One of the bodyguards grabbed a chair and smashed out a front window. Ferguson heard an automatic rifle popping behind him somewhere. He grabbed at Corrine and helped throw her through the window.

Their driver and escort—more embassy Delta boys—had pulled the Mercedes up. The escort leveled an M249 squad-level machine gun at Ferguson as he came out with the others.

"He's with us!" yelled a marine. "He's ours!"

A distinct look of disappointment registered on the man's face.

Corrine kept insisting that she was all right and could run on her own, but no one listened. They wedged her in the back, all six of them in the Mercedes. Their second vehicle, an SUV with a local driver, pulled up behind them, but there was no time to parcel out the seating arrangements. The Mercedes driver stomped the gas, and the car whipped forward. One of the marines screamed as his ankle got caught in the door, but he managed to get his foot inside as they skidded forward.

Four blocks later, the Mercedes and SUV veered onto a side street so that they could rearrange themselves. Ferguson pulled himself out of the back and flipped over into the front.

"Not here, not here!" he yelled. "This is the last place we want to be. That's a mosque. Get us the hell out of here. Down the block, go. Go! Go!."

The driver gave him a dirty look.

"Go!" said Ferguson. He pulled his gun up, the small one, though the driver probably didn't appreciate the difference.

"Listen to what Ferguson says," Corrine yelled.

"Left, quick right," said Ferguson, struggling to get his bearings straight as the car lurched into gear. They made it over to Abou Ali Square and headed south.

"All right, there's a place we can get to beyond the town and get a helicopter in," said Ferguson. "It's scoped out."

"I'm not leaving," said Corrine.

"Bullshit you're not leaving. Somebody just tried to kidnap you. Or assassinate you."

"So I'm supposed to run away?"

"I don't necessarily disagree with your attitude," said Ferguson, turning around. "But given that you're not here for any real reason except to kick in my teeth, I think you ought to get out while the getting out is good. You're just a target now."

Corrine, seated between two marines, realized Ferguson was right. But leaving town felt too much like running away.

"Hell, you were going tomorrow anyway," said Ferguson, pulling out his phone. "Besides, it'll get you out of another one of those tours."

Corrine laughed, more out of relief than anything else.

One of the Delta boys had been shot in the arm; one of the marine boys had sprained or possibly broken his ankle in the escape. Otherwise they were unharmed. Ferguson told Corrigan to hustle in the MH-6 helo they had stationed offshore for an emergency bailout. It was sitting on a barge about ten minutes' flying time away; they made it to the rendezvous point three minutes before the helo did.

"Who do you think did this?" Corrine asked as they waited for the chopper.

"Ordinarily I'd say the Syrians, but they looked a little surprised."

"There were Syrians in the club?"

"They followed you in. Second bet would be some of the people you had dinner with."

"They were government people and businessmen."

"Is that supposed to rule them out?"

"Was it Khazaal?"

"If blaming him will get me permission to kill him, then sure."

"Ferg."

"No, I doubt it was Khazaal. He's not here. Probably it was some group of local crazies trying to score big who heard that you were around." He could hear the helicopter in the distance. He pointed at two of the bodyguards. "You two guys are on the ground with me. Everybody else goes home."

One of the men started to object.

"No, listen to what he says," said Corrine. "He's with the CIA."

"Well, don't tell everybody." Ferguson smiled. The helicopter had already started to glide in. "There's not enough room for everybody in the chopper. It's all right. You're safe with me. I've had my rabies shots."

Corrine started for the helicopter, then turned back. "Thanks," she told Ferguson.

"For what?"

"For saving my life."

"I was saving my own. You just got in the way."

"You don't give up, do you?"

"Not unless I'm out of ammo."

"I wanted to tell you something. I saw a man in the hotel whom I saw with Mossad."

"Probably an officer," said Ferguson. "Maybe he runs some agents up here."

"He denounced me."

"What?"

"He denounced me." Corrine had to yell to make herself heard over the chopper. "He said his name was Fazel al-Qiam and he'd been a rep to the UN, an Arab. He denounced me."

"Did he spell that?"

"No."

"I'm just kidding. Thanks, I'll check it out."

"Can the helicopter get me down to Beirut?"

"Why?"

"I'm supposed to be there tomorrow."

"It'll take you to Oz if you want. Go."

"Thanks, Ferg."

"Yeah. I'll hate myself in the morning." Ferguson turned to the marine and Delta bodyguard staying behind. "Beer's on me boys. But let's find a place with a calmer floor show."

CIA BUILDING 24-442, VIRGINIA

The CIA and American intelligence in general were often faulted for not knowing much of what was going on in the world, but to Thomas Ciello, the criticism was not only unfair; it was wrong-headed. The CIA and its brother and sister agencies knew a great deal, so much, in fact, that it was impossible to know exactly what they knew.

Which was the real problem. Even someone like Thomas, who had made a career of knowing what the Agency knew, couldn't possibly know everything. All he could do was skim and skim and skim, use search tools that made Google look like a disorganized orangutan, and occasionally— only occasionally—take wild guesses.

The wild guesses usually led nowhere. The search engines, however, helped him match the name of a Russian weapons expert with a place he didn't expect to find him: Syria. Northwestern Syria, as a matter of fact, where Jurg Vassenka had booked a ticket on a rare flight to Latakia from Cairo via Damascus.

Vassenka was an expert in several weapons systems. The one that was most interesting in this case, given the Iraqi connection, was the Russian R-11/SS-1B, more popularly known as the Scud.

Thomas soon realized that Vassenka's arrival in Latakia would not actually be all that unusual; the Syrian resort on the Mediterranean was a popular place for arms dealers, one of the many facts that the CIA knew that he didn't. But by then Thomas had found more data on Latakia, including intercepted e-mails from several months before between Khazaal's Iraqi group and a mosque in the city.

As he started to type the information into a brief report, he glanced at Professor Ragguzi's manuscript on his desk. After he spoke to Corrigan, he promised himself, he would write an e-mail to the professor and point out his error on the UFOs. Surely a man as great as Ragguzi would appreciate knowing that he had made a mistake . . . as impossible as that was to contemplate.

TRIPOLI

Even if he hadn't already made up his mind that Lebanon was a wrong turn, the kidnapping would have cinched it for Ferguson. Had it been successful, the attempt would have brought down the wrath of the local authorities on the radicals in town, something Khazaal wouldn't have been foolish enough to want.

Figuring out precisely who had made the attempt on Corrine was a problem for another day, if not an entirely different agency. Ferguson's goal at the moment was to get out of the country without expending any more ammunition. Syria was the logical destination, but going over the nearby northern border involved document contingencies that would be hard to finesse for his two companions, Special Forces/Delta Sergeant Gordon Ranaman, and Marine Corporal Winchester Abbas. Ferguson decided that it would be considerably quicker to smuggle them across the border in the mountains to the northeast, which involved a great deal of driving, or go by sea, which not only would have meant procuring a boat but also would have deprived him of the car. So he chose the mountains.

There were many things Ferguson could have done with Abbas's name, but the marine had won a rather unfortunate tag from a drill instructor upon his initiation to the Corps: Grumpy. Ranaman was already using it, and Ferguson saw no reason not to do so himself. Ranaman's name was pronounced like *rain man*, thus suggesting Monsoon.

Nicknames decided, Ferg parceled out shifts for driving and sleeping. Two of the three men would stay awake while the other caught what rest he could in the backseat.

Which was how Ferguson came to be woken by this conversation:

"You know where we are?"

"On the road he told us to take."

"You think we should stop?"

"They're going to shoot us if we don't."

"They may shoot us if we do stop."

"Looks to me like we can count on it."

Ferguson bolted upright in the backseat. "Floor it," he yelled, pulling out his big Glock.

They'd come upon a preborder checkpoint manned by Syrians to cut down on smuggling. Fortunately, the checkpoint was manned by only two soldiers who were a bit sleepy and slow to realize that the Mercedes wouldn't stop. Unfortunately, the men a half mile away were much more awake, considerably more numerous, and better shots. They proved all three as the Mercedes rounded a curve down the pass on a narrow road leading to the border. The first few shots missed. The second set of rounds bounced harmlessly off the armor-plated hood. The next hundred or so, all fired by a light machine gun, did varying amounts of damage to the fenders and door but did not slow Grumpy, who was driving like a true marine: foot hard on the accelerator.

"Go, just keep going," Ferguson said, pulling on his night glasses. There was an obstruction set up in the middle of the road, but Grumpy managed to get the Mercedes past it by plowing through a ditch, sideswiping the Syrians' vehicle, and then barreling through a fence and down an embankment. When the car finally stopped, Ferguson grabbed his pack.

"End of the line guys, come on." They jumped out into the field and began to run, about twenty or thirty seconds ahead of the Syrians.

"What if this a minefield?" said Monsoon.

"Hey, good idea," said Ferguson. He reached to his belt and pulled out one of his small pin grenades. As he pulled the pin, he screamed in Arabic, "Mines! Mines!" and rolled the grenade on the ground, following it with a second and more warnings.

After the second grenade exploded, Ferguson cupped his hand around his mouth in a way he hoped would throw his voice and began yelping that his leg had been hurt. Whether his crude attempt at ventriloquism worked or not, the Syrians didn't bother following.

"Now what do we do?" asked Monsoon when they were finally sure they were clear.

"One rule from now on," Ferguson told them. "Never let me sleep through the good parts of the movie. Wake me up. OK?"

"Yes, sir," said Grumpy.

"It's all right. I forgot marines drive faster than most normal human beings," said Ferguson. "I thought I had another half hour before we got close to the border."

The other men laughed.

"All right. Next thing we do is find ourselves another car. And figure out where the hell we are." He glanced at his watch. "But first I have to call home."

The GPS device said they were about five miles from An Nabk, a small town on the road north of Damascus. Or as Corrigan put it, the middle of nowhere.

"I can tell you used to work for Rand McNally," Ferguson said.

"We have a theory."

"Who's we?"

Corrigan explained what Thomas had found out about Latakia.

"Thomas admitted Vassenka might be a coincidence," said Corrigan. "But he does know how to set up Scuds. He's an expert on the fuel systems. So if the Iraqis had some of the missiles but needed help using them, he'd be able to get them on track."

"He would, wouldn't he?" said Ferguson. "Do we think Khazaal has some?"

"No. But you know there were at least two dozen that were never accounted for properly. At least. You could have parts buried in the desert somewhere."

"I'd think of Khazaal more trying to sell them than use them," said Ferguson. "He's more meat and potatoes: rocket grenades, car bombs. According to the estimate I read, he's supposed to be on his way out."

"A Scud would change that."

Sure would, thought Ferguson, especially if it were aimed at Baghdad when the president was there.

Or Israel.

"Thomas got this on his own or after talking to Fouad?"

"Thomas doesn't talk to anybody," said Corrigan. "Not in any language they can understand."

"Fair enough," said Ferguson. "We'll be up there by the afternoon. Get me some rooms, backup gear, whole setup. I have two friends with me. Get Thera and the boys over there, too."

Ferguson told Corrigan about the Mossad agent Corrine had encountered in the Tripoli hotel.

"No diplomat of that name exists," said Corrigan after a quick check on one of the databases.

"Gee, no kidding, Jack. Here's the thing, either the guy is a legitimate Mossad agent who was worried about having his cover blown, or he's a double agent who Mossad ought to know about. Either way, we have to talk to Tischler about him. I just want some more information before I do it."

"You're going to talk to him?"

"Who do you suggest?"

"Um, Corrine said she would. She already has the call in."

"Jeez, Louise, get her a real job, would you?" Ferguson pressed his lips together. "All right. Make sure she knows about the double-agent angle. Tischler won't admit it, so she shouldn't expect him to. Maybe I should tell her. Where is she?"

"En route to the embassy."

"She should have been in Beirut hours ago."

"She was. She got up early, and she's on her way to Damascus."

"What?"

"She was going there anyway. State's going to file a formal protest with the Lebanese and—"

"Save the details for another time. I have to go steal a car."

Smugglers in Syria were generally assumed to be heading east toward Iraq, which was one thing in Ferg's favor. The second thing in his favor was the unexpected availability of a car bearing the faded but still visible indicia of the local Red Crescent society, the Arab world's equivalent of the Red Cross. Ferguson didn't steal the car; he bought it for five hundred Euros from a service station/junkyard/chicken farm that had just opened for the day. The vehicle, a ten-year-old Fiat with multicolored fenders, was a veritable bargain even considering the large rip in the backseat and the fact that it burned a quart of oil every two hundred miles.

Monsoon's Arabic was quite good, his accent smoothed out by a year's service at the Beirut embassy and considerable practice. Grumpy, on the other hand, knew only a few words, and even Ferg had a hard time understanding them. The marine's grandfather had come from Iran, and Grumpy claimed to know Farsi very well. Ferguson didn't know the language beyond a few rudimentary phrases, but he guessed that most people they encountered wouldn't either. The mix of language skills suggested a potential cover story: they were relief coordinators on an inspection tour, Monsoon working with the UN from Damascus, Ferguson an international visitor from Ireland, Grumpy an Iranian.

The story wouldn't have withstood very deep questioning, but it wasn't put to the test; they made decent time north, bypassing the city of Hamāh and cutting straight toward the coast and the region north of Tartūs. Ferguson did the driving and got mildly lost only twice, both times because the car's engine started acting up and he decided it would be better to break down off the main highway.

North of Baniyas the engine began overheating, and despite suggestions from Grumpy on how to nurse it the car finally died about ten miles south of Latakia. The distance was walkable, but after a mile they found a bus stop and joined a group of workers heading to town to fill night jobs in the tourist industry.

Tourism in Tripoli had ancient roots, but it had a very temporary feel there; the grayness of the town around the major hotels and the very visible scars of the Israeli occupation seemed to hang like a shroud at the edges. Latakia, by contrast, was brighter. You could see the money in the freshly paved highway and the sleek lampposts, along with the neon Western-style signs and the glittering domes of two new mosques, recently built by devout nouveau riche businessmen.

Tourists from the Middle East and southeastern Europe found their Euros went ten times as far in Latakia as in European hot spots: the casinos paid off a little better and neglected to report earnings to foreign tax authorities. The tight control of the Syrian government made the area extremely safe for tourists; there was no question of kidnapping or crazed suicide bombers here, unless they were under the direction of the government. The dictator and his family owned interests in several of the major resorts and casinos, further encouraging local prosperity. It might be terrible to live under a dictatorship, but playing here was not so bad. Arms dealers and other shady characters had flocked to the city over the past two years, finding the government mostly benign as long as the informal taxes were paid and the occasional favor rendered.

Corrigan found them a suite at an older hotel in town called the Taib, which translated roughly into English as "good," an apt description. A business-class hotel that had a sedate, understated staff, Taib was around the corner from one of the main streets at the southeastern end of the city. The building's thick masonry and plaster walls made listening devices harder to place, and the main clientele made them mostly a waste of time. Ferguson's sweep turned up only one in the suite, and it had dead batteries. He placed white-noise machines in the two bedrooms and common area, then told his companions to rest up while he went scouting.

"You're not tired?" Monsoon asked as Ferguson tried to work the wrinkles out of a sports coat for his evening forage.

"Nah. I slept on the plane," he told him. "I have the key, but I'll knock like this when I'm back."

He rapped on the bureau, mimicking the first bars of "Jug of Punch," an old Irish folk song.

"I may even sing to you."

"What do we do if it's not you?" asked Monsoon.

"After you shoot the person knocking, there's a dock at a new hotel called Versailles about a mile and a half from here on the water. If something happens, you call this number and go there."

Ferguson wrote down a local phone number and gave both men a copy.

"What do we say?" asked Grumpy.

"Nothing. Make sure the call is answered, then hang up. Someone will look for you at the dock. The person there will say your name and will know your social security number. If not, kill him. If you're not already dead."

4

DAMASCUS

Corrine studied her reflection in the mirror. Her blond hair had grown a trifle long; she reached into her toiletry purse and retrieved a scissors to trim the bangs.

The puffy bags under her eyes were a more difficult problem to solve. She daubed on a light veneer of makeup, then rubbed most of it off. Corrine ordinarily wore very little, and even the light touch looked artificial to her. She decided that the excitement of the night before would excuse a pair of heavy eyes, and if they didn't, tough.

The Lebanese had bent over backward with apologies. When she insisted on continuing on to Damascus, everyone, from the security people to the ambassador, looked at her as if she were insane. But she saw no reason to change her plans. She wasn't about to let the attempt on her life—if that's what it was—influence what she did.

The fact that people thought it was appropriate to treat her as a piece of delicate china pissed her off. That was the way she thought about it: *pissed off*. Profanity and all.

Corrine closed her bag and checked her dress. She was scheduled to attend a small reception at the president's palace with the ambassador that evening. American-Syrian relations had started to thaw with the incoming administration, although the country remained on the U.S.'s sanctions list for dealing with terrorists.

A knock on the door startled Corrine. She reached instinctively for the small pistol in her bag, even though she was in the embassy, but it was only the steward.

"Ma'am, you have a phone call from Washington," he said through the door. "I believe it's the White House."

"On my way," she replied, placing the gun back in the bag.

"Miss Alston, assure me that you are all right and that the rumors of your demise are greatly exaggerated," said the president as soon as he came on the line.

"Mr. President, I'm fine. I hope there are no rumors to the contrary." Corrine forced a smile for the ambassador, standing next to her in his study as she took the call.

"I was deeply concerned to hear that there was a problem," said McCarthy. "Deeply concerned."

"I'm fine." Corrine summarized the incident briefly. While there were several competing theories, Corrine and the security chief at the embassy favored the one proposing that a group had wanted to kidnap her and hold her for ransom, most likely for political gains but possibly simply for financial. "It comes with the territory," she said. "I would expect that things will be even more restless in the next few days and weeks, as the outlines of your plan become known. Many people are not interested in peace."

"Restless does not begin to cover it, my *deah*, though it is an interesting turn of phrase," said the president. "I assume your presence had something to do with the arrest of the individual we spoke of in Washington."

"Something to do with it, yes."

"Well, it would be very good timing to have him arrested," said the president. "Very good timing indeed. His trial would underline the commitment to democracy and the future." *Future*, in the president's full Georgian drawl, sounded like a country on the distant horizon filled with precious things. "But you and I spoke of your personal safety before you left."

"I'm fine, Mr. President."

"Now don't get your back up, *deah*. I know you can take care of yourself."

"I can, sir." Corrine felt her face flushing. She felt constrained by the fact that the ambassador was nearby. "Really, Mr. President. I am fine. And I am very capable of taking care of myself."

McCarthy chuckled. "I would *nevah* say anything to the contrary, *deah*."

5

LATAKIA

"Ferguson, is that you?" said the man, spreading his arms in wonder. He spoke in English, with a heavy accent that most people took as Russian, though he was actually a Pole.

"Birk, pull up a chair."

"I am surprised to see you," replied Birk Ivanovich, still standing.

"You should be," said Ferguson. The last time Birk had seen him had been at the end of Ferguson's trip here a year before, when Ferguson disappeared into a blazing sunset, ostensibly the victim of a bomb blast. "Have some champagne with me."

"Is it good luck to drink with a dead man?"

"Only with his ghost," said Ferg.

"I didn't set that bomb," said Birk. He glanced at his two shadows, motioning with his head that they should find seats elsewhere in the elegant club room of the Max Hotel.

"If you had set the bomb I wouldn't be here," said Ferguson. The waiter came over with a fresh champagne flute and poured a drink for Birk, who was here so often that he had a regular table at the far end of the room.

"To your health," said Birk, raising the filled glass.

"And yours."

"Still have the yacht?" Ferguson asked.

"A new one. You should come see it some time. After all, your money helped me buy it."

"Still have the one-eyed Greek as the captain?"

"Fired him. And the hands. I run it myself."

"You do?"

Birk shrugged. "For now. You must sail out to see me. It is offshore, of course. I call it the *Sharia*."

"Islamic justice? You do have a sense of humor, Birk."

"I try," said Birk, downing the champagne. "What are you in the market for today? More missiles?"

"Always looking," said Ferg. "How hard is it to get things into Iraq?"

Birk made a face. "Why would you go there?"

"Me? I wouldn't. How hard is it?"

Birk shrugged. "Not hard. But the market there is as bad as ever. What are you bringing in? Milk? Penicillin? That could get a good price. Not as good as under Saddam but still decent. Aspirin . . . you would be surprised."

"I was thinking more along the lines of what you trade in."

Birk made a face. "The Iraqis don't buy. They sell."

"You sure?"

"It is the same as when you were here last. They have plenty of small arms. The quality is so-so, but you can make it up on volume. I get my RPGs from there. Cheaper than Russia or Georgia. Ukraine, well, sometimes you can still find a bargain there."

RPGs were rocket-propelled grenades.

"You buy a lot from them?" Ferguson asked.

"Usually not." Birk shook his head. "Rifles, yes, if I can find a large lot. But even there, you must be careful. Some of the ones who come here to sell don't even know the guns themselves. That is the depressing thing. They are not trying to cheat you; they just don't know. Imagine that!"

"So what are you selling to Khazaal?"

"Khazaal?"

"The Iraqi resistance leader."

"I know who he is. Please." Birk shook his head. "You think I don't know my business?"

"I know you know your business. That's why I'm here."

The arms dealer squinted at him in a way that was supposed to suggest that he had no idea what Ferguson was talking about; it had exactly the opposite effect.

Birk drained his champagne. "Business calls," he said, starting to rise. "Another time—"

Ferguson clamped his hand on Birk's forearm. "Come on, Birk. Don't hold out on me. It's bad form."

The two bodyguards seated at the table behind Ferguson started to get up.

"Better tell them to get back," said Ferg.

Birk signaled with his head that the men should relax. Ferguson let go of his arm. "There's a convention in town that I want to be part of."

Birk shook his head. "Too dangerous even for you."

"Are you invited?"

"They would roast me first."

"A drink?" said Ferguson. He signaled to the waiter. "Something more serious than the champagne?"

"Why not? Bombay Sapphire. On the rocks."

"Gin now? Last year it was vodka."

"I like a change of pace."

Ferguson took the barest of sips from the gin, then asked Birk what he knew. The Pole told him that he didn't know much, only that no one should go near the castle north of town for the next few days. After gentle and not-so-gentle prodding and several more drinks, Birk told him that he had heard several Islamic fanatics—he used a Polish word whose most polite connotation was "maniacs"—were either already in town or en route. They were trying to do something in Iraq, but what it was, no one could say.

Birk hastened to assure Ferguson that he did not deal with such men directly, though occasionally he might facilitate arrangements with go-betweens. None, he claimed, were currently buying.

"Is Khazaal in town yet?" Ferguson asked.

"I cannot afford to keep track of which crazy is here or not here."

"You can't afford not to."

Birk shrugged. "I heard, yes, but I don't see him. He may not be a gambler."

"When's the meeting?"

"Maybe three days from now, but my information is sketchy as always. Try the secret police."

Ferguson had the waiter bring over a full bottle of the gin, but this produced no more information. Finally he mentioned Jurg Vassenka, the Russian expert Thomas had discovered who was heading toward Latakia.

"An overrated Russian on his way out," said Birk.

"You say that about all Russians."

"I would not deal with him. He pretends to know systems that he does not know. He passes himself off as an expert, when he is an imbecile."

"By birth, right?"

Birk nodded solemnly. Though he did business with them all the time, he did not like Russians.

"Is he going to the meeting?" Ferguson asked.

This possibility surprised Birk, though he frowned quickly to hide it. "I doubt it. Is he in Latakia?"

"He will be."

"For that information, I owe you a favor," said Birk.

"And I'll be sure to collect," said Ferguson.

6

NORTH OF LATAKIA
SEVERAL HOURS LATER . . .

Crusaders had started to build the castle in the twelfth century but abandoned it in favor of other, better sites farther up and down the coast. Its four walls ranged from six to twenty feet high and were doubled in places. There were two covered keep areas, but they were not much larger than a fair-sized bathroom. Overall, the footprint was perhaps a tenth of the size of the famous Krak des chevaliers, the medieval castle farther south near Tartūs, which had been built around the same time.

Ferguson leaned forward against the rocks a half mile away, watching through binoculars as two men worked on the approach to the old fort, apparently laying mines along the long, narrow road that led to the only entrance. Built on a rocky promontory overlooking the Mediterranean, the castle had only two doorways: one above a very narrow staircase cut into the stone that led up from the sea and the other at the end of the long road where the men were working. A sharp, clifflike drop near the castle wall and a rocky ravine helped isolate the narrow road, which had been constructed with a pair of switchback curves that could be covered from the old walls. Nobody without an invitation was crashing the party.

Ferguson flipped up the antenna on his phone. "How's my U-2 doing?" he asked Lauren back in Virginia.

"Leaving Cyprus in about ten minutes. We're going to get a Global Hawk to share time so we have around-the-clock coverage. Your devices planted?"

"Yeah, but you're not going to see much from here that they won't. I can't get close enough to bug the place. I'm on that bluff a half mile away; ten feet from here they'd be all over me. I figure no more than four guys in there right now, counting the people planting the mines."

Ferguson had planted a pair of low-light video cameras to keep the road under surveillance. Small transmitters fed the images into a satellite system that relayed them back to the Cube.

"What do you think?" Lauren asked.

"B-52 as soon as they're all there. Get all the bees while they're in the hive."

"What do you really think?"

"That's what I think," said Ferguson. "Best pest eradicator in the business."

"Have you talked to Ms. Alston?"

Ferguson grunted. "I will." He glanced at his watch. "I'm going to get moving. Where's the rest of the team?"

"Should be getting to the Taib any minute."

"Uh oh. Who do you figure is the best singer on the team?"

"Singer?"

"Better give me Guns. Marines at least know how to hum."

When Ferguson got to the hotel an hour later, he discovered that Rankin had decided to take the backup room on the second floor and wait for Ferguson to arrive rather than test the Delta boy's ability to pick out a tune from a knock. This was just as well; Monsoon nearly clipped Ferguson even though he hummed along with his knock.

"You're too close to the door," Ferg told him as he walked in. "I would've flipped you on your back."

"I would have shot you first," said the bodyguard.

"Want to try it again?"

Monsoon wisely declined. Guns and Grumpy were soon trading marine drinking stories while Ferguson huddled with Fouad to discuss the layout and possibilities. It appeared that the castle was intended as a meeting place only. The ruins had nothing in the way of amenities, not even an outhouse. This suggested that the people coming in for the meeting would be spread around town and that therefore the best thing to do would be to look for them and with luck find someone they could bug or get close enough to eavesdrop or follow, on the theory that he would lead them to Khazaal. The more people they were looking for, Fouad argued, the easier it would be for them to find someone.

"Can't say no to that." Ferguson grinned at the Iraqi, thinking his father would have made the same point. He felt an ache suddenly to know more about his dad, what he might have done here, but it would have been out of place, too indulgent, to ask.

"Fouad, why don't you and Rankin take a tour and arrange some of the backup stuff we need. Thera, get some party dresses, something you'd wear to buy a suitcase nuke. Everybody else hang tight." Ferguson leaned back on the couch. "I'm going to catch some z's. Somebody wake me up at six, all right?"

And with that, he closed his eyes and gave in to sleep.

Fouad had not been in Latakia for several years, and he found that what little he remembered of the place was wrong. He and Rankin rented two different cars and bought bicycles and other items, squirreling them around town for emergency use. Rankin explained that the contingency arrangements were often handled by a separate advance team, but Syria was a place that the Americans found difficult to operate in, a fact Fouad could have guessed on his own.

When their chores were done, the Iraqi led Rankin to several coffee houses, sitting quietly and listening for openings in nearby discussions he might use to gather gossip. It was a task that took patience, and it was clear to Fouad that the American did not possess much of this, though he was wise enough to suffer in silence. Fouad gained little information anyway, learning only where the most devout mosques were; he was clearly a stranger, and his Baghdad accent was probably cause for even more suspicion.

Fouad was not like Ferguson, who could make someone's suspicions play to his advantage. He was not like Ferguson at all, unable to fake his way deftly through a maze of traps. He lamented this shortcoming to Rankin as they traveled back to the Taib hotel.

"I wouldn't compare myself to him," said Rankin. "What he's good at is lying."

"He's good at many things. Like his father."

Rankin, not particularly interested in hearing Ferguson's praises, said nothing.

Fouad wondered how a man so different from Ferguson had become one of his closest associates. But that would make sense, he decided: a man as wise as Ferguson would seek a shadow with different qualities. Rankin was brave, not braver than Ferguson but at his level, and he had proven himself resourceful and watchful.

"It's almost six," Rankin said. "We'll get something to eat and head back."

Soon after Ferguson woke up, Corrigan reported that two SUVs had been spotted going into the castle. Ferguson decided to have Rankin, Fouad, Monsoon, and Guns trail the SUVs with the help of the U-2. He and Thera would troll for information in the casinos and clubs. When Grumpy protested that he didn't want to stand guard in the suite doing nothing, Fouad volunteered to change places with him. The old Iraqi said he would be only too happy to sit and watch the local TV.

"No, sorry. Grumpy doesn't speak Arabic well enough to talk himself out of anything," Ferg told him. "There'il be plenty of time for excitement down the line."

"How do you know this isn't the meeting?" said Rankin.

"Because my luck's been too crappy to get that lucky," said Ferguson. "Take the laptop and the backpack. Corrigan will set up a download so you can see them in real time. The spy plane has to stay off the coast, but he can see into the city from out there all right."

"If we find Khazaal, can we shoot him?" asked Rankin.

"No. Better to lose him than shoot him."

"That sucks."

"Tell me about it."

NORTH OF LATAKIA
TWO HOURS LATER . . .

Having the spy plane overhead simplified things a great deal. Rankin didn't have to get too close to the castle and in fact decided it was much safer to stay along the highway a half mile away. He split his force into two elements: Guns and Monsoon in a car to the north, he and Grumpy to the south. The image from the spy plane was downloaded via satellite to the small antenna he'd unfolded from his rucksack nearby. The image was decent, though not quite as clean or detailed as that available back in the Cube, and Corrigan had an analyst on the satellite radio line relaying information. The men in the castle were simply checking out arrangements, walking around the area, probably making sure it would be secure and examining the area for bugs and the like. The interior could not be seen by the spy plane, but the men didn't bother to stay in there very long, moving around the old battlements and nearby land, probably inspecting it for the upcoming meeting.

"I think they're moving," Corrigan told Rankin over the radio's satellite frequency.

"All right. We're on it." Rankin had already seen it on the First Team laptop, which received a download over a separate satellite circuit. He closed the case and switched the radio to the team frequency. "Our guys are leaving," he said. "Guns? You ready to dance?"

"Always."

"Coming out," said Corrigan. "Truck one is going north. Truck two . . . south."

"They split up," Rankin told the others as he put the laptop into his pack. "Guns, they should be past you in about sixty seconds. We're just following," he added. "Keep far back. And remember that's a Ford you're driving, not an M1A1."

LATAKIA

Birk's most serious competitor in Latakia was a Syrian who had grown up in Germany and went by the name of Ras. He tended to lie more than Birk but had better connections with the Syrian police. Unfortunately, a good deal of what they told Ras were lies.

Ras generally spent early evenings in the Agamemnon, a small, plush hotel on the Blue Coast north of Latakia. He owned a table in a room they called the Barroom, a lavish, nineteenth-century dining room with crystal chandeliers and tuxedoed waiters. Ras usually had a ship captain or two at his side; a good deal of his arms were sold to foreign concerns and traveled through Latakia's port. But this evening he was sipping a vodka martini alone. He frowned when he saw Ferguson but brightened considerably when he realized Thera was with him.

"Mr. IRA," Ras said to Ferguson in German-accented English as he approached the table. "Your wife?"

"I wish," said Ferguson. He pulled out the chair for Thera. Unlike Birk, Ras believed the cover story Ferguson had used on his last visit.

"A most beautiful woman," said Ras, standing and taking her hand to kiss it.

Thera played along as Ferguson had coached her, saying nothing and sitting down; the strong, silent type intrigued Ras and left him howling for more.

"Perrier," Ferguson told the waiter.

"Is that all?" said Ras.

"With a twist. Thanks."

"I will have a bourbon on the rocks," said Thera. She wore a flowered two-piece skirt set whose silk was too tight for her to hide more than one small pistol on her inner thigh.

Ras's face lit up as he pushed his drink aside. "The same for me. Good bourbon. American. Your best."

The waiter bowed and went off.

"I hear you had some excitement in town the last time you were here," Ras told Ferguson, even as he stared at Thera.

"Every day is an adventure."

"I had nothing to do with it."

"Guilty conscience?" Ferguson leaned back in the chair, observing the rest of the room. Besides the Syrian intelligence agents on semipermanent assignment here, he thought he recognized someone from the French military intelligence agency and a Czech who sold information to the Russians.

"If I had wanted to kill you, I assure you I would not have missed," said Ras.

"Everybody tells me that."

Their drinks arrived. Ras made sure to clink glasses with Thera, who took the tiniest possible sip.

"So who was gunning for me?" Ferguson asked.

"You have many enemies here. Many."

Thera watched as the two men boxed around a bit, Ferguson letting Ras steal long glances at her before prodding the conversation along. When he finally got around to why they had come, it seemed like an afterthought, catching up on gossip: he'd heard the Russian Vassenka was in town.

"Vassenka?" Ras's face momentarily blanched. "An idiot. I hope not."

"Doesn't like you much, does he?" said Ferguson, going with the reaction.

"An idiot."

"Well, you should have paid him," said Ferguson.

Thera thought it was a guess, but it was a masterful one. Ras shook his head and held up his glass for another drink.

Ferguson now moved in for the kill, still subtle but more aggressive. Given that Ras believed his old cover story, it was natural that he was interested in Vassenka as a competitor. But even before Ras's refill arrived, he could tell that the Syrian had no useful information. He lingered a bit, finishing his seltzer before rising to go.

"Leaving so soon?" asked Ras.

"At some point, perhaps we will be interested in rifles," said Ferguson. "A few days."

"I can offer so much more," said Ras, looking at Thera.

Ferguson took her arm proprietarily.

"Didn't get much from that," said Thera as they made their way to Buenos, another casino nearby.

"Sure I did."

"Like?"

"Vassenka's not here yet, and no one around town has been talking him up. Ras doesn't know about the meeting, probably because the Syrians haven't told him. He'll tell the Syrians about Vassenka, and they'll be looking for him. If they find him, they'll tell Ras, and Ras will tell me. If I need him to. That enough for you?"

"It's OK."

"You get all the credit," added Ferguson. "Dress looks good. I'm starting to get a little sweet on you myself."

She laughed, thinking he was joking.

9

The first truck made a U-turn soon after heading onto the highway, which left both trucks going south in the same direction, separated by about a half mile. Alerted by Corrigan, Rankin delayed leaving his hiding place, guessing that the idea had been to catch anyone following the second SUV. It was absolutely the right move, but it would make it more difficult to track them closely if they split up later on.

Both the U-2 and the Global Hawk that alternated with it used an integrated sensor suite built by Raytheon for surveillance work. The sensor set had an active electronically scanned array (AESA) that allowed moving targets to be identified and tracked at long range. The multihyperspectral electro-optic infrared sensors (in layman's terms, a very good digital camera that could see in the dark) transmitted a stream of images to the satellite unit and from there back to the Cube and the team's laptop. More refined though similar to the units that had been used for battlefield and bombing assessment during the 2003 Iraq War, the system provided a commanding view of what was going on in the city. But no matter how advanced, technology had its limits, as became apparent when the trucks pulled into a lot containing similar vehicles just outside the city.

A car lot, where the vehicles had been borrowed or stolen from hours before.

"There's a bus coming," said Corrigan.

Rankin cursed and stepped on the gas, but by the time he got close enough to see the bus the men were aboard and it was moving.

"We'll tag along, see if they get off together," said Rankin, though he knew it was hopeless. "Best we can do."

10

Ferguson was just about to call it a night when a large man in an ill-fitting suit walked into the Milad, a crowded club on the Blue Beach. The pale-skinned, pimple-faced European looked out of place here, but then he probably would have looked out of place at his own funeral.

"Birk wants to talk," said the man. "At the Max."

"Very good," said Ferguson. "We were just on our way over."

The Max awed Thera. The place was one part European grand hotel and another part Las Vegas fun palace.

"Nice place," she said as Ferguson tugged her inside.

"It'll do. Don't say *anything* in Russian. Or about Russia. And count your fingers when we're done."

Birk was sitting with Jean Allsparté, an Algerian who specialized in arranging transport for items large and small. Ferguson remembered from his last visit that Allsparté spent almost all of his time in town gambling; clearly he was here now for a deal. Birk dismissed him as soon as he saw Ferguson arrive: Allsparté slipped away before Ferguson could get close enough to ask how his luck was running these days.

"Ferg, a pleasure," said Birk rising. "And with such lovely company tonight." He took Thera's hand as gallantly as Ras had but then turned to Ferguson and said, "She leaves."

"She's with me."

Birk shook his head. "No."

Ferguson gestured to Thera that she should go over near the bar. "Not too far," he said. He watched her leave, then turned to Birk. "So talk to me."

"Recently on the market. Very nice."

"I know you're speaking English, Birk, but I'm not getting the words."

"*Mashinostroenia.*"

"Russian weapons manufacturer," said Ferguson. "Speak English. Or I'll speak Polish."

"The P-120 Malakhit 4K-85—the Siren cruise missile. One has recently become available."

"That's nice."

The weapon Birk was referring to—known to NATO as the SS-N-9 Siren—was an antiship cruise missile that entered Russian (at the time, Soviet) service in 1969. The weapon carried a five-hundred-kilogram conventional warhead, or nuke. Primarily a ship-launched missile, it was also carried aboard Russian "Charlie II"–class submarines. Depending on how it was launched, it had a sixty-nautical-mile range, with inertial and radar-terminal homing, meaning that once fired it could find its own way to the target.

According to some sources, the Russians had experimented with a video guidance system for the weapon that allowed it to be steered to a precise aim point (though in practice the target would have had to be fairly large: a house as opposed to a door, for example). It was a potent missile, though weapons such as the "Switchblade" (Kh-35 Uran, a Harpoon knockoff) had made it technically obsolete in the Russian inventory.

"Come on. You would like one, no?" prompted Birk. "You bought the SA-2s last year."

"Different program," said Ferguson. "What sort of warhead?"

"What would you like?"

"What can you get?"

Birk laughed. "I like you, Ferguson, really. You dance like one of us. You *are* Polish, no? Tell me you are, and I slice ten percent from the price."

"Not according to Mom. But she might've had reason to lie."

"Perhaps we should go into business as partners."

"You'd trust me as your partner?"

"Of course not. That is why you would make a good partner."

"Maybe when I retire."

"One million."

"Too much."

Actually, the price was low, and under other circumstances Ferguson would have grabbed it. But he had too many other things to worry about and doubted he could talk Corrine Alston into the idea.

"I will find many buyers," said Birk. "There is a primitive launching system included; no need for elaborate preparation."

"You have the Titanit radar, too, huh?"

"No, but this is not a serious deficiency. A GPS kit has been installed. There is internal guidance as a backup and—"

"Whose GPS kit? American?"

"Russian, actually," said Birk. GPS stood for "global positioning satellite" and technically referred to a group of satellites launched by America. But the initials had become shorthand for any system using satellites for target guidance. The satellites and the radios that got their bearings from them had many uses; civilians were familiar with the GPS system from mapping programs used for getting directions in high-end automobiles. The U.S. military had pioneered the use of relatively inexpensive "kits" that could be added to otherwise simple weapons: an iron bomb, for example, could be turned into a precision-guided munition with such a system steering its tail fins. The Russians had a satellite network named Glosnass that worked the same way.

Satellite guidance had not been invented when the Siren was first put into service; even if it had been, the Russians wanted the weapon to strike ships, which presumably wouldn't stay at a fixed point on the earth's surface very long. But on the black market, such a system would make the missile more desirable to anyone wishing to hit a fixed target. Not only would it be more accurate, it would be easier to use.

A five-hundred-kilogram warhead (a bit more than a thousand pounds) could obliterate a decent-sized building. A nuke could take out a good-sized city.

"Can you get a satellite kit for other missiles?" Ferguson asked.

"Everything is for sale." Birk sighed. He hated it when negotiations moved off point. "As I understand it, the Siren missile is aimed in the proper direction, then launched. After a certain time the guidance system takes over. The accuracy is very good. Within three meters, guaranteed."

"Or my money back, right?"

Birk smiled.

"You have an EUC for the missile?" Ferguson was referring to an end-user certificate, a document used by governments to certify that weapons systems had been bought legally. The usual fee for one—fraudulent, of course—started at one hundred thousand dollars.

"That would be pointless in this case," admitted Birk. "There were not so many made: five hundred, eight hundred . . . I lose track."

"I'll bet."

"A very good deal for you, Ferguson. A dangerous weapon in the wrong hands."

"Whose hands?"

Birk shrugged.

"The warhead on the Siren, a nuke?"

"Conventional, alas. But something of this size is very hard to come by.

Five hundred kilograms. It would leave quite a hole. And of course you could always remove the conventional payload and replace it with something more to your liking."

"Do you have more?" asked Ferguson.

"Only the one."

"If there are so few, where did this one come from?"

"That is always a question I do not ask. One would believe a government," said Birk. "But I do not deal direct."

"And the person who has this has only one?"

"Had one. It is now in my possession."

"What about the guidance system?" asked Ferguson.

"Part of the package."

"Are there other guidance systems? I might be interested in buying a few."

"What missile would you like them for?"

"How about a Scud?"

Birk made a face. "An inferior product. I would not sell you one."

"The guidance system or the missile?"

"Either. The Scud is a piece of junk."

Not, thought Ferguson, if it were guided by a GPS system, though admittedly this would take a bit of tinkering. "Who *would* you sell it to?"

"I have no Scuds. Today, I'm selling the Siren. Tomorrow, who knows? Are you a serious buyer?"

"I'll talk to my superiors and see what we can do."

"You have a superior?" Birk laughed. "I don't believe it. Not even God would be your superior. As a show of good faith, one piece of interesting gossip," added Birk. "First, a vodka."

"Back to vodka?"

"One strays but always comes home. Drinking is like marriage."

They shared a shot of an obscure Polish vodka that Birk claimed was the best alcohol in existence. To Ferguson it tasted one step removed from potato peelings—and a step in the wrong direction.

"Look for your friend Khazaal in a mosque," said Birk.

"Which one?"

Birk shook his head. "You are supposed to be the spy. I cannot keep track of these mosques. They are all alike to me."

Ferg got up, winking at Thera.

"Five hundred thousand, firm," said Birk.

"I'll see what I can do."

11

Corrine tried twice more to get hold of Tischler without getting a response. When she told Ferguson about it, he didn't seem surprised.

"His man may have already filled him in," Ferguson told her.

"Wouldn't it be polite to return my call? He doesn't know what it's about."

"It would be *smart* to return your call, because he doesn't know what you want, even if he thinks he does," said Ferguson. "But Tischler doesn't *do* polite. Think of it this way: he figures you're going to tell him his man is a screwup."

"How is he a screwup?"

"He should have skulked away without seeing you, taking the chance that you wouldn't notice or might not remember, and knowing that even if you did, you're supposed to be an ally and ought to know enough to keep your mouth shut. This way there was no chance that you wouldn't notice him."

"I thought Mossad people don't screw up."

"They're human," said Ferguson.

"If he's not going to call me back, the hell with him."

"I guess," said Ferguson. He paused a moment, then changed the subject. "Listen, I need a million dollars."

"What?"

"I can probably get the price down a bit, but it's going to be in that neighborhood."

"For what?"

Ferguson explained that he wanted to buy the Russian ship-to-ship missile Birk had for sale.

"I'll have to talk to Washington," she said doubtfully.

"They're going to tell you it's not in the budget," said Ferguson. "The program to buy nuclear-capable cruise missiles ran out of funds eight months ago."

"Well, then, why are you asking me?"

"Because it's an opportunity to take a pretty potent missile off the market," said Ferguson. "And because it'll make my next request seem much more reasonable."

"Which is?"

"First, let me ask you: are you still ruling out an air strike? Van says he can get some Stealth Fighters overhead in a half hour. Personally, I prefer B-52s."

"Absolutely, positively not. No aggression on Syrian soil. Nothing like that. We're trying to improve relations, not end them for all time."

"All right. I'm going to need a hundred thousand dollars, greenbacks, in the next couple of days. I can't finesse it with local counterfeit or Euros."

"For what? Another missile?"

"No. I need some mortars and some other weapons, along with some Semtex, and I'm going to have to overpay to get them."

"Mortars? You're out of your mind."

"That has nothing to do with it," said Ferguson. "The sooner the better. I'll make the arrangements myself if you tell Corrigan it's cool."

"It's *not* cool."

"Look, I need the money. Otherwise I'm going to have to rob a bank, and I don't really have time."

"You *wouldn't* rob a bank."

"I will if I have to." Ferguson gave her a brief rundown of what he needed the money for. "I know it's a rip-off, but beggars can't be choosers, and I want to make it look at least plausible that a rival group hit them. With Fouad's help, I'll start spreading the rumor tonight that there's another group coming to town. We'll make some rentals, set up a paper trail. All we have to do is give the Syrians a few little tidbits so they can claim it wasn't the U.S., and we'll be all right."

"The U.S. government cannot condone the operation of an international outlaw, much less make a deal with him. You can't go and buy mortars, for cryin' out loud."

"Jeez, Madame Counselor, where have you been for the last century? Even Washington bought arms on the black market."

"You are not George Washington."

"You were just going to check on a cruise missile."

"You said it could carry a nuke." Corrine sighed. "Tell me you're not going to kill Khazaal with these mortars."

"Never mind. I'll rob the bank."

"Ferguson, don't blackmail me."

"Now there's an approach I hadn't thought of."

"Are you going to kill him?"

"Not if I can help it. And not with the mortars."

"Every cent better be accounted for. Every cent."

"I'll get the invoice in triplicate."

"Be serious, Ferg. You can't cause an international incident here. You cannot."

"That's why I need the money. Look, this is basically what we did to get Kiro in Chechnya."

"That was in Chechnya. No one cares what happens there."

"The Russians do."

Corrine realized that he had her checkmated at every turn. Once again, she felt like a complete amateur and not, she had to admit, without reason. She thought that she had proven herself in the dirty-bomb operation. And she had—with everyone *but* the most important person, Ferguson. She was never going to win him over. In his eyes, she was always going to be the outsider, the "suit" he had to work around to get his job done. Which was baloney.

"You live dangerously, Bob. I respect that. And I appreciate the fact that you saved my life. But if you go too far here, I'm not going to be there to reel you in."

"He who lives by the sword, right?"

She could just about see his smirk in front of her.

"I need you to do one more thing for me," he added. "It's a little dangerous, so I'll understand—"

"What?" she snapped, angry that he was manipulating her so transparently.

"There's a Russian coming into Damascus in a few hours. I was going to send Guns and one of the rentals I picked up from you down there, but I have him working another angle. If you could help out—"

"What do you need?"

"I'm going to use two people who are agents of ours in town, but I don't want to give them more information than necessary, especially ahead of time," said Ferguson. "All you have to do is point out who they have to follow, put them on the plane, and that's that."

"What if he doesn't take the plane?"

"Same deal. They should be able to handle it. I'll have a photo sent to the embassy."

"All right."

"One other thing."

"Yes?"

"He'd be easier to follow if he had a tracking device. One's being delivered to you personally in half an hour. You twist it to turn it on. Tell them not to twist it until they're ready to leave it. The battery's pretty limited. It's a tiny little bug, smaller than your fingernail. Well, smaller than my fingernail."

"I have small fingernails."

"There's nobody in the airport I trust to get it on his baggage behind the scenes, so it has to go on him."

"How am I supposed to do that?"

"Not you, *them*."

"How are they supposed to do it?"

"They'll figure it out. I don't need to know operational details."

"Very funny."

"You sure you can do it? If not, I can get someone from the embassy. I just don't trust the people there."

Was this some sort of test, she wondered.

"I can handle it," Corrine told him. "Look, I appreciate the fact that you saved my life."

"Yeah, well, don't rub it in. We all do things we regret."

"You can't turn it off, can you?"

"Would you respect me if I could?"

She killed the connection before he could hear her laugh.

LATAKIA

The operation Ferguson had sent Guns on was a long-shot play, one of those stabs in the dark that you made every so often in hopes of winning big time.

The mosque Thomas had linked to Khazaal was Al-Norui Khad in the southwestern corner of the city. Fouad's brief foray into gossip made it seem possible; the mosque's resident imam, or teacher, was considered one of the more strident in town, though whether that translated into support for the Iraq resistance was a fair question.

One way to answer that question, Ferguson thought, was to send in a visitor who spoke Russian and could be mistaken for Vassenka.

"It's either you or me," he told Guns. "Your accent's probably better, and my face has been in town before."

"I'll do it."

"We'll send Fouad in with you. And Monsoon," added Ferguson. "Because Monsoon's Arabic is good, right?"

Monsoon ripped off a passage from the Koran.

"All right then," said Ferguson, echoing his lines. "Blessed be to all of us, peace to the good people of the Book."

Like many mosques, Al-Norui Khad was actually a collection of buildings interconnected and related, all gathered around an old wall. Though not a very large mosque, even for Latakia, Al-Norui Khad had a good-sized minaret, the tower traditionally used to call believers to prayer. A small dome sat over the sanctuary at the western end of the complex, and there were three other fair-sized buildings that extended inward from the walls. An old inlet from the sea extended in a lagoon along the southern wall. There was only one entrance from the street, which made it easy to watch the mosque. Rankin planted a pair of video cameras in lampposts on either side of the block.

Fouad rambled in first, unarmed but with a bug so they could hear any advice he gave. An elaborate mosaic with blue, yellow, and white stones marked the pathway through the gate and opened into a bricked space beyond the wall. A pair of two-story yellow stone buildings sat on either side of the entrance, looking as if they had grown out from the wall. One was being used as a school, infirmary, and social center; the other, much more dilapidated, seemed not to have been used for some time. Fouad kept up a running commentary, as though he were a crazy man talking to himself as well as others. There were a dozen or so men on the grounds, some on their way to pray and others on errands related to the school or other concerns. A man watched over a book stall; another handed pamphlets out to visitors. Fouad found an administrator's office and mumbled the route as he retraced his steps. This was where Guns should go and mention that he had recently come from Chechnya and was looking for a place to stay.

The mosque itself sat just beyond the school building. Like several other holy sites in the Middle East, its stones had been converted to Islamic use from an earlier faith, in this case a small church built by Christians sometime around A.D. 600 or 700, which itself was erected over the site of a temple used by Zoroastrians. The Muslim alterations had enlarged the basic footprint and raised the walls as well as added the dome. Had it not been for a plaque declaring that the building had once belonged to Christians, only an expert would have known. The *qibla* wall oriented the faithful toward Mecca when they prayed; the space around the courtyard or *sahn* was dominated by thick pillars that held the roof.

Fouad left his shoes and joined the others purifying themselves at the fountain before going to pray.

"God is greater," prayed Fouad. "All praise be to Allah . . ."

He had learned the words as a child, but at many times in his life they came to him fresh, their meaning revealed again. Today was one of those times: as the prayers proceeded, so did his understanding. The words from the al-Talbiyah ("Compliance") were like ringing truth: "Here I am, God, at your command. Here I am!"

What did God require of him? The men he was here to find invoked God. Was it the same God? How could they be so badly mistaken?

But they were mistaken. The Prophet (peace be unto Him) had preached only necessary war, had forbidden the killing of innocents, had offered peace to those who would live in peace with the faithful.

Sadness overcame Fouad, as if he were responsible for the others' sins and mistakes in addition to his own.

"Glory to my Lord," he said, flattening himself prostrate on the stones. "Glory to my Lord, Most High."

Guns timed his arrival so that he came through the gates just after prayers. He headed toward the administrative office, shadowed by Monsoon. Since Fouad hadn't seen any weapons detectors, or guards for that matter, they went in with pistols under their flowing Arab-style clothes, along with bugs similar to the one Fouad had been given. They milled around the outside of the building for a moment, as if looking for someone, then Guns went to the office and, in Chechnya-inflected Russian, explained that he had just come to the city and desired guidance on a good place to stay.

The man at the desk didn't understand a single word he said.

Guns repeated it, nearly word for word. The man shook his head.

Guns now tried, haltingly, to say in Arabic where he was from and what he wanted. Ferguson had told him not to worry about his pronunciation, for the important thing was to make clear that he was from Russia, which he did by taking his passport from his pocket and using it as a prop. He then asked if the man spoke French; this won him another blank stare.

"Englishki?" said Guns. "Speak Eng-lush?"

"English?" said the man.

"*Dah, un* little. From Russia. I am from Russia." He continued in half Russian, half English to mention the town in Chechnya he'd come from and the path he'd taken through Georgia to Egypt, which duplicated the route Corrigan had said Vassenka would take. The man at the desk simply nodded.

"Rooms?" said Guns finally.

"We are not a hotel, my brother."

"Where? A hotel?"

The man wrote down the address of a place in town. As he did, the phone on his desk rang. He frowned, then picked it up. After a few moments his eyes widened in alarm. He hit the receiver button, then tapped the keys, talking quickly when someone came on the other line.

"I am very sorry," he said, rising and handing the paper with the hotel to Guns. "I have an emergency."

Guns followed the man out of the building, toward the mosque, where a crowd had gathered. A siren wailed above the walls. People began to shout. Guns turned and saw an ambulance backing through the narrow passage into the courtyard. A man was carried from the mosque as the rear of the ambulance was opened and a stretcher brought out.

The man they laid on it was Fouad.

13

DAMASCUS

Even before they came near her, Corrine realized that the two men in the terminal were the agents Corrigan had sent to trail the Russian. That, she decided, was not good; if she could identify them with just a glance, wouldn't he?

She went back to reading the paper she'd bought. One of her two embassy guards sat in the chair next to her; the other was a row away, watching.

"Ms. Alston?" said one of the men, standing next to her.

The man smiled down at her. With a white shirt and tie, he looked more like a detective than a spy.

"Can I help you?" she asked.

"Are you Ms. Alston? Do you have something for us?"

Corrine glanced sideways at the guard, one of the Delta men who had escaped from the club with her. He had a perplexed look on his face. Clearly he couldn't believe it either.

Corrine glanced at her watch. The Russian's plane was due in twenty minutes.

"Plans have changed," she said. "Give me a phone number where I can reach you."

I'm sorry, Ms. Alston, I didn't quite catch that," said Corrigan.

"I said, who the hell were those guys?"

"Egyptians. They've done some work for us before. All of our people are tied up chasing down security leads related to the president's visit and—"

"You're serious? Those were legitimate agents?"

"We've gotten information from them. The Agency has, not Special Demands. Ferg didn't give me much time. We have to take what we can get sometimes."

"No. We don't. I'll take care of trailing the Russian myself."

"Uh, ma'am, do you think that's a good idea?"

"He's only being trailed to the airport, right? In Latakia?"

"Well, yeah, but—"

"I think I can handle that." She killed the connection as he continued to protest.

Corrine saw the Russian come off the plane, watching as he walked toward the boarding area for the flight to Latakia. The small aircraft, an Embraer EMB-120 Brasilia, held only thirty passengers, and Corrine had already reserved places for herself and the two Delta bodyguards. In order to be prepared in case Vassenka changed his mind at the last minute, the men were outside in rental cars, poised in different spots in the lot. Corrine's job was to watch him inside and to plant the tracking device.

Not difficult work, she thought. All she had to do was follow along, get behind him in line, and slip the tiny bug onto his sweater. The exterior of the device looked like a burr, the sort of thing you might pick up walking through a field in the fall. Corrine had it perched between her fingers but worried that she would drop it on the carpet. She had no backup.

As the Russian reached the main hallway, he stopped to get his bearings. Corrine started to stop as well, then realized this was the perfect opportunity. She raised her hand slightly, bug ready, and walked into the Russian's back. Pretending to be startled, she jerked her hand back, glancing at the bug to make sure it was planted before twisting and falling down.

"Ow," she said.

The Russian spun defensively, nearly tripping over her. He sputtered something in Russian that Corrine didn't understand, though she assumed he wasn't asking for a date.

"Excuse me. I'm sorry," she said. She got to her feet unsteadily, dragging out her rise as if she were uncoordinated. "I didn't see you there."

He frowned at her, said something else in Russian, and then in English told her she was a clumsy oaf. Then he realized how pretty she was and extended his hand.

"Are you OK?" he asked.

"I'm fine, yes. Thank you. It was my fault."

"You are an American," he told her. "Funny you should be in Syria."

"Syria is a lovely country."

"Not for Americans."

"I'm on business."

The photo she had gotten from Corrigan made him look a little older than he was in real life. He wasn't unattractive, though the thick scent of vodka on his breath was a turnoff.

So was the grip on her arm.

"I have some time," he said.

"You're going to let go of me now," said Corrine.

He smiled in a way that convinced her he wasn't going to. Corrine smiled back and then stomped her heel into his instep. As he started to jerk back, she kicked again, this time zeroing the heel into the ankle of his other foot. She shrugged as he fell to the floor.

Several Arab men passing nearby came up to assist her, but it was unnecessary. She thanked them, calmly rearranged her scarf, and walked across the concourse, trying not to smirk.

Corrine waited until the Russian had gone to the gate to call her shadows outside. "I think just one of you should come in and fly with me," she said. "I don't trust him not to bolt or get off the plane."

"You're coming with us?" said one of the men.

"All I have to do is fly to Latakia. Ferguson will take it from there."

"Uh—"

"Charles, you're with me," she said. "Danny, we'll see you in a few hours."

14

The power of money had always impressed Judy Coldwell, but in the Middle East it could be absolutely intoxicating. A folded hundred-dollar bill could get one on an airliner that was supposedly booked; two would stop a customs agent's inquiries. A single fifty-dollar bill was enough to ensure that her registration at the hotel was entered under a name different from the one on her passport—Benjamin Thatch.

Yesterday, Coldwell had stopped in Athens, Greece, where she visited a small pawnshop on a backstreet seldom traveled by tourists. She had retrieved a small suitcase, sewn into the lining of which was a list of accounts as well as the name of a local bank and a bank officer who did not ask many questions, as long as they were accompanied by the right number of hundred-dollar bills. Within an hour he had confirmed that the accounts in Morocco and Austria were accessible. Together, they held about two hundred thousand dollars. Unfortunately, that was a small sum compared to the task that needed to be accomplished.

Coldwell took off her shoes and reached to undo the top button on her blouse. She was tired from the journey, which had included stops in France and Egypt as well as Greece. She would take a bath and then sleep. Tomorrow she would resume her mission.

And do what, exactly? Make herself visible, surely. Find the places where the demons swarmed. She would go to the merchants of hate, mention her brother's name. Eventually, the contact that Benjamin had made would come to her.

And then what? Would he scoff at thousands when millions were needed?

Coldwell got up from the chair and went to the bathroom. As she leaned over the tub she felt her hands begin to shake. She stared at her fingers; they seemed gnarled, foreign, not hers at all. Fear shot through her; she was not up to the task.

The room turned to ice. Coldwell felt as if she were falling. She had experienced this sensation several times in her life, always at moments of great stress. The first had been as a five-year-old, when she discovered her mother in the basement, her head wrapped in a plastic bag taped tightly so she could not breathe.

Suicide, though the five-year-old had no comprehension what that meant.

Coldwell found herself sitting on the floor, paralyzed. She was a little girl again, staring at the dead body, unable to go back up the stairs.

"I have faced great problems in the past," Coldwell said aloud. "I can overcome this."

Still she did not move. She tried thinking of achievements, of struggles. Not a year after she had been hired by the oil company, she had arranged for her boss (a slime and reprobate) to be freed from a Cairo jail after that unfortunate incident with several local boys. That task had been extremely difficult: harder than this, surely, and with greater personal risk. One man had held a knife at her throat and drawn blood.

If she could succeed then, she could succeed now.

Coldwell tried to rise but could not. Little had been at stake in Cairo beyond her life and that of her boss. This . . . this was an entire millennium waiting to be born.

That was all the more reason that she would succeed, wasn't it? For she had the great weight of history on her side. Change was coming; it was inevitable. All she had to do was play her own small role in it, a droplet of rain in the stream.

"I can do it," she said. "I will not falter."

Slowly, unsteadily, Coldwell rose. A bath would feel wonderful. And after that, bed.

15

LATAKIA

Monsoon sidled up next to Guns in the courtyard between the mosque and the outer wall. There were twenty or so men crowded around the ambulance, trying to see what had happened to the man the medics were working on.

Guns sneezed, then reached for a handkerchief. "Fouad," he whispered to Monsoon. "Find out what happened."

Monsoon didn't acknowledge but shifted forward slightly, craning his head to get a better view. Then he asked a man in Arabic what was going on.

"Allah has called him," answered the man.

"What?"

The man clutched at his heart. "His time," he said. "It is a sign of holiness and worth to be called while praying," said the man approvingly. "Perhaps the brother's greatest wish was granted."

Listening in the van, Ferguson turned to the small laptop computer he was using to track the signals from the locator devices planted on Fouad, Guns, and Monsoon, making sure they were working. He'd known the moment Fouad collapsed in the mosque that the Iraqi wasn't faking; he'd gasped and made a muffled chirp like a young bird that had fallen from its nest. He upped the audio and heard him breathing irregularly, struggling for life.

Ferguson couldn't help thinking of his father, who'd had a heart attack at home. He'd lain on the floor of his study for three days before the housekeeper found him.

A terrible thing, to die alone.

Ferguson pushed his headset to the side so he could talk on the sat phone to Corrigan back in the Cube. "You getting anything from our phone tap?"

"They called for the ambulance."

"Nothing out of that office Guns went into?"

"We have all the lines you tapped. If that includes that line, we'll get it. There's no calls. You should have just planted a bug there," Corrigan added.

Ferguson hated explaining things he thought should be obvious. "If I put the bug in there, and we're right that Khazaal is going to be going there at some point, they'll find the bug," he told him. "Then we have to go back to square one."

"They're low probability of intercept," said Corrigan.

"Did you read that out of the sales brochure?" Ferguson snapped. It was really a waste of time to get into details with other people, really a waste of time. "Listen, I need you to do something that's going to seem strange, but it's very important," he told Corrigan. "I want you to call a number and give someone the access code so they can call my phone."

"You sure?"

"Corrigan, do what I tell you. Here's the weird part: the number is in Cuba."

"Ferg—"

"If I explain it to you, I'll have to kill you. So just do it. All right?"

He gave him the number.

"Am I looking for a response?" Corrigan said.

"You'll get a machine. Give the access code, nothing else. Make it a one-time–use code."

"Yeah, I know that."

"Coming out," muttered Guns, just loud enough so it could be picked up by the bug he was wearing.

The ambulance started to move. Ferguson put the laptop down and moved to the front of the van, where Rankin and one of the marines they'd borrowed were sitting.

"Skip, you take the con back here, OK? Keep monitoring the area, checking the bugs, but don't go in," said Ferguson. "When Thera checks back after renting the hotel rooms, tell her to come over and spell you guys. Don't keep the truck here too long. I'll be back."

"Where are you going?"

"I can't let Fouad go to the hospital alone."

"He's just an Iraqi."

It was really useless to explain anything to anybody, Ferg thought, moving to the back door.

The ambulance took Fouad to Al Assad University Hospital. The hospital, a satellite of the larger and more famous facility in Damascus, had facilities on par with the best hospitals in the U.S. and Europe and was considered one of the outstanding hospitals in the Middle East.

Beyond the high level of care, the university connection presented Ferguson with an opportunity for a convincing cover: the Syrian government's Ministry of Health sponsored a number of programs for visiting doctors, including an exchange with the Syrian-American Medical Society. A sign in the lobby directed doctors attending the society's convention to proceed to Suite A-21; Ferguson didn't need any more hint than that to stroll down the corridor in search of the meeting. Unfortunately, he was dressed somewhat poorly for a visiting doctor, and so he began ducking his head into the offices that he passed, looking to exchange his stained, Arab-style coat for a shorter jacket. It took three tries before he found a snappy blue blazer beckoning from a rack. Two doors down he found a stethoscope, but it wasn't until he took a wrong turn and bumped into a laundry cart that he completed his costume with a pair of green scrub pants. A bit much maybe—especially since they were large enough to fit over his "civilian" pants and then some—but sartorial excess could be excused in a heart specialist.

Suitably dressed at last, Ferguson decided to forgo the seminar—in his experience, always boring once the donuts were exhausted—and instead took up rounds, venturing toward what he hoped was the emergency cardiac care unit. He intended to tell anyone who stopped him that he was a visiting doctor simply here to observe procedures, but no one stopped him. In Syria, as in much of the world, a stethoscope and purposeful expression were enough credentials to sway most people without a medical degree.

Contrary to the opinions at the mosque, Fouad had not died, though admittedly his pulse was weak and his breathing very shallow. He was wheeled into an emergency unit for treatment. Shadows passed around him and voices hummed in his ears, but Fouad couldn't make sense of anything except the tremendous pain surging through his body. It came in waves, starting as an excruciating bolt that knocked the wind from his lungs; from there it increased tenfold and then a hundred times beyond that. He wondered why he was putting up with it. Couldn't he just sleep? Shouldn't he sleep?

The hums grew louder. He felt himself moving away from the pain: the pain didn't subside, just moved across the room somewhere, physically distanced from that part of him that was thinking.

"Hey," said a voice, whispering in his ear.

Fouad turned and saw his neighbor Ali. They'd been boys together in Tikrit, blood brothers since the day they stole the teacher's pen and were caned for it.

Ali had died in the Iran War. But long before that his spirit had been broken, depressed by what had happened to their country under the dictator. Like Fouad he worked for Saddam, first as a government inspector and then an army officer. His sense of fairness was too highly developed, Fouad thought. Everything about the regime pricked at him day and night, until finally his soul seeped from his body around the clock. The day he'd volunteered to go to the front and face the fanatics, Fouad had shaken his head for a full hour, already sure of his friend's fate.

But now his boyhood friend smiled at him.

"You're going to make it, Fouad," said Ferguson, kneeling down next to his gurney and whispering in his ear in his Cairo-scented Arabic. Ferguson knew he was lying, but the urge to say something positive was so strong he couldn't resist. He held the Iraqi's hand. "You're going to make it."

Fouad didn't see Ferguson; he saw his boyhood friend. It was a happy day when they were nine, sipping water. Nothing special, just a happy day.

So I have done my duty, sometimes well, sometimes not. And that is the total of what I am: a small man who navigated between the difficult rocks. That is what God gave me to do, and I have done it. And now I go to play with my friend, a reward neither special nor exalted but a reward I cherish all the more . . .

As the machine monitoring Fouad's heart began to flat-line, Ferguson reached for the tiny bug implanted near the lapel of the agent's coat, tugging it from its perch with a discreet but strong pull. He stepped back as the others in the room tried to revive the Iraqi, a task they knew would be fruitless yet felt compelled to undertake.

Ferguson's eyes felt hollow. For a moment he stood in space, unaware of where he was, unconscious of the danger he himself faced if caught.

Were the others working for Fouad or for themselves? Why was it so necessary to defy death?

If you didn't struggle, what else did you have?

Ferguson faded out of the room. He found an empty lounge, scanned for bugs, then turned on the sat phone.

A number was waiting. The international code indicated it was in Austria, though that would be only one stop along the way. He punched it in.

"Hello, Michael," he said when a man on the other end of the line picked up.

"Fergie. I've been thinking about you," said the man. His voice was that of a man in his early sixties whose English mixed hints of Europe and the Middle East.

"Good thoughts, I hope."

"Always."

"Listen, I need a favor. A very big favor."

"I owe you my life. What can I do?"

"I need information about a man who may be working for Israel. I know what you're going to say, but here's why I need it: I want to rule out the possibility of Mossad being involved in an assassination attempt on a member of the administration."

"They would not do that."

"I have to rule it out."

Ferguson glanced up at the doorway, making sure he was alone. He had debated whether to pull this string, since it might set off other repercussions, but in the end he needed an answer; he could accept only so many coincidences.

"The name?" asked Michael.

"Fazel al-Qiam."

There was a long pause. "You are asking a great deal."

"Could you get me a photograph?"

This time the pause was even longer. "I don't know about that. It would depend on too many factors to say."

"The cover's a public one."

"Still—"

"I'll give you an e-mail address. I owe you one."

"The debt is still heavily in your favor. But you have asked a great deal."

Ferguson gave him the e-mail address, then killed the line and hot-keyed into the van. "Rankin?"

"It's Guns, Ferg. Rankin's doing a reecee."

"Fouad died. Heart attack."

"Man, that sucks."

"He was smiling," said Ferguson. "For what that's worth."

"Yeah."

"What's going on?"

"Corrigan called. The guy I talked to inside the administrative building called the Riviera hotel and told someone in a room there that a Russian had come in. He told him about the hotel he'd given me."

"Bingo."

"Corrigan says the Riviera's a tourist hotel, high class," added Guns. "You think he's there?"

"Maybe they're giving him the corporate terrorist rate."

"What about that hotel the guy at the desk suggested? You want me to check in?"

"No, that may be too dangerous," Ferguson told him. "We'll get some video bugs in the lobby and tap the phones and see what shakes down. Where's our Russian missile expert?"

"Plane should be leaving from Damascus in about ten minutes. Corrigan's still tracking it."

"Once you get confirmation that he's on the flight, take Monsoon and get over to the airport so you can track him. Be careful with this guy; he's been around the block a few times and he served in Chechnya."

"Will do."

"One other thing: there should be an e-mail coming to one of my addresses in a few minutes. I want you to forward it to Corrine's e-mail address. To do that you're going to have to open it and cut and paste, because the address I'm using is good for one shot only. Ready? There's a lot of numbers in this."

Guns took the address down. "Will she know what it's about?"

"No. I'll have to tell her. I'm trying to figure something out, and I want to make sure I'm looking at the right person. All right?"

"Yeah, but—"

"My butt or your butt?"

"I don't know how to forward e-mail."

"You kidding?"

"No, this system—"

"All right. Have Rankin do it."

"Thanks, Ferg."

"Watch what he does, OK? It's rocket science."

The Riviera was a chic hotel catering largely to very well-off Europeans and Arabs. Located in the center of the city on 14 Ramadan Street (the number being part of the street name, not the address of the building), it had an extensive staff, including a private security force, one of whose members frowned at Ferguson's scrub pants as he sauntered into the lobby, checking his watch and taking a seat as if waiting for a friend. A casual glance showed there was little possibility of getting beyond the lobby to the elevators without elaborate preparation; the way was guarded by two men wearing bulky sweaters over bulletproof vests.

Nor was Ferguson given much of a chance to assess the situation. Within sixty seconds of his sitting down, a squat clerk with a twitchy moustache came toward him to ask what he was doing.

Ferguson jumped up and took his hand in greeting, pumping vigorously.

"Dr. Muhammad," he said in English, throwing an Irish lilt to it. "I am looking for Dr. Muhammad, who is going to the conference at the hospital. He is an old friend from Cairo I studied with many years before. I could not believe my good luck at finding him registered for the conference."

The man replied—in Arabic and English—that the esteemed doctor was unknown to him as a guest in the hotel.

"No?" Ferguson scratched his chin. "Could you look? Muhammad."

"That is a very common name. Like Smith in your country. But I assure you, he is not staying here. Our guests are all well known to us."

"Smith isn't common in Ireland," said Ferguson, trying to establish himself as Irish, not American. "I come from the south and Smith would be British—English. English, you know?"

The man didn't know, but finally went to the computer under the weight of Ferguson's spiel. Ferg's attempt to catch another guest's name failed; the computer screen was small and turned from his view.

They had no Dr. Muhammad, and in fact no doctor at all. The clerk named several rivals. As Ferguson lingered, one of the men with the bulky sweaters came over and grabbed his arm. Ferg only just managed to stay in character, yelping but not pulling the man over his shoulder.

A good move, as it turned out, for the man was simply clearing the way for a phalanx of bodyguards who swept through the lobby. Ferguson stared at the men, who were all dressed in light brown fatigues, expecting to see Nisieen Khazaal in the middle of the group.

Instead, he saw a face he recognized not from this mission but from another a year and a half before: Meles Abaa, a Palestinian wanted for murdering ten Americans and two Israelis in an attack on a tourist bus in Ethiopia, and even more in another attack on an airliner headed to Rome from Israel three months ago.

The latter attack had taken place after Ferguson's team, faced with a decision about whether to go after him or pursue their primary objective, had decided to bypass a chance to get Meles and concentrate on their objective, which was recovering several ounces of enriched uranium. Ferguson hadn't made the decision—he wasn't in charge of the mission, which took place before Special Demands existed—but he had agreed with it. Meles wasn't on the "get" list at the time, and they needed approval to try and capture him, let alone assassinate him, which his presence on the list now entitled Ferguson to do.

The security man let go of Ferguson and walked back to his post without an apology or even a glance toward him. Ferguson straightened his coat, said thank you to the man who had helped him, and went quickly outside. But Meles was gone.

Ferg took a turn around the block, sizing up the area and finding the telephone line into the hotel so they could set up a bugging operation once it got dark. The line came into the second floor, which was inconvenient. He was just deciding how inconvenient when his sat phone vibrated in his pocket.

"Ferguson," he said, leaning against the wall to talk.

"Ms. Alston should be landing at the airport in about ten minutes," said Corrigan.

"I'm sorry. What?"

"She's following the Russian. They'll be landing at the airport in ten minutes."

"What the hell is she doing following the Russian?"

"There was a problem with the agents I lined up."

"Oh, for cryin' out loud, Corrigan. Jesus."

"She's not going out of the airport. I thought I better tell you, because Guns mentioned—"

"Yeah, all right. I'll take care of it. Next time she tells you she's going to do something like this, tell her no, OK?"

"She's the boss."

"That only means you can't slap her," Ferguson told him. "Unless you have a very good reason; and this would qualify."

orrine sat two rows behind the Russian, and she spent the entire flight watching him. Neither alcohol nor food was distributed on the flight, but he'd come prepared with a flask bottle, sipping at regular intervals. He didn't look like a weapons engineer to her; he looked more like an alcoholic, and a classic one at that.

When they touched down, she stayed with him into the terminal, following as he headed to the baggage area, apparently to claim luggage that had already been checked through. By the time he got it, Charlie had hooked up with Guns. When the Russian passed her in the baggage area of the small terminal, Corrine made eye contact, stopped, and crossed her arms. The Russian laughed and grabbed for his foot as if it were all a joke, then continued past.

Corrine, playing her part, shook her head and walked around the side to where her suitcase was waiting. As she reached the end of the hall someone grabbed her from the side.

"Never turn your back on an asshole."

"Ferguson!" she said.

"Not that I'm the asshole in question." Ferg smiled at her, then noticed one of the attendants eyeing them. "Make like you're happy to see me."

"You're not—"

He kissed her. As their lips parted, she reared back and slapped him.

"That was in the line of duty," he said.

"So was that."

"Step into my office, dear, so we can have a proper quarrel." Still holding her elbow, Ferguson steered her toward the side hall. Corrine pulled her arm away as they walked. He stopped next to the men's room.

"What do you have? A death wish? What are you doing in Latakia?" Ferguson asked.

"Can we talk here?"

"I got the two bugs they had down here already, but that's a good point. It's been a whole ten minutes." Ferguson reached into his pocket and took out his bug scanner. The area was still clean.

"Why are you here?"

"You needed help; I helped."

"Corrigan sent two people to do the job."

"They were buffoons."

"Says you."

"Do you know them?"

"Even if you were right, you should have let Charlie or someone else handle it. I'm sure he's done crap like this before."

"You're forgetting I was in Russia."

"I'm not forgetting anything. You were stopped there, too. Sooner or later your luck is going to run out."

"What about yours?"

"I don't need luck."

"You're such a bullshit artist. I have to go. I have a plane to catch."

"Wait." Ferg grabbed her as she turned away. "Since you're here. Something new has come up."

He told her about Meles. "I want to take him down."

"No," she said. "You can't."

"No? He killed a hundred and twenty people in the airplane that crashed going to Rome. A lot of them were Americans. He's on the list; I can take him. I don't need permission. That's the idea of the list."

"You can't jeopardize this mission. Khazaal is more important."

"No, I don't think so," said Ferguson. "Meles is more of a threat. Khazaal stays in Iraq. Besides, I'll figure a way to get them both."

"It's too close to the president's visit to the Middle East. The political repercussions will be too much."

"What repercussions? It's just pest eradication."

Corrine shook her head. "I'm not chancing it."

"He's on the list."

"I'm overruling the list."

"Why is Khazaal different?"

"He's not. You're just arresting him and turning him over to the Iraqis."

"Then I'll arrest Meles," said Ferguson, though he knew this would be even more difficult than getting Khazaal.

"No."

Ferguson folded his arms in front of his chest. "You don't even know what I'm going to do."

"Neither do you, I bet." She, too, folded her arms. "It doesn't matter."

"I have to tell you, Corrine, it's taking a hell of a lot of self-control here not to slug you."

It took just as much self-control on her part to simply turn and walk to the airline counter for her flight back to Damascus.

"If anything happens to her, I'm going to take it out of your hide," Ferguson told Charlie, the Delta bodyguard. "Because I want her around so I can stomp her ass when this is done."

16

LATAKIA
SEVERAL HOURS LATER . . .

Rankin leaned back against the side of the building, rubbing his chin. They'd gotten rid of the van, figuring it might be a little too conspicuous after a few hours and were taking turns milling around near the mosque entrance. So far, neither Khazaal nor Meles had been spotted nor had any bodyguard types. When night fell they'd be able to plant better surveillance cameras on the wall, and the job would be considerably easier. For now, though, all he could do was shrug off the stiffness and try and stay alert. He rambled down the block. He'd donned a headdress and a Bedouin's long robes to alter his look. He had papers showing he was looking for work if stopped.

He paused at a street vendor, pointed to a kebab, and thrust a bill into the man's hands. He ate the food hungrily, not realizing how famished he was.

As he turned back to walk up the street, a white Mercedes pulled up to the curb, followed by two Toyota SUVs. The doors opened and a set of bodyguards got out, checking the block. Rankin stopped, concentrating on his food for a moment, or so it appeared. He hooked his thumb beneath his coat, holding it up as two men got out of the last car.

One was Meles Abaa. The other was the man whose face he'd seen a few hours before, when he'd helped Guns forward the e-mail to Corrine: Fazel al-Qiam.

17

LATAKIA
A FEW HOURS LATER . . .

"I can't believe the Israelis are gaming us," said Corrigan. "I can't believe it."

"Yeah, well, maybe they are and maybe they're not, but they definitely have somebody inside, and they definitely didn't give us a heads-up when they had a chance," said Ferguson. "And I'm still not entirely exonerating them for the attack on Alston in Tripoli."

"No way, Ferg."

Ferguson didn't believe it either, but he was surely in the middle of something he didn't completely understand. Fazel al-Qiam's real name was Aaron Ravid. Ferguson was reading between the lines, but it looked like he was a long-time operative who had been infiltrated into Syria several years ago. He had impeccable credentials as an Arab "intellectual" (read "closeted terrorist"). He had even been to the UN as he told Corrine. The CIA file on him was extremely thin, and it was only because of the UN assignment that he had been ID'd as an Israeli plant, a fact the Agency would not inform Mossad about, since it might inadvertently reveal information about bugging at the UN's New York headquarters.

Why had he been in Tel Aviv? Had the pass in the building been a coincidence or a hint too subtle for Corrine to get?

Or a pass for his benefit, so he saw his target?

Why had he shown up in Lebanon? That couldn't be a coincidence.

And what was he up to with Meles?

Corrigan asked Ferguson the same question.

"I don't know," Ferg told him. "It was some sort of meeting. He's at the Versailles, one of those posh places on the beach up north. Meles went back to the Riviera. The Russian hasn't hooked up with them yet, and I still don't know where the hell Khazaal is. I'm beginning to think he's a figment of our imagination."

"He'll turn up," said Corrigan.

"Yeah. Meles has to have a ton of money to take over half a hotel."

"Just two floors," said Corrigan. "We're pretty sure from the phone taps it's two floors."

"All right, so he only has a half ton of money."

"Maybe the Syrians are subsidizing him. Or the Saudis. Or a whole bunch of other people. You going to grab him?"

"Alston says I can't."

"What? He's on the list."

"I know. It's not settled," added Ferguson. "I'll work something out."

"Ferg—"

Ferguson changed the subject. "Anything from the taps?"

"Nothing so far. You figure Khazaal's in the mosque?"

"I think it's a pretty good bet. We'll have to get some bugs inside if the taps don't turn anything up."

The National Security Agency used a computer program as well as translators to transcribe important intercepts or wiretaps, and the NSA's experts had been called in here to help. But all the bugs and translators in the world were useless if the people you were listening to weren't talking.

Ferguson put his legs out on the coffee table and glanced at his watch. "Speaking of Alston, why don't you connect me to her? It's pumpkin time."

"Yeah, she's supposed to call in from the embassy. She went to another reception."

"Call me back," said Ferguson, snapping off the phone. He gazed across the room, staring at Thera curled into the corner of an upholstered chair.

He needed another Iraqi liaison to make the arrest, but the president's upcoming visit to Baghdad had stretched the already thin intelligence corps to its limit. It was a BS problem, Ferg decided. They could paper over it by depositing Khazaal with the Iraqis once they had him, and the Syrians and political considerations be damned.

All considerations be damned. His job had nothing to do with *considerations*.

Tell the people who died in the plane Meles had blown up about *considerations*.

Fouad had smiled when his monitor began to buzz. Was it a real smile or just a reflex?

The poor guy's body was on ice in the hospital and would remain there for at least a few days. They couldn't recover it without endangering their gig. The fake ID Ferguson had given him claimed he was a Saudi, but anyone who checked would hit a dead end.

His phone buzzed. Ferguson flipped up the antenna and answered.

"Hello, Cinderella. How was the ball?"

"It was quite lavish," answered Corrine. "The president of Syria is quite a gentlemen."

"He's also the kind of gentleman who encourages problems to disappear in the middle of the night."

"So what's new?"

"Have you looked at your e-mail?"

"It's definitely the guy."

"His name is Aaron Ravid," Ferguson told her. "He's a Mossad agent."

"Well, we knew that."

"Here's something we didn't know: he's in Latakia, and he just met Meles."

"You're kidding."

"Yeah, I'm doing stand-up. Did Tischler return your call?"

"No. I would have told you."

As he'd told Corrine, Ferguson had first interpreted Tischler's reluctance to return Corrine's call as an indication that his agent had already fessed up; avoiding talking to her not only meant that he didn't have to say he was sorry but also made unnecessary the obvious lie he'd have to tell about the man being an agent. But this was too much.

One thing bugged Ferguson: they hadn't picked up any trail teams or shadows or Mossad people lurking in the shadows behind Ravid either in Beirut or here. Which maybe meant that the poor sod was on his own. Or that Ferguson wasn't doing as good a job as he should be.

"You have to go to Tel Aviv and have it out with Tischler," Ferguson told her. "Find out why he has an agent meeting with Meles."

"You think he'll tell me?"

"Bring a baseball bat with you. A big baseball bat."

"All right, I'll try. But—"

"You tell him you saw him in Tel Aviv, you saw him in Lebanon, and then say we ran into him again here. Tell him to stop screwing with us."

"And if he doesn't tell me what's going on?"

"Tell him we think he's a double agent, and we're going to take him out."

"You can't kill him," said Corrine.

"Why not?"

"Ferg. Tischler will see it's a bluff."

"It's not."

"It better be, *especially* if he's a Mossad agent."

"Either he's a double agent, or there's something going on that they're not saying. Either way I don't want to get screwed."

"Maybe he's just trying to gather information."

"Yeah."

"*Bob*—"

"Just play it like that, all right? Try it. If it doesn't work, it doesn't work. Worst case: if he *is* a double agent, they know about it."

"You think he's a double agent?"

"I'm not sure," admitted Ferguson. "The odds are against it. Mossad's pretty thorough. But I don't know what they're doing here. You change your mind about Meles?"

"Bob, you can't take him."

"It's a bad decision, Corrine."

"Why, because it's not the one you would make?"

"Because people are going to die if I don't take him."

"You think I haven't thought about that? It's not as simple as you think."

"I don't think it's simple. I think I can knock him off. I don't think there's going to be another chance. You're worried about international-law BS. I'm worried about reality."

"This isn't a legal issue. Khazaal is more important. And you don't even know where he is yet."

"I will." Ferguson hung up abruptly, corralling his anger. There was something to be said about keeping the focus on Khazaal, but, damn it, he had Meles cold. He could take him, blow up the entire stinking hotel if he had to, blow it up and be done with the slime.

He got up from the couch and walked over to the half bath, pausing to peer at Thera's curly hair and almost cherubic cheek. Inside the bathroom, he turned on the cold water, letting it run as he dialed the general's home number.

The answering machine picked up. It was about half-past five at night in the States; the general would probably still be at the office.

"Hey, General, it's Ferg. Look, I have a question for you. Kind of appreciate your getting back to me. I'm in your favorite place without a paddle."

He hesitated a second, then hit the end button.

Back in the suite room, Thera had started to snore. Ferguson lifted her up and carried her into one of the bedrooms, kneeling so he could lay her gently into the bed. He smoothed her hair back behind her ear, then reached down and pulled her boots off, leaving the gun holster in place. She mumbled and rolled over as he threw the cover over her.

"Cute," she said in her sleep.

"Yeah, you're damn cute yourself," he told her. Then he got out of the room while he still could.

LATAKIA

The hot water scalded his back and legs, but Ravid remained under the shower. It wasn't an act of purification but just the opposite: the outer layer of his skin needed to be hardened; the epidermis needed to be deadened so it could survive. Only by singeing his body could he make himself impervious to the filth of Meles and his ilk.

In the car, Ravid had come close to strangling the Muslim madman. The only weapons he had were his hands, but the impulse to do so had been nearly too strong to resist. He kept reminding himself that he had not exercised or trained in nearly two years, that he had lost some weight and muscle in that time, and that he might not be able to finish the terrorist, who was himself in good shape. His instincts argued against his logic, suggesting that he might use his teeth and his knees and legs and feet, every ounce of his strength, and if he did this, surely he could not lose. Twice he had been almost ready to give in, but the car had stopped and the chance lost.

It was not his job to kill Meles; quite the opposite, in fact. If he struck he would most likely ruin everything. Tischler would not forgive him.

Ravid knew all of this, but these things did not influence him. He cared little for what Tischler thought. If he struck, Tischler and the others would be irrelevant; even if he succeeded, the terrorist's bodyguards would kill him on the spot.

As the water went from scalding to lukewarm, Ravid fantasized about letting his instincts win and saw himself struggling with Meles. In his daydream, he killed the terrorist. Then, as the bodyguards killed him—a quick and merciful shot through the head—he realized he was not satisfied. He'd been cheated, he thought, of any real revenge for his wife and child's deaths.

Was that the real reason he had hesitated? The death of one man, however despicable a murderer he might be, would not sufficiently quench his thirst for justice.

Not justice. Revenge. There was no such thing as justice. God, if He existed, provided justice. He did not exist, and therefore there was no justice, just brute emotion.

Ravid wavered as the water turned cold. Perhaps he would have felt relieved after all. Perhaps his muscles had atrophied and he simply didn't want to admit it. His stomach, once taut, hung toward the ground.

He turned off the water and got out of the tub. Drying himself, he thought of Khazaal, the Iraqi murderer, and the jokes he had made about Jews.

"Oh yes, the Jews," Ravid had replied, speaking as a closeted terrorist himself. "What can we say about them?"

Khazaal had brought jewels with him from Iraq as part of a complex arrangement brokered by Meles and others to furnish the Iraqi resistance with a catastrophic attack on the new government. Among the stops they had made today was one to a jeweler who might estimate their worth. Ravid had arranged the meeting. Even though he had not seen the jewels—they were kept in a small briefcase—he knew from the jeweler that they were worth two or perhaps three million dollars.

Would that much money fund revenge?

Ravid wasn't sure. It would surely buy serious weapons—Khazaal was proof—but it was a matter of buying the right weapons. How would they be used? Where? Would killing a hundred, a thousand, a million Muslims satisfy him?

The question was too difficult to face. Instead, Ravid considered how he might get the jewels. Stealing them would require killing the bodyguards:

impossible, as the theft would immediately be noticed. Better to switch them somehow.

Impossible. There wasn't enough time now. And besides, he was watched too carefully. If he got the jewels, he would never be able to use them.

Ravid tried to put the idea out of his mind as he finished dressing, but it remained with him. It was comforting in an odd way, an abstract problem to occupy his mind, a theoretical danger to divert him from the great peril his mission here posed. It distracted him as well from the thirst that kept creeping into his mouth, the desire simmering in the distance of every thought and emotion. He wanted a drink nearly as much as he wanted revenge, possibly more, definitely more, as hard as he tried to banish the idea. He defeated the desire a dozen times a day, but always it was there, sneaking back, whispering from a distant room. Thinking of the jewels and Khazaal helped push it away.

By the time he was ready to leave the rented apartment for a round of late-night visits to the local cafés, Ravid had come up with several different plans to swap the jewels just before the Israeli action began, and even knew where he might find the substitutes.

His fantasies died with the first step he took from his house. Two Arabs were watching from across the street. He pretended not to notice, continuing toward the main boulevard a block away. These were almost certainly Meles's men and thus not difficult to lose, but his best course was to let them follow; they would report back to their master exactly what he wanted them to say. He ground the molars in his mouth together and pushed his gaze toward the pavement, narrowing his world to the small space before him as he walked.

TEL AVIV
THE NEXT MORNING . . .

Corrine was not shocked to find her plane met by a Mossad officer when she landed. She acted as if she expected no less and kept her lawyer face on as she was led, without explanation, down to the secure conference room once again. This time it was empty. Corrine stared at the wall, her expression as blank as she could possibly make it, until Tischler came in and closed the door.

"Fazel al-Qiam," she said.

"I'm afraid I don't understand," said Tischler.

"Unfortunately, I don't have time to play chess this morning, Mr. Tischler," she said. "I realize that you have a great number of obligations, which surely explains why you don't return my calls. I, too, am busy. I've stopped on my way to Baghdad because some of our people tripped over Fazel al-Qiam in Latakia. After he tripped over me here and in Lebanon. What exactly is going on, Mr. Tischler?"

Tischler remained silent. She smelled the same hint of shaving lotion that she had on their first meeting, but now it seemed part of an act, too contrived, as if he thought he could impress her by dressing nicely and keeping every strand of hair in place. He wore a nice watch and a handsome ring on his pinkie, along with a thick wedding band: all props, she thought, to help put her off.

"It might have been helpful if you had informed us that you were in Latakia," she added. "You knew we'd end up there."

"I really wouldn't want to get into a discussion of operations," said Tischler.

"I hope for your sake that al-Qiam is not a double agent," she said. "We've heard rumors that he is better known as Aaron Ravid."

Tischler said nothing. Corrine waited a moment, then pushed back the chair and went to the door. He remained at his seat as she left the room.

This was the way she had to act from now on, she told herself: harder than the people she was dealing with. Otherwise they were going to treat her like a pushover. And if they thought that, her own people were in jeopardy.

Corrine was in the lobby heading for the exit when one of the plain-clothes guards stopped her.

"I believe you left something behind downstairs," said the man.

"No, I don't think that's true," she said.

"I'm told it is."

The man smirked, and if the patronizing tone in his voice hadn't sealed her decision, that did. She smiled at him and then patted his elbow. "Afraid not, thank you. Mr. Tischler knows how to contact me . . . if he wants."

The pat was a bit over the top, but if she was going to play the hard-nosed bitch it would be better to be so obvious that no one missed the point. Corrine walked to her car and told her driver to take her to the airport, where the chartered plane was waiting.

She expected Tischler to make another try, this one in person. But he didn't.

Once aboard the civilian Cessna Citation that had been leased to take her to Baghdad, she called Corrigan and told him what had happened. She also put in a call to Slott, deciding to personally update him on the meeting. She also felt it possible that Tischler would choose to deal with him rather than her. But Slott's assistant answered the phone. The time difference meant that it was still quite early in the States. The aide asked her if it was worth calling and waking him at home; Corrine said no.

"Tell him that Tischler declined to say anything, and tell him to call me as soon as he can. I'm en route to Baghdad."

She clicked off the phone. The copilot had come back to see if she was ready to leave.

"There's some lunch in that fridge over there," he said. "Sandwiches. They're fresh."

"Thanks," she told him. "Maybe later."

"We'll be in the air in ten minutes."

"Whenever you're ready."

She sat back in one of the plush seats. By the time the Citation's wheels left the runway, she was fast asleep.

LATAKIA
SHORTLY BEFORE NOON . . .

Rankin didn't realize the stooped old man with thick glasses and cane outside the mosque was Ferguson until the man pressed his fingers into his forearm.

"You oughta cut your nails," he grumbled.

"Let's go say our prayers. I'm a little slow, and you're deaf and dumb," Ferguson told him.

"*Hmmph.*"

"I know you can do dumb. It's deaf I'm worried about."

Always a wise guy, thought Rankin to himself.

Ferguson smirked at Rankin's frown but noticed that he kept his reaction to himself. They'd done the deaf man routine on an earlier mission, and Rankin had pulled it off very well.

The pair made their way inside the compound, moving slowly toward the mosque. Rankin felt uneasy, not because of the mission—that was a given—but because they were going into a holy place. It was the kind of thing that ought to be out of bounds; even if the crazy idiots didn't respect that, *someone* ought to. He'd thought that in Iraq, too, though it was a real luxury there.

Not that he'd let it stop him.

Ferguson mumbled his prayers in sing-songy chat as they paused to take off their shoes.

"I'm gonna fall," he told Rankin.

"Uh-huh."

Ferguson crumbled to the ground. As Rankin knelt to help him, Ferguson pulled out a pair of shoes from beneath his long *dishadasha*, or robe, and placed them in the corner, making sure the camera hidden in the toe of the left shoe had a good view of the entrance to the mosque.

"I'm all right," Ferguson said in Arabic as others came up to help Rankin with the frail old man. "All right. My grandson is deaf, but a good lad. He didn't mean to drop me."

Several of the men close to Rankin shook their heads and berated him for not taking proper care of his grandfather. Rankin glowcred at them, even though he was supposed to be deaf.

Ferguson babbled away as they walked inside. He told the others that they were pilgrims from southern Egypt, seeking to travel to as many holy places as possible before God called him to rest. His patter soon wore out his listeners, and they were left alone to purify themselves and join the faithful in prayer.

His cover now established, Ferguson played the role of devoted pilgrim and tourist after prayers. He examined the old pillars carefully; he wanted to find a second spot to plant a video camera if the first failed. Shimmying up them without being seen would be impossible, however, as there were at least four rather discreet guards milling through the hall, large men who probably had weapons hidden beneath their clothes. Ferguson managed to catch the eye of one of the men, nodding at him, but the man didn't nod back.

"You oughta not get in their face like that," Rankin said as they put their shoes on outside. "Guy looked like he wanted to kill you."

"Can't kill me for praying," said Ferg.

"You weren't praying."

"Sure I was, Skip. You weren't listening."

They walked to the left of the interior courtyard, in the direction of the abandoned building, which seemed to Ferguson the most likely candidate to be hiding Khazaal. They got as far as the long, low step that led to the door before someone yelled at them to ask where they were going.

"Don't stop," Ferguson whispered, still shuffling ahead. "You're deaf."

"Umph," said Rankin.

The person shouted again. This time Ferguson stopped and turned toward him. He raised his head slowly, looking up and down, and then started to turn back.

"You fool. Where are you going?" said the man, grabbing Ferguson's cane.

Ferguson repeated his earlier story about being a pilgrim and tourist, exploring the holy shrines of Islam with his devoted though deaf and dumb grandson. . . . A man who, alas, was not sharp in the mental department, perhaps as a result of being kicked by a Jew when he was young.

Even this last bit failed to win the sympathy of the man who had stopped them.

"This place is off limits to the likes of you," said the man.

"Is it a shrine?" asked Ferguson.

"It is an empty building, fool," said the man.

He pulled Ferguson's cane from his hand. Rankin grabbed him. Fear sprang into the man's face.

"No, no," said Ferguson, tapping his ersatz grandson's arm. "No, no. Peace be unto you, brother. Peace be unto you."

Two other men came over. Both were dressed in business clothes. The taller of the pair began to speak, using calm tones and introducing himself as the imam's son.

Then he started asking Ferguson about which mosques he had been to.

This was not a difficult question in and of itself, for as it happened Ferguson had been to many. He began with the expected, saying how the greatest experience in his life had been Mecca: an obligation for every able Muslim but, more than that, an experience of joy and faith impossible to duplicate elsewhere on earth. He then moved through Saudi Arabia, then to Yemen and then to Egypt. The Imam's son still had not tired—in fact he seemed genuinely interested—and so Ferguson found himself in Beirut, where the Omari Mosque was incomparable.

"God must have been very pleased to take it from the nonbelievers," said Ferguson.

"That happened here," said the Imam's son.

"So I've heard. But there was no trace."

"Oh, yes. Come."

By now, Rankin had a truly bad vibe about the Imam's son. He tried to signal this to Ferguson by tugging at his arm, gently at first, and then more insistently. Finally his pull became obvious to everyone.

Rather than using it as an excuse to leave, Ferguson began berating his grandson, threatening to lash him with the cane and saying that it was not time to eat yet. Rankin did his best not to react, cringing like the long-suffering grandkid he was supposed to be.

The Imam's son gently pulled Ferguson away, starting him toward the mosque. Ferguson wrapped his arm around his and planted a small audio "fly" and a tracking device on the man's jacket.

What the hell is he doing?" Monsoon asked Thera out in the van. They were parked two blocks to the north, barely in range of the bugging devices they were using. "He should be getting the hell out of there."

"It's a calculated risk," Thera told him. "He hasn't found what he's looking for. Khazaal has to be inside. He's the only one Meles would have come to meet. At least that's what Ferg thinks."

"Sounds to me like the guy's trying to trap him. He's asking too many questions."

"Probably he doesn't believe him."

"We don't have enough people to get him out if something goes wrong," Monsoon said.

"He knows what he's doing. Ferg's been in this kind of situation before."

Monsoon took a sip from the bottled water. As a Delta op, he'd been involved in some difficult operations, including a hostage rescue in Peru that had gone sour. But these people pushed things too far; if they saw a hairy situation, they tried to make it ten times worse.

"He have a death wish?" Monsoon asked.

Thera turned and looked at the Delta soldier. She was going to scold him but held back.

"He might," she said. "He might."

ankin could feel his heart pounding as they walked slowly along the pillars in the mosque, the Imam's son pointing to the stones left from the older church. These guys didn't believe they were who they said they were, but they were stuck now; cutting and running for it wasn't going to get them out alive. Besides the two plainclothes guards at the back of the prayer hall, Rankin had spotted four men with Kalashnikovs outside.

He glanced at Ferguson, still hamming up the old man act. There was no sign that he was nervous. He could've been on the stage in a high school play, yapping out rehearsed lines.

Rankin had had a bit in a high school play once. He'd flubbed the five words he had to say.

Ferguson seemed to fall against him. Rankin grabbed at his arm, then realized that Ferg hadn't fallen, but was bending forward to spit on the rocks of the Christian church.

"No, you shouldn't show such disrespect," said the Imam's son. "They are children of the book, even if they are wrong in their conclusions. Jesus Christ was a great prophet. Peace be unto him."

Chastised, Ferguson bowed his head, then spontaneously dropped to his knees and rubbed up the spittle. As he did, he slipped the knife secreted up his loose sleeve to his hand, ready to be used. The Imam's son gently tugged him to his feet.

A moment of decision: there might not be a better opportunity to grab him by the throat.

The tug was gentle. Ferguson remained in character, mumbling his apology and begging forgiveness, practically doubling over even as he rose, admitting he was unworthy and a fool besides.

"No, old man, you are not a fool. I am sorry I yelled at you," said the Imam's son. "You are a devout believer, a faithful child. God will smile on your soul."

He led them back outside, and offered a place to stay. Ferguson thanked him profusely, saying that first they must complete their visits to the other mosques in town and then with God's grace return.

Outside the mosque, Ferguson started for his shoes. Four men with AK-47s were milling nearby.

"Just a minute," said the Imam's son, grabbing Ferguson's forearm tightly.

Guns pushed his glasses up, trying to peer across the street through the doorway of the outer wall without making it too obvious that he was staring inside. Ferguson had told him to remain outside if at all possible; even in disguise there was always the chance that someone would remember him from yesterday.

Two men with AK-47s, stocks folded up so the weapons looked more like machine-pistols than rifles, walked from the left and came through the opening. Guns took off his glasses as if to clean them but stayed where he was for a moment as the men checked the block. One of them put his hand to his ear—he had an earphone there though Guns couldn't see it—and then both men came out of the doorway, heading eastward on the street.

Guns kept his glasses off and walked the other way, catching a glimpse of the knot of men in black shirts and pants as they came out. A pair of cars came around the corner, accelerating and then stopping in front of the mosque.

"You seeing this?" Guns whispered to Thera.

"Oh, yeah. There's our boy. Just keep walking. We'll have the Global Hawk tag the car in its ID system. Once we recover Ferguson we can find out where it went."

Ferguson pushed his teeth together as the Imam's son let go of his arm. Khazaal had passed not more than five yards from him, but he was gone now, the bastard.

"Strong arms," said the Imam's son, staring into Ferguson's face.

Ferguson smiled and bowed his head.

"You have much hair," added the man.

"Were every strand a prayer to holy God, it would not be a tenth of what I owe," answered Ferguson.

"A van will take you to the next mosque," said the Imam's son. He snapped his fingers and shouted directions to one of the men nearby. Ferguson protested lightly, saying he was unworthy to accept such kindness but then accepted with gratitude.

One of the men with the AK-47s came over from the courtyard, walking with them to the street. Two other guards were nearby; the Imam's son bade them good luck and farewell, then turned abruptly and went inside the administrative building. Ferguson took hold of Rankin's arm, stalling for a moment to size up the layout, but it was clear that if they ran for it they'd be cut down before they made the street.

C omin' out," said Guns. "Finally."

"We see," Thera told him from the van. "Four guards."

"Shit."

"It's all right. Take a breath and hold it. Ferg is talking."

Guns started walking behind a group of smartly dressed women, paralleling Ferguson and Rankin. The two ops were sandwiched by men with guns. Thera was right; Ferguson was chatting up a storm.

Guns hopped into the street, deciding to cross and get closer. He moved without thinking of the traffic, which though light wasn't nonexistent. He just missed getting run over by a battered Renault, whose driver swerved and laid on the horn. Guns put out his hands in apology as another man leaned out the window and cursed him and his children's children for being so careless.

One of the men with Ferguson pulled open the sliding door to a white Toyota van and prodded him inside. Ferguson pulled himself upward and got in, groaning all the way. Rankin followed. The van had three rows of seats: two guards got behind them; the other two crammed into the front with the driver.

"We better follow," said Guns.

"We're taking it," Thera told him. "You hang back. Go up to that café at the corner and relax."

Relax? Yeah, sure, thought Guns. He'd put that on the agenda, but it didn't look like he'd be getting to it anytime soon.

T hey'd gone about two blocks when Rankin felt the barrel of a gun pressed against his neck.

"You heard that horn," said the man behind him. "I saw you."

Rankin turned in the direction of the gun but said nothing, clinging to the last vestiges of his cover. The men in the front turned and started yelling at the gunman.

Ferguson started to laugh.

"He hears with his eyes and fingers," Ferguson told the others, still laughing. "Shoot the gun and you will see. He hears it. Watch."

Ferguson clapped his hands together. Rankin jerked his shoulder up in reaction.

"He's a fake," said the man in the back.

The man behind Ferguson reached forward with his gun. Ferguson, still feigning amusement, turned and insisted that the men must fire the weapons and see what he was saying. "You will see, you will see. Shoot."

"We're *not* firing in the Imam's van," said one of the men in the front.

Ferguson leaned across to the front seat. The man near him grabbed his hand as he reached for the horn.

"Beep it," urged Ferguson. "Watch. He hears the air. It is quite phenomenal. Watch. Watch!"

The driver hit the horn. Rankin now practically jumped upward in the seat.

The man in the front who was in charge told the driver to stop up ahead near an open lot. He pulled in. The men got out. Rankin let himself be jerked from the van, a bewildered look on his face. He landed in a heap on the dirt, then slowly got to his knees.

"Fire the guns and watch," said Ferguson as he got out of the van. "Watch him. He will jump."

"Maybe we should fire at you," said the man who'd first put the rifle at Rankin's neck.

Ferguson took his prayer hat off his head and pushed out his chest. Then as a final gesture tossed down his cane. "Accept my soul, my Lord God. Thank you for this favor," he said. "Thank you for sending the angel to deliver me to Paradise."

The man leveled his gun at Ferguson's face, then pushed the barrel down before shooting. Bullets splattered into the grounds a few feet from him, ricocheting wildly.

Ferguson didn't flinch—much.

"Old fool," said the man. "Let them walk."

They got back in the van and drove away.

Ferguson bent to pick up his cane. Rankin got up and reached it before he did.

"We're still being watched," Ferguson whispered. "I don't think the Imam's son totally bought the act. But those idiots did."

He straightened, then pointed up the street. "Thera can pick us up after we go into that café at the corner. We'll dump our disguises in the back and come out there."

He began to walk. Within a few steps he had fallen into a rhythm and begun to hum.

It took Rankin half a block to realize it was "Finnegan's Wake." He hoped to hell the people watching them didn't know any old Irish folk songs.

21

LATAKIA
LATER THAT DAY . . .

"So, were you nervous?" said Ferguson as they headed back to the hotel in the van. He'd waited until they reached the other mosque, where he changed out of his costume and made sure the people trailing him had left before getting Rankin.

"I wasn't nervous," lied Rankin, "but next time don't tell them to shoot me."

"I didn't tell them to shoot you, just to shoot the gun. There's a difference."

"I doubt they saw one."

"The Global Hawk tracked the van with Khazaal up to the castle," said Thera. "Meles is on his way in that direction, too."

"What about the Russian?"

"Hasn't left the hotel."

"He may have a way around the sensors," said Ferguson.

"Or maybe he's not in on this meet," suggested Rankin. "Maybe this is about Khazaal and Meles. Your source said the meeting wasn't until tomorrow. Maybe they're getting together before the rest of the players."

"Do we still want to scare them out of there, Ferg?" asked Thera. "If they go to the mosque, we're in worse shape."

Ferguson took the laptop and paged through some of the video showing Khazaal. One of his men had a small briefcase with him.

"Hey, Rankin, this look like a case for an Uzi to you?"

Rankin looked at it. "Maybe a mini Uzi; it's so thin. But why? It's not like they need to fool anyone."

"Probably has the jewels in it," said Thera.

"Yeah. That's what I'm thinking. So riddle me this, Batgirl," he added. "Iraqis don't buy, they sell."

"What's the riddle?"

"Iraqis don't buy, they sell," repeated Ferguson. "But our Iraqi is going around with a case that has so many jewels in it, he doesn't leave it with the people in the mosque. He doesn't even trust Meles, you see?" Ferguson pointed to the pictures. "He's keeping it out of his reach, away from Meles's people. These guys travel in a separate car."

"Might be his lunch, Ferg," said Rankin.

"Assume it's not. What's he going to buy here?"

"The Russian," said Rankin. "He needs him to run some missile system."

"Corrigan's guess."

Rankin frowned. He wished Ferguson hadn't mentioned that.

"That's not a reason to reject it," added Ferg. "But ordinarily, you don't pay in advance for services rendered. Maybe he's trying to buy something, too. Either way, if we snatch the case, we stop the deal."

"Just as easy to snatch him," said Rankin.

"No," said Ferguson. "Because I can't touch him. I don't have to be so careful with the guards; they're not going to stand trial."

He was making a fine distinction—a very fine distinction—but hadn't that been Corrine Alston's point? The administration wanted Khazaal to stand trial in Iraq.

She wouldn't like the fact that the guards were killed, if that happened. But in the context of everything else, she'd accept it.

Maybe.

Definitely if he got Khazaal alive.

Snatch the jewels, and even if he missed Khazaal he'd change his plans. The Iraqi would be more vulnerable if he had to improvise, infinitely more vulnerable.

"So what's he buying?" Thera asked.

"Something he doesn't have," said Ferguson, thinking of Birk's offer.

While Ferguson was washing the gray out of his hair back in the hotel room, Guns and Grumpy added booster units to pick up signals from the bugs Ferg had left in the mosque. The boosters, each about the size of a cigarette carton, took the signals and broadcast them to the satellite system. Ringing the target area with the boosters not only provided insurance if one of the units malfunctioned or was discovered but also allowed them to plant even smaller audio flies inside later on.

Guns had one more unit to place, this one on the water side of the compound. An ancient wooden waterwheel stood about ten feet from the road on the north side; it looked to Guns the perfect place to put the booster, assuming he could get out there. A narrow stone ledge that had once been part of a dock or walkway ran almost all the way toward it, but what exactly would he say he was doing if someone came down the road and saw him?

He sat for a few minutes, puzzling this out. Then he hit on an idea: he'd claim he had dropped something into the water and hoped to fish it out. To make it more authentic, he dug into his pockets looking for something. He didn't come up with anything, at least not that he felt he could afford to lose, so he took off his watch. It was a cheap plastic model, but it had been a present from his brother. Rather than throw it in he pocketed it. If he got to the point where he was being searched, the watch was going to be the least of his worries.

Guns reached over to the wall and pulled himself up. His foot slipped off one or two of the stones, but he managed to make it to the wheel. There he took the booster from his belt, activated it, and slipped it into the rung at the top.

As he started back he saw that the wall angled toward the land just beyond the wheel, forming a wedge that ran to a small rocky beach. A chain-link fence blocked off the beach, but from where he was he could just see the edge of a boat in the angled inlet made by the wall. As best he could remember, the boat had not been in the photos he'd seen earlier from the Global Hawk. Guns decided to reconnoiter, though the only way to do this was to go back the way he came, walk around several blocks, and then slip into the back of the large building above the fenced-off beach. The building was a laundry. Guns got past it without any problem, then hopped the fence and walked onto the rocks.

From the other side, it had looked as if he could just reach across to the boat from the rocks. But now that he was here, he saw it was actually six or seven feet from the shore. He also saw that there was a doorway in the mosque wall that opened right above the boat.

Guns took off his shoes, rolled up his pants, and plunged into the water. He took about two steps before he realized it was deeper than he'd thought, far deeper—it came above his knees—and with the next step dropped off to his chest. He was committed, though; he pushed down and swam to the wall. He pulled himself up on the slimy stones, twisted a bug so it would work, and stuck it in the wall. The boat bobbed nearby. He was tempted to take it, and then had another idea: why not plant a fly in it?

As he reached into his pocket, he heard voices coming from the other side of the wooden door. He quickly tossed a pair of flies into the boat. Then, not knowing what else to do, he slipped down into the water, took two long strokes, and dove under the surface.

Guns swam as far as he could underwater, then stayed down for two more good strokes before coming up. He took a gulp of air, then slid back down, pushing as strongly as he could. He repeated this two more times, until he felt the water starting to push him forward. He broke the surface and found that he was now about thirty yards beyond the boat. He pushed backward, kicking his legs beneath him. The speedboat had backed away from its mooring and circled toward the sea. By the time it passed him it was riding the waves at a good clip, heading northwestward along the coast.

Guns took a deep breath and began swimming back to the beach where he'd left his shoes. Four strokes later, he realized he hadn't made any progress against the tide.

Meles is moving," said Thera, knocking on the door to the bathroom. Ferguson grabbed a towel and pulled on pants, then went out to the common room, where Thera had been watching the feed. The Global Hawk surveillance system showed two SUVs parked in front of the Riviera. The computer processing the unit's images could be programmed to track and zoom in on up to one hundred different objects within its viewing range; it could distinguish objects roughly a meter square, which made tracking trucks relatively easy, though the city streets could complicate things.

"Khazaal's still at the castle," said Thera. "You think that's where he's going?"

Ferguson studied the feed. If they were meeting—a good guess, given that Khazaal's vehicles were at the castle—then if he went to take Khazaal, Meles would be fair game.

So that was the solution. Except he wasn't ready.

"Wake up Rankin and Monsoon," he told Thera. "Where's Guns?"

"Still down by the mosque with Grumpy."

Ferguson bent down to the laptop and selected the area. But the resolution was not quite fine enough to see people.

"He have a bug showing where he is?" Ferg asked Thera.

"Supposed to."

He picked up the sat phone and called Guns's phone. There was no answer.

Rankin and Monsoon, sleepy-eyed, came over.

Ferguson fiddled with the computer, looking for the screen that would show where Guns was. A signal came up offshore, north of the mosque.

"I'm going to take a run out there," Ferguson told Thera, grabbing his gear. "See if you can get ahold of Van and make sure he's ready for a pickup. Keep Khazaal and Meles in view if you can. Khazaal's more important. Rankin. Monsoon. You're with me."

It didn't seem possible that the tide could be this strong. Guns thought it must be some defect in the way he was swimming, not curling his hand right or something. But no matter what he tried, nothing worked.

After nearly fifteen minutes struggling against the tide, Guns felt his arms starting to cramp. He tried to relax, coasting for a bit, but the weight of his pants and long shirt dragged him down. He decided he didn't need the pants, and stripped to his military-green shorts, then off came his shirt. He had a pistol strapped to his waist and another at his leg; he pulled off the one at his stomach but kept the other. He turned and started stroking with the current, but this didn't take him any closer to the shore.

"I hate the water," he said out loud. "If I wanted to die in the water, I would have been a sailor."

You're not going to die, he told himself quickly, but once the idea had been planted in his head it began to grow. He tried to fend it off by concentrating on the job at hand, which was to find some way—any way—out of the current. But with each stroke his arms got heavier and his legs more tired.

"Goddamn it," he said. "Let's go, marine. Stop being a sissy."

The pep talk worked for about two minutes. He tried to float to rest, kicking his legs and leaning his body out nearly flat against the surface. When he started to swim again he saw a large boat on the horizon about a half mile offshore. He decided that was his destination and that once he reached it he would be saved. So all he had to do was stroke for a few more minutes, he told himself, ten or fifteen at the most. Then he would get there and give them some cock-and-bull story about falling off a tourist boat, completely in Russian, and be saved.

He'd be ribbed about this forever. Served him right for jumping into the water. He should have had Grumpy covering his butt.

His arms were lead and stiff and dead.

A motor ripped in the distance. Guns turned to see where it was. As he did, his arms collapsed and he sunk below the waves. Something hard grabbed him around the neck and shoulder and dragged him upward.

The air felt like a shock when he broke the water.

"Don't they teach marines how to swim?" yelled Ferguson. He was swimming alongside him.

"Ferg, man, am I glad to see you."

"Yeah, no shit. Kick. Come on. We have to grab that rope. See it? Rankin can't steer to save his life."

Guns managed a feeble kick, but it was Ferguson who did all the work, towing the marine to the rope and then pulling them both to the boat, where Rankin and Monsoon fished them from the sea. Guns collapsed against the side of the vessel.

"I owe you one, man. I owe all you guys," said Guns.

"Bet your ass," said Rankin.

Ferguson stood and tried knocking the water out of his ears. The harbor would not rank among the world's cleanest, and he was covered with a film of oil. The only reason he couldn't smell it was that the stench of raw sewage and dead fish was too strong.

"Where's Grumpy?" asked Guns.

"Not where he was supposed to be," said Ferguson.

"It wasn't his fault," said Guns. "I left him on the other side of the mosque and told him I'd be back."

"We left him where we stole the boat," said Ferguson, only slightly mollified. "I told him if the owner came back he should offer himself in trade."

"You shouldn't have told him that," said Guns.

"Why not?"

"He's a marine. Trained to follow orders. I don't think he's got much of a sense of humor."

22

LATAKIA

The scent of the vodka nearly overwhelmed Ravid. When he had started out this evening to get a sense of what the arms dealers were doing, he had felt strong, even dismissive of the need for liquor. But now desire clawed up from his chest, more powerful than sex, more powerful than the will to breathe when underwater. He wanted, he needed a drink.

Was that why he had given himself this assignment after all? Because he knew he would succumb? Because he had to succumb in the end?

Ravid tried to ward it off. He returned to the plot to take Khazaal's gems, but its elaborate twists no longer interested him. He thought of his wife and his son, forced his mind's eye to reconstruct their pictures. He thought of revenge, the need to annihilate his enemy. He wanted justice—

No, all he wanted was a drink. He didn't even care if it damaged his cover. Why would it? Many Muslims, especially those who had tasted the luxuries of the West, sinned by drinking. It might even be argued that it helped his cover, for what spy would dare to sin openly?

He didn't care. He wanted a drink.

Ravid turned around as if he were here to meet someone.

Who? One of the arms dealers. Birk, the notorious Pole. Andari, the half Italian, half Armenian whom everyone thought was a Jew.

Perhaps he would go up to one of them, just as a diversion, just to keep himself from giving in.

But if he didn't want a drink, why didn't he just leave? He was free to walk out. He could easily walk out.

He should walk out, he told himself. And yet he felt he couldn't.

The bartender tapped Ravid's arm from behind. Ravid jerked around, as if jolted by lightning.

"Drink, sir?" asked the man in English.

Ravid stared at him for twenty seconds, thirty. "Vodka," he said.

As soon as he pronounced the word, blood rushed to his head. He felt warm, almost hot. Relieved and ashamed at the same time.

A woman brushed by him. Ravid turned quickly, his eyes following her as she made her way toward one of the arms dealers, Birk.

The bartender put the vodka down behind him. Ravid forced himself to stare after the woman, ignoring the greater temptation.

He would never stop at one drink. His mission would be lost. Very likely he would lose his life. Tischler would have nothing to do with him. Any chance of revenge would be lost.

What chance, though, did he have of revenge? He knew several people, many people, men in similar situations, who would help. He could form an army of the wrathful, he thought. Together they could take their revenge.

If he had the strength. Not to gather them—that was nothing, that was a child's task. The strength he needed was to not drink. Not to remember his wife and child. Not to remember but to stay focused on the present.

The smell of alcohol rose around him, overwhelming everything else. He put his hand to his face, closing off his nose, trying to force the scent away. He wanted to leave yet his legs seemed glued to the spot. Finally he got himself moving, eyes riveted on the woman who had just bumped into him. He began following her, telling himself she was attractive and reminded him of his wife. A lie, but useful.

The woman—Judy Coldwell—stopped at Birk's table. It had taken her much longer than she had thought to find him, and now she had to screw up her courage just to speak. But with the first word, the rest flowed; it was if she were an actress, playing a part, and that made it easy.

"Do you remember me?" she said first in Arabic, then in English. Her Arabic was still rusty—far too rusty, really, to be properly understood—but Coldwell knew that using it before English was generally helpful.

Birk didn't know quite what to make of her. She was attractive, and while he thought it possible she was some sort of journalist, he decided he might amuse himself for a few moments while it was still relatively early. He swept his hand across the table, inviting her to sit.

"Do you remember me?" she repeated as she sat.

"I should, with a face as lovely as yours," said Birk. "But I'm afraid I do not."

"Three years ago, I worked for a firm that needed to equip its security workers," said Coldwell. "We needed to get around some inconvenient regulations and some nosy officials. You were able to sell us some items."

"Of course," said Birk. He didn't remember the transaction, but that was unimportant. "And now you find yourself in need of more. I have to say that inflation has taken quite a toll—"

"I'm here for something else entirely," said Coldwell. "I'm taking the place of Benjamin Thatch. He's been delayed."

"The name is unfamiliar."

"Perhaps not with others. I was hoping perhaps you could mention it."

"Mention it?"

"Some people may be looking for Thatch instead of me. Of course if this is inconvenient, we could arrange to pay for your time."

Birk could tell from her accent that the woman was an American. Could this be a hopelessly lame attempt by his friend Ferguson to trick him?

"You're a reporter?" he asked.

The woman's face blanched. "Absolutely not."

"CIA?"

"No. I am with a group called Seven Angels. We assist different people."

Birk laughed. "A charity?"

"Not exactly, no."

A few yards away, Ravid slid back in toward the bar. The bartender saw him and approached once more, holding the drink out this time. "No, thank you," said Ravid. He reached into his pocket and pulled out a few bills. "For your troubles. And if I might have a seltzer, no alcohol."

The bartender shrugged. Ravid straightened, straining to hear the conversation at the table. He could hear no more than a few words, *Seven Angels* among them.

They struck him because they were the name of a group mentioned in the background briefing as he brought himself up to date. An American group had made some contact with a number of Islamic groups, including members of the cells meeting in Latakia. Seven Angels wanted to provoke some sort of apocalyptic dawn by funding attacks in the Holy Land. It had been rolled up completely by the Americans following a freak event in Jerusalem around the time he had been recalled.

Ravid leaned closer, trying to hear, but the interview was over; she was already getting up.

Ravid began to follow, slowly first, then quicker, pushing toward the exit, and his future.

BAGHDAD

When Peter Bellows saw Corrine at the airport, he shouted to her. He felt almost as if he were her uncle, though he hadn't seen her more than once a year over the past decade.

For her part, Corrine didn't feel like a niece; Bellows was her father's friend, not hers, and since receiving the president's instructions had tried to distance herself even further mentally, thinking of him as the "American ambassador to Iraq," not her father's old chum. She smiled bashfully and put out her hand, but Bellows wrapped his arms around her and kissed her cheek.

"It's been so long, Corrine," said Bellows. "How are you, hon?"

"Very well, Mr. Ambassador. Yourself?"

"Oh, stop that Mr. Ambassador stuff. Peter's fine." He winked at her, indulging in an almost fatherly pride at how far his friend's little girl had come. "Your father says hello," Bellows added. "I spoke to him just last night. He claims you never call."

"He always says that."

"God, you look good. Now I don't mean that in a sexist way."

"I wouldn't think so," she told him.

"Would you like to freshen up back at the embassy or look around town?" he asked.

"I'm fresh enough."

"You said it. I didn't," said Bellows, leading her to the cars as a swarm of bodyguards followed.

Two years after the formal turnover of government to the Iraqis, the city remained pockmarked and battered from the occupation and the continuing struggle with a hodgepodge of insurgents. The Iraqis were clearly making progress, and in fact two-thirds of the country was arguably as calm as any place in the Middle East. The area around Baghdad remained the exception; while it wasn't anywhere near as dangerous as it had been even a year before, Americans were still targets here. A sizable portion of the remaining U.S. military presence was concentrated in and around the capital. American troops and dignitaries traveled in convoys whenever possible, their routes never announced in advance.

But Bellows seemed jubilant and even carefree as they rode from the airport and toured the sprawling city. He spoke in glowing terms of a new housing development that, in Corrine's eyes at least, already looked run-down. From there they drove to a new shopping mall outside of town. Corrine realized that the ambassador wanted her to be impressed, hoping that she would interpret what she saw as a sign that normalcy was returning to the country.

The empty shelves and idle clerks in the mall had the opposite effect. There were at least three dozen Iraqi government soldiers in the building and another dozen Americans, outnumbering the shoppers nearly twenty to one.

Iraq might be on the road to democracy, but it was a long road, with many twists and turns, and it would be years before the country rose from poverty, let alone began to live up to its economic potential. In two months, the bulk of the remaining American troops were scheduled to withdraw. Corrine couldn't help but wonder what would happen when they were gone. Besides reducing security, their removal would hurt the local economy, which was benefiting from cash payments for bases as well as from the GIs' personal spending.

Bellows shrugged off the question.

"A few hiccups, nothing more," he said as they rode back to the embassy. "I have a few meetings I can't duck. Should we get together after dinner? Late? I'd love to catch up."

"Sure," said Corrine. "That'd be good. I have a few things to do myself."

The embassy complex—it had been built at the end of the occupation, one more spur to the economy—was so new that it smelled of plaster as well as fresh paint. There were three small dormitory-style residence buildings for VIPs. Though Bellows suggested she take a room in the ambassador's residence near him, Corrine demurred; she planned on using the secure communications facilities, which were located in the basement of the largest of the VIP buildings (the Yellow House, so called because of the exterior color). Staying there would make it easier to come and go. She also wanted to keep a little professional distance between herself and Bellows, though she didn't tell him this.

Like its predecessor, the embassy had extensive secure facilities manned twenty-four hours a day and located in an elaborate bunker. Corrine found her room, then went down and checked in with Teri, her secretary at the White House. Teri ran through a long list of calls and then demanded to know if the rumors were true that she had been shot at.

"No. There was some sort of fracas in a nightclub, but my bodyguards hustled me out before things got too crazy," said Corrine, crossing her fingers in front of her.

"Is that really what happened?"

"Would a lawyer lie?"

"Ha."

After she managed to allay Teri's fears, she phoned Corrigan to see what was up with Ferguson. The First Team leader wanted to talk to her, Corrigan said. Corrine kicked off her shoes and curled her legs up in the chair as she waited for the connection. The long day had her tired out already, and she was a little disappointed by the ambassador; he hadn't taken her questions seriously.

Or maybe he had, and that's why he was putting a smiley face on everything.

"How do you like sunny Baghdad?" said Ferguson cheerfully when the line connected.

"It's all right. What's going on?"

"I know where Khazaal is staying, a mosque in town."

The word *mosque* swept away her fatigue. "You can't blow up a mosque."

"I didn't say I was going to. Can I make the arrest without a replacement for Fouad?"

"Go ahead, but don't do it in a mosque. Not in a mosque."

Ferguson said nothing.

"Unless you really have to," she added finally.

"I don't think I will. I'll talk to you." He snapped off the line.

Corrine rose and went upstairs in search of a shower.

LATAKIA

As it turned out, Khazaal left the castle around the time Ferguson was grabbing Guns from the riptide. Meles, meanwhile, didn't go there, visiting a small cottage a mile outside of town, apparently to see another delegate to the upcoming conference.

The flies Ferguson attached to the Imam's son's clothes yielded nothing except for a few jokes at the old man's expense. Good fodder for the CIA Christmas party, but of dubious intelligence value.

The flies that Guns tossed in the boat, however, provided several interesting tidbits when the boat returned from a trip to the port area. According to the transcript Corrigan forward to Ferguson:

> sbj a: [garbled] . . . Tomorrow night
> sbj b: All of them?
> sbj a: As many trucks as you can get, yes. And brothers who are trustworthy.
> sbj b: The Yemen? [series of indivuals named by pseudonyms or nicknames, none identified as yet . . .]

"Which you think means what?" Ferguson asked Corrigan.

"Thomas thinks it means the meeting is set for tomorrow. He's found an airplane that was leased in Turkey a week ago with money from Morocco that came from Iraq. That airplane has a flight plan filed for Latakia tomorrow night. That jibes with what your source told you."

"The airplane is going to pick up Khazaal?"

"That's Thomas's theory. It landed somewhere in Lebanon a few days ago, but then flew back to Turkey."

"Near Tripoli?" That would have made sense if the men they had apprehended were to meet Khazaal there.

"I asked Thomas, but he accused me of jumping to conclusions without facts. It seems logical, right? But those guys you grabbed still aren't talking. Slott won't send them over to Guantanamo and Cor—Ms. Alston won't approve, uh, coercive methods."

Ferguson's plan, still vague, was to grab the Iraqi as he came out of the meeting. That was problematic, however; Khazaal would be on his guard, and once the attack started he'd fight to the death. The plane represented a better opportunity, but by then Khazaal might have completed whatever deal the jewels were intended to cement. The trick was to think of them as separate events.

"Tell Thomas he did a good job," Ferg told Corrigan.

"I'm afraid to encourage him. He has yet another UFO theory."

"Hey, I have some of those myself. What does he think the jewels are supposed to buy?"

"Just the usual: weapons. I have a theory," added Corrigan.

"Fire away."

"I think it's mercenaries. They'll bring in suicide bombers from Hamas or something."

"They have plenty of whackos in Iraq already," Ferguson told him. "Iraq is a net exporter of crazies. Just like guns."

"I think you're wrong. It's not easy to get people to blow themselves up, Ferg."

"When does that plane land?"

"It takes off around six p.m., and it should be there within one to two hours. A bit of time to turn it around on the ground . . . it gets back here somewhere between ten and two."

"Thanks for narrowing it down for me. My money set?"

"Wired in, with Ms. Alston's approval."

"All right. I have to talk to Van and then I'll get back to you on what else I need. Definitely the Global Hawk or U-2. An Elint plane would be nice."

"There's no signals coming out of there, Ferg. With the president's trip next week and everything, it's a real bear to spring resources. And even Special Demands has a budget."

"Corrigan, do you pay for this stuff out of your pocket?"

"No, Ferg, but you know what Slott is going to say."

"Does *he* pay for it out of his pocket?"

"He's going to say if there's no high probability of data, resources would be better conserved—"

"To which I say, 'use it or lose it.' I like my saying better."

"Yeah, but I'm the one he's going to yell at."

"No, he's going to yell at *Mizz* Alston," said Ferguson, snapping off the phone. He looked up at Thera, who was watching the video feed on the laptop. "Hey, beautiful, did you buy just that one dress the other day?"

"It's a skirt set," she told him.

"Is that a no?"

"I can't wear the same thing?"

"Don't be gauche." He grabbed the blazer he had borrowed from the hospital. "Come along. Uncle Sam is about to take us shopping."

Thera found a gorgeous blue dress in the Versailles shop that fit so well she was ready to spend her own money on it, until Ferguson whispered the price. They put her conservative Arab clothes in a bag, along with the weapons that wouldn't fit beneath her dress without creating unsightly bulges. Ferguson found a blazer next door and a shirt to go with it. For Monsoon and Grumpy, along as shadows and sartorially challenged, Thera selected a pair of brown suits and black shirts that made them look like rap stars trying to look like bouncers. Not a bad effect, Ferguson thought.

"We check our weapons at the door," Ferg said as they rode in a taxi to Agamemnon. "The Barroom is a very posh place, which means we can't bribe the help but we can slide the guns in through the window in the men's restroom."

Ferguson made a show of handing his big Glock to the attendants at the hallway entrance to the club, then went through the metal detector and set it off. They pulled him aside. "Oh, it was probably this," he said, holding up a penknife. "Sorry about that."

They took the knife and wanded him with a handheld metal detector. Not satisfied even though it didn't beep, they patted him down.

"Tickles," said Ferguson, who finally passed through the gate without setting the machine off. Thera was waiting for him.

"Did you do that on purpose?" she asked as he took her arm.

"What do you think?"

"I know you must have, but I can't figure out why."

The maître d' approached them, nodded graciously, and then showed them to a table overlooking the bar.

"I want them to remember that I was clean," said Ferguson as they sat. "And I wanted everybody in the place to get a look at how cute you are, especially Ras."

"Ha-ha."

"Look, he's coming to us tonight. Perrier with a twist," he said as a waiter fluttered toward them.

"I'll have a champagne cocktail," she said.

"No bourbon?" asked Ferguson.

"The night is young," said Thera. "How are we going to get our guns?"

"Monsoon'll figure it out." Ferguson rose. "Ras, how are you?"

"Mr. IRA and wife," said Ras, sitting. "So lovely." He asked Thera what she was drinking and then ordered the same.

"You don't strike me as a champagne cocktail kind of guy, Ras," said Ferguson.

"Mr. Ferguson, I have to say, you have impeccable taste in women. Your wife is so intoxicating she makes me forget who I am."

"Too bad I don't have the same good judgment when it comes to picking business associates."

"How so?" asked Ras, making a not very subtle attempt to stare down Thera's cleavage.

"I mean that you have not been completely honest with me," said Ferguson. "You told me you had not heard that Vassenka was in town, and now I hear that he is."

"If he is or not, that's not my concern. I didn't know that he was when you asked."

"So now you do?"

Ras waved his hand. "The Syrians may think so. I have an open mind."

"What do they say about Suhab Majadin?"

Ras didn't recognize the name.

"An Iraqi," said Ferguson. "A Shiite."

"You are dealing with him, Mr. IRA?"

"I always deal with the highest bidder. But I have other business with Suhab Majadin. Personal business. Business that I would like to conclude, especially if I had the opportunity by chance to meet him here."

They sipped their drinks for a while. Ras asked Thera some questions about her background. Thera said that she was from Turkey but was otherwise purposefully vague.

As Ras glanced at his watch, Ferguson leaned forward. "If you sell anything to Suhab, you're going to make a lot of people very angry," he said. "And by sell I include trade, loan, or gift."

"One never makes a gift in this business," said Ras.

Ferguson leaned forward on the table. He said nothing and made no gesture that could be interpreted as conventionally threatening. Yet even Thera felt a tingle of fear.

"Where's Suhab?" whispered Ferguson.

Ras shook his head.

"You're dealing with him?"

"I don't even know him."

Ferguson straightened, then leaned back in his seat, staring at Ras. Then he grinned, in effect releasing him. Ras strode away, his composure not quite restored.

"Can we bug him?" Thera asked.

"He'd find it." Ferguson sipped his seltzer.

"So what are we going to do now?" Thera asked.

"Dance the night away," said Ferguson. "Then go for a swim."

LATAKIA

Despair seized Judy Coldwell as the taxi approached the hotel. For the first time since receiving the Reverend Tallis's message she doubted, truly doubted, her ability to carry out the task.

It was not that the meeting with the Polish arms dealer had gone badly. On the contrary, while clearly he didn't remember her or the AK-47s and grenades he had supplied her employer three years before, the Pole seemed to have taken her seriously. He had even tried to sell her a weapon.

She thought he had. Surely he hadn't been just making conversation by mentioning he had a cruise missile for sale. But that was what had depressed her. He claimed to want five million dollars for it.

Five million dollars!

A serious buyer would surely bargain him down—if she remembered correctly, the rifles had sold for about half his initial asking price—but even so: who would be impressed by a few hundred thousand dollars when millions were needed?

A hole opened in her stomach as the taxi pulled up in front of the hotel. She must not lose hope, she told herself. The weight of history was on her side.

Coldwell gave the taxi driver a good tip. Inside the hotel, the short man at the desk smiled at her lasciviously. She forced herself to smile back.

A man trotted across the lobby toward her as the elevator arrived. She got in, then grabbed the door to hold it for him.

"Thank you," said the man. He reached for the floor button and pressed five, even though she already had.

"The Pole is not a very reasonable man," said the man as the doors closed. "But he is willing to bargain, which is a plus."

Startled, Coldwell asked if he had been sent by Birk.

"No, not at all. But perhaps we can work together."

"I'm not quite sure what you mean," she said.

"Seven Angels?" said the man, Aaron Ravid.

"Yes," managed Coldwell.

The door opened on her floor. Coldwell stayed frozen in place. When the door started to close, Ravid put his hand out to stop it. "We should find a place to talk. Your room is surely bugged."

When they finally reached a part of the beach Ravid thought was safe from eavesdroppers, they stood together for a few moments without speaking. It was Coldwell who spoke first, suspicious yet feeling almost confident, as if she were an actress playing out a well-known part.

"Who are you?" she asked.

Ravid gave his cover name, Fazel al-Qiam.

"I am here for Benjamin Thatch," said Coldwell. "To complete the arrangements."

"Yes," said Ravid.

He waited for her to continue, but she did not. Finally he saw no other choice to push the conversation but to admit that he was not the person she was apparently waiting to meet. As soon he did, however, a frown appeared on her face. He volunteered that he had heard of Seven Angels and knew that the group was willing to help those "with the proper agenda" in the Middle East.

Coldwell listened to him carefully, believing that he was lying now about not being her contact. Benjamin would have presented the group as being sympathetic to the Islamic goals of jihad; it could be counterproductive to explain the true nature of what they wanted, though Coldwell believed most groups would take their money anyway. She was afraid that when she told him she had only two hundred thousand dollars, he would simply walk away.

After a few minutes, Ravid decided that he had gotten all the information from the woman that he was likely to get. She was an amateur at best, a poseur at worst, and if she had real money it would surely be fleeced off of her by one of the many snakes in the seaside hotels within a few days. He watched her face, thinking of how to best break this off. As he did, a light on the water caught Coldwell's attention and she turned away. The sweep of her head took him by surprise: he saw not Coldwell but his wife. As Ravid pulled himself back to reality, back to the present, Coldwell turned her head back to him.

"I have little money," she said, deciding to state the situation simply and get it over with. "I can get two hundred thousand, no more."

"It's not enough," said Ravid. He thought of Khazaal's gems. For a moment, only a moment, he inserted her into the plans he had thought of the other day.

"What would your target be?" Coldwell asked.

Ravid looked up at her. "Mecca."

Coldwell didn't understand. She thought she had heard wrong. Before she could say anything, Ravid flew at her. He gripped her blouse and pushed her down, his rage erupting. Two years of anger flashed into his hand as he pushed it against her chest. The suicide bomber, the Muslims, his keepers at Mosaad—everything erupted.

Coldwell looked up at him, unable to speak, certain that she was to be killed. She put her hands against his chest, starting to push him off, knowing it would be futile but determined to have her last act on earth be one of courage.

"Yes," said Ravid as she pushed against him. He let go and stood back. His wife would have fought that way, too.

The rage vanished. In its place was something logical and cold, another kind of wrath, one with a chance to be fulfilled.

"I want to destroy Mecca," he told the woman. "And you can help me. In this way, both of us can benefit."

A layer of thin clouds obscured the moon over the eastern Mediterranean. Water lapped against the side of the boat. The breeze made the air a bit chilly. It was a fairy-tale sort of night, the kind that makes you think nothing can go wrong anywhere in the world, the sort of night that makes even a cynic feel safe while slumbering in bed.

Zrrrpp . . .

Zrrpppp . . .

The two guards fell to the deck of the boat, paralyzed by Taser shots from fifteen feet away. As they hit, a man in a frogman's suit leapt up the ladder of the boat they had been guarding. In his right hand he carried a weapon that looked like a rubberized M79 grenade launcher, which was more or less what it was. He leveled the launcher in the direction of the bow, where two other guards were sitting, and fired. A large shell sped from the barrel, striking the bulkhead just beyond them. As it hit, a nylon and metal mesh net mushroomed from the canister, along with a heavy dose of gas derived from the same chemical family as methadone. The victims struggled for a moment, but they had had a long day and had been close to sleep even before the attack; the effect of the gas was overwhelming.

The frogman bent to the two men who'd been hit by the Tasers. The men were still conscious though paralyzed. He pulled a hypodermic needle from the pouch at his belt, tore away the plastic guard and slammed it home in the first man's leg. He repeated the process with the second man. The drug took effect within three and a half seconds of being administered. By that time, the frogman's two comrades, Thera and Monsoon, were aboard. In their hands were weapons that looked like oversized spearguns covered in rubber: Tasers designed for working in water.

"Monsoon, you have the deck," he said. "Thera, let's go find Sleeping Beauty."

———

Birk Ivanovich hated to be woken up before ten a.m., even if it was by a beautiful woman who looked as if she'd just stepped out of a dream.

A wet dream, as a matter of fact: she had on a tight-fitting diving suit, and her hair and upper body were still damp.

"Who are you?" he said, simultaneously trying to rise from the bed in his cabin on the *Sharia*.

He wasn't successful, because Ferguson had taken the precaution of re-straining his hands before waking him.

"Rise and shine, Birk ol' buddy," said Ferguson from the foot of the bed. "Time to do some business."

"Ferguson, how did you get onto my boat?"

"You invited me the other day, remember?"

"My guards?"

"Upstairs sleeping," said Ferguson. "I keep telling you, Polacks guarding Polacks is never going to work. By the way, when are you going to hire a full crew? You have only four bodyguards on duty. That's fine for the Syrians, but what if a real enemy came calling?"

"Undo my chains," grumbled Birk.

"Just belts," said Ferguson. "You're a really heavy sleeper, Birk. You're lucky I didn't do something you'd regret."

Ferguson nodded at Thera, who leaned over and undid them. Birk stayed motionless for a moment, then grabbed for her. Thera, prepared, had no trouble fending him off with a hard punch to the chest, calculated to stun rather than incapacitate. Birk fell back, blinked a few times, then rolled to the other side of the bed, grabbing for a weapon.

"I got it already," said Ferguson, holding up the pistol. "So the Walther P1A1 has the arms dealer's seal of approval?"

"A gun is a gun," said Birk. "Why are you here?"

"I want to make a purchase."

Birk's face brightened and he sat up. "What do you want?"

"Is the missile still for sale?"

"Yes," said Birk.

"When can we take delivery?"

"Three days. Or maybe four."

"Three days?"

"I need a day or two to make arrangements You know how it goes."

"Is that how long it's going to take you to get the missile for the Iraqi?"

Birk made a face. "What Iraqi?"

"Khazaal."

"I told you, I'm not dealing with him."

"You shouldn't. It would decrease your life expectancy. And you see how defenseless you are."

"I'm not dealing with him, Ferguson. I haven't been invited to their party. I'm not trusted, and I don't care to be. Not there."

"Why is the Russian in town?"

"I don't know. Honestly."

"Are the Israelis involved?"

"Mossad? Here? You believe the stories that they are supermen. That is a myth they like to spread. They were powerful once. Those days are gone."

"How much do you want for the missile?"

"A million. As I said the other night."

"Three hundred thousand."

"Be reasonable. I have others interested."

"Oh really? Khazaal?"

"There is a good market for a weapon like this," said Birk. "Someone offered me five tonight."

Ferguson laughed.

"I can get two million," said Birk, annoyed not that his bluff was called but that he had made such a halfhearted attempt. He was not at his best when first waking. "You must meet my price."

"I don't know how high I can go," said Ferguson. "If you're serious—"

"Very serious."

"I have talk to the bean counters."

"You were to do that the other day."

"No, the other day I had to get clearance from my superiors. Now that I have it, I can see what's in the piggy bank."

"You're becoming more like the Russians every day, Ferguson. This is not a good direction to take. What happened to the man I was going into business with? Where is the boldness?"

Ferguson smiled. "In the interests of goodwill, I'd like to buy some other items."

"Not on credit," said Birk.

"Considering that we're doing business—"

"Not on credit, Ferg. No, no, no. You know better."

"We can roll it into the other deal, with a little interest."

Birk shook his head.

"All right. But I need to take delivery by this afternoon," said Ferguson.

"It will be figured into the price. What do you need?"

"C4—"

"I have a Czech substitute. Very high quality."

"Acceptable. I need something along the lines of the M252, the 81mm mortar."

"I can get you two of the British designs. Same weapon. How many rounds?"

"At least four good ones. High explosives. I'd like some training rounds and an illumination round or two."

"Training rounds? Why?"

"I'm out of practice. I need some rifles."

"M16s? Or will AK-47s do?"

"Well, what do you have?"

"Oh, we have many things," said Birk, finally warming to his role as a dealer. "If you want a machine gun, I have these very nice H&Ks made in Mexico. I came by them just the other day."

"Mexico?"

"Your army chose the Minimi over it, but I think the trials were rigged."

"Yeah, but Mexico?"

"Labor is cheaper there. What can I say?"

"I'll take two, but I need regular rifles as well. Kalashnikovs. Couple of thousand rounds. And something like a MILAN antitank weapon."

"Now we are becoming serious," said Birk. This was his way of saying that he did not have the item, but could find suitable substitutes. "Not RPGs?"

"I need something better. Longer range."

"Battle tested."

"Sure, if I don't mind being flattened by the return fire."

"Handled properly, there will be no return fire." Birk knotted his brow. "I have a pair of older Gustavs. Good weapons. Hard to find ammunition."

"How many rounds?"

"Just two. But I can let you take them very cheap."

"I'll bet."

The Gustavs—M2 Carl Gustav recoilless rifles—were Swedish-built antitank guns. They fired an 84mm round to about 450 meters; the missile could penetrate up to eighteen inches of armor.

"Are you going to war with all of this?" asked Birk.

"More or less. I need some crappy radios, too. Something easy to intercept. Russian."

Birk rolled his eyes. "As you wish."

They haggled for a bit over price after Ferguson finished giving him the shopping list. The mortars were very expensive: the list price on the versions that the U.S. used was just a shade under $25,000, and while Birk couldn't get quite that much for a used British model, he held out for more than half. Ferguson got some throw-ins, including a pair of white phosphorous rounds, but he was not in a position to haggle and probably wouldn't have gotten a much better deal elsewhere in the city if he had been. Birk claimed to be taking a beating by selling the Gustavs for only five thousand dollars apiece, which was actually a fair deal, especially as an RPG-7 (the basic lightweight Russian rocket-launched grenade) would have cost about the same. The total—as Ferguson had predicted several days before—came to just under a hundred thousand dollars.

Thera, tiring of the back and forth, went topside to check on Monsoon. He had removed the mesh from the two guards at the bow and stowed it in a canvas bag. Though it covered about ten square feet, the thin filament filled the space of a large skein of yarn.

One of the men moaned. "Think he needs another shot?" Monsoon asked Thera.

"Nah, we're out of here. You can OD on that stuff." She could tell from Monsoon's expression that he didn't think that would be a particularly bad thing; in his eyes, an arms dealer's goon was as much of a scumbag as a terrorist was. "Killing him would be counterproductive in the long run," Thera explained. "It's not worth the risk."

"He's not going to be happy when he wakes up anyway."

"Ferg's call."

By way of conversation when the deal was concluded, Ferguson asked Birk what other gossip he had heard about the meeting. Birk mentioned some minor terrorists as he dressed.

"What about Meles Abaa?" asked Ferguson. "I hear he's at the Riviera."

"Another person I would not deal with."

"Why not?"

"The Israelis would not like it. It doesn't pay to anger them."

"I thought you said there weren't any Mossad agents in town."

"That would get back to them. They do not like Meles. That is the difference between you and the Jews, Ferguson. You say you do not like someone, and you watch what he is doing. The Jews, *chrtttt*, they slit his throat."

"I should be more like them, huh?"

"I don't tell anyone how to run their business."

Up top, Birk looked over his bodyguards and shook his head. "I can't even fire this one," complained the arms dealer, kicking the biggest one. "Tomanski is my brother-in-law."

"You're married?" said Ferguson.

"My sister's husband."

"You don't look like the type to have a sister," said Ferguson. He pulled out a wad of Syrian bills. "If I leave this to cover their medical expenses, will they get to spend it or will you?"

"Tell me how much it is, and I'll dock it from their pay."

"Fair enough. I don't feel like swimming back, so I'm going to borrow your boat. I'll take your brother-in-law with me. He can bring it back when he wakes up. When will things be ready?"

"In the afternoon. Three o'clock."

"I'll meet you. Where will you be?"

"The Versailles, but . . ."

"Not a problem," said Ferguson, understanding that Birk would be doing business. "I'll just call. Same number?"

Birk nodded.

"Come on, Sleeping Beauty." Ferguson bent down and picked up Brother-in-Law.

"Not him!" yelled Thera. "He's almost conscious."

It was too late. Whether awake or in drug-induced sleep, the man grabbed Ferguson's neck in his arms. Ferg leaned forward, spun to the side, and when that failed to release the stranglehold, pushed off the boat, taking Brother-in-Law with him.

The cold water revived the bodyguard enough to panic, and he tightened his grip rather than loosening it. Ferguson jerked his elbow hard against the man's side, expecting that would release him, then kicked upward. His progress upward could be measured in micrometers. Brother-in-Law was a real meat and potatoes kind of guy, with emphasis on the potatoes; he weighed a hundred pounds more than Ferguson.

"Cover him," Thera told Monsoon, gesturing at Birk as she dove off into the water to help Ferguson.

By now Ferguson had decided he actually needed air and so took extreme measures, bowing his head down and ramming Brother-in-Law into the side of Birk's boat. That did the trick: Brother-in-Law's grip didn't loosen but the rest of his muscles sagged, and Ferguson was able to kick them both upward to the top about a half second before his lungs would have imploded. Thera fished for the back of Brother-in-Law's shirt, grabbing it as Birk threw a line down into the water.

"He weighs a ton," complained Ferguson, ducking back down and finally extricating himself from his grip.

"Keep him," said Birk. "Get him out of here."

"Is he alive?" whispered Thera as they pulled Brother-in-Law into the small skiff.

"Don't check until we're out of Birk's sight," said Ferguson. "He'll add the funeral to the bill."

Brother-in-Law was alive and managed to open his eyes a few minutes later as they headed toward Latakia's commercial port area.

"Sorry I had to hit you," Ferguson told him.

Brother-in-Law said something in Polish. Polish wasn't one of Ferguson's languages, but it didn't sound much like "have a nice day."

"You speak English, or do I have to speak Russian?" Ferg asked.

Brother-in-law spit. "Speak Arabic before Russian," he said in English.

"I'm going to make up for getting you in trouble with Birk but not for slamming you against the yacht; that was self-preservation," said Ferguson. The next sentence was in the universal language: he took out five American hundred dollar bills and held him in front of Brother-in-Law's face. "I need a little help onshore. Nothing you'll get in trouble for."

"What?"

"I need some bicycles and a pair of trucks. I can't drive the trucks at the same time. One bill now, the rest later."

Thera stared at Ferguson. Was he crazy? How could he trust this guy when he had just about killed him ten minutes before?

"OK," said Brother-in-Law reaching for, the bills.

Ferg gave one to him.

"Where are we buying these trucks?" Thera asked.

"I wouldn't use the word *buy*," said Ferguson. "Borrow, maybe." Ferg was going to take them from a so-called charity organization that was actually a fund-raising front for terrorists funneling money into Palestine and Iraq. "But Brother-in-Law and I are going to take care of it on our own. You and Monsoon are going to the toy store at Versailles. The shops in the hotel mall there all open at eight. I don't want you hanging around; in and out first thing, OK? Don't be in the lobby, don't walk the halls, nothing. In and out."

"You think a toy store's dangerous?"

"You'd be surprised," said Ferguson, who actually didn't want them seen by Ravid. "I saw a remote-controlled car there. Get as many of those as you can. Even better would be an airplane. If you see one, grab that, too. But make sure it's good one; the cheap models'll only go to seven hundred and fifty feet. We want the high end. Twenty-five hundred if you can."

"What about a boat?"

"Only if you're planning on taking a bath," said Ferg. "After you go shopping, take a nap. You need all the beauty rest you can get."

B irk's brother-in-law turned out to be unusually adept at jumping cars and even relished the idea of victimizing the Charitable Brotherhood, which even he knew was nothing more than a collection of slimes masquerading as concerned citizens. Ferguson had him follow in the second truck as he drove across town, first north and then west to a residential area at the edge of the city. He'd taken Brother-in-Law along not as a gofer but as an insurance policy in case Birk had been lying about dealing with the Iraqis or otherwise became curious about the Americans' location in town; the trucks were a misdirection play that would keep someone hunting for them busy while Ferguson set up the operation.

"Hungry, comrade?" asked Ferguson as Brother-in-Law climbed into the cab. He said it in Russian, and the other man reacted immediately, practically spitting as he said in English that all Russians were dogs and he would do well to wash his mouth out after using the language.

"Don't like them, huh?" said Ferguson.

"Phew."

"Something personal, I hope."

Brother-in-Law didn't reply. Ferguson took the road to the coast, then instead of going south took a right on the highway.

"You look hungry," he explained. "We'll get something to eat."

Brother-in-Law grunted, but then told Ferguson that there was a decent place for breakfast a mile up the road, one where there weren't too many Russians or Syrians.

"If you don't like Syrians and you don't like Russians, why are you here?" Ferguson asked. "Family obligations?"

This drew a long, convoluted story about the need for the family to recover a farm it had lost during World War II because of the Russians. To Brother-in-Law, Syrians were Russians with head scarves and robes (even if the majority in Latakia didn't wear them).

"How about the Iraqis?" asked Ferguson. He ran his fork through the scrambled eggs. Apparently Brother-in-Law liked runny yolks and potatoes so crisp they endangered fillings.

"All Iraqis are idiots," said Brother-in-Law.

"But Birk deals with Iraqis all the time."

Brother-in-Law made a face but didn't answer.

"Sometimes?" said Ferg.

Brother-in-Law knew better than to say anything, but if Birk had a deal going with Khazaal he either didn't know about it or didn't realize Khazaal was Iraqi. The latter seemed pretty far-fetched; the former remained a possibility.

After breakfast, they drove to a bicycle shop in the center of town where he bought a dozen used bicycles and had them loaded into the back. From there they went back to the dock where he'd tied up the boat.

"Give my regards to Birk," Ferg told Brother-in-Law as he handed him the promised money and another hundred for goodwill. "You probably ought to tell him I gave you a hundred to help. Knowing Birk he'll want a cut."

The Brother-in-Law smiled and slammed the door.

Thera and Monsoon returned to their hotel with an armload of toys and a large bag of batteries. By the time Ferguson returned—he'd stashed the bicycles in several strategic locations and parked the second truck near the first—Guns and Grumpy were racing two of the cars around the suite.

"I have to go check in with Van," Ferg told them. "Then I'm going to catch some z's. Give those to Rankin when he wakes up. And don't wreck them; he needs them to make some bombs."

INCIRLIK, TURKEY

Colonel Van Buren had just come back to his office when the call from Ferguson came through. He checked his watch. It was a little past ten a.m.

"You're up early," he told Ferguson after he picked up the phone.

"Haven't been to bed," said Ferguson.

"No wonder you sound tired."

"Nah, must be the connection. Listen, Van, I've been thinking. I can't blow them up when they're meeting, right?"

"Right."

"But they don't know that."

"OK," answered Van Buren, not entirely sure where Ferguson was going.

"So what I do is, I make them think they're being attacked, which gets them the hell out of there on our time schedule. We follow Khazaal, who probably heads back to the mosque—"

"You can't take him there either, Ferg."

"I'm not going to. We're going to set up so that it looks like we will, though. Move people in and out of the area, make sure they're seen."

"Then what?"

"He's going to do the logical thing and go for his airplane. I take him there. We compromise the air conditioning so it shoots dope into the cabin. The only question in my mind is whether we do it on the ground or in the air."

"Ground is easier and safer," said Van Buren. "I can put two platoons of Rangers at the airport, land them near the plane. We'll use the civvy 737 you guys dropped out of. I think it can land on that field."

They worked out the arrangements and contingencies, talking over the various options. While taking him on the ground at the airport would be easier than doping him in the air, it was likely to lead to political complications if things went wrong, since there would be plenty of people around to notice. But as they worked the possibilities back and forth, it still seemed a better bet.

"I have to separate him from the jewels in case this doesn't work," added Ferguson. "That's the tricky part. I have to do it before the meeting starts."

Ferg explained that the Iraqi kept the jewels near him but not with him, clearly not trusting any of the people he was dealing with. Ferguson needed a plan to separate the cars before the meeting, while he still knew where the jewels were.

"What if he changes the way he does things before the meeting?" asked Van Buren, sensing from Ferguson's dismissively breezy tone that he hadn't finished thinking the mission through. "Maybe that's the one time he brings them with him."

"It's possible," said Ferguson.

"What are they trying to buy?" Van Buren asked.

"That's what has me beat. There's at least one serious cruise missile on the market here, and a Russian expert who should know how to use it is in town. But the guy who has access to them claims he hasn't been approached."

"Like an arms dealer never lies, huh?"

Ferguson laughed. He was tired; the laugh was way too loud. Van Buren worried that Ferg was pushing himself too far. You had to be a little reckless to do what Ferguson did, but it was a controlled kind of recklessness, and despite his goofy veneer Ferguson was one of the most controlled people Van Buren had ever met, much more deliberate even than the anal drill sergeants who had introduced him to the army a million years before.

Recklessness, controlled or uncontrolled, left little room for mistakes.

"You OK, Fergie?" Van Buren asked.

"I'm more than OK. I'm the best."

"Yeah, I know all that. You OK?"

"I'm all right. A little tired. I have to take a nap. How's your kid? Signed with the Red Sox yet?"

"He's got to go to college."

"I'd tell him to take the money and run."

"That's why you're not his dad," said Van Buren.

"Lucky for him."

LATAKIA

TWO P.M.

The alarm on Ferguson's watch beeped incessantly, growing louder until its owner finally found the button to turn it off. He stared up at the ceiling, momentarily disoriented.

Did I take my stinking pills, or not?

He couldn't remember. The need to travel lightly had simply made the compartmentalized pill minders impractical, but there were times when even he could have conceded they were useful. Ferguson, still not sure, took a dose just to be sure; better to be a little hyper than seriously dragging, which was the effect missing even one round of the T3 replacement had on him lately.

Outside in the common room, Rankin was dismantling the remote-control cars. "I assume there are going to be explosives to go with these," he said by way of greeting.

"Yeah, I have to go pick them up. You didn't take apart my airplane, did you?"

"Wouldn't dream of it. Why the hell don't we use a real setup instead of this cobbled together crap?"

"Two words: *plausible deniability*."

"Sounds like bullshit to me."

"That's one word," said Ferguson. "But it'll do."

Ferguson intended that the weapons that he used would suggest the tactics favored by some of the insurgents in Iraq, specifically the southern Shiites who had access to some of the British equipment left behind in the war. His visit to Ras was intended to introduce the name Suhab Majadin to the local authorities. Ras hadn't recognized it, but the Syrian intelligence service would. Suhab was the leader of a faction that hated Khazaal and vied with him to head the insurgency. A thorough investigation would show that Suhab was back in Iraq and had in fact been paid off by the present government to tone down his activities. But a thorough investigation was unlikely in Latakia.

"Where's Thera?" Ferguson asked.

"Still sleeping."

"Wake her up, will you? I have another errand for her and Grumpy."

"Why don't you wake her up?" said Rankin.

" 'Cause if I go into her room I'm not sure I'll come out," said Ferguson.

Forty-five minutes later, Thera and Grumpy found themselves in the casino of the Versailles, playing the slots with bogus slugs and watching for Birk. Thera's appearance had changed considerably: most notably her hair was now fiery red and stretched well down her back. The effect was startling, even with the black lipstick. Unfortunately these changes were accompanied by one far less flattering: she had gained what looked like fifty pounds, the smooth curves now considerably rounder under her long skirt.

Even disguised, Ferg had warned her that Birk might recognize her if she got too close, and so she let Grumpy do the hard work, betting colors on the roulette wheel, where the video bug that had replaced the button in his shirt could get a good view of Birk, who was testing his skill at calling sevens on the nearby craps table.

From what Thera could see across the room, Birk was alone, except for his bodyguards. Ferguson wanted to know who he was meeting here. He suspected Ravid, since he was staying at the hotel, though Thera wouldn't have been surprised to see Khazaal or Meles or even one of the men from the mosque.

Birk was still alone when Ferguson's phone call came. Birk took the call, listened, said something, then hung up and continued playing. Ten minutes later, he cashed out his chips—he was ahead—and went into one of the lounges. Thera followed, with Grumpy right behind her. The lounge was tiered; they took a table together on the top tier, diagonally cross the room from Birk and positioned so that Grumpy's video bug would catch the face of anyone sitting at his small table.

"I was in the middle of a run, you know," said the marine. "A few more rounds and I could have retired."

"Don't even joke about that," said Thera, surveying the room. She realized from his silence that he'd taken her seriously. "I was kidding. What would you do if you won a fortune? Go fishing?"

"I hate fishing. Too boring," said Grumpy. "I'd learn how to play golf and play every day."

"Golf?"

"I always thought that would be a good thing to waste time on."

Across the room, a woman approached Birk. Thera turned to summon a waiter so she could get a better look. The woman was tall and with light features, almost surely a Westerner, and, thought Thera, vaguely familiar. "You getting that?" she asked Grumpy when she turned back.

"I think so."

"Keep watching," said Thera. "I'm going to the restroom."

She got up and took a circuit of the lounge area and bar, and even went back into the casino and the hotel without seeing Ravid or any of the others she might have suspected. By the time she returned to the table, the woman who had been meeting with Birk was gone and the arms dealer was on his cell phone.

"Talked for a few minutes, then said bye-bye," said Grumpy. "Didn't look all that happy. What do you think? Unsatisfied customer?"

Thera shrugged. The image would be looked at by analysts back in the States, who would compare it to known agents and others on their watch lists. Most of the players in international arms smuggling were male; Thera guessed the woman was a go-between for someone, maybe even a stranger picked at random to deliver a seemingly innocuous message or help check surveillance.

They had another hour and a half before they had to meet Ferg. Until then, they'd stay with Birk as long as he was in the hotel. Birk had ordered a bottle of champagne and clearly wasn't going anywhere. "Let's get ourselves another round of Cokes," said Thera, signaling to the waiter. "And then maybe you can explain what's so interesting about whacking a defenseless little ball into a black hole all day."

After he called Birk, Ferguson rented a car from a rental agency in the center of town and took it to a shipping company in the port area. At the start of the operation he'd had a "goodie box" sent up with different tools of the trade, mostly obscure items that were impractical to carry around but potentially of use. The box did not include any explosives or weapons, since they would have likely been detected by X-rays or more sophisticated scans.

The shipper was reasonably secure and reliable, but most of the companies in the port area were subject to occasional scrutiny by the local police, with everyone in and out noted. There was no way around this, and so Ferguson decided to take the job himself, figuring he was the most likely to be able to bail himself out of trouble. He dropped Monsoon two blocks away, and told him what to look for. Sure enough, he saw the pair of Syrian plainclothes security types sitting in their battered sedan as he drove up.

But things went quickly at the counter inside, without the telltale frowns and eyeblinks that typically gave away an undercover operation. Ferguson took the box—it was the size of a microwave, though not quite as heavy—boosted it up on his shoulder, and carried it outside to the car. He'd gotten it into the trunk when he heard an approaching muffler that had a vaguely official rattle to it. When he slammed the trunk and turned around, the two plainclothesmen he'd spotted were getting out of the car, which they'd positioned to make it impossible for him to leave.

"*Ahalan*," Ferg said cheerfully in Arabic as they approached. "Hello."

Neither man smiled. Ferguson switched to English, putting his Dublin-laced brogue into it. "Good afternoon, gentlemen. How are y'today?"

"Passport," said the man nearest him.

Ferguson took out his Irish passport and presented it, smiling brightly. Monsoon had stopped across the street and was looking on.

"Your visa is not in order," said the man.

"I got it at the embassy," said Ferguson, acting surprised. "I must have made a mistake somehow."

"Why would an American be in Syria?" said the other policeman.

"I'm from Ireland," said Ferguson. "Dublin. I'm on vacation."

"If you are on vacation, why are you accepting a package for business?"

The dimensions of their scam—or, more specifically, their demand for a bribe—were now clear: the policemen would charge Ferguson with violating his tourist visa unless he offered to make up the difference between what the document cost and what an imaginary short-term business visa would. This could be quite expensive, but the real cost to Ferguson was time; he had a number of things to do this afternoon. So there was a slightly testy note in his voice as he expressed surprise and assured the men that he wanted always to comply with the law.

"Then you will let us search the car," said one of the policemen.

"The car? Why not?" said Ferguson, holding up his hands. "Go to it."

Across the street, Monsoon leaned against a car watching as Ferguson dealt with the police officers. He had a small Taser in his hand. The basic guts were similar to the weapons he and Thera had used to subdue Birk's guards, but its range was limited to a little over twenty feet because the dart it shot was attached to the device via wires. More important, he'd only be able to take out one of the policemen.

But Ferguson seemed to have it under control. Monsoon watched as the Syrians went through the rental, which of course was clean since they'd just gotten it.

"What are you doing?" asked a man in Arabic behind him.

Monsoon scratched his ear and turned slowly. A Syrian almost exactly his height glared at him from a few feet away. The man had expensive shoes and a shiny watch; Monsoon guessed that he was the owner of the car he'd been leaning against and apologized in Arabic.

"What do you have in your hand?" the man asked, pointing to Monsoon's crossed arms.

Monsoon rolled his eyes but decided it was best to make a discreet exit. As he took his first step, however, the man identified himself as a customs agent and reached to the back of his belt. As it turned out, he was only going for an ID, but Monsoon couldn't afford to take a chance. He brought up the Taser and fired point-blank into the man's neck, jolting him to the ground.

Ferguson had seen the little fiasco developing across the street. He was ready, therefore, when the police officer nearest him reached for his gun. Ferguson dropped him with an elbow to the side of the head, barely having to move. The blow was hard enough to pry the gun from the policeman's hand.

Ferguson caught it in midair, barrel first, and used it as a hammer to make sure the policeman would stay down. By then the other man had scrambled around the adjacent car, fumbling for his radio as well as his gun. Ferg took one of his mini tear-gas grenades from his belt, pulled the pin, and threw it under the car.

"Take the car," Ferguson shouted to Monsoon as the canister exploded. He threw the keys to the Delta boy then jumped in the police car and backed it up far enough to move the other car. As he did, the policeman began emptying his service pistol into the vehicle; the tears in his eyes hurt his aim, but he got close enough to the car to send bullets through all of the windows. Ferguson dove out on the passenger side, rolled, and jumped to his feet, running to the rental car as Monsoon pulled out. He managed to get the back door on the driver's side open before the policeman could reload. They raced down the block, then had to pull a U-turn and go back because it was a dead end. The policeman managed to get one shot in the trunk.

Six blocks later, Ferguson told Monsoon to pull over and pop the trunk; even if the cops hadn't gotten a good description of the vehicle, their compatriots would soon be stopping every rental in the city.

"We'll walk to the minibus station up the street," Ferg shouted as he went to grab the box.

"You sure that's a good idea?" asked Monsoon.

"Probably not. Let's run instead."

The president's voice sounded almost tinny on the secure communications system when Corrine spoke to him from the basement of the Yellow House.

"Miss Alston, I trust that you are well," he said after an aide had made the connection for him.

"Fresh as a peach," she said, throwing one of his expressions at him.

"Well put, Counselor." She could just picture his grin. "And how is Baghdad?"

"Ready for you, such as it is." She gave him a quick summary of what she had seen around town yesterday, along with the highlights of an informal briefing from the ambassador. "I didn't get into security matters about your trip," she added when she finished.

"That's quite all right. The Secret Service will see to that. They've already blabbed my ear off."

Corrine wanted to tell him to stay in the States. She knew he wouldn't take her advice, but she felt as if she ought to say that, ought to somehow go on record with him that she was concerned for his safety. Not that Iraq was as dangerous as it had been even a year before, just that he was such a huge, tempting target. If fanatics could try and kidnap or blow her up in Lebanon, imagine what they might do to him in Iraq.

Or Jerusalem and Palestine when he went there.

But she couldn't tell him any of that. If she did he'd say something along the lines of *Now, now, Miss Alston, don't be a frightened pony. The snakes look bad but they don't bite.*

So why was he allowed to act like a fretful hen on her behalf?

"And the personnel matter related to our representation in the region?" the president asked.

"I'm working on it."

"I'd like to know one way or another when I arrive."

"I'll try, Mister President," she said.

"That's all I can ask," he said, hanging up.

30

LATAKIA

AROUND 2000 (EIGHT P.M., LOCAL) . . .

Unlike the vehicles that Meles had used to check out the castle, Khazaal traveled in SUVs owned by the mosque. After analyzing the video recorded over the past few days, the gurus back at the Cube had realized that Khazaal used two specific trucks, probably because they were armored. The trucks were kept in a parking lot across from a police station several blocks from the mosque. The lot was guarded only at the entrance, which made it easy to penetrate: a chain-link fence covered the back and front, and the lot was deep enough that the vehicles could not be easily seen by the guard. It would be a simple matter to go over the back fence and tamper with the truck, at the same time preparing a diversion for the guard if his suspicions were aroused. It would take little more than ten minutes to tune the vehicles to First Team specifications, said specifications including a radio-controlled device that would choke off the flow of exhaust through the tailpipe, thereby making the engine run slower or stop completely.

While customizing the electronic ignition or fuel system would be more efficient, tampering with it would be much more involved. Placing an electromagnetic unit designed to interfere with the system would also work, but was likely to be spotted during a bomb check. The inserts, included in the "goodie box" Ferguson had retrieved, had diaphragms that would mechanically expand on command. Inserted into the tailpipe with the help of a flexible stick that looked like a tightly coiled spring, the devices were impossible to see without taking the exhaust system off or X-raying it.

The flexible stick had a grapple at the end that gave Rankin a hard time on the second truck: it failed to release after he had positioned the unit. He started to pull the stick out but something snagged. He pushed the stick in and tried again, only to have it stick farther in, just at the edge of his fingertip.

"Got movement at the door of the station," said Grumpy, who was acting as lookout. "Four guys coming in your direction."

Rankin crawled behind the truck, then, deciding to take no chances, he climbed up over the four-foot fence and lay on the ground as the men approached. It was a good thing, too; the men were the drivers of the vehicles. They checked for bombs, but when making sure the tailpipes weren't obstructed used their eyes rather than their fingers and didn't see the black probe jammed deep inside.

"Tell Ferg they're on their way," Rankin told Grumpy. "I'll meet you at the bikes."

O verhead surveillance was being performed by both the U-2 and Global Hawk, giving them backup as well as lengthening the scope of their coverage area. There was also an EC-130H Commando Solo aircraft orbiting at much lower altitude offshore. Its equipment could pick up a variety of radio signals, eavesdropping on Syrian military channels as well as any longer-range radios or phone systems Khazaal and the others used. The aircraft could also jam radios and other devices if things got hairy. For tonight's mission, equipment had been added to tie an operator aboard the aircraft into the command network used by the First Team. The man and his relief had real-time displays from the Global Hawk and U-2 so they could relay information to the ground ops.

"Subject cars are en route," said the operator in a Texas twang.

"You have to be from south Dallas," said Thera, drawing out her Houston accent. She and Monsoon had disabled the boat at the rear of the mosque and were now in the van, monitoring the feed a few blocks away.

"Ma'am, you have me dead to rights."

Thera switched back and forth between the feeds. Ferguson had to know which car Khazaal got into, which meant watching the video bugs. But with the two SUVs about ten minutes away, a truck pulled up and blocked the bug with the best view. Thera switched to the backup, but the shadows from the light obscured the street, and she couldn't be absolutely sure she would see it.

"Time for plan B," she told Monsoon, adjusting a headset beneath her scarf. "You hear me, Dallas?" she asked the operator aboard the EC-130.

"Loud and clear, ma'am."

Thera and Monsoon got out of the van and began walking down the block. They waited until the trucks were about thirty seconds from the mosque. Thera nodded at Monsoon and began to run, turning the corner just as the first vehicle came down the street. There were armed men near the wall of the mosque compound. Two turned to challenge her.

"Help me, help me," she cried in Arabic, her Houston twang subverted into the hysterical scream of a Syrian woman wronged by a stranger. "My husband has beat me. He's a monster."

The guards had been interested if not sympathetic until the mention of her husband; as modern as Syria might be, women were still expected to do as they were told in marriage. The man nearest Thera flung her aside; she managed to keep her balance long enough to see Khazaal get into the lead SUV.

Just as he had the other day, another man carried a briefcase and got into the second vehicle. The men left Thera in a heap against the wall as the trucks backed down the road. She got up quickly, making sure she was positive which SUV had Khazaal and which had the briefcase.

"They're on their way," she said. "Khazaal is in the lead car. The target is in truck two. Ferg, you got that?"

"Thanks, darlin'," he said. "Remind me to beat the daylights out of your husband when I see him."

———

The SUVs carrying Khazaal and his bodyguards turned off their headlights after they reached the highway, making it difficult for the lead vehicle to keep track of the trail car as they started to separate. The muffler restrictor's effect was difficult to calibrate, and the vehicle didn't fall behind significantly until the dial on the device reached fifty percent. Ferguson, sitting below the ridge a half mile from the castle, followed the trucks' progress on the team's backup laptop, retrieved from the goodie box.

"Move that up to about sixty percent," he told Guns, taking the remote-controlled airplane in his hand. Powered by a two-stroke gasoline engine, the small plane took several tries to start, and when it finally did, the propeller nipped Ferguson's finger. He threw the plane aloft and then grabbed the controls, steadying it into a stable though light flight pattern.

The toy plane had a range of about 2,500 feet but with easy-to-fly controls designed specifically for rich parents who wanted to impress their offspring for the weekend. Even so, Ferguson struggled to get it to go exactly where he wanted, using the tiny running lights as a visual guide. He wanted the people on the ground to think that a UAV was spying on them. The trick was to get it close enough to be noticed, but not so close that it could be seen as a toy. From a distance, the plane's small size would be interpreted as meaning it was higher than it actually was.

"Sixty percent," said Guns.

"Check the second SUV," Ferguson asked, still getting the hang of the remote airplane. "How far behind?"

"Two hundred yards. Lead vehicle is just a mile away from us."

Ferguson nudged his right wing down and took the plane into a bank, turning northwestward and flying back toward his position. Then he slid around back to the south, confident now that he had control of the craft, or at least enough control to accomplish his goal. As the airplane came back over the road, the LED lights flickered and went out. Grumbling, though he could still see the aircraft, Ferguson flew it toward the lead SUV as it came around the turn, then headed toward the castle.

"Somebody in the lead car saw the aircraft," reported the controller aboard the EC-130E. "They just broadcast a heads-up."

Ferguson piloted the plane directly over the castle wall. He issued the commands to make it bank back, but the box had been wildly optimistic about the controller's range; the airplane was now on its own and continued out to sea.

"We have a half mile between the cars," said Guns. "Truck two is almost in position alpha."

Ferguson threw down the control. "Go to one hundred percent. Stop the truck." He put his hand over the earpiece. "Jam the radios," he told the crew on the Commando Solo. "Let the party begin."

While the gear aboard the electronics aircraft obstructed the frequencies Khazaal and pals had just used to communicate, Ferguson dropped to the ground next to the 82mm M2 Carl Gustav antitank gun. The recoilless rifle had a short forward bipod that helped steady it as he sighted for the road.

"Truck's still moving, Ferg," said Guns. "Slow. I can't get it to stop."

"Not a problem," said Ferguson, zeroing in on the road. "Truck one?"

"Around the bend, turning down the road to the castle. They're out of sight."

"Hang on." Ferguson fired at the SUV. As the missile whizzed away, he realized he'd blown it. Worried about the tendency of the rocket to fly high, he'd overcompensated and fired into the ground a good fifty yards from the road. He tossed aside the launcher in disgust and picked up the backup weapon.

"Stand back," he told Guns. He peered through the telescope at the side and let loose from a standing position. This round scored a bull's-eye: the three-pound, twelve-ounce shell hit the base of the hood and windshield, one of the weak spots in the armor treatment. The rocket obliterated the front half of the vehicle.

"Let's ride, boys," said Ferguson. "Skippy, cue the light show."

R ankin had hoped to wait until the SUV was inside the castle to begin his simulated attack, but the truck stopped about a hundred yards from the entrance and began backing up the access road, probably concerned about the trail vehicle.

"Mortar," he told Grumpy, adjusting the focus on his night optical device to see if he could make out who was in the truck.

Grumpy dropped the first shell into the British weapon. The round whipped into the air with a hoarse *whu-thumpppp* and fell just outside the walls of the castle, where it exploded with a more satisfying *thrappp*. He followed up with two dummy shells, which landed in the same general area, and then another live round close enough to a minefield on the northern flank of the access road to set off several mines.

Rankin, watching the shells hit through his night optics glasses, had Grumpy adjust to the south; the Delta sergeant got the white phosphorous shell precisely in the middle of the roadway about twenty yards behind the SUV.

"They're taking cover," said the controller in the EC-130E, interpreting the images from the Global Hawk.

"Start the tape," said Rankin.

A crewman aboard the aircraft turned off the jamming gear. In its place, he began broadcasting a prerecorded set of radio signals that made it sound as if a platoon-sized group was maneuvering outside the walls. The voices were in Arabic, and the frequency was the same as that used by the Syrian army. "Commander Suhab" was mentioned several times in the brief conversation, just distinct enough for anyone recording to make out.

"Ready on the machine guns," Rankin told Grumpy. Two men with automatic rifles had come out, crouching near the entrance.

"Sure I can't hit them?" asked Grumpy, hunching over the weapon's tripod.

"No," said Rankin.

"Shame," said the marine, firing at the road.

Ferguson and Guns rolled off the hill on the sturdiest bikes he'd bought. Even thirty yards away they could feel the heat.

"How long is it going to burn for?" Guns asked.

"Not sure. Guess I should've brought a fire extinguisher, huh?"

The flames settled for a moment but then flared into a fireball. Ferguson got off the bike and reached into the oversized knapsack he'd taken with him for their small chain saw.

"Going to be hot as hell, Ferg," said Guns as the flames died down.

"Yeah. But I'm kind of in a hurry." Ferguson walked around the truck, trying to figure out where the briefcase would be.

A flare shot up from the castle, illuminating the night. The gunfire there intensified.

Ferguson triggered the saw blade and started in on the roof and then the door. Rather than pulling it out he was able to kick it to the side and down, singeing but not burning his boot. The scent of burned flesh hung over the car, overpowering all of the other smells, even the exhaust from the buzz saw.

The briefcase was right near the rear door, attached by a handcuff to the guard's charred wrist. Guns grit his teeth together and grabbed hold of the briefcase, pulling on the chain hard enough to snap several bones in the dead man's hand and free the case. He dropped it on the ground and spun to his knees, his stomach suddenly queasy.

The briefcase was barely a foot and a half wide and less high, no thicker than a large paperback book. Ferguson picked it up, examined the lock, and took out his picks. The lock took some work—forty-five seconds—and Ferguson had to balance the small case upright on his knee. When the clasp snapped open it fell, spilling most of its contents to the ground.

A jumble of gold chains, watch bands, necklaces, and loose jewels spilled out. There were sapphires, a number of small diamonds, emeralds. Most were fairly small, but that would only make them easier to sell. There were some gold rings and chains as well. Ferguson guessed conservatively that they must be worth close to three million dollars, maybe considerably more.

It was also a lot more than Khazaal would need to travel in Syria or to hire Vassenka.

Ferguson scooped them back into the case, then took a quick snapshot with his digital camera. Guns got his stomach settled and came back.

"Wow, that's a lot of gold," said the marine.

"Yeah. Hang on to it for me," Ferguson told him, handing him the case.

"Me?"

"Don't trust yourself?"

Unsure what else to do with it, Guns stuffed the briefcase beneath his shirt.

"We have to get out of here," said Ferguson.

"Hey, you forgot that," said Guns, pointing to a bracelet on the ground.

Ferg scooped it up with one hand and grabbed the chain saw with the other. "We have to get out of here. Now."

Van Buren secured his seat belt only a second or two before the 737's wheels hit the cement runway. The plane settled with a jerk, the pilot fighting a rush of turbulence as he brought the plane onto the unfamiliar runway. His official flight plan had him landing at Damascus, but they'd been rerouted with the help of an agent there who had bribed a controller to order the pilot to hold pending a military investigation of another plane on the runway. The 737 pilot had then declared a fuel emergency and been rerouted here. The fact that Damascus had ordered the rerouting meant no questions would be asked about the plane's sudden arrival.

If questions were asked, any one of the forty-two heavily armed men in the rear of the plane would gladly provide an answer, complete with explosive punctuation.

Van Buren threw off his restraints as the jet trundled onto a taxiway. He went forward to the cockpit, where the copilot told him that the controllers had directed them to a hangar area near the terminal ordinarily used by Syrian National Airlines for its weekly flights to Damascus and Cairo.

"They say we can refuel there. It's about a mile from your target," said the copilot. He showed Van Buren the location on a simplified diagram of the airport they had prepared before the mission. The plane's crew were contract workers on retainer for the CIA.

"We want to get out before we get there," Van told him. "Just in case they have any people working at the hangar. Can you swing it?"

"Not a problem. There's a holding area just up ahead," said the pilot. "We'll stop there long enough for your people to slip out, and claim we're getting our bearings if anyone asks. You'll be a half mile from your target."

"Let's do it," said Van Buren.

G rumpy fired through half the box of belted ammo before stopping. "Nice gun," he said of the H&K machine gun, picking up a second to fire from the hip.

Rankin grunted. So far, the pseudobattle belonged to the attackers, who had clearly caught the small force inside the castle by surprise. But that wasn't going to last forever; the defenders had very powerful motivations, beginning with the briefcase of jewels. The two men at the gate to the old fortress had been joined by six or seven more. As soon as Monsoon's gunfire stopped they sprinted down the road, sprawling on the ground.

"Give them another blast, and let's get out of here," Rankin told him. He pulled up his mike as the gun spat shells at the road. "Jammers still off?" he asked the controller in the EC-130.

"Roger that."

Rankin had prepared a series of improvised explosive devices and rigged them to detonate with the help of the radio controllers in the toy cars, a simple but effective trick he'd learned from *hajji* slime in Iraq. When the wheel on the control unit was turned all the way, the signal on the other side closed the circuit and flashed the igniter, detonating the small block of explosives he'd placed by the road. The units had a limited range—three hundred feet was pushing it—but in this case it was the idea and flash that counted.

"Here they come," said Grumpy, jumping up from the now bulletless gun. He ran and grabbed the bike, kick starting the small engine.

Rankin was already rolling down the hill. When he got to the road he slapped the switches on and detonated his bombs. The hillside began popping as if it were the Chinese New Year.

As the attack on the castle wound down, Thera and Monsoon launched a raid of their own. It began with two garbage cans hauled innocently down the street by Monsoon, who placed them near the mosque wall and walked away. Thera, having doffed her *jilbab* to reveal black fatigues, drove a stolen pickup truck down the block, stopped near the entrance to the mosque compound, and ran back up the street. One of the men watching the mosque shouted at her to stop, but the explosion of a small bomb in one of the garbage cans persuaded him not to press the issue.

A moment later, a fire in a box at the rear of the pickup truck began cooking off bullets. Fed by oily rags and a collection of gasoline-drenched cardboard and wood, the fire in the truck worked itself into a bonfire, igniting the thousand or so rounds of ammunition scattered in the back like firecrackers.

When Thera reached the end of the block, she unfolded the stock on the AK-47 she'd been carrying and aimed it at the power transformer on the nearby pole. It took her three shots to find exactly the right spot on the device to make it arc and explode. The night flared white, and then the entire block and mosque went dark.

They've called over to the Syrian police, trying to figure out what's going on," the controller on the EC-130E told Ferguson. "They think it's a robbery."

"It is," Ferguson said. "Make the call to the army. Tell them that radicals have attacked the president's hotel. Give them the castle location."

"Yes, sir."

Ferguson and Guns had ridden their bikes back up the hill, where they could see the men in the castle regrouping. He picked up one of the Russian radios he'd gotten from Birk and began improvising a one-sided conversation about a pickup truck approaching behind the team making the attack, addressing "Commander Suhab" and asking for directions on what to do next. He pressed down the talk button and fired his AK-47 right next to it, then threw the radio down.

"Jam all their communications," Ferg told the controller in the EC-130E. "Jam everything within fifty miles. Rankin, you out of there?"

"We're clear."

"Get to that turnoff and wait."

"You think I forgot what I was supposed to do?"

"You never know, Skippy. This stuff is so much fun even I forget what I'm doing sometimes."

Van Buren had split the assault group into three elements, each named after their primary task. "Field," composed entirely of Rangers, had been charged with securing the area near their target plane and then preventing an escape by the subject in the second phase of the operation. "Plane," a team of Delta troopers drilled in taking over aircraft, had been assigned to secure the aircraft itself. They would also take Khazaal after he arrived. "Support" would cover contingencies as well as provide scouting and security around the planes during the operation.

The men fanned out across the airfield. Van Buren and a communications sergeant stayed with Support, moving into position about twenty yards from the tarmac where the target aircraft, a Rockwell Commander, was being fueled. The flight crew had not taken the precaution of posting guards, and the only complication was the tanker truck, which had just arrived to deliver fuel. But even this worked to the assault team's favor; the truck and its driver occupied the pilot and copilot as the attack team shifted forward.

Captain Melfi snuck around the driver's side of the fuel truck with three of his troopers. As the man who had come to fuel the plane spoke to the pilot, Melfi and the others sprang out, shotguns point-blank at the men. The guns were loaded with nonlethal rubber shot. As the pilot started to turn to the aircraft, Melfi and one of his men fired, sending the man in a lump to the ground. The copilot and fueler surrendered without a struggle.

"Plane is secure," Melfi told Van Buren.

"Roger that," said the colonel. It had gone even easier than he had hoped. "Now all we have to do is hope the rooster comes back to the hen house."

Guns and Ferguson had cycled about five miles south when the controller in the EC-130 warned that two police vehicles were heading their way. The Americans pulled off the road, hiding in the brush until the vehicles had passed. Then Ferguson pulled out the laptop and got the feed from the Global Hawk, taking stock of the situation.

Realizing they were no longer under fire, the men in the castle had swarmed over the burned-out SUV; several cars and trucks, including Kha-

zaal's, were parked near it on the road. One well-placed bomb there, Ferguson thought to himself, and a dozen of the world's worst scumbags would be sent to their final reward.

Unfortunately, another dozen would eagerly take their place.

Meles's Mercedes and several other vehicles were still inside the compound.

"What do we do if they stay there?" Guns asked.

"Eventually they have to leave," said Ferguson.

"You think he'll go without his jewels?"

"If he thinks Suhab Majadin has them, he may, because he'll figure he knows where to find them," said Ferguson. "But we'll have to see."

"Hey, look at this," said the controller.

Ferguson and Guns hunched over the screen. The Syrian police vehicles that had passed him had driven right up to the burned-out SUV and were now enveloped in tracers. There was a flash: one of the visitors had used an RPG on the police car.

"The odds on his bugging out just improved considerably," Ferguson told Guns. "Let's get into position for phase two."

T hera threw her gray *jilbab* over her shirt and pants, and donned a two-piece scarf. Then she and Monsoon headed toward the Riviera, intending to see how the rest of Meles's contingent had handled the situation. But they found the streets near the hotel filling up with police and Syrian soldiers. They drove around the area, made a report, then went over to the hotel where the Russian weapons expert had been staying. He didn't appear to be in his room. Thera decided a little reconnaissance was in order. She left Monsoon on the street and went inside, walking through the lobby briskly as if she were a guest. She got off the elevator on the first floor and took the stairs to the third. By the time she reached the Russian's room she had slipped a set of lock picks from her pocket.

A hard rap failed to get an answer. Thera rapped again, saying she was from housekeeping and had been sent up with an extra pillow. When she didn't get an answer, she slid a pick into the lock, nudging upward with a flair of body English. The lock gave way but the door didn't; she took a wedge-shaped pick and opened the fifty-year-old dead bolt above it. Picks back in her pocket, Thera pushed the door open and stepped in, scooting it closed behind her and locking the door.

As she turned around, the light went on, and she found herself staring at the curved barrel of a Czech-made CZ52. Though a reasonably large pistol, it looked rather small in the big, beefy hand of the Russian weapons expert Jurg Vassenka.

Rankin and Grumpy rode their bikes to a strip of storefronts three miles north of the castle area. Two of the three stores here were empty, but the third housed a Syrian convenience store where customers could buy a variety of fast foods, groceries, and even clothing and hardware items. Unlike in America, the store's hours were highly irregular, and the owners who manned it had gone home long ago. This was fine with the Americans, who took their bikes around the back and caught their breath.

"They're mounting up," the controller in the aircraft said a few minutes later. "Looks like they're going south in one big convoy: Khazaal's truck, Meles, the whole lot of them."

"You got that, Rankin?" asked Ferguson.

"Yeah, I got it."

"Hang loose until they clear past the police. If you can get into the castle to take a look around without too much trouble, do it. Otherwise, bag it and meet us back at the airport. Don't cut it too close."

"Not like you, huh?"

"Not like me."

The Russian held the gun in both hands as he approached Thera. There was no question of reaching for one of her weapons under the long Arab dress; at this range, the 7.62mm rounds in his gun would make her look like Swiss cheese long before she could return fire.

The Russian said something to her; she replied in Arabic that there must be some sort of mistake. The Russian yelled at her, and after pulling the chain across the door, slapped her across the face with the pistol. The blow sent her to the floor. While Thera could have done without the pain, she was able to slide her hand to her waist, where she had a small Smith & Wesson. But as she tucked her thumb under the button on the *jilbab* to get at it, the Russian hauled her up by the hair and tossed her against the wall, this time hard enough stun her.

"What's going on?" said the Russian in broken English. "What are you? Police?"

"My room," said Thera, her brain too scrambled to give her a better alibi.

The Russian grabbed hold of the back of her *jilbab* and pushed her toward the door. He pressed his gun against the side of her face and told her, half in English and half in Russian, to open it. When she did, he pitched her head into the hall as if dunking her into the water, obviously intending that anyone outside shoot her before him.

"We go," he said.

Thera coughed. "Where?" she said in English.

He said something in Russian that didn't sound very promising.

"Where are we going?" she asked again. She wanted the others on the radio circuit, including the EC-130E and the people back in the Cube, to hear.

"Move," he said, propelling her into the hall. She started for the elevator, but he grabbed her, pointing her toward the far end of the hall. "Move."

"Outside, yes. I'll do as you say." A large window sat at the end of the hall. Thera walked to it. The window had a fire escape outside, but it was also wired to sound an alarm if opened. A small sign in Arabic and English warned of this; Thera pointed to the sign and tried to explain.

The Russian didn't buy it. He yelled at her, pointed the gun at her head, and opened the window himself. As the alarm began to sound, he cursed and threw her out onto the grate, quickly following.

31

CIA BUILDING 24-442, VIRGINIA

Corrigan hated this part of an operation. He had literally a world's worth of information at his fingertips—feeds from the Global Hawk and the U-2, near real-time transcripts of intercepted transmissions from the EC-130E, the First Team's radio chatter from the scene—but it served mostly to remind him how far removed from everything he was. All he could do was sit and watch.

He rubbed his eyes, staring at the screen. He had a large map of Latakia open on the desk to help him keep a visual image of the operation in his head. Van Buren and the Special Operations forces were at the airport several miles southwest of the city. They had just radioed in that they had control of the airplane Khazaal was going to use to get back to Iraq. The police and army were responding to the castle and several sites within the city. A contingent was moving to shut off the port, but so far forces had not been sent to the airport. The security there had not been notified, thanks not only to the jamming by the EC-130 but a selective cutting of the lines by Van Buren's people.

Thera and Monsoon were on the south side of the city, searching the hotel where the Russian had been staying. Ferguson and Guns were at the northern outskirts of Latakia, waiting for the convoy that was heading down the highway from the north. Ferg suspected that it would bypass the city and head straight to the airport. He and Guns were still on their bikes but had a car stashed not too far away that they could use if necessary. Rankin and Grumpy were north of the castle on bikes. In a few minutes they would move down to check it out if they could.

"Something's going on with Thera," said Thomas, the First Team analyst who'd come down to the Cube to help monitor the data. He was sitting in the second row of temporary desks to Corrigan's left. "Listen in to channel two."

Corrigan hit the preset, which isolated on her microphone. "I don't hear anything."

"Yes," said Thomas. "Don't you think that's very odd?"

Corrigan looked at the analyst, then hit Ferguson's preset on the communications panel.

"Ferg, I think we have a problem."

LATAKIA

"Five million dollars is a very large sum." Coldwell pushed the drink that had been set down away. She had not ordered it, but she was glad now to have a prop. "Two million dollars."

"Considering the capabilities of the missile, it is quite cheap," said Birk. "Five million dollars—the weapon cost more than five times that to make."

"The price includes the associated systems?"

"Enough systems to launch the weapon, yes." Birk forced himself to smile. He did not like the way she said that. Clearly she had been coached, but that was to be expected, surely.

Not by Ferguson, he thought. Ferguson would simply have handled this himself.

Who then? He had to be careful whom he sold to. Or rather, he had to make sure the price was commensurate with the risk. Five million was a handsome payoff, but was it handsome enough?

As long as the target was not Israeli, he thought, he would be safe. The Europeans and Russians were so inept that they would have trouble even discovering what hit them, let alone mounting any sort of revenge. The Arabs were more or less the same. The Americans were capable of being nasty but were slow and clumsy, as Ferguson proved. Besides, the woman had hinted that the target was Arab, which suited Birk just fine.

He would travel for a while in any event. Perhaps he would retire. With a good sale here, he could.

Try his luck in Asia in a year or two? Get rid of his family relations, find a nice native woman to see to his needs?

Why not?

"Five million is too much," said Coldwell. "Two million."

"Ah well," said Birk, leaning back. It was so easy to tell when amateurs were bluffing.

"I simply don't have five million," said Coldwell. "Two million."

"Two million?" Birk hesitated a long moment. Two million was a fair price on the present market, but should he settle for a fair price? In truth, prices were depressed right now, especially for large pieces of hardware. In the old days (two or three years ago), a missile like this might fetch five million easily.

But Birk was not one for nostalgia.

"Two. Done."

Coldwell had been prepared to go higher—Ravid said three—but the secret to a good negotiation was to make the other person think he had won. "Very well," she said. "If we can work out the arrangements."

"What arrangements?" said Birk.

"The turnover, and I will need technical information."

Birk shrugged. He hated these riders in the end game. Always there would be some chiseling down the line: ten thousand dollars for missing wires, one hundred thousand dollars to compensate for an antiquated GPS system. "I'm sure we can work the details out."

"Very well." Coldwell rose.

"Where are you going?"

"I'll contact you when I'm ready to take delivery."

"Wait, now," said Birk. For a moment he feared he had been set up and would be arrested.

"I must make other arrangements. I'll be in touch."

"Hold it now, please," said Birk. He realized that his voice had nearly cracked and smiled at himself. This was either part of her negotiating tactics or just the by-product of her being a naïf. Either way, there was no reason to panic. Certainly not.

Coldwell stared at Birk. He didn't trust her, but that was to be expected. She didn't trust him. It was the basis of their relationship.

The one person she did trust was Ravid. She hadn't until he told her why he wanted to destroy the Muslim holy city. There was no emotion in his voice when he told her of the death of his wife and child; his tone had been flat and unaffected. That was how she knew he spoke the truth. She didn't even hold his attack against him; it was to be expected in his position.

"Who are you working with?" Birk asked.

"I'm not at liberty to say. I'll be in touch."

"Tell me that it's not Khazaal."

She shook her head.

"An Arab?" Birk asked.

"I can't say."

But he saw it in her face: not an Arab. "You'll be in touch?"

"Yes."

"Yes, be in touch," said Birk expansively. "Have some champagne before you go."

"Another time," said Coldwell.

BAGHDAD

"This brandy is very good."

"I'm sure," Corrine told Bellows. "But, really, I can't."

"Still on duty?" The ambassador put the snifter down, and went over to the chair. "It is after ten."

"The president's counsel is always on duty."

"McCarthy runs everybody ragged, I hear."

"I wouldn't say that. He has high standards."

Bellows swirled his glass gently, then took a sip, savoring the liquor. "So tell me, Corrine. Why exactly did he send you?"

"To take a snapshot of the Middle East before the president arrives."

"The State Department has a regular advance team for that."

"The president likes a personal touch."

Bellows nodded but added, "There's a rumor that you work for the CIA."

"Well, there's a rumor I'd like to encourage." Corrine laughed. "I hope you've helped spread it."

"Well, I did think it was preposterous."

"I don't think it's *preposterous*," said Corrine. "I think I'd make a very good spy."

"You would, you would." He took another sip. "But, seriously, why are you here? You've been traveling throughout the Middle East. It's not because of the trade legislation. That's clear."

"The trade legislation is part of it," said Corrine.

"The initiative between Israel and the Palestinians?" asked Bellows. If that were the case, he thought, she was in way over her head. Corrine was a good girl but young, and certainly unschooled in the nuances of diplomacy, let alone the Middle East. Not that he would tell her that.

"I'm just familiarizing myself with the area," said Corrine. "It's been quite a while since I was in Israel and Egypt. And I've never been to Iraq. Or to Syria, which turned out to be a much more beautiful country than I had realized."

"It's rumored that the president is going to appoint someone to shepherd his peace plan for the Palestinians and the Israelis," said Bellows, deciding to cut to the chase. There was no reason not to be forward with her; she was his friend's daughter, practically his niece. If she could help, she surely would. "Am I in the running?"

"Would I know?"

"Would you?"

"Well, I guess if I were a spy, I might."

Bellows was a veteran of several administrations, democratic as well as republican, and he knew a prevarication when he heard one.

"I do want the job. I would take it if you're here to offer it," he said.

"I'm not."

"Will you recommend me?"

"You're an old family friend. You don't think the president would take a recommendation with a grain of salt? Or a barrelful?"

"Iraq has turned the corner," said Bellows, reprising a speech he'd given on their tour after she arrived. "The country is stable. It's an example to the Middle East."

"You don't think the resistance is lying low until after the last of our troops are withdrawn?"

"Not at all."

"You can be honest with me."

Bellows put down his drink. "You've seen the city. What do you think?"

"I haven't been here long enough to form an opinion. I'd be more interested in what you think."

"Well, I think Iraq has turned the corner, as I said." Bellows didn't have a real opinion of Iraq. He knew only that the secretary of state believed it was useful to cite progress and that it was therefore useful to him to do the same, especially if he wanted a more important position.

Like peace envoy. And then maybe secretary of state.

The beeper at Corrine's belt began to buzz. Corrigan or someone else on the First Team wanted to talk to her.

"I have to return this call," she told the ambassador. "I'm sorry. I have to go down to the bunker."

"Of course. We'll chat later on."

"I'd like to."

"And you can have some brandy."

"We'll see about that."

34

Rankin and Monsoon were heading back toward the castle when Corrigan called Rankin on the radio.

"Ferguson wants you to head down toward Latakia. We may have a situation with Thera. We've lost contact with her."

"Where's Monsoon?"

"He's outside the building where the Russian was holed up. Thera's inside somewhere."

"I thought the Russian was at the meeting."

"We're working on it. Just get there, OK?"

"Yeah. We're going."

When Monsoon had seen the lights go on in the hotel room, he assumed that it was Thera. But she'd gasped a few seconds later, the sort of sound a person made when they tripped, he thought. From that point on, her radio had been dead.

He went to the side of the building when the fire alarm began to ring, looking for a way to get in. Then he heard someone on the fire escape and saw it was Thera and the Russian.

He slid to the corner of the building and took out his radio unit to dial into the shared team circuit. Before he could, Ferguson buzzed in on the man-to-man line.

"Watchya got goin', Monsoon?"

"Thera's in the Russian's building. He must've been inside. He's got her and taking her up the fire escape. Him or someone else. I couldn't tell."

"Track them. Don't get too close. Tonto and I are two miles away," said Ferguson.

"I don't know if I can get her back without shooting him."

"He's dead as far as I'm concerned," said Ferguson. "Don't hit her, though."

"That's fine." Monsoon slung his AK-47 over his shoulder and ran around to the fire escape, leaping up to pull the ladder down.

Thera moved up the fire escape slowly, partly because she was still disoriented from being slammed against the wall and partly because she thought it would give Monsoon and the others time to catch up. The Russian grumbled and pushed, but, overweight and not in particularly good shape, he stopped every few rungs to catch his breath.

When they reached the sixth floor, Thera felt the rattle on the metal below and realized Monsoon must be following. Now she changed her tactics and began scrambling upward. But the Russian was too close. He reached up and grabbed her ankle, pulling her down. She kicked at him; he punched back.

"Hey!" yelled Monsoon below.

The Russian answered by firing two shots from the CZ52. The slugs clinked off the metal.

Thera scrambled upward, reaching for her pistol beneath the bodice of her dress. Vassenka, huffing, caught up and managed to grab her leg, pulling hard enough to make her lose her grip. She fell against him, clawing but sliding past to the steel deck. The Russian fired blindly at Monsoon below, then started to climb again.

By the time Monsoon reached Thera, she had gotten her gun out and struggled to her feet. Her knee had twisted and a stream of blood was spurting madly from her nose.

"Let's go," she told Monsoon, half hopping and half running for the ladder. "Come on."

"You stay here. Your face is bashed."

"It's just my nose," she said, pulling herself up the ladder ahead of him.

At the airfield, the Delta Team bound the plane's crew members and the fuel truck attendant, then carried them into the nearby field where they would be out of the way. They drove the fuel truck up the ramp area and outfitted it with an explosive device so it could be blown up as a diversion if necessary. Two men pulled on civilian clothes that made them appear to be pilots. By the time they were dressed, two canisters and a delivery system had been connected to the ventilation system. The canisters would deliver a mixture of oxygen and Enflurane into the cabin. Enflurane was a fast-acting general anesthetic used during operations. The mixture would incapacitate everyone in the pressurized cabin within a minute if not less.

After checking the aircraft, Colonel Van Buren trotted over to the support team, huddling with his communications sergeant as he checked in with the group watching the approach. The 737 pilot reported that he was ready to go; he had the engines idling.

"Colonel, we have some contacts here we thought you'd like to know about," said the operator aboard the EC-130E. "We have a pair of Dornier DO 28, liaison/transport types flying very low to the water, offshore on a line to Latakia airport. I'm advised that Israel operates this type of aircraft, designated as the Agur, and uses them for maritime patrol and occasional transport. They have the capacity to land on a short runway and can carry up to fifteen troops, sir."

"Are these aircraft Israeli? Are they heading here?"

"We're not sure," said the controller. "Neither plane has answered radio calls and I'm informed they don't have functional IFF."

The friend-or-foe identity device was essentially a radio beacon declaring who the plane belonged to. The fact that the devices were not operating and their pilots were not talking, strongly suggested that they were Israeli aircraft and that they were on something more serious than a routine training mission.

"Sir, the F-15 escorts have the aircraft in sight and are requesting guidance. They can shoot them down at this time."

"Negative," said Van Buren. He turned to the communications sergeant. "I have to speak to Corrigan, right now."

Ferguson threw down his bicycle in an alley near the hotel. He had his gear, including his MP5, in the large rucksack on his back; he pulled two stun grenades from one of the pouches on the back of the pack but left the submachine gun inside, not sure whether he'd have to go into the hotel or not. Guns was just coming down the block.

"Monsoon? Thera? What's up?" said Ferguson over the radio. He reached to his belt to select their channels; neither answered.

"EC-130 control, are you in contact with Thera?"

"Negative. I have Sergeant Ranaman."

"Monsoon? Ranaman? Where the hell are you?"

Monsoon's out of breath voice responded. "We're on the fire escape. He's getting away."

"Where's Thera?"

"She's here. She's banged up but OK."

"Where's the Russian?"

"He just reached the roof."

"I'm on my way. Don't go up until you hear from me. Don't shoot him if you don't have to."

"But you said—"

"That was then; this is now. Relax. Everybody get on team frequency. This is a sharing time." Ferguson pulled off his rucksack. Guns had just arrived. "I'm going up to the roof," he told him. "Watch the door. We want Vassenka alive if we can get him. We may be able to get him to play with us after Van takes Khazaal. Rankin and Grumpy are on their way."

Guns glanced at the big Glock in Ferguson's hand. "I thought you wanted him alive."

"This is for persuasive purposes only," said Ferguson, sticking it in the belt of his black fatigues. He opened the pack and took out his sawed-off shotgun and a package of plastic bullets. He also grabbed a gas mask, slinging it around his neck but not donning it.

Guns took out the grenade launcher and packed it with a large, nonlethal round, thick enough to stun a horse.

Ferguson trotted to the hotel, lowered his shotgun so that it was at his side, and walked in. The desk person said something to him. Ferguson put up his empty hand, signaling as if to say "one minute," and kept walking.

A bellhop ran up toward the elevator as Ferguson pressed the button. The man looked as if he weighed three hundred pounds and wanted to pound Ferguson into the floor. Ferguson raised the shotgun, which persuaded him that following the stranger into the elevator would be very foolish.

By the time he reached the top floor, Ferg had taken out a flash-bang and removed its pin, holding it in his left hand. The door opened on an empty corridor.

"Monsoon, where are you?" he said into the radio headset.

"We're just under the roof."

"All right. I'm at the stairwell," said Ferguson. "Let me see if I can sneak onto the roof. When I'm ready, you draw his fire. Don't forget: we want him alive if we can take him that way."

"You sure?"

"No, but let's pretend I am."

He reached for the doorknob, turning it slowly with the hand that held the small pin grenade. He pushed into the space, once more throwing himself to the ground, ready to fire; once again there was no one there.

Third time is going to be the charm, he thought, grabbing his night glasses and putting them on awkwardly as he went up the steps to the roof door.

Thera reached through the blouse of the long Arab dress and took two smoke grenades from the webbing sewn inside. As she gave one to Monsoon, the Delta trooper gave her a slight nod.

Something in his face at that moment attracted her. It was hard for her to say later on exactly what it was, but she could always pin it to that look, that one moment.

"Ferg says 'go'," said Monsoon.

They threw the smoke grenades over the top. Monsoon raised his rifle, fired to the side, then ducked.

Ferguson opened the door slowly as soon as Monsoon began to fire. He was facing away from the end of the edge of the roof where Thera and Monsoon were.

He didn't see the Russian.

The smoke spread from the other side as he crawled out. He moved a few feet to the right, then farther, almost to the edge. Still nothing.

"Vassenka! Listen to me," he yelled in Russian. "Listen, I'm here to make you a deal. We're not the Syrians. We want to do the deal with you. One hand washes the other."

There was no answer. Ferguson told him again in Russian that he wanted to make a deal and that they would pay him twice what the Iraqis were willing to spend.

"I have references," he added. "Good ones."

Still no answer.

"A deal?" he said in English.

Silence.

"Monsoon?" said Ferguson.

"We're on the roof. Don't see him."

"All right, be careful. This is me, here." He waved his arm.

"We see you."

"Guns, you got anything down there?"

"Negative."

"Keep your eyes open."

Twice Ferguson saw shadows he thought were Vassenka; both times they were nothing. Finally he began looking over the side and found an open window.

"Guns, he's off the roof," said Ferguson. "We're coming down."

Guns stood about twenty feet from the entrance to the hotel in a shadow cast by the light from the front. He saw the doors open and raised his weapon as two women in long black robes with heavy veils came out.

Perfect disguises, he thought.

"Wait," he said in Russian, running after them. "Wait."

The two women turned to see a man with a large gun running after them. One fainted; the other stood frozen in fear. Guns tore the scarf from the head of the one who remained standing, then stooped to pull the veil off the other one, sure he had found Vassenka. He felt a twinge as he reached, a warning. He jerked away, pulled his gun up, almost firing point-blank at the prostrate body. At this range, the force might very well have killed her.

Her, not him. The fabric fell away from the woman's face. It *was* a woman, not Vassenka.

Guns heard footsteps and looked up. Someone was running from the front of the hotel toward a cab that had just stopped to let out a passenger.

"Stop!" he yelled. Guns leveled his weapon to fire, but Vassenka grabbed the man who had just gotten out of the cab and held him as a shield, pulling him into the car. As Guns began to follow, the cab backed up wildly, made a quick U-turn, and began driving in the other direction. In desperation, Guns leveled his grenade launcher and fired. The plastic bullet blew out the back window, but the cab didn't stop.

Corrigan's voice usually hit a higher octave when he was excited, and he was excited now.

"Israeli liaison says he knows of no operation," he told Van Buren.

"Do this," said the colonel calmly. "Tell them that my fighters have two aircraft in their sights. They will shoot them down if they are not Israeli aircraft. Give them their location."

Before Corrigan could acknowledge, the controller in the EC-130 broke into the line. "Colonel, the cars are approaching the gates to the airport. They're a mile away. Very light traffic at the moment. Police still haven't responded your way."

Van Buren turned to the communications sergeant. "Tell the teams the caravans are a mile away."

"Israeli aircraft have turned into an orbit," added the controller. "Some sort of holding pattern just offshore. In Syrian airspace, but apparently undetected by the radar. No radio signals from them that we can detect."

"I have Ms. Alston on the line," said Corrigan.

"Corrine, the Israelis—"

"I heard. Jack, put me through to the liaison."

"Yes, ma'am."

Van Buren heard Corrine tell the Israeli—a duty officer for Mossad—that he had exactly five seconds to acknowledge that the aircraft were his, or they would be shot down as a threat to her operation.

"Yes, ma'am."

"Yes, they're yours?"

"Yes, ma'am."

"Thank you," said Corrine. "Jack, get me Mr. Stein. Colonel, please pass the word that the aircraft are friendly. As long as they don't interfere, they should be permitted to proceed."

"Thank you."

"At the gate," said the controller, referring to the cars.

"Here we go," said Van Buren.

As the words left his mouth, an explosion rocked the western end of the airport near the entrance. It was followed by a larger explosion and then two more. The ground under Van Buren shook as badly as if he were in the middle of a California earthquake.

"What was that?" asked someone on the shared radio channel.

"Our target," said Van Buren, even though he wasn't close enough to see.

ACT V

His kingdom was full of darkness; and they gnawed their tongues for pain.

—Revelation 16:10 (King James Version)

1

"There's been an explosion outside the airport at Latakia," Wu told Corrine from the Cube. "I'm looking at an image of it now. Several vehicles have been destroyed. It looks like there may have been a large truck bomb near the vehicles."

"Was it the convoy we were targeting?"

"I believe so, yes."

"Give me Mr. Corrigan," said Corrine.

"Uh—"

"Now."

The line clicked.

"What's going on?" Corrine demanded.

"We're working it out. We don't know, exactly."

"Did we do this?" said Corrine.

"No."

"Where's Ferguson?"

Corrigan hesitated, but then said that Ferguson and the other members of the First Team who had gone into the city to rescue Thera were still at the hotel.

"They're still there?" Corrine asked.

"I'm trying to figure it out. This is all happening right as we speak and—"

"Connect me to Colonel Van Buren."

"With all due respect—"

"Do it, Jack."

Once again the line clicked. The connection now had a slight buzz of static, and there were background sounds.

"Ms. Alston?" Van Buren sounded subdued.

"What's the situation?"

"All of the vehicles in the caravan were destroyed. Khazaal appears to have been among them. There were no survivors."

"You're sure? This isn't a trick?"

"It isn't a trick. Someone came and checked all of the vehicles."

"It had to be the Israelis," said Corrine.

"Wouldn't be a bad guess," said Van Buren. "The Syrian army has responded from their part of the base, and I've been told by the EC-130 to expect the local police force. We're going to get out. My men are boarding the 737."

"What about Ferguson?" asked Corrine.

"Our contingency called for them to find another way out. I think it would be safer for them to stay away from the airport at this time."

"What happened to those two Israeli planes? Were they involved?"

"The last I checked, they were still offshore. Ma'am, at the moment—"

"Yes, I realize you have a lot to do. Please proceed."

"Thank you."

Corrine leaned back in her seat.

It had to be the Israelis.

Or Ferguson.

Certainly it had been the Israelis: they had aircraft offshore, a deeply covered agent in the city, . . .

So why was she so mad at Ferg?

LATAKIA

"There was an explosion at the airport," Corrigan told Ferguson. "The caravan with Khazaal was targeted. There was at least one bomb, probably several."

"The Israelis," said Ferguson. It was a statement, not a question. He finally understood what Ravid was doing here, what had been going on all around him. It was the sort of puzzle he should have figured out, could have figured out, if only he'd taken a step back.

"Why would they hit Khazaal?" Corrigan asked.

"They didn't. They wanted Meles," Ferguson said. "He hit the Israeli airliner bound for Rome, remember? Just like we were willing to take him if he went along with Khazaal for a ride, they got our guy, too. They're probably going to want to be thanked."

"I don't think Corrine liked it much."

"Tell me about those planes we spotted off the coast. Where are they?" Ferguson shouldered his backpack and picked up his bike. Thera and Monsoon were standing next to him. Guns had grabbed his bike and ridden after the Russian. Ferguson switched the radio to Rankin's direct channel and told him what was going on. "Don't go to the airport. Meet us back at the hotel."

According to Corrigan, the Israeli aircraft had stopped orbiting and were now flying southwestward, back out to sea.

"They were backups in case the bomb missed," Ferguson told him. "We probably messed up their timing. Ravid must have figured out somehow that Meles was going with Khazaal on the airplane. Pretty good work. They must have a bunch of people sprinkled around, enough to spot the caravan and ignite the bomb."

"Why didn't they tell us, Ferg?"

"Maybe they did, and we just didn't understand."

"When?"

Ferguson started to pedal without answering. The most likely scenario, he guessed, was something along these lines: Mossad had been targeting Meles and stumbled across Khazaal. They felt an obligation to tip off their American allies but withheld enough information—which meant just about everything—so they wouldn't jeopardize their own show, which was a takedown of Meles. They tracked Khazaal first, or tried to—the First Team operation probably crossed them up then, too—then came here and got him.

Parnelles had probably been informed or at least given some sort of indication.

And Corrine?

Corrine had probably told him everything they had told her. Whether she should have been able to read more into it or not was another question.

He rode up toward Souria, where the taxi had stopped. Guns was waiting; the Russian was long gone.

The driver and the man he'd grabbed were not. Both had rather large bullet holes in their heads.

"I lost him, Ferg. I'm sorry," said Guns.

"It's all right." Ferguson unzipped his backpack and fished out the small attaché case. "Take this back to our hotel," he told Thera and Monsoon, who'd ridden up behind him. "Guns and I are going to ride up to the train station on the traffic circle. We'll meet you in the room. Be ready to rock. You can pack the nonlethal stuff away."

Ferguson handed the briefcase with the gems to Thera but didn't let go.

"Give us exactly two hours," he told her. "You don't hear from us, you leave. The blue boat at the Versailles Marina is ours. You go fifty miles due west, exactly due west, and there'll be a cruiser waiting for you. That's our lifeboat. Corrigan knows. You got it?"

"Two hours," she said. "Blue boat."

He could tell from the way she was looking at him that she wouldn't go. He turned to Monsoon. "Two hours. You got me?"

"Yes, sir."

"You drag her if you have to." He turned back to Thera. "If something goes wrong and you don't leave, I'm going to personally smack that pretty cheek of yours, you got it?"

"Suck an egg," she said, grabbing the briefcase away.

3

CIA BUILDING 24-442, VIRGINIA

Thomas replayed the Global Hawk imagery at his workstation several times, watching again and again the destruction of the caravan. He was not so much interested in the event itself, a rather conventional, if spectacular, remote detonation of very large bombs in tractor-trailers parked along the road leading to the airport gate. What fascinated him, even unnerved him a little, was the fact that the Mossad operation had proceeded in parallel to the First Team's without being detected.

In retrospect there would certainly be plenty of clues. They had practically tripped over it several times: Ravid, the airplanes. But they'd been so intent on their own operation that they hadn't seen what was in front of their faces.

It was not, he reasoned, a bad thing from their point of view: while politically it would have been better to capture Khazaal and put him on trial, the ultimate goal was to eliminate him as a threat. And he had been eliminated.

But was there more to the picture now that they weren't seeing?

The Russian hadn't been at the meeting. Had he not been invited? Had his deal already been set?

Corrigan, who'd been standing over his shoulder for several minutes, became exasperated that he couldn't get the analyst's attention. "Thomas!" he said, practically screaming.

"More important, what was the deal supposed to be?" said Thomas, finishing his thought out loud.

"What are you talking about?"

"Why wasn't the Russian at the castle?"

"Maybe he was due later. Listen, there are going to be all sorts of questions about the attack on the caravan. I need you—"

"Too busy," said Thomas, waving his hand.

"What?"

"I have to go check something."

He turned and left the area on a run. Corrigan shook his head, once more ruing the day he had recommended the eccentric for his job.

LATAKIA

Vassenka wasn't at the train station, or anywhere nearby. Ferguson decided it wasn't worth spending any more time at the moment looking for him. As they rode back to the hotel, Guns berated himself for letting the Russian get away, angry that he had gone after the women rather than hanging back and waiting.

"Could've been a brilliant guess," offered Ferguson. "And you could've ended up like the taxi driver."

"Nah."

"Even marines don't win every battle," said Ferguson.

"Yeah."

"I can hum a few bars of 'Halls of Montezuma' if it'll make you feel any better."

Guns laughed, but it was a forced laugh, and Ferguson gave up trying to cheer him up.

By the time they got back to the hotel, Rankin and the others had gotten an update from Corrigan. Van Buren and the assault team had taken off, successfully eluding the Syrian authorities. Intercepts from the EC-130, still orbiting offshore, indicated that the Syrians' preliminary guess was that the Israelis were responsible. There had been as yet no mention of the incident on Syrian TV, which was not unusual; the media was government controlled.

Not knowing what to expect, Rankin had stacked guns and ammo on the coffee table. The rest of their gear was packed and ready for express departure. Thera, sitting cross-legged on the floor, back against the wall, monitored the video flies that were covering the lobby and street.

Ferguson changed from his black fatigues into Western-style civilian clothes, then sat down in one of the chairs in the common room, considering what to do. The odds heavily favored checking out now; the police were sure to come down on every foreigner in town. But the fact that Vassenka hadn't been at the meeting interested him.

Had he been late for his date? Or was Khazaal supposed to pick him up on the way from the castle?

Or was he not involved at all?

That seemed like far too much of a coincidence.

Meles was planning something big; he was a big kind of guy. Did the fact that he was working with Khazaal mean he was going to help Khazaal in Iraq, or did Khazaal have something to help him elsewhere?

If it weren't for the jewels, Ferguson would have figured it like this: Khazaal had several old Scuds and wanted to get the best deal he could for them. He hooked up with Meles. Vassenka would be brought in to fix them up once the deal was completed. The fact that he was already in town meant they wanted to move pretty quickly.

That scenario made sense, except for the jewels. Vassenka would be expensive, but three million bucks was more than he was worth.

Unless they were meant to buy something else as well. Like a few of the missiles Birk was selling.

Birk had claimed there was only one.

"Hey, Ferg. You know that Israeli undercover agent, Aaron Ravid?" said Rankin. "He's walking on the street outside about twenty yards from the hotel entrance, staggering around. Looks like he's been shot."

BAGHDAD

Corrine placed a call through to the White House to alert the president to the situation. She reached Jess Northrup, the assistant chief of staff, whose main mission in life was to keep the president from falling more than a half hour behind his daily schedule.

He hadn't succeeded yet.

"I'm afraid I have bad news," she told Northrup. "I have to talk to the president personally."

"All right."

When the president came on the line, Corrine plunged into the situation, telling him everything she knew. Uncharacteristically, he didn't interrupt her.

"Well, now, Miss Alston, I would say that this is less than optimum," he said when she was finally done. "Reminds me of a bear harvesting a cornfield: not practical or pretty."

"No, sir."

"Although I suppose there is *something* to be said for the fact that the individuals in those vehicles will not have to be dealt with again. I suppose that, down the line, we may even think that Israel did us a *favah*. But that would be *fah* down the line."

"Yes, sir."

"Does the State Department know?"

"We've informed them."

"Very well. Let us move on," said McCarthy. "Get the rest of your people out of danger. I will see you in Baghdad Tuesday, will I not?"

"Yes, sir. I'll be here."

"Very good, then, Miss Alston. Keep me informed."

6

LATAKIA

Ferguson took a step out from the shadow as the man staggered past him, touching him lightly on the shoulder and then backing away. It was definitely Ravid, and the Israeli looked very much the worse for wear: he was bleeding from the forehead; the side of his face looked battered; and a patch of black blood stood out on his shirt beneath his jacket.

"What the hell are you doing here?" Ferguson asked him.

Ravid tried to focus. "You're an American."

"Yeah, cut the bull. I know you're Mossad. One of my people saw you in Tel Aviv."

"I don't know what you mean."

"I'm not in a mood to play games tonight," Ferguson told him. "For one thing, you guys just blew my operation. And for another it's past my bedtime."

"Police—"

"You don't want the police."

Rankin had circled around the block from the other direction. He raised Ferguson's shotgun and steadied it against Ravid's head.

"I could take that gun from your man," said Ravid.

"Then I'd have to kill you," said Ferguson.

"It's clear, Ferg," said Guns over the radio. He and Monsoon had checked the area to see if Ravid was followed. "Nothing, not even a wino or a cat."

"All right. We're going to take him upstairs. After we check him for bugs and see if this is blood or catsup."

Ravid's wounds were minor but real, scrapes that could have been from shrapnel or simply falling down, said Rankin. He wouldn't say how he got them.

"Why did you guys take down Meles Abaa without telling us what was going on?" Thera asked. "We could have helped."

Ravid looked at her as if she'd suggested the earth was flat.

"The real question is, why'd you come here?" Ferguson asked.

"I didn't."

Ferguson would have sooner believed that pigs could fly than that Ravid had simply wandered by. But there was no sense arguing with him; he was good enough that he wouldn't say anything he didn't want to.

"Go inside and lay down," Ferguson told him.

"I want to leave."

"Yeah, I know. Inside." Ferguson thumbed at the bedroom; Ravid got up reluctantly and went in.

"Hell of a coincidence him showing up here," said Rankin.

"Ya think?" Ferguson snorted.

"Maybe those aircraft we intercepted were supposed to take him out."

Ferguson shrugged. He doubted it. And if they were, the Israelis would have had a backup, and a backup for the backup.

"Hey, Ferg, you better take a look at the feed from the video bug you planted in the lobby," said Monsoon, who'd taken the watch. "Two plain-clothes guys and a squad of soldiers just walked in the front door."

Some people choose hotels because of the room service; others look for marble bathrooms and king-sized beds. For Bob Ferguson, multiple escape routes were the deciding factor. He sent Thera, Guns, and Rankin to the stairway, telling them to go to the roof and cross over two buildings before descending to an alley that ran to the next street over, where the team's safe car had been parked. He and the others, with Ravid, took the elevator to the next floor down, where Ferguson jammed it so it couldn't close. They went to the backup room, where the windows overlooked the side alley.

Ferguson tied a rope to the leg of the coffee table, opened the window, and threw it down.

"Monsoon, you go first. There should be a Dumpster down there. If it looks soft enough, we'll throw Ravid here down."

"I can climb," said the Israeli.

"Come on, let's go. The Syrians are used to chasing people. They're pretty good at it."

The Dumpster was there, which meant it was only a two-story climb. Ferguson sent Grumpy down next.

"What's your game?" Ferguson asked Ravid.

"I'm not playing a game."

"Can you climb, or should I throw you?"

"Climb."

Ferguson watched him go down. Then he went and unhooked the rope, deciding they would do better not to leave any telltale signs of their departure.

Ferguson glanced down into the alley, where the others were waiting, then pulled out his sat phone and called Corrigan.

"Ferg, why are you using the phone? Is there a problem with the radio?"

"I don't know. Ravid showed up at the hotel. The Syrian police just came in, and they look like they're looking for him."

"Aaron Ravid?"

"Yeah. Maybe you better see if *Ms.* Alston can ask Tel Aviv to figure it out for us. In the meantime, I'm going to assume he's just too proud to ask for help and take him out with us."

"You think that's what it is? He needs a bailout?"

"I really doubt it."

It was possible, of course. Maybe Ravid had been close to the airport when the bombs went off, expecting the planes offshore to pick him up there. Now he was desperate to get away.

Maybe.

"What are you guys doing?" asked Corrigan.

"Right now I'm jumping into a pile of garbage," Ferguson said, dropping his backpack down into the Dumpster. "I'll get back to you."

When Ferguson got down, he found Monsoon and Grumpy but not Ravid.

"Where's the Israeli?" he demanded.

Monsoon turned just as Ravid came out from around the corner, where he'd relieved himself. "Nature," said the Mossad agent.

"Don't let him out of your sight again," Ferguson told the others. "Not even for 'nature.' Let's go."

R ankin led Guns and Thera across the block to a car he and Fouad had rented.

"Everybody stand back," he told them, kneeling down next to the driver's side and feeling underneath for the magnetic box that held the key.

"You think it's booby-trapped?" asked Guns as Rankin rose with the key.

Rankin didn't answer, just glanced to make sure they were back far enough. He didn't think it was booby-trapped and hadn't seen any signs that it had been tampered with when he checked it before the night's operation, but you never knew.

After he got it started, he rolled down the windows and opened the other doors; you never knew. He'd seen a car in Iraq that had been set up to go off only when the rear passenger door was opened. Two Americans had driven around in it for days before the bomb was discovered. SOBs were journalists, and they bugged out the next day.

It was four a.m. and the streets were deserted. They headed in the direction of the Côte d'Azure de Cham, a well-known tourist hotel on Blue Beach or Shaati al-Azraq. Two truckloads of soldiers had cordoned off Palestine Square, and all the traffic that ran near it. They ducked it by going up one of the side streets. Figuring that there would be more patrols on the main roads in the middle of town, they crisscrossed their way toward the western part of the city. But this strategy could only get them so far. To get to the beach they had to get on the highway, where they were sure to run into another roadblock. Even though their papers were in order, they couldn't take the chance of bluffing their way past tonight. The soldiers would be under orders to apprehend any foreigner they saw.

Or shoot them.

"Easiest thing to do is take a boat," said Guns when they stopped to discuss it. "We can grab one near the water. It's either that or walk up the railroad tracks."

"Tracks are safer," said Rankin.

"It's ten kilometers," said Guns.

"It's not that far."

"I think we ought to steal a boat," said Thera. "It might come in handy later on."

"If we're in a boat, we have no place to hide from a patrol. The Syrians have a navy. They'll be running up and down the coast."

"It's a risk," said Guns. "But so's walkin'."

"I say we walk." Rankin got out of the car, reaching into the back and taking his pack.

Thera and Guns looked at each other. "I think he's just tired," said Guns.

"He's going to be even more tired when we get up there."

Ferguson planned to go south along the main road, cut across the railroad tracks, and then go down the beach about a half mile to an old jetty, where a small rigid-sided inflatable boat had been stowed as part of their emergency escape package. But as they reached the tracks he heard a train whistle and got a much better idea.

"Here comes our ride, boys," he yelled to Monsoon and Grumpy. "Got your tickets?"

"We need tickets?" said Grumpy, his timing so perfect it sounded rehearsed.

"I can tell you're a marine. Ravid, you're with me." Ferguson pointed to a spot to their right. "He'll come around the bend down to our left and start up the hill here. It's not too steep, but it should slow him down. Don't lose your packs. If we get split up, drop off up near the hotel, Côte d'Azure de Cham."

"How will we know it?"

"It's the first big building you're going to see once we're out of town. Big building," Ferg told him. "Come on. We have to cross the tracks so we won't be seen from the road."

The train was loaded with empty automobile carriers and going faster than he'd thought, but not so fast that they couldn't jump it. They spread out and Monsoon went first, followed by Grumpy, who pulled himself up against one of the support beams.

"Let's go Ravid," yelled Ferguson, pulling the Israeli agent up from his crouch.

"I don't know if I can."

Ferguson gave him another push. Ravid picked up his speed, swung his hand tentatively, then finally grabbed on to the ladder at the rear of one of the cars. Ferguson waited until he was sure he was on, then turned and grabbed hold of the ladder of the next car. He swung his feet up, hung off for a moment, then flattened against the train as it headed under a highway overpass.

The train swung out toward the Mediterranean, then banked back inland. There were troops posted at several of the road intersections as they passed, and others down by the river.

Ferguson worked his way over to Ravid.

"How far?" asked Ravid.

"Six or seven miles," said Ferguson. "Be there in no time. How'd you know where to find us?"

"I didn't."

"Why didn't you guys tell us you were after Meles? We could've helped."

Ravid said nothing. He had narrowed everything down to the space immediately in front of his eyes; he knew nothing beyond that. For the next twenty-four hours—for eternity if he had to—he would focus only on that space.

"You come to me so I can drag your butt out of here in one piece, and you're going to be ungrateful?" said Ferguson.

"I didn't come to you for anything."

"Jump off the train then."

Ravid stared at him, but made no move to get off.

A n old Russian army truck sat near the front of the hotel when Ferguson got there, but he couldn't see any soldiers.

That didn't mean some weren't around, but he guessed that if there had been a decent-sized contingent they would have at least set up a checkpoint in and out of the hotel and probably stopped traffic through the local tourist area as well. Not that there was much traffic at five o'clock in the morning.

Ferg didn't see Rankin's car in the parking lot. He left the others outside and went into the building through a service entrance near the back. Walking through the back hall, he checked the stairwells and then came out into the lobby as if he were a guest on his way out to a morning appointment. On the way out he spotted a soldier who'd presumably come with the truck sipping from a ceramic coffee cup and chatting with the nightman at the desk.

The car still hadn't shown up. Ferguson walked to the side of the building and pulled out his sat phone to check in with the Cube. Instead of Corrigan he got Lauren.

"Hey, beautiful, what happened?" he asked her. "Corrigan had a date?"

"No, he went down to talk to Slott at Langley. The Mossad connection has everybody torqued."

"Yeah, I'm pretty torqued myself." He glanced at his watch. "How's the Dayliner doing?"

"We can pick you up within a half hour. Just say when."

"You know where Rankin is?"

"He just checked in. They're two kilometers from the hotel."

"Are they crawling?"

"They ran into trouble with patrols. They walked up the train tracks."

"Skippy." Ferguson shook his head. Rankin was dependable, extremely good with his hands, and a dead shot but very cautious. Ferg glanced at his watch. "All right. Let's say six-thirty on the pickup. Get me a room somewhere, will you?"

"A room?"

"Yeah, I've never been much for sleeping on the beach."

"Slott wants you out. Corrine, too."

"Uh-huh. You know what? Make it the Versailles. I like the view from their beach."

"What's going on, Ferg?"

"I'll tell you when I figure it out."

Ferguson found the others sitting on rocks near the water, looking very much like day laborers waiting for the start of work. He told them that their boat was on its way, then went down to the sea, where he dipped his hand into the surf and used it to down his pills. The tang of the salt felt good and he splashed some over his face and hair.

"Stuff'll kill you," said Monsoon.

"If I'm lucky," said Ferg.

"You want me to go find Rankin?"

"Nah, they'll find their way. How's our guest?"

"He wants to leave," Monsoon said, thumbing toward Ravid. "I told him not to while you were gone. I promised to break his legs if he did."

"A promise is a promise," said Ferguson. "Maybe we'll get lucky, and you'll get to keep it."

He climbed up the shoreline to where Ravid was sitting. The Israeli narrowed his eyes as he approached, watching him the way a hawk might focus on a mouse in a field before pouncing.

"What's your story?" asked Ferguson. "You don't want to be rescued?"

"I haven't been rescued. I told you, I didn't want to go with you."

"There's a Syrian inside having a cup of coffee. You want me to turn you over to them?"

Ravid didn't even bother answering. He stared ahead, intent on his course.

"How'd you know where we were?" asked Ferguson.

"I didn't."

"We'll save you anyway. You don't even say thank you."

Rankin, Guns, and Thera appeared a short time later, directed by Lauren to their location. Ferguson told them to keep an eye on Ravid after the pickup.

"You sure he's really Mossad?" asked Rankin. "Maybe he works both sides."

"A possibility," said Ferguson, though he doubted it. "I put a locator tag on him when we cleaned him up. If he really wants to run, let him go."

"Figures. They screw us, and we save their butts," said Rankin.

"Way of the world, Skippy. Way of the world."

7

CIA HEADQUARTERS, VIRGINIA

Corrigan had just started to explain what had happened for the second time when the phone behind Slott's desk rang. The deputy director for operations of the CIA guessed it was his opposite number at Mossad returning his call.

"This will be Adam," Slott told Corrigan. He reached over and picked up the phone. The CIA telephone operator confirmed that indeed Adam Rosenfeld was on the line. "Put him through," Slott said.

Corrigan, unsure of the protocol, started to get up.

"No, no, stay," Slott told him. "This won't take long." Slott wanted Corrigan to hear his end of it to emphasize that he fought for his people, even if he had been effectively angled out of First Team operations.

"Adam, what the hell were you doing in Syria? Excuse my French," said Slott as soon as the other man came on the line.

"I might ask the same question."

"We alerted you to our interests. You should have done the same."

"We made it possible for you to pursue your interests," said the Mossad official.

"Oh, don't give me that. And don't trot out your luncheon speech about living in a complicated world either."

Corrigan stared at his hands as Slott scolded his opposite number in Israel, claiming that the Mossad operation had not only sabotaged a delicate mission by the U.S., but had put the lives of his people in danger. Corrigan had joined the CIA only a year before, coming over specifically to work in the newly created job of "desk coordinator" for First Team operations. It was a jack-of-all trades job, running interference for the First Team in the field, helping coordinate missions, and arranging support. As originally conceived, the real power rested with the field officer in charge of the mission, who had almost unlimited authority once given an assignment. The missions were supposed to flow directly from a finding signed by the president. In the last administration, the findings had consisted of language so brief and open-ended that Corrigan had been shocked by the first one he saw: *Recover illegal arms.*

No location, no time frame, nothing but those three words.

President McCarthy had gradually asserted more control, first by more narrowly defining the missions and, within the last few months, inserting Corrine Alston as the conscience and de facto boss of Special Demands. Slott hadn't quite recovered; part of his frustration now was being expressed indirectly in his conversation with Rosenfeld.

"We have one of your people with us," Slott told Rosenfeld, changing his tone to make the information seem almost incidental, though it was anything but. Bailing Ravid out—which was the only possible interpretation of what had happened, Slott believed—was a four-aces hand in the unspoken competition between the agencies. "Aaron Ravid. Or Fazel al-Qiam, as he's known. We'll take him to Cyprus. I don't expect you to acknowledge him," added Slott. "But you may want to make arrangements."

Rosenfeld didn't reply.

"I'm still not happy," Slott said, realizing he was rubbing it in. He hung up, feeling vaguely unsatisfied.

A statue of a gargoyle sat in the corner of his desk, a Father's Day gift from one of his sons after a visit to Notre Dame in Paris, where they'd admired the gargoyles in the heights. The boy had been fifteen at the time; now he was thirty, married, with a boy of his own.

Monsters in the shadows of the wall.

Gargoyles were common in medieval cathedrals, but according to the guide who'd led them on the tour that day, no one was actually sure why. There were many theories on what they were: devils denied access to the holy church, old gods, tokens to frighten demons away. It wasn't even clear that the men who had carved and put them there knew exactly why they were doing so.

"There's got to be a lot more here than they're telling us," offered Corrigan.

"That goes without saying." Slott picked up the phone. "I have to relay this to Parnelles. If you'd stretch your legs for a minute, I'd appreciate it."

8

LATAKIA

After the boat picked up the others, Ferguson went to the hotel to use the shuttle bus into town. Along the way he changed the jacket he was wearing for a longer coat he found hanging in a men's room. In the lobby, he appropriated a cap. He didn't look Syrian at all, but he could have been a Turk or Greek worker, and the policeman standing near the shuttle didn't stop him. The ride down to town took less than a half hour. The checkpoints had been removed already.

The most logical place for the Russian to hide, Ferguson thought, would be the mosque, and so he made his way back there on foot from the center of town. But when he got to the block, he found it cordoned off, with a large contingent of soldiers on the street outside the wall. A few attempts to ask passers-by what was going on drew nothing but shrugs.

Ferguson walked back over to the hotel they had escaped from the night before. He didn't go in; instead, he tried to figure out where Ravid had been before he passed by. It didn't make sense that he had walked from the airport—the field was twenty-five kilometers or so from town—but clearly he hadn't just materialized on the street either. The immediate area was mostly devoted to business; the residential section that began a few blocks away was solidly middle class. A bus line ran nearby, but there had been no buses at that hour of the night. No cars in the vicinity of the hotel bore any obvious signs of having been close to an explosion.

If Ravid hadn't come there specifically to find them—by far the most logical explanation—then either he had been nearby to see someone or he had been dropped off by another agent as they escaped from the Syrians. Ferguson couldn't rule either possibility out; he spent a frustrating hour wandering around before putting the quandary on hold and having a late breakfast. His clothing—and unshowered stench—drew some stares, and so his next stop was a nearby secondhand shop, where the proprietor was quite surprised to see the raggedy patron pull out a thick wad of cash to expedite the sale. Using his Irish passport, Ferguson then rented a car—the double take was milder here—and went up to the Versailles. It was still before check-in, but the man at the desk clearly preferred having him upstairs rather than in the lobby. He showered and after changing into his new clothes did a little additional shopping at the hotel mall.

Among his purchases were a pair of swim trunks and a snorkeling set, which he tested off the Versailles beach, far off the beach. So far, in fact, that he finally had to pull himself up on the side of the nearest boat he could find. Which not so coincidentally happened to be the *Sharia*, Birk's yacht.

"Greetings," he said to the two guards, who responded by leveling their submachine guns at him. "I was in the neighborhood, so I thought I'd say hello."

The men were not particularly amused. Fortunately, Birk was sunning himself on the rear deck, smoking a fat Cuban cohiba.

"One of these days, Ferguson, you're going to push things much too far. Much, much too far," said the arms dealer, looking over from his chair. "Let him go."

"Can I get a towel?" Ferguson pulled off his gear and sat in the empty seat across from Birk. He declined the offer of a cigar.

"They don't make them as well as they used to," complained Birk. "Standards have slipped since Castro got worried about lung cancer. Something to drink?"

"Water would be nice."

"A bottle of Pellegrino for our guest," Birk said. His brother-in-law scowled but went below to fetch it.

"I notice you hired a few new guards," said Ferguson.

"Rough neighborhood. Why did you blow up Khazaal?"

"I didn't. The Israelis did. They wanted Meles, and he happened to be nearby."

"I might believe that," said Birk. "But no one else will."

"Did you pay the men for the trouble I caused?" said Ferguson as Brother-in-Law came over with the Pellegrino. He made sure his voice was loud enough for the others to hear.

"I wouldn't cheat my men. Not very good business," said Birk. He signaled that Brother-in-Law should leave them.

"So everyone thinks I killed Khazaal?" asked Ferguson when they were alone.

Birk shrugged. "What other people think, I couldn't say. The Syrians are looking for Jewish spies. But they are always looking for Jewish spies."

"The Syrians weren't in on it, were they?"

"The Syrians and Israelis working together? That would be interesting. Very interesting." Birk didn't laugh.

"Was Khazaal here to sell or buy a Scud?" Ferguson asked.

"Bah. Neither, I would think. Obsolete equipment."

"You're not answering my question."

"Ferguson, truly, if you want junk, talk to Ras."

"You couldn't get me a Scud if I wanted one?"

"I can get you a real missile."

"How would I get a Scud?" Ferguson asked.

Birk sighed. "You wouldn't."

"If I wanted one."

Birk studied his cigar. "I suppose that if you honestly and truly wanted one, it could be had."

"From?"

"The Koreans. You could perhaps purchase a Scud-D SS-1e, seven-hundred-kilometer range. The design is not actually the same as the Russian . . . I'm afraid I don't retain details I'm not interested in."

"Why aren't you interested?"

"No one wants to buy such a missile. The liquid fuel is very difficult to obtain and to handle. The weapon I can get you, much better."

"The Siren?"

"I have another buyer. You'll have to act fast. The price is going up."

Ferguson took this as a ploy and was annoyed. "I want a Scud."

"Perhaps the Iraqis can help you. You should reconsider about the Siren. I have a genuine offer on the table. Five million."

"Right."

"But I would give you a very good deal for old time's sake," said Birk, deciding he would much prefer to sell to the American CIA. "Two million."

"Three times too much."

"Two million is a bargain."

"What happened to one million?"

"One million," repeated Birk. No, he decided; that was too much of a discount.

On the other hand, considering what the Israelis had done . . .

"Perhaps, for old time's sake," said Birk. "Perhaps for a million."

"I need a few more days," said Ferguson.

"Oh," said Birk, genuinely disappointed now. But here was the consolation: he would make four million dollars more, and more than likely the Jews were buying it anyway. Yes, this must be so. They did not fool around the way the Americans did.

"Who's your other buyer?" Ferg asked.

"Oh, there are always buyers."

"Come on, don't try and bluff me," said Ferguson.

"I have other buyers," said Birk. "You will see I am serious, Ferguson."

"Right."

"We'll see then."

"You're not a very good liar, Birk. That's your one flaw as an arms dealer."

"It isn't a flaw; it's a reason to do business with me: I'm honest." Birk once more looked at the tip of his cigar, frowning as if there were something wrong with the gray ash.

"Tell me about Vassenka," said Ferguson.

"Again?"

"Who was he here to meet?"

"I didn't even know he was here," said Birk, protesting a bit. "You told me."

"I'd like you to do me a favor," said Ferguson, taking a swig from the bottle. "I'd like you to pass a message to him. Tell him I'm ready to make that deal."

"To Vassenka? He would never talk to me."

"Sure he would. Professional courtesy."

"No. I doubt this."

"Try. Tell him I'm ready to make that deal."

"He'll know what you're talking about?"

"If he has a good memory. Tell him I can get him out of the country. Vouch for me."

"Why would I do that?"

"Because you're a great guy." Ferguson rose.

"Are you sure he wasn't killed?"

"I know he wasn't killed, and I know you know every Russian in town, even though you hate their guts. Tell him my offer stands. And I'll get him out."

"If you need a Russian—"

"I need that Russian," said Ferguson, pulling on his flippers. "I'll check with you tonight, in your office."

"I'm always there."

9

APPROACHING CYPRUS

Ravid said nothing the whole way to Cyprus, shaking his head and not answering when asked if he wanted anything to drink. He sat alone, walked the deck alone, and in general kept to himself. After watching him for a while, Rankin decided that the Israeli felt humiliated that he'd had to go to the Americans to escape. It was possible that something had gone wrong in the operation, as well: how had he gotten injured? But Rankin decided he wasn't in the mood to question the guy. If he was going to be a jerk and not say anything, well, the hell with him.

Maybe if he'd been in the same position, he'd've kept his mouth shut, too. The boat that had picked them up was a nice-sized yacht, the sort of toy Rankin had seen a lot of in Miami and fancy places like that on vacation. The crew had obviously been briefed to ask no questions. There were bunks below where they could sleep if they wanted; only Thera took the offer. The others sat on the deck, drinking coffee and looking at the view. Except for the reason that they were there, it would have been a hell of a little vacation.

A CIA handler met them at the dock in Cyprus, along with two men in civilian clothes who were actually PMs-in-training, paramilitary CIA employees doing grunt work as part of their initiation rites. Ravid, still not talking, followed along passively and didn't object when the handler—he claimed his name was Paul F. Smith, emphasizing the "F" as if that would make them believe him—said they'd like to debrief him before sending him on his way.

Ravid didn't argue. Smith took them all to a British clinic to be checked out by a doctor. Ravid, the only one among them who was injured, went into the nurse's area to take off his clothes and have his wounds attended to. When the doctor came for him five minutes later, he was gone.

"We can use the tag," said Thera, reaching into her bag for it.

"Waste of time," said Rankin, pointing to Ravid's shirt on the changing bench. The two tags Ferguson had placed on him were there.

10

Thomas stared at the e-mail from Professor Ragguzi, which had come on his "blue computer," a unit used for nonsecure communications with the outside world. (All communications and other use were subject to strict monitoring to make sure security rules weren't violated.)

He had hoped for a response, but could not have guessed that it would be quick. Or so blunt.

You're wrong.

That was it. No explanation, no hedging. Thomas's own e-mail, which he had carefully vetted with two internal security officers and Corrigan, had filled two screens. Without citing any classified information, it made a careful argument calling the Turkey sightings into question, politely wondering if perhaps the professor could clarify.

Thomas felt as if his entire foundation of knowledge of UFOs, carefully built over decades, had been thrown into doubt. If Ragguzi was wrong—worse, if he refused to acknowledge that he *might* be wrong—what could Thomas believe?

The CIA analyst tried to concentrate on his work. He rose and began pacing around his office. He had no sense of what time it might be: somewhere in the morning or afternoon, he thought, though perhaps it was midnight.

How could he be wrong?

If he'd overlooked something, perhaps. That was possible. It had happened in Latakia, surely, since they had missed the Mossad operation completely.

Not completely. They had seen pieces but failed to put it all together.

Thomas sat down at his computer and began rummaging through the various lists he had compiled. Corrigan had asked him questions about Vassenka and his abilities; they'd checked into the Scuds, of course. It was logical because of Iraq, though there seemed no possibility, no possibility whatsoever, of there being any remaining in the country. Or, if there were, they would be in pieces. Worse, they would lack the rocket fuel.

Fuel.

Thomas keyed over to the satellite photo of the city. One of the things that made Latakia unique in Syria, and in the Middle East in general, was its train line.

Exactly the sort of thing that you would need to move rocket fuel.

Thomas pulled his chair closer to his desk. *Wrong*, indeed.

LATAKIA

Ferguson had just gotten back to the beach outside the Versailles when his sat phone rang. He stared at it cross-eyed for a moment, as if he wasn't sure what it was, then pulled open the antenna.

"Talk to me."

"I have a weird Thomas theory," said Corrigan. "Can you talk?"

"Better let me get upstairs," said Ferguson. "I'll call you back."

Fifteen minutes later, Ferguson rested his head against the outside of the bathtub, listening to Corrigan talk about rocket fuel formulations as the room filled with steam, the by-product of an impromptu white noise system, otherwise known as a running shower. Thomas's theory, in a nutshell, was that Vassenka hadn't been hired simply for his expertise; he was supposed to supply the fuel for the Scuds as well. The Americans had looked for the rocket fuel fairly carefully during the occupation, literally checking every tanker and railcar capable of holding it in the country and using special ground-penetrating radar to look for hidden underground tanks. The thorough search didn't mean there wasn't some hiding somewhere, but the stuff was not particularly easy to store. Highly toxic, it ate through metal and could spontaneously catch fire when it came in contact with organic material. Bringing a fresh batch in from outside the country would be the way to go, especially if you had many rockets.

And two or three million dollars' worth of jewels would buy fuel for quite a number.

"The thing is, we can't find a railcar with either red-fuming nitric acid or inhibited red-fuming nitric acid," said Corrigan. Those were the main ingredients in the rocket fuel used by all but the very earliest Scud missiles. "Thomas has gone over every lading notice, shipping document, you name it. He's been all over it."

"I'll bet he has," said Ferguson.

"Is it a false lead?"

"No. It's just not in a railcar."

CYPRUS

The men had to double up, but Thera got her own room at the hotel near the British base. She lay down on the bed in her clothes and fell fast asleep, plunging into a thick unconsciousness that felt like burrowing into the ground beneath the dirt.

Several hours later, she heard the phone ring and ignored it. A few minutes later, someone knocked on her door. She ignored that, too. Then she heard the door open.

She grabbed for the pistol she'd slid under her pillow.

"Hey," said Guns, "it's just me. Ferg needs to talk to you. He's been calling on the sat phone and the room phone."

"Oh." She slid the gun down.

"You leave the safety on when you're sleeping, right?" asked Guns.

"Why would I do that?"

Guns went back to his room. Thera, her eyes burning, sat up on the bed and pulled out her phone. She hit the preset combination for Ferguson, who answered on the first ring.

Not that he said hello.

"You still have that attaché case?" were the first words out of his mouth.

"Yeah." Thera glanced at it. It had fallen on the floor right next to the bed.

"You feel like coming back to Latakia tonight?"

"Tonight?"

"Bring the jewels. Meet me at the Agamemnon, at the bar with the green marble, not in the Barroom. Wear something that will make the mullahs think they've found something better than Paradise."

"Who am I dressing for?"

"Me."

LATAKIA

Ferguson watched her come down the steps, her blue dress clinging to her hips, her hair held up on one side by a jeweled pin that made her look like royalty. He watched her looking for him, admired the way she gazed at the room as if she owned it. And she might have, he thought; more than a few of the men nearby were staring at her. Finally Thera saw him and acknowledged him with the slight upturn of the corner of her mouth: not a real smile, but it was pretty nonetheless.

"I've been looking for you," she said, walking up to him.

"That the most original line you could think of?" Ferguson asked.

"It'll do. What am I drinking?"

"Champagne?"

"What are you drinking?"

"Coffee," said Ferguson. He held up the glass; he convinced the bartender to pour some into a tumbler with ice.

"Could I have a whiskey sour?" she asked the bartender.

"A whiskey sour?"

"I always wanted one."

"Don't fall asleep on me. I'll feel obliged to take advantage of you."

"*Hmmph*." Thera had taken the precaution of downing a "go" pill, prescribed by Agency doctors for situations where a CIA officer had to stay awake no matter what. She wondered if Ferguson did; he didn't seem to have had a chance to get any sleep.

"I see you brought our friends." He pointed to the attaché case.

"You told me to. I was worried I would have to open it up at the door."

"They don't check for weapons here because of all the tourists. It's downstairs where we'll have a problem. I already got us a locker on the other side of the casino. We'll put it there."

"What are we doing downstairs?"

"Going to see Ras. We're a bit early."

"How early?"

"Early enough to finish your drink and tell me what happened with Ravid."

Thera told him what she knew. It was almost word for word what Corrigan had said.

"How's the drink?" Ferguson asked.

"Very sweet. Too sweet."

"I know the feeling. Come on."

Ras had someone with him, but he did his swoon act over Thera as they approached, and the guest was quickly forgotten. After Ferguson ordered his usual Perrier and twist, Ras asked to what he owed the pleasure of basking in Thera's loveliness.

"Mr. IRA has finally decided to buy, perhaps?" he asked.

"Yes, and I want to buy something special," said Ferguson. "Red-fuming nitric acid."

Ras continued to sip his drink.

"What ship captain would bring it in?" Ferg added.

"I don't even know why you would want such an item," said Ras.

Ferguson leaned across the table and smiled. "You want to end up like Khazaal?"

Ras's hand trembled slightly as he put down the glass. "You had something to do with Khazaal? The Syrians told me Mossad was behind it."

Ferguson stared at him.

"It would be very bad business to betray a trust. Very bad business," said Ras.

"Better bad than dead."

Ras sat back, his face pale. "If I wrote down the name of a sea captain, could you find his ship?"

"I don't know," said Ferguson. "Could I?"

Now what?" asked Thera as Ferguson steered her out of the hotel.

"Now we go up to Versailles and meet Vassenka."

"He's going to meet you?"

"Supposedly. Somebody called my room and left some heavy breathing on the machine. I took that to mean he'll be here."

"You gave him your room number?"

"I gave him yours." Ferguson smiled. "I left word with two dozen people that he should contact me. What I'm hoping is that Meles and Khazaal getting stomped on killed his deal."

"What good will he be in that case?"

"We can still find out who he was dealing with and where the Scuds are. We'll have this ship tracked down and find out how much fuel is on it. My guess is that there'll be quite a lot. Which argues for a lot of missiles."

Ferguson called Corrigan with the information from the beach. The Versailles was within walking distance; they made it into the casino with ten minutes to spare. There wasn't a lot of leeway: Ferguson hoped to take the Russian out twelve miles in a small boat and get aboard a helicopter. The helicopter had to come all the way from Turkey, and would only be able to stay on station for about forty-five minutes. The backup plan was to take the boat all the way to Cyprus: not impossible, certainly, but not as convenient nor as quick.

"Are we running late?" Thera asked, noticing he was checking his watch after they took a seat in the lounge above the poker tables.

"We're on time."

Ferguson ordered a Turkish coffee. Thera scanned the room and searched for something to talk about. "Is Rankin always so angry?"

"Somebody took his bottle away when he was a baby and he never got over it."

"Monsoon is nice. Sergeant Ranaman."

"Ranaman, yeah," said Ferguson. "You like him?"

"Yeah, I like him a lot. He's . . ."

Her voice drifted in a way that made it obvious to Ferguson that *like* meant something more than he wanted it to mean. He glanced at her face, turned away from him in profile. The curls came down behind her ear so gracefully, it was as if a painter had placed them there with a brush.

"Yeah, Monsoon's a great guy," said Ferguson, finishing the sentence for her. "Maybe we should have him work with us more. It's hard to get Arabic speakers, good Arabic speakers."

"You got me."

"I rest my case." Ferguson smiled at her and leaned back to survey the room.

An hour later, Vassenka hadn't shown up. Ferguson gave him ten more minutes, then another five, then went to the men's room and called Corrigan. The helicopter had already gone back. They'd arranged for the EC-130E to fly off the coast again; Ferguson wanted an early warning if the Syrian police decided to raid all of the Western hotels. They hadn't heard anything.

"Find my ship?"

"You were right about Tripoli. It was there a few days ago."

"And now?"

"I can't just snap my fingers and get information, Ferg. It's not that easy."

"Let me give you a hint where to look: heading for Iraq."

"Yeah, I know."

"Well, get on it, Jack."

"I am. Say, when do you sleep, anyway?"

Ferguson laughed at him and went back to Thera at the table.

They gave the Russian another half hour. Ferguson decided they would hit some of the other clubs to see if they could drum up some information about him, but first they had to stash the jewels, which Thera had in the case. So they went upstairs to Ferg's room. Thera tapped on the wall of the elevator all the way up.

"You took a 'go' pill, right?" Ferguson asked, waiting for the door to open.

"I was afraid I'd fall asleep. I'm OK, really."

"No driving for you. Come on. I'm down the hall."

The room Lauren had reserved was small, with only a bed and a table too small to spread a napkin. Thera kicked off her shoes and sat back on the bed.

"Is that piece in your hair from in here?" he asked.

"Of course not." Her face turned deep red. "It's glass."

"Don't get offended. I was just asking. It'd be all right if you borrowed it."

"I don't borrow things. I didn't even open the briefcase."

"Why not?" asked Ferguson. He opened the small in-room safe. The case was a little too wide to fit.

"You trust a safe?" Thera asked.

"Of course not. But I've never believed that 'Purloined Letter' stuff. You leave something out; it's gone. The safe will keep the amateurs at bay." He took up the case, set it down, and took out his picks. He opened the case and though he continued to smile at her, he realized immediately something was wrong: there weren't as many jewels, and it struck him that they weren't the same.

He snapped it closed. "Your turn," he told her, as if he'd noticed nothing. He flipped it over to her on the bed. "You open it."

"Why?"

"I want to make sure you can."

"All right."

Ferguson watched as she took the picks. She hadn't had much practice, that was clear, but she didn't act like she was completely incompetent either; she snapped it open in about a minute.

Thera handed it to him.

"I should make you do it again. You're a little slow."

"Are we going to play locksmith or look for Vassenka?"

"Vassenka," said Ferguson. He started scooping the jewels into the safe.

There was definitely a different mix than the last time he'd seen them. Or was it, Ferguson wondered, just that he was tired now and he'd been in a rush then?

The sat phone rang as he closed the door on the safe. "I hope this is room service."

"Ferg, they found Vassenka in a shower in a dump off 14 Ramadan Street," said Corrigan.

"The police raided him while he was taking a shower?"

"No. He reached for a bar of soap and got a grenade instead. He's in pieces."

ACT VI

They are the spirits of Devils, working miracles . . .

—Revelation 16:14 (King James Version)

1

BAGHDAD
THE NEXT MORNING . . .

Abu al Hassan, the new Iraqi prime minister, was about as physically different from Saddam Hussein as possible: tall and thin, bald, with no facial hair and a soft whisper of a voice. The State Department briefing papers presented him as a "dynamic individual" and a "political survivor." But the CIA duty officer Corrine befriended in the communications center rolled his eyes when she asked for his opinion, and Corrine saw why as soon as she met him. Hassan studiously avoided meeting her gaze while they spoke; his answers to even simple questions were so convoluted and hedged that Corrine wondered if the point wasn't to make her forget what she had asked. To a man, his staff's body language made it clear they didn't have any better an opinion of him. He and his government weren't going to survive their first political crisis. A five percent dip in world oil prices—already forecast after the run-up of the past few years—would be enough to upset the country's loan payment schedule and threaten the social and rebuilding programs necessary to keep the economy moving ahead. But it wouldn't take something nearly that severe: if violence stoked up again around Baghdad, if Iran rattled its sabers, if the Kurds complained that their semiautonomous state was too semi and not autonomous enough, the fractious parliament would divide. Hassan, Corrine now realized, had only been chosen because he was such a nonentity the different factions couldn't object. Under any sort of pressure he would wilt.

Not a good situation, she thought as he led her on a tour of the new government building. Corrine made the proper admiring noises as they walked through the building, which was architecturally quite impressive, then left with the ambassador to continue the scheduled tour of a hospital in the city.

"I have to leave Iraq for a day or so," she told Bellows. "Something's come up."

"More important than Iraq?" said Bellows, surprised.

"It's trivial, really," she lied. "But I have to take care of it. Can you drop me off at the embassy?"

The ambassador leaned forward and lowered the window separating them from the driver. He gave him the new instructions but left the window open. As he started to lean back, Corrine gestured toward the window. Bellows trusted his driver a great deal—a former Delta Force bodyguard, the man had been with him for six years, through many different assignments—but he closed the window to make her more comfortable.

Corrine closed it so they could talk.

"What do you think of Hassan?" she asked.

"A very solid man."

"He's a milquetoast."

"Appearances can be deceiving," said the ambassador lightly. "He's very astute politically and very strong."

"Are you telling me that because you think it's what I want to hear? Or because you believe it?"

"I'm not sure how to answer that," said Bellows.

"Is it me? Are you just not taking me seriously?"

"Corrine, of course I take you seriously," said the ambassador, shocked that she thought that. "Why wouldn't I take you seriously?"

"Can Hassan survive a crisis?"

"He's strong. He has a lot of support throughout the country."

Corrine gave up, and they drove back to the embassy in silence. She still hadn't decided whether he was deliberately trying to mislead her or had deluded himself by the time she reached the secure communications center.

"Where've you been?" Ferguson asked her.

"You wouldn't want to know. What's the situation?"

"Vassenka's in the morgue. On the bright side, we found the ship we think has the rocket fuel. It's about twelve hours from Basra."

"Stop it."

"You think so?" said Ferguson, in his familiar mocking tone. "I was toying with the idea of letting it sail into the horizon."

"Bob—"

"It's Ferg. Even my enemies call me Ferg. Rankin and Guns are on their way to give an assist to the navy team that's going to board the ship."

"You think of me as your enemy?"

"Depends on the day. What's with the Israelis?"

"I have a meeting tomorrow with Tischler to iron this out. Parnelles suggested I talk to him in person."

"How is the general?"

"I don't know. Slott passed the message along." Corrine knew Ferguson meant Parnelles, of course, but she wasn't sure why he called him "general." As far as she knew, the CIA director didn't have a military background. But this wasn't the time to ask him about it. "Ferg, I'd like you in Tel Aviv for the meeting."

"Really?"

"Yeah. Don't you think you ought to be?"

"If it fits into my schedule."

"Make sure it does."

He didn't answer.

"The meeting is at nine a.m.," she continued. "You want to meet at the airport, or—"

"I'll meet you at the building. I have some stuff to do."

"So do I." She clicked off the phone, then went upstairs to change into less formal clothes.

OFF THE SYRIAN COAST, NEAR LATAKIA

Judy Coldwell sat with the handbag between her knees, pressing her hands together as the small boat approached the yacht. Her chest began to tremble, and for a moment she feared she was having a heart attack. She closed her eyes and took a long breath, trying to calm herself.

She could do it. She would do it. It was all ridiculously easy. All she had to do was have faith.

Finally the boat drew alongside the yacht. Birk came to the side as she climbed over the ladder, extending his hand and helping her aboard.

"Ms. Perpetua, how are you this early morning? Well, I trust." He positively beamed. "Come. Have some champagne."

"Thank you, no," she said.

"Bottled water, then. Or tea, perhaps tea?"

"Some coffee, maybe."

"Coffee, yes. Of course. Coffee."

Birk led her into the cabin sitting area, where a bottle of Dom Pérignon was on ice. He opened the bottle and poured himself a glass as he ordered one of the bodyguards to make some coffee.

"Do you have the weapon?" said Coldwell.

"Of course," he told her.

"Is it aboard?"

This was one difficulty of dealing with amateurs, thought Birk: they did not understand the protocol. Still, they did overpay.

"It is accessible," said Birk. "That is not a problem."

"Is it aboard? I'm told it's very big."

"The crates that carry it are large, yes," said Birk. "No, it is not on board."

"Where is it?" Coldwell clutched her handbag, fearing that she had been swindled somehow.

"It's not far. Your agents can pick it up as soon as I give the order."

"We must pick it up before I pay."

"You have the money?"

"Jewels."

"Yes, jewels. Forgive me. Do you have them?"

"I will get them as soon as the transaction is completed."

"I'm afraid that is not how it works," said Birk. "You will tell me where they are now. I will retrieve them. Then you will be directed to the missile."

"You don't have it on the ship?"

"It would clutter the deck. Now. Where are the jewels?"

Coldwell opened her bag. For a moment Birk thought she might actually have them with her, but she—or more likely the person she was working for—was not quite so foolish. She handed him a man's wristwatch.

"The alarm screen has the GPS coordinates," she said. "Don't push the mode button more than once, or it will be erased."

Ravid watched through his binoculars as the American woman handed over the watch with the coordinates for the small boat where the jewels had been stashed. It should not be more than a few minutes before Birk's minions had them and cleared the rest of the transaction.

The gems were the real ones Khazaal had brought to Syria. Birk would never have been fooled with the fakes.

He had not counted on the Americans when he had made his plans, but their complications helped him in a way: their presence gave him a natural excuse to stay behind. Someone had to keep watch over the slippery Mr. Ferguson and his minions; even Tischler could not object to that.

After finding that the bodyguards had been waylaid, Ravid realized what was happening and acted without hesitation, a man desperate to obtain the means to his revenge. He already knew the general area where the CIA people were operating; he had only stumbled around for an hour or so before finally finding the proper hotel. Anticipating that he would be searched by the Syrians inside, Ravid had left his substitute jewels outside the hotel and picked them up when he excused himself to answer nature's call. Swapping them in the boat when the others were taking him to Cyprus was child's play.

Birk would make a radio or phone call soon, and the next phase would begin. The moment of ultimate decision was at hand. There could be no hesitation after this.

There would not be.

Ravid turned to the men in diving gear at the rear of the boat. "A few more minutes," he told them. "Be ready."

Birk answered the phone on the first ring.

"Three million at least," said his brother-in-law. "One or two are fake, but most are real. Small diamonds and a few rubies."

Birk smiled. By this time tomorrow, he would have exchanged the jewels in Turkey. After taking care of a few odds and ends, he would head toward the Greek islands where he would have the leisure to plan a more distant voyage.

"Well?" said Coldwell.

"There is a barge at this location," Birk told her, taking a piece of paper from his pocket. "Those are GPS settings. Use my phone to call your contact, and I will see you off."

"I'll use my own, thank you."

"As you wish," said Birk.

As she left the *Sharia*, Coldwell felt the muscles in the back of her neck relax. For the first time since she had heard of her brother's death—for the first time in two years, really—she could relax. It was in the Mossad agent's hands now. Her mission was complete.

The small speedboat rocked as the engine kicked to life. Coldwell gripped the railing and then her seat, but for balance only; she no longer had any fear. She gazed at the shoreline, a hazy shadow in the distance. When she returned she would have a long bath, then take a very long nap.

It was amazing how prescient the old religious writers had been. She was the woman clothed in the sun of chapter 12 in the book of Revelation, the Christian prediction of the new age. The dragon awaited her child, but the Lord God protected her.

Was it blasphemy to think of herself as holy as that? As she considered the question, something grabbed her around the neck. The man in the boat had taken a garrote from his pocket and pulled it tight around her throat.

For the first few moments, Coldwell struggled. She grabbed the wire with her fingers and tried to pry it off, instincts getting the better of her. And then she heard a voice that sounded like her brother's whispering in her ear.

"Let it be," it whispered. "We will rise again in three days time, the Temple rebuilt."

Coldwell relaxed her arms. An angel appeared before her, his body a bright light that shone warmly, a fire of faith and reverence. Behind him stood the new world, the shining tabernacle where there would be no sorrow, no death, no pain. He held his hands out to her.

"My God!" she exclaimed. "Thank you for bringing me to this moment."

She extended her hands toward the angel. As she did, his face tore in two. She saw that it was a mask covering the hideous aspect of a dragon: the Devil incarnate. She began to scream and back away, but the angel's wings had turned to snakes and held her fast for the burning fire behind him.

The man with the garrote, sensing Coldwell was dead, replaced the wire with a thick metal chain weighed down by iron dumbbells, then pushed her off the side of the boat.

Having gotten up early to consummate the business deal, Birk found it impossible to go back to bed. He decided he would amuse himself by taking the wheel of the *Sharia* as he set sail northward. The yacht was a large vessel, but a fleet one, and as he laid on the power he felt a rush of adrenaline.

One of his regrets about leaving the area for an extended "vacation" was that it would deprive him of the most rewarding part of his business: meeting interesting characters such as Ferguson, the American agent who had so entertained him of late. What would life be like without such stimulation? Birk was not one to romanticize danger, but if truth be told he would miss that aspect of his business as well or at least the elation he felt when the time of anxiety had passed.

"Two boats, small ones," said Birk's brother-in-law, coming into the wheelhouse area behind the helmsman.

Birk turned to look. The boats were small speedboats.

"Break out the weapons."

The helmsman reached to his shirt to draw his.

"No, not you," said Birk. "You take the wheel while I see what this is about. Probably nothing."

As Birk turned, the man fired point blank into the back of his head.

B y the time Ravid got to the *Sharia*, the shooting was over. Birk, his brother-in-law, and the two bodyguards loyal to him had been killed.

So had the American woman, strangled by one of the bodyguards Ravid had infiltrated among Birk's men. Ravid had debated before deciding this. The woman had to be killed as a matter of operational security as well as tidiness. The fact that she was a fanatic and aimed ultimately at the destruction of Jerusalem weighed heavily against her as well. The world was better off with one less fanatic.

On the other hand, she had released something in him, allowed him to function again, allowed him to really work, he thought. This went beyond simply helping him obtain the missile. Speaking to her of his need for revenge had freed him somehow, and he felt real gratitude: a liability in his profession, but still he felt it.

He hadn't wanted a drink quite so badly since that night either. Whether that would last or not, he couldn't say. He wouldn't count on it.

Coldwell's pocketbook had been brought to him. Ravid examined it now. She had a few thousand dollars in Euros, less than a hundred American, four credit cards, and a passport which might be of some use in the future.

"Set the course south," he told the others. "Weigh the bodies down and send them overboard at nightfall. Except for Birk; we will need his to make his ship appear as if it was robbed. Find a place where his body can be stuffed conveniently. Quickly. I must leave as soon as possible."

LATAKIA

Ferguson had one indisputable point of reference: the digital photo he had taken when they retrieved the case. He avoided looking at it—he avoided dealing with the problem at all—while he tried to psyche out who had killed Vassenka. Ras provided a semiuseful theory: the Syrian authorities believed Vassenka had tipped the Israelis off to the meeting at the castle and the incoming airplane, and this was payback.

The theory was wrong, but it told Ferguson that there were probably additional Iraqis and/or fanatics associated with Meles who had escaped Mossad's revenge bombing. He and Thera spent the early morning hours placing new taps on the local police phones; the NSA already had a healthy operation harvesting information from the central authorities in Damascus. Sooner or later the rest of the scum would turn up in the net.

There was a legitimate question to be asked, though: how much of this effort was truly worth it? With all of the major players out of the picture and the rocket fuel about to be confiscated, the immediate threat had vanished.

Asking the question was another thing Ferguson didn't bother with until he put Thera on the ferry for Cyprus. Unlike the yacht she and the others had taken the day before, this was a public vessel, a recent enterprise aimed at tourists but mostly used by Syrian workers who found they could earn twice as much on the island as they could in Syria. Which wasn't saying much.

Thera held his hand at the dock, as if they were sweethearts.

"See you," he told her as the small crowd began to press forward.

"When?" she asked.

"Probably tomorrow. But who knows?"

"You look like you need a vacation."

"Think I can get a good deal at Versailles?"

"Ha, ha. I'm serious." She looked up at him, as if expecting a kiss. "We're done, right?"

"We're never done."

He held her hand for a moment. She had changed into Muslim dress to blend with the Turkish women going home; the comb she'd had in her hair the night before was gone.

Why would she have stolen the jewels? Ferg thought.

Besides the obvious reasons, like greed.

"We're saying good-bye, right?" Thera told him in Arabic. That was the cover they'd worked out for the plainclothes police who watched the dock.

"Yeah," he said, and he took her in his arms and flattened his lips against hers.

The taste of the kiss was still in his mouth an hour later when he showed some of the jewels to a pawnbroker in the old part of the city. The man closed his eyes when he saw the stones; Ferguson pulled them back across the counter.

"How about these?" he said, taking out two of the diamonds.

The man considered them. "Twenty Euros apiece."

"Come on, they're worth more."

"Your accent is Egyptian," said the man. "But your clothes tell me you are from Europe."

"Ireland. I grew up in Cairo. Will that get me a better price?"

"Fifty Euros would be the best I could do. They are decent but not real."

"What about this?" said Ferguson. He took out the bracelet that had fallen on the ground the night of the operation. The man's eyes and greedy fingers told him immediately it was real.

"For this—" started the merchant.

"Don't even tempt me. It's not for sale," said Ferguson, pulling it back.

Of all the covers Ferguson had ever adopted, playing a doctor had to rate among the best. It wasn't just that people seemed to easily accept it; they became positively voluble, offering all sorts of information. And so Dr. Ferguson not only gained a great deal of insight into the autopsy procedures at the university hospital but was also treated to a full tour of the area where corpses were held. In the course of this tour, the assistant to the assistant head pathologist revealed that they had handled an important case just that morning, working on a body that had unfortunately met its demise by coming too close to a hand grenade.

Dr. Ferguson recalled experiences with mines in Bosnia as a young intern volunteering his time. This pressed the cover story to the limit— Ferguson was actually too young to have been there in the time frame when it would have taken place—but the assistant assistant wasn't keeping track of dates. Ferguson moved on to a discussion of plastic surgery, a specialty he had not indulged in but often wondered about. The conversation flowed a crooked road of techniques and wounds and reconstruction, until at last Ferguson found himself staring at the face of Jurg Vassenka, who was not Jurg Vassenka.

They'd been had. The Russian had managed to slip away.

THE PERSIAN GULF, SOUTH OF IRAQ

The U.S. Navy had special teams trained to board and inspect ships on the high seas, and Rankin was content to ride shotgun with one as it approached the *Chi Lao*. Guns chafed a bit at the seamen's haughty commands when they went up the ladder from the rigid-hulled inflatable boat, but then the whole idea of sailors doing what by rights should have been a marine job didn't sit well with the leatherneck anyway.

The freighter had started its journey not in North Korea as Ferguson had originally suspected but the Philippines, where it had docked not far from one that had recently come from North Korea. This was all documented in the papers the captain presented to the ensign in charge of the boarding party, as were the stops it had made in the Middle East. It hadn't docked in Tripoli or Latakia, but Rankin already knew from Thomas's work that there was enough slack in the ship's itinerary for it to have lingered a few hours offshore, presumably to get a payment or for instructions. In any event, the papers weren't what he and Guns had come to see.

"We want to look at the cargo," he told the ensign.

The ship captain's English, which just a moment ago had been perfect, suddenly became strained. He managed to communicate that he had nothing but televisions and cooking oil aboard, and was already overdue.

"Then you better help us take a look quickly," suggested the ensign, "or you'll be even later."

Rankin gripped his Uzi as they went down the ladder to the forward cargo spaces. There were shadows everywhere, and while the destroyer they'd come from sat less than a hundred yards away, the boarding crew was very much on its own amid the shadows and cramped quarters below deck. They went to the stacked boxes of cooking oil; the crew directed one of the skids to be opened for inspection. The captain asked if they wanted it done there or above on deck.

"Neither," said Rankin. "Where are the televisions?"

The ensign shot him an odd look. The captain's English once more failed. The boarding crew, however, had already located them in the next hold; the crates were arranged so that they would be easily unloaded.

When they finally reached them, the captain began to protest that an inspection would make them even later.

"Tell you what then," said Rankin, raising his Uzi, "I'll just fire at random through them. What do you say?"

Guns grabbed the captain as he jerked away and threw him to the ground. The sailors who jumped on him grabbed a small pistol from his pocket.

The first set of boxes they opened contained thirty-two-inch televisions manufactured in South Korea. The second set seemed to as well, until the picture tubes were examined more closely. The flimsy cardboard that protected the rear of the TV sets covered a large plastic piece at the back of the picture tube. The first sign that it was different from that on the legitimate sets was the fact that it screwed off rather than pulled. The second sign was the kerosenelike stench that quickly spread through the hold when it was off. Rankin put the cap back on gingerly.

"Better get this place vented," Rankin told the ensign in charge of the boarding team. "This stuff catches fire pretty damn easy."

5

CYPRUS

Thera got back to the hotel just as Monsoon and Grumpy were taking their gear out to the van that would run them over to the British military airport at Akroti. A jet there would take them to the States, where they would have a few days off before rejoining their units. Surprised and disappointed that they were leaving, Thera tried not to show it. She kissed Grumpy, which surprised him, and then kissed Monsoon, which didn't.

"I hope I see you again," she told him.

"That'd be nice."

"You have an e-mail address?"

"Sure."

Upstairs, she tucked the address into her wallet, then went to take a shower. Catching a glimpse of herself in the mirror as she undressed, she saw a woman with drooping eyes and a puffy mouth: an old, tired, lonely woman.

Exhausted by the last several days, feeling the aftereffects of the pill she'd taken to keep herself going last night, she burst into tears.

6

"The problem with you Americans is that you think you don't have to get your hands dirty. You think you can deal with a problem by talking about it rather than taking action, when only action will solve it: strong action, eradicating action. You would have kept Khazaal and Meles alive, risking their escape. We have dealt with them efficiently. We have provided you a solution to the problem which you did not have the stomach to take."

Ferguson sipped his coffee in the secure room beneath the Mossad building as the Israeli's rant continued. One thing surprised him: the lecture was coming not from Tischler, who sat stone-faced across from Corrine, but from Aaron Ravid. The slime had not only made good time getting back to Israel but also put the effort into polishing up a speech.

Corrine listened impassively. She didn't have a lot of experience as a courtroom litigator; most of what she did had come from pro bono work in local courts representing poor people accused of very minor crimes. But she knew how to act during a prosecutor's summation: nonplussed, occasionally sipping from her water, once in a very great while taking the time to look incredulous.

"Is that the position of the Israeli government?" she asked Tischler when Ravid finished.

"We don't speak for the government," he answered.

Corrine pushed her chair away from the table and got up to leave. As she did, she turned to Ferguson. "Is there anything you want to say?"

"Only that this is the best coffee I've had in the Middle East. It's not Starbucks, is it?"

I can't believe they blew us off like that," said Corrine outside the building. "I can't believe it."

"Relax," said Ferguson. "Walk with me."

He turned to the left, leading her down the block, away from the car.

"We're supposed to be allies," said Corrine. "We're supposed to work together."

"Yeah. That happens sometimes. Not as much as you'd think."

Corrine pressed her lips together. She wanted to admit that she wasn't really sure what to do, but she couldn't say that to Ferguson. Making herself that vulnerable to someone who not only didn't like her but also resented her would be suicidal.

"You noticed that Tischler didn't say anything?" asked Ferguson.

"And?"

"That's what's important for the next step. Whatever that is."

Corrine stopped in the street, squinting because of the sun, which poked through the buildings and hit her in the eyes. Ferguson saw the squint and interpreted it as her attempt to look tough, which he thought made her look just the opposite. If it weren't for stuff like that, she might actually be all right to deal with.

Not better than all right, but all right. On a good day.

"What's next is we figure out where the Russian went," said Ferguson. "He's not in Latakia."

"You don't think back to Russia?"

Vassenka could have gotten down to Damascus, hopped a plane to Cairo, and then flown just about anywhere in the world. Alternatively, he could have taken a boat to Turkey or Lebanon or even Israel, driven north in a car, even taken a train.

"Let's say Khazaal's friends didn't kill him. On the contrary, they helped him get out of town. Seems logical. If that's the case, then he owes them a favor."

"We have the rocket fuel."

"True. But we don't have the rockets."

"How many could there be?"

"You tell me. There was enough fuel for a dozen at least. You have them in parts? Who knows?" Ferguson still thought that Khazaal had over-paid for the fuel and for Vassenka. But the fact that he had to get the rocket fuel from Korea showed that maybe the stuff was getting harder to come by these days because of the weapons export agreements. When the Russians had first started mixing the stuff using German recipes, it had cost about twenty cents a kilogram, which would work out to less than a thousand dollars a missile. Clearly, the stuff was harder to come by these days.

"One thing I want to take care of in Syria," Ferguson added. "The cruise missile Birk's offering for sale. I want to buy it."

"For a million dollars?"

"That's cheap. Not only do I take it off the market, but I also can find out where he got it. As far as we know, nobody's manufactured copies of the SS-N-9 Siren, and it's never been exported. If we have this one, we may find out differently. Not to mention the fact that we'd be taking a pretty potent weapon off the market. The Siren has a range of over 110 kilometers, carries a 500-kilogram warhead; it'll do a lot of damage."

"All right. I'll fix it with Parnelles."

Mildly surprised, Ferguson told her that he was sending Rankin and Guns to Iraq to see if they could figure out who was supposed to pick up the fuel and to poke around for Vassenka. He mentioned Thera in passing, saying he was keeping her in Cyprus in case he needed backup.

Which was the truth, just not all of it. He hadn't decided what to do about the jewels yet.

"Ferg, let me ask you something," Corrine said, trying not to look at her watch. "What do you think about Iraq?"

"It's a hellhole."

"Do you think the government there is going to last?"

"You were just there. You tell me."

"The ambassador claims it will. He seems pretty confident."

Ferguson laughed. It was the only answer he gave and the only one she needed.

Since Ferguson had to make a complicated dance to get from Israel to Syria anyway, he made a virtue of necessity and stopped in Cairo for a few hours that afternoon. The new CIA deputy station chief who met with him had recently discovered the pleasure of the pipe, and spent much of their meeting in the café puffing away, to Ferguson's amusement. Unfortunately, that was about the only thing he got out of the meeting. If Vassenka had stopped in Cairo on his way out of Syria, no one had spotted him.

There had been no fallout from the Fatman incident. "Dead is dead" went an old Egyptian proverb. It might have lost a bit of color in the translation, but it retained all of its meaning.

"That was related to that whacko Christian thing, Seven Angels, right?" asked the deputy between puffs.

"Yeah," said Ferguson.

"Did the FBI find that lady or what?"

"You lost me there."

"They had a heads-up the other day, travel-advisory thing, about this woman they were looking for. Real vague. It got flagged because it was related to your run-in. Routine stuff."

"Yeah, routine. You find her?"

"She didn't come to Cairo."

"You sure?"

"Not on any of the lists. You can check with Dave downstairs if you want. I don't even remember her name."

Neither did Dave downstairs, who had to look it up: Judy Coldwell.

It didn't click with Ferguson either, but it did with Thera.

"That's the woman I visited in the States. Thatch's sister," she said immediately when he mentioned the name. "The bureau said she wasn't connected with Seven Angels. Why is she traveling overseas?"

"And why the hell don't we know about it?"

Two hours later, Ferguson had his answer to the question: the FBI had considered the First Team's involvement in the case over and therefore hadn't bothered to inform them. He also knew that someone had used Thatch's name to register at a hotel in Latakia.

"The FBI really dropped the ball, Ferg," said Corrigan as he finished filling Ferguson in. "They really screwed up."

"Yeah. Where is she now?"

"Unclear. Thatch checked out. We're trying to see if we can trace any credit cards that were used."

"Get back to me when you know something."

Ferguson called Thera in Cyprus to see if she knew anything else about Coldwell. When he told her that Coldwell had been in Latakia, she volunteered to go there and look for her.

"No," he told her. "Not now."

"When?"

"I don't know. I'm not sure she's still there."

"Hell, Ferg. Why am I on ice here?" she asked. "You think I screwed this up somehow?"

"You're not on ice."

"Well, why I am here when everybody else is on the job?"

"Just get some rest."

"I'm sorry I screwed up."

"I didn't say you screwed up."

The emotion in her voice sounded genuine, so convincing, that it was hard for Ferguson to imagine that she could do anything wrong. But it wasn't easy to figure out if someone was lying from the tone of their voice. Ferguson, who made a science of lying, knew you could never go by what someone said, or even how they said it; you needed the whole context of what they did, and even then it could be a tough call.

Few people were above suspicion where millions of dollars were concerned. Then why didn't he think Guns or Rankin had taken them? He couldn't even consider that possibility. Neither was a good liar, but that wasn't the reason: he knew where they would draw the line. He'd seen them under fire, been next to them through a lot of mud and thunder.

He'd seen Thera under fire, too, though not for as long. Maybe he was just being harder on her, or more distant, because he realized she was in love with Monsoon.

"Just hang loose," he told her. "Work on your tan. He also serves who sits and waits."

"Whoever said that was blind," snapped Thera. She killed the connection before Ferguson could tell her she was right.

NEAR JERICHO, THE WEST BANK

The building looked no different—absolutely no different—than a public school in America. In fact, as she walked through the halls Corrine couldn't help but think of her own childhood. They paused at the door of a classroom where the students were learning English; third-graders were reading a storybook about ducklings that would have been appropriate in any American class.

Corrine realized that the officials who met her might distrust and even hate the U.S. The deputy prime minister had chided her for starting her day in Israel rather than coming directly from Baghdad or Jordan. But the children who turned from their lesson to stare at her did so with curious eyes; they were neither suspicious nor particularly troubled by her presence.

"I know that story," she said from the doorway. "I read that when I was your age."

She hesitated and then walked into the classroom. The children rose in respect, something that she thought would never happen in America.

"Oh, no, please sit," she told them. She went to the teacher, a young man about her age. "Might I read that?"

The teacher, embarrassed, turned to her escorts, who besides the school principal included the deputy prime minister and the American ambassador. By the time he told Corrine that he would be honored, she had already taken the book and pulled over a chair to the children, beginning to read. When she was done, she told the children that she had gone to a school in California just like theirs.

"The paint was not as pretty, but I think the teachers worked nearly as hard as yours." She smiled. "Do you have any questions? What would you like to know?"

For a moment, she felt as if she might be able to change things, to affect the children in some way with some simple answer about her own hometown or youth. If they knew that she was just like them, she thought, then when they grew older they might be able to see America as their friend, which it should by rights be.

But the moment wilted. The children had no questions for her, and Corrine began to feel foolish. She glanced at their teacher, then back to them. When no one said anything after a few more seconds, she asked if they got homework every night. There were a few nods, and she said something innocuous about how she used to hate homework but did it anyway.

Later, the officials took her to a refugee camp to the west of the city. The camp looked more like a tightly packed city at the foot of the mountains than a camp, but the incongruity that struck Corrine was the great beauty of the towering hills behind it. It was as if God had placed a reminder of His power and abilities in front of the citizens.

But whose God? The God of Abraham: the God of Jews, of Muslims, and Christians. They shared this land and this God but had nothing but strife to show for it.

The deputy prime minister had other appointments and took his leave. "I will pray for peace and a full agreement," he told her as he said good-bye.

"I'll pray with you," said Corrine.

8

It wasn't exactly a case of déjà vu, but when he stepped off the helicopter, Rankin remembered the last time he'd gotten off an aircraft in Baghdad, roughly two years before. Then he'd been hunting for one of Khazaal's rivals, though he didn't know who Khazaal was at the time. He didn't know who anyone was in Iraqi. He thought he did; that was the problem.

When the war started, Rankin was assigned to work with a Special Operations task group searching for Saddam. When the dictator was found, Rankin was shipped out to Afghanistan for a few months. After catching two members of al Qaeda, he was "rewarded" by being assigned to lead the team hunting for the Crabman back in Iraq.

The Crabman's real name was Fathah Tal Saed, but everybody used the dumb nickname. It came originally from the way the *hajji* slime had looked in one of his pictures. The picture turned out not to look much like him at all, but that was beside the point.

The Crabman had tried to collect on a reward offered by Osama bin Laden for the assassination of Paul Bremmer, the American ambassador and civilian head of the occupying government before power was turned over to the Iraqis. A lot of people actually were gunning for Bremmer, but the Crabman and his band of murderers had come a little too close for comfort.

It took two weeks to find the town north of Tikrit where he had fled after his latest attempt failed. It took three weeks to find out where he was in the town. It took five minutes to kill the son of a bitch. And it took a lifetime to get out of there once they did.

For the record, the after-action report claimed it took only three days and nights to "exfiltrate" once the assignment was completed. But those things never ever got the story right, even when they were written by the people who'd been there.

Especially not then.

Two years had changed the airport, turning it into a facility that might actually be considered efficient and attractive somewhere else. Once they cleared customs and the security area, they found a suite of car-rental desks; Corrigan had arranged for a car, which turned out to be a tiny Ford Fiesta. Guns took one look at the vehicle and went back inside to negotiate an upgrade. This proved surprisingly easy, and they were soon on their way into town.

Guns yawned. "Doesn't look as bad as you said it would."

"They built a few new things." He flinched involuntarily as a car zoomed close to pass.

They were staying in the equivalent of a Days Inn, a new motel at the north of town. Applying a move from Ferguson's playbook, Rankin took two double rooms on opposite ends of the second floor. For security they would stay together, but this gave them a backup to use just in case. They were walking from the car to the room when a voice Rankin hadn't heard in a lifetime echoed against the freshly sealed macadam.

"Hey, Sergeant. Hey, Rankin! Steve?"

Rankin turned slowly, as if acknowledging the voice meant more than simply recognizing it. But when he did, and when he saw James Corning, he smiled, genuinely glad to see him.

"What the hell are you doing here, James?" Rankin asked.

"Same old, same old," said James. He held up his scrawny hand and gave Rankin a mock high five.

"Still pissed off at the world?" asked James when he saw Rankin's scowl.

"You still writing lies?"

"Oh, you betcha. Bigger the better. What are you here for? Do something wrong?"

"Yeah. I got to work it off."

They looked at each other for a moment, Rankin towering over James, James practically dancing back and forth as if he were buzzed on amphetamines, though in reality he didn't even drink coffee.

Alcohol was a different story.

"I have an interview with the new prime minister, so I can't hang out," James told Rankin. "But we should have a drink."

"Maybe."

James thought that was funny and started to laugh. "You here for the president?"

"No," said Rankin.

James thought that was even funnier. "What are you here for?"

"Looking for Scuds. You see any?"

James thought this was a joke—it did sound like one—and he laughed twice as hard as before. "You got a sense of humor in the last two years. I'll give ya that. Listen, I'm in two-ten. Knock on the door. Same old, same old." He did the goofy thing with his hand again, slapping at the air, and walked off.

"What's he, some sort of reporter?" Guns asked as they checked out their rooms.

"Yeah. Except he's OK. He was with me north of Tikrit when I got Crabman."

"The whole time?"

"Whole time. He's OK."

Guns nodded. He had heard the story in bits and pieces, the only way Rankin told it. Even though he had worked with the guy for going on nine months, he still didn't know everything that had happened.

"He's not the guy who shot the woman?"

"No. That was Colgan. James shot the kid that tried to turn us in, and the two policemen who came for us."

"Oh," said Guns. "I didn't know journalists could do stuff like that."

"I told you he's OK, right?"

"Whatever." Guns shrugged. He didn't have any feelings about journalists, one way or another.

Rankin finished scanning the room with the bug detector. He put his gear into one of the drawers, setting a small motion detector in the lower corner so he could tell if it had been tampered with.

"James is the guy who dove on the hand grenade that turned out to be a dud," said Rankin. "Did the ultimate good deed and lived to tell about it."

"Wow."

Guns hadn't heard *that* part of the story at all. He waited for Rankin to explain, but the other man simply went to the door. "Let's go to Iraqi intelligence and get that bit of BS over with."

9

The analysts had tentatively identified the alias Judy Coldwell had used to travel to Europe and then the Middle East: Agnes Perpetua. She had used a Moroccan passport. But no one by that name had registered in any of the hotels in Latakia.

"What about the rest of the country?" Ferg asked Corrigan.

"Jeez, Ferg, Syria is a big place."

"Immense," said Ferguson. "Try Damascus."

"Well, there I'm ahead of you, because I did already, and she's not there. Not in any tourist hotel."

It wouldn't be hard to register under a different name. If the Syrians were more cooperative, and if they had infinite amounts of time, they might be able to find her. But neither was true. Ferguson needed a shortcut, but couldn't think of one.

"Did you try Thatch?"

"Of course we tried Thatch," said Corrigan. "We also tried her maiden name and some other different combinations. And we've looked at flight lists. Nada."

"What's she do again?"

"She's an accountant."

"Any hints from her clients? Where's her husband?"

"Jeez, Ferg. Let us do our job all right? Next you're going to ask if we started tracking her credit cards."

"Did you?"

"Screw yourself, of course we did."

"Keep looking for her," said Ferguson. "Check back with me when you find her."

"*If* I find her."

"Better make it *when*, Corrigan."

Ferguson rented a boat and took a spin out to the area where Birk generally anchored his yacht. It wasn't there.

Back at his hotel, Ferguson was just taking a cola from the minibar when his sat phone rang.

"Ferguson," he said, grabbing it.

"There are times, Bobby, when you sound so much like your father it sends a chill down my spine."

"Hey, General. How are you?"

"Incredibly busy, distracted, and forgetful, unfortunately," said Thomas Parnelles, the head of the CIA. "How are *you*?"

"Probably the same. Except for the forgetful part."

"Memory and concentration run in the genes. I understand you had some difficulty the other night."

"Our party got crashed."

"Shame."

Ferguson had known Parnelles all his life, and it was difficult when talking to him to separate the vast bulk of their relationship from the fact that Parnelles was the head of the CIA. The two roles—surrogate uncle, director of intelligence—were quite opposed to each other. Parnelles had no problem: he'd been segregating his life since before Ferguson was born.

"I had a call from Tel Aviv," continued Parnelles. "I spoke with David Tischler. We hadn't spoken in many years."

"Good friend of yours?"

"Not particularly. He was rather junior when I knew him. Your father liked him. They worked on a project or two together and did some traveling. But I've always been at arm's length with everyone at Mossad."

Tischler had never mentioned Ferguson's father. Good discipline, Ferguson thought; he wanted to keep everything at arm's length.

Ferguson's approach would have been entirely different.

"He was very impressed with Ms. Alston," Parnelles continued. "He had something he wanted to share, but she was in transit, to Palestine, and he didn't know where to get a hold of you."

"So he called you?"

"As a matter of fact he did. I was surprised," said Parnelles, in a tone that suggested the opposite. "They had a radar plot of an aircraft taking off from the Latakia airport two nights ago."

"Funny, the Syrians said it was closed."

"I heard that as well. The airplane went northward, toward Turkey, before it was lost on radar."

"You wouldn't happen to have a time on that, would you?"

"Only that it was very late. You can't have everything."

"No, but you can ask."

They were telling him about Vassenka, Ferguson guessed. Too bad he'd already figured it out.

"You called me the other night, Bobby. Was something wrong?"

You tell me, thought Ferguson, but he said, "I think it's resolved itself."

"That's very good to hear. I have a great deal of confidence in you. And Ms. Alston. She's the president's representative on Special Demands."

Yeah, thought Ferguson. She's the designated guillotine victim if something goes wrong.

"I have to be going now, Bobby. You take care of yourself. We should have a drink when you get back. I have a new single malt I'd like to try."

"I'll be there."

10

CIA BUILDING 24-442, VIRGINIA
THREE HOURS LATER . . .

If the airplane had gone directly to Iraq, it would have been easy to trace. The fact that it had gone to Turkey made things slightly more difficult. Thomas had already requested access to all of the radar and other aircraft intercepts over the border. He could look not only at the summaries but also at the raw data and could call on three different people to help interpret them. But all of the flights over the Iraq border had departed from Syria. It seemed pretty clear from the Israeli data, which he had by now verified with separate NATO intercepts off Cyprus, that there had been a flight out of Latakia to Turkey—Gaziantep, to be specific; not the largest airport in the country but not a dirt strip either. It had its share of regular flights, mostly to other places in Turkey but in about a dozen instances to countries around the Middle East.

Thomas's mind drifted to Professor Ragguzi and his theory about the Turkey sightings or rather, to Professor Ragguzi's two-word response to his query. It was unbelievably arrogant. Because he was right, wasn't he?

Of course he was.

Thomas went back to the list of flights. There were none into Iraq. So either Ferguson was wrong about the plane having Vassenka, or he was wrong about Vassenka going to Iraq. Either way, wrong.

Not that it would bother Ferguson, probably. Thomas knew him only from what Corrigan told him, but it seemed like nothing would bother him.

Unlike Professor Ragguzi, obviously.

The plane was a four-engined turboprop, probably an An-12BP "Cub," though someone had erroneously called it a Hercules C-130. Obviously, the plane had taken off again, nearly right away. But where was it? Not in any of the intercept sheets. A plane that large would be relatively easy to detect unless it flew very, very low. Frankly, it wasn't a good choice for sneaking across a border, unless you had to carry something pretty heavy. It was more the sort of airplane you might use as an airliner or heavy commercial transport.

Did Professor Ragguzi know something he didn't know? Nonsense. Thomas had a record of *every* spy flight out of Turkey, beginning with modified B-29s and running through to the U-2s. The spaceship sighting corresponded indisputably with a series of U-2 flights. Encouraging the UFO stories to take attention away from the U-2s was pure CIA, precisely the sort of thing the Agency used to do during the cold war. And would still do now. Any intelligence agency would.

Even an extraterrestrial one?

Was *that* what Professor Ragguzi was getting at? Were the aliens using the U-2 missions the way the CIA used the UFOs? Hiding in plain sight?

In "plane" sight?

Thomas began hammering his keyboard, realizing where the plane had gone.

Corrigan winced when he saw Thomas coming through the door. The analyst looked even more wild-eyed than normal, assuming there was a normal.

"Ha! Ha!" shouted Thomas.

"Are you all right?" asked Corrigan, carefully positioning himself behind the monitor.

"Ha!" he yelled even louder.

"I really don't have time to guess what's going on," said Corrigan.

"In plain sight. Hiding in plain sight. *Plane* sight. Ha!"

Corrigan knew that if he could remain calm and not overreact, Thomas would soon calm down enough to tell him what it was he had discovered. But staying calm while a man was yelling "Ha!" at the top of his lungs in an ultrasecure bunker was a task that would try a Zen master. And Corrigan wasn't a devotee of Eastern religion.

"Ha!" shouted Thomas.

"No more. What have you found?"

Thomas shook his head. Corrigan could be so slow at times. "The UFOs used the spy missions to hide their flights."

"I have no idea what you're talking about."

"It was a scheduled flight. The plane from Syria landed in Turkey. Eight hours later, it took off for Iraq. Tal Ashtah New," he added. "Took off a few hours ago and is back in Turkey. It's a scheduled flight. The one from Iraq wasn't; that's what threw me off. I thought smuggler, and that's what I looked for. It was a regular flight. A big plane. Four engines."

"Great," said Corrigan, who wasn't about to open Pandora's box by asking what that had to do with flying saucers. "Let me get Ferg."

"Tell him Thatch used his credit card this afternoon in Tel Aviv."

"What? Thatch? The Seven Angels suspect who was blown up in Jerusalem?"

"Ha!"

LATAKIA

Jean Allsparté gave Ferguson a look of mock horror as the American CIA op slid in at the end of the table at the King Saudi Casino, putting down a stack of chips and pointing at the dealer. The game was blackjack, and Ferguson's luck ran hot for the first five hands; he won four of them. Now armed with a decent stake, he began betting more strategically, keeping better track of the hands and adjusting his wagering accordingly. After a dozen or so hands, his pile of chips had grown considerably.

Allsparté was both amused and annoyed at this, and kept glancing at Ferguson. He began betting haphazardly. Ferguson waited until Allsparté had a particularly lucky win—he hit sixteen and got a five—then announced in a very loud voice, "I can't believe you're counting the cards. And so blatantly."

"I don't count cards," said Allsparté in Algerian-accented French.

The dealer stepped back to take a sip of water. A manager came over and had a word. A larger card chute was ordered over and more decks added to the deal. This annoyed Allsparté immensely: the desired effect. He tried hard not to be flustered, but the larger deck threw off the Algerian's system, for contrary to what he told Ferguson, he *did* count cards. After a string of losses, he could no longer contain his impatience. He grabbed his drink from the table and stalked up to the tiered lounge area a short distance away.

Ferguson played two more rounds, collected his chips and went up to the table.

"What do you want?" asked Allsparté in his native French. He did not use the polite pronoun.

"Birk," said Ferguson. His sat phone, set on vibrate, began to buzz, but he ignored it. "I'm looking for him."

"You ruin my night because of him?" said Allsparté, using even less polite pronouns.

Ferguson scratched the side of his temple.

"I need to find him."

"What was he going to sell you? I will get it ten percent cheaper, just to be rid of you."

"Missiles," said Ferguson. "Scuds."

Allsparté made a face and picked up his drink, but at last he was being serious. Ferguson watched the Algerian calculating what to say.

"The Polack is not so crazy as to sell Scuds," said Allsparté finally. "And not to you."

"To who then?" Ferguson mixed real questions with dodges, making it more difficult for anyone to follow his trail.

"He has none. Birk would never sell a Scud."

"Did Vassenka buy from someone else?"

"Which agency do you work for? MI6? Or the Americans?"

"I have my own interests."

"Which are?"

"I'm looking to blow up something very big."

"The only thing that Birk had that would interest you was a cruise missile," said Allsparté. "He mentioned to me that he would sell it soon."

"An American missile?"

"Don't be absurd. A Russian weapon."

"Where did he keep it?"

"Around."

"In the port?"

Allsparté shrugged. "I don't inquire too deeply."

"Did you transport it for him?"

Allsparté shook his head.

"Is it still for sale? Or did Vassenka buy it?"

"You should know that Vassenka is not a user of missiles."

"Khazaal."

Allsparté shrugged.

"Did Khazaal buy some rocket fuel or Scud parts?"

"You have an obsession with Scuds; you must work for the Americans."

"I can pay a good price for Scuds."

"You should talk to Birk. He is the seller, not I. I move things at his request."

"What have you moved lately?"

Allsparté shook his head. "Very little."

"You know where he is?"

"I do not keep track."

"What about the Siren missile. I want it."

"Really, you should address your questions to him."

"I need a serious missile," Ferguson told Allsparté, deciding to push things as far as he could. "Birk was going to sell me a Siren missile. But Birk disappeared."

"A shame."

"Where can I find something similar?"

"Have you spoken to Ras?"

"Claims he can't help me," said Ferguson, which was true.

"Well, then, neither can I."

"Did Birk sell the Siren to Khazaal?"

"What would an Iraqi do with a cruise missile?"

"Same thing I want to do."

Allsparté shook his head. "If I knew where Birk was, I would tell you just to get you away from me. I can't stand your odor. But I do not."

Ferguson leaned very close and lowered his voice almost to a whisper. "If I find out you're lying, it's not going to be pretty."

Allsparté stared at him for a moment, then nodded almost imperceptibly. "I don't know where he or the missile is."

The aircraft the Israelis had tracked and that Thomas had traced was large enough to carry a Siren cruise missile and its associated hardware. Which suggested to Ferguson that whoever had helped Vassenka had purchased the missile from Birk and taken the weapon with the expert to Iraq. Birk might even have sold the weapon to Vassenka himself, provided the Russian would pay the undoubtedly steep premium he would ask. Birk complained a great deal about Russians, but in the end money was stronger than his prejudices.

Ferguson plied the casinos for another two hours, but failed to hear anything about where Birk was. Nor did the bugs pick up activity in Coldwell's room. The video image had been tentatively matched against a driver's license picture. The match was not perfect, but for Ferguson the ID was synched by the fact that Coldwell had disappeared from her Chicago-area home. He didn't think she had bought Birk's weapon and wasn't surprised that she was missing again: Coldwell had probably approached someone with a less well-developed sense of propriety or humor than Birk and paid for her insanity with her cash and life.

"I have been wondering when you would show up again," said Ras when Ferguson walked into the Barroom. "But where is your wife?"

"She has a headache," said Ferguson.

They bantered back and forth a bit, Ras noting that the town had been quiet of late.

"Funny you should mention that," said Ferg. "I hear your competition is hiding out."

"What competition?"

"Birk."

"Why would he hide?"

"Supposedly because he supplied the Israelis with the weapons that were used to blow up the Iraqis at the airport."

"Birk? Never."

"It's what I hear."

"I would not believe that."

"Someone told me he's hiding out in the yacht he sold to buy the *Sharia*. It's called the *Saudi King* and anchored near Jezira," said Ferguson.

"Why would he hide there? Everyone knows he sold it."

"I think that was the idea. Then again, maybe not." Ferguson poked the lime twist in his drink. "People tell me things, and I believe them. I'm just a gullible fool."

———

An hour later, Ferguson slid a small speedboat around the ships moored off Jezira, a floating dock large enough to earn the Arab name for island. Corrigan's photo analysts had not been able to find *Sharia* anywhere off Syria. Clearly the yacht was gone, but was Birk? Linking him to the attack at the airport was the surest way Ferg could think of to find out if Birk was or wasn't in Latakia; if the authorities came looking for him here, then clearly he was nowhere else to be found.

Of course, there was always the possibility that Birk *was* aboard his old yacht. Ferguson decided to eliminate that possibility before the police arrived. He drew up next to the large craft and hauled himself aboard. The vessel was empty, but it took longer than he'd planned to check it out. There were several large crates in the cabin area, and for a few minutes Ferguson thought he had actually stumbled onto part of the cruise missile. This did not prove to be the case, though the discovery did pique Ferguson's interest: the crates contained naval mines. He took some photos with his digital camera to be used for future reference and went below to see if some sort of mechanism had been set up to disperse the mines, as impractical as this seemed. It had not, nor was there anything else aboard to explain the mines further. Ferguson decided it wasn't worth puzzling out at the moment, and returned topside to leave.

As he untied his boat, he saw a large shadow about a half mile away, close enough for him to see that it was a Syrian corvette that operated out of Tartūs to the south.

Its guns could make mincemeat of Ferguson's boat in about thirty seconds, but the ship wasn't half the threat the two Zodiacs he spotted coming from the shore were. And to prove that particular point, bullets began to fly from their bows.

12

BAGHDAD

Rankin heard noises inside the room that suggested James was not alone.

He knocked anyway. When James didn't answer, he knocked again.

"Go away!"

"Hey, James, I gotta talk to you."

"Rankin, buddy. I'll be with you in half an hour."

"Gotta talk to you now."

"Can't do it."

The girl who was with him in the room giggled.

"I'm coming in," said Rankin. "I have a key."

He was bluffing, though he did have a set of picks. Unlike Ferguson and Thera, he wasn't very good at undoing locks. It'd be easier for him to simply break down the door.

"All right. Hold on."

The girl James was with sat in a chair in the corner when the door was open, watching quietly from under a blanket. She looked awfully young, but Rankin wasn't in a position to ask for a driver's license. James stood near the bed in a pair of jeans and no shirt, his pigeon chest heaving. He took a swig from a bottle of red wine.

"I need a translator," Rankin told him.

"So?"

"Somebody I trust."

"You don't mean me."

"It has to be somebody I trust. The army guys, I just haven't worked with them. And I'm not working with these civilians."

"Stephen, come on. This is a different place."

"No, it's not."

"I'm not army. I'm not anything."

"But I trust you."

"Screw that. I'm kind of busy." James took another swig of the wine, then offered it to Rankin. "Want some? It's French. It's pretty decent. Cost fifty bucks a bottle in the States."

"I need you to come with me, James. I really do."

"Listen, Stephen, I love you and everything, but, no." James went over to the girl and whispered something in her ear. She nodded, then went into the bathroom, her bare behind poking through the blanket as she walked. Rankin started to speak, but James put up his finger to quiet him. The girl emerged a few minutes later in a long Arab dress that made her look even younger. James pressed money into her hand, then gave her a kiss.

Rankin stared at the floor as she left.

"I need your help," Rankin said when James closed the door.

"Nah, come on. Let's go get drunk. There's this really great strip joint a mile from here. Where's your buddy? We'll have a party."

"James."

"Aw, for Christ's sake." James shook his head, but Rankin knew from the way he did it—from the frown on his face, from the look in his eyes—that he was coming. James was the guy you met in Hell who wouldn't let you down. "Can I write about it?" he asked.

Rankin shook his head.

"Stephen, Jesus."

"Maybe in a couple of years you could write about it."

James laughed. It was a bitter, tight, very quick laugh. "I'm not going to be alive in a couple of years."

"Depending on what happens, you might be able to write about it in a couple of years."

James cursed. "All right. Wake me up when it's time. I'm *not* driving. I hate driving in this country."

"It's time. Come on. I have a gun for you."

"We're going *now?*"

"I have a machine gun. Guns is getting the Humvee."

"No Humvee."

"It's an armored one. We may need it."

James shook his head, but Rankin had already started out of the room.

13

Ferguson knew Ras's contacts with the Syrians were good, but he hadn't realized they were quick as well. He'd thought he would have another ten or fifteen minutes at least before they could get anyone out here, and then it would only be policemen who might fire their guns once a year if that. The people firing at him now were coming incredibly close to the yacht and to his small boat, close enough, in fact, that he decided to plunge into the water and begin stroking toward a group of boats two hundred yards away. By the time he reached them the Syrian marines in the Zodiacs had reached the yacht. Rather than confiscating his small boat, they perforated the bottom and watched it sink.

In the meantime, the corvette drew closer and began playing searchlights across the water. Ferguson saw another pair of Zodiacs headed up from the south and figured there would soon be a boat from the corvette as well. There were sure to be soldiers or policemen on shore. His best bet seemed to be swimming north.

Fortunately, it was a pleasant night for a swim, and he began stroking to the north. Unfortunately, the Syrians had sent another pair of Zodiacs from that direction. He reversed course and did his best freestyle back to the boats, pulling himself into the nearest dinghy as the rigid-hulled inflatables began crisscrossing the area. Lying on his back in the bottom of the boat, he pulled out his sat phone and called 911.

Actually, it was Van Buren, who was orbiting offshore in the MC-130.

"How about we try that diversion?" suggested Ferguson.

"When?"

"Ten minutes ago would have been great. But now will do."

Ferguson stowed the phone and listened to the Zodiacs approach. His arms and shoulders were sore, and his neck stiff; hopefully his muscles would respond better once he got back in the water. He didn't particularly feel like going back in, but it was better than the alternative.

———

Guided by the GPS signal in the phone, the MC-130 zoomed toward shore. Roughly three miles from the mooring area—and well within range to be detected by the corvette—it fired off a shower of flares. This was followed by a hard bank as the corvette began peppering the air with flak. One of the bullets from the gun struck the plane and its fuel tank exploded, sending it spiraling into the water.

Or so it appeared from the water. The MC-130 had actually jettisoned a large disposable fuel tank that had been rigged to explode in flames; a pair of small parachutes kept it airborne just long enough to heighten the effect. Ferguson thought he could hear a whoop of elation from the Zodiacs over the roar of their engines. Three of the four that had pulled up near Birk's old yacht immediately began racing for the supposed wreckage. He slipped over the side and began stroking south, angling toward shore.

The cramp in his neck disappeared, but his arms remained tired; even his legs felt drained. He pushed on, his goal the rocky beach. But within a few minutes he realized he wasn't making much progress at all. He thought he felt the temperature of the water abruptly change. Remembering the riptide that had taken Guns, he started to get serious about cutting across the current. When that didn't work, he rested for a minute. This wasn't a mistake because he really had no other choice, but the tide took him back to the north in the direction of the corvette's searchlights.

A minute wasn't much of a rest, but it was all he was getting. Ferguson threw himself into it, pushing directly toward the beach. Head down, he slammed his hand against the shallow rocks sooner than he thought possible. He wrapped his arm around the stone and held on, the water tugging at him, still trying to pull him out to sea. After awhile he pulled up onto the rocks, wincing because of his bare feet. He made it to a relatively level portion of land and sat down, leaning against a boulder and thinking he would rest a few minutes before heading south along the shore and returning to the hotel. But his arms were too heavy to move, and his legs felt pasted to the ground.

Ferguson remained there, a sodden mass, for a half hour, watching the headlights that occasionally swept along the road above. He'd climbed up next to a boat landing. Studying the lights he eventually realized that if he'd gone just six or seven feet farther to the south, he could have walked up a paved path from the sea. Crawled, more likely.

He was just thinking that he was in an exposed, easily seen position when a set of lights turned down the ramp. Too tired to run, he slipped to the side behind the rock, trying to hide as two men got out and came down to the water, only a few feet from him.

The men had seen him on the ground and came over, shouting at him that they were policemen and he was in a great deal of trouble. One kicked him in the ribs, asking in Arabic if he was drunk or drowned. The other grabbed him and started to pull him up; as he did, the sat phone fell from one of Ferg's pockets. The man dropped Ferguson in a heap and picked up the phone. The phone had a thumbprint reader as well as a password number for security, so there was no chance of it working. The man fiddled with it for a few minutes, then tossed it to his companion, who threw it out into the sea.

When the first man returned and tried to pick up the drunkard by the shirt, he suddenly found himself flying in a somersault toward the rocks. Ferguson jumped up and aimed a kick at the other man, bare foot connecting with the Iraqi's knee. The man grabbed Ferguson as he fell and managed to pull him down with him. Ferguson kicked at his chest but the man held on, his fingers like metal clamps. The fatigue that had immobilized Ferguson just a few minutes ago vanished; he rolled and smashed the man's head with his fist, pounding him into unconsciousness with three blows to the temple.

In the meantime, the first man drew his pistol and began firing wildly, the bullets sailing well over Ferguson's head. Panicked, he quickly emptied the magazine. As the gun clicked empty, Ferguson threw himself forward and plowed headfirst into the Syrian, knocking the wind from him. Two sharp blows to his head put him out for good.

Ferguson grabbed the gun and looked at the man's belt for more ammunition. All he could find were a pair of handcuffs. He cuffed the man's arms behind his back and did the same to his companion. Then he sized up the men and borrowed the clothes of the larger. His pants were too wide but more than an inch short; the shoes, at least, fit snugly.

Smaller than an American vehicle and without the bubblegum light at the top, the police car nonetheless came fully equipped with everything Ferguson wanted at the moment: four wheels, a full tank of gas, and a key to save him the trouble of jumping it.

Ferguson turned the wrong way out of the road leading to the ramp and found himself driving north rather than south on the highway. The easiest way to correct this was with a U-turn in the middle of the road. He misjudged the distance and went off the other side, the tire slipping down into a ditch and taking part of the exhaust with it. The pipe clattered along loudly. Ferguson was no mechanic, but he found a suitable solution by veering off the side again, scraping the pipe sufficiently to leave it and the muffler behind.

Except for its effect on Ferguson's ears, the noise wasn't a problem on the highway; given that the hotel was only a mile or so away, he figured he could tough it out. But as he neared the hotel he saw a pair of military vehicles at the front entrance and decided to keep going.

The sat phone would be sending a GPS signal out because it had been tampered with. If he didn't call in soon, Van Buren would initiate the bailout plan. Unfortunately, Syria wasn't very big on roadside telephone booths. Ferguson drove all the way to Latakia without spotting a place to park. Finally, he parked on a side street near the train station and got out, figuring there would be a phone inside. He had to put his hands in his pockets to keep the borrowed pants from ending up around his ankles, but there was a phone at the corner, and he called the number that signified he was OK.

Feeling a bit like a homeless man living in a borrowed set of pants, Ferguson walked south through the city, looking for a place where he might hide out and sleep. After several blocks he thought of the hotel they had escaped from and the bikes they had left in the alley nearby. As he turned down one block, he caught a glimpse of the moon. The sight of it between the buildings and his fatigue played on his mind, and within a block he was softly humming "The Rising of the Moon."

> Death to every foe and traitor
> Or would strike the marching tune—
> And we'll arm our boys for freedom
> 'Tis the risin' of the moon . . .

The bicycles were still there. He took one and pedaled south, riding for nearly an hour until his legs felt so tired he thought they might fall off. He found a spot of brush near the water on the other side of the railroad tracks to hide.

Ferg lay on his back, staring at the stars, the words to "The Rising of the Moon" still echoing in his head.

14

The guards who challenged Rankin, Guns, and James on the road into the airport at Tal Ashtah New had American M16s and sidearms, but everything else about them was Iraqi. Rankin stared at their ill-fitting pants and their untucked shirts as their sergeant checked the ID cards. In Rankin's opinion the Iraqi army was good at one thing and one thing only: running away. All the real fighters joined the resistance groups.

The guard gave the cards a cursory glance, then handed them back. Rankin gave him the name of the air freight company they were looking for, seeking directions; the Iraqi simply waved at them, not wanting to be bothered.

"There can't be many buildings here," said James, leaning forward from the backseat between Rankin and Guns. "And what's here'll be falling down."

Contrary to James's prediction, the first building they saw was in good shape, and the second was brand new.

"That way," said Guns, seeing the sign for Mesopotamia Express, the name of the company that flew the aircraft Thomas had tracked. The macadam road turned to concrete; the company's building sat to the left, in front of a large ramp area. A four-engined aircraft sat in the back. After spending much of their day yesterday tracking down useless leads about people who might have been connected to the shipment of the rocket fuel, this felt like they were really on to something. Even though Guns realized it was unlikely they would find Vassenka or the cruise missile Ferguson had told them about here, he checked his M4, making sure it was ready for action.

"Let's check the plane first," said Rankin.

They drove over and parked alongside. There weren't any guards or even employees nearby. A high-winged design that looked like a slimmer version of the American C-130, the Russian-made An-12 dated from the late

1950s. This particular plane had been around since the mid-1960s. After serving in the south of Russia for more than a decade, it had been transferred to Iraqi military service. It was now on its third owner, a company run by a pair of former Iraqi pilots, one of whom had received a bonus from the dictator after the first Gulf War for running to Iran with his MiG. The plane had been well maintained mechanically but looked a bit of a hodgepodge on the outside, with the remains of old paint schemes and even different ID numbers littered along its fuselage. There was a door on the pilot's side beneath the high wing. This was generally reached with the aid of an exterior ladder. There were no ladders nearby, and the wheel fairing made it difficult to climb high enough to get a foothold, but Rankin got enough of a foot- and handhold to reach the recessed handle.

The freshly risen sun streamed shafts of light through the windows into the long, bare interior. Ropes lay scattered around the tie-downs, but otherwise the cargo bay was empty.

The warehouse doors at the rear of the company's building were closed, but the front door was open. Rankin, Guns, and James walked past the small reception area into the back, Rankin thinking of what Ferguson would have done in this situation, the others glancing around warily. Guns held his M4 at his side, as if there were any way to be discreet when carrying an automatic weapon into a building.

Two panel trucks that looked like downsized UPS vehicles sat to the right. Assorted pipes, small boxes, bundles of Arabic-language newspapers, old wooden crates, and a pile of rubber mats were arranged opposite them. None of the boxes was big enough to hold a surface-to-surface missile or its related hardware. Rankin was just going around to check the trucks when a fat man in mechanic's overalls came out from around one of the vehicles and demanded to know what they were doing there.

"Looking for someone?" asked Rankin in Arabic. The phrase came easy on the tongue; he'd said it a million times in Iraq. "What are you doing?"

"You're the intruder," said the man, switching to English. "What is it you want?"

Rankin took a step toward the mechanic, who made the mistake of starting to square off as if to punch him. The American's reflexes kicked in, and within a split second he had the Iraqi on his stomach, arm pinned behind his back. Rankin drew his pistol and pointed it at the man's face, though given the fact that he hadn't been intimidated by Guns's rifle this was probably a useless gesture.

"I think we'd all be better served if we asked a few questions calmly," suggested James. "I doubt there's much here for anyone to get very upset about, much less shot."

He repeated the words in Arabic. The Iraqi, somewhat more subdued, shrugged. He said that he worked on the trucks and knew nothing about the aircraft.

"We don't want to know about the aircraft," Rankin said in English, letting James translate. "We're looking for a very big package."

"A package that was supposed to go to us but didn't," added James when he translated, adding justice to their claim for information.

Guns went over to the desk near the window and rifled through the drawers. He found a strongbox with some bills and a notebook, and a larger ledger divided into columns. The writing was in Arabic. He held it up.

"Hey, James, can you read this?"

The journalist came over and struggled through a few lines. They were cities and what he thought were the names of the drivers or the person responsible for the delivery.

"Let our friend here read it," said Rankin.

He jerked the mechanic to his feet. The man stared at the ground.

What would Ferguson do? Rankin asked himself.

Probably be able to read it; the SOB seemed to know every stinking language going. But if he couldn't, he'd bribe the man to get him to help.

Unlike Ferguson, though, Rankin didn't travel with a wad of counterfeit local currency. He reached into his wallet and took out fifty dollars American, half of the money he had.

"Read it for us," he told the mechanic, holding the money toward him. But Rankin hadn't handled the exchange deftly enough; the incident became a matter of pride for the Iraqi, who would have refused a bribe of a hundred times that amount. Rankin, angry at himself as well as the man, tossed down the money. "Take the books. Let's get out of here," he said.

They found a schoolteacher to translate the ledger books. The woman thought they were a bit eccentric until James explained that they had found the books along the side of the road and were trying to figure out where they should be returned. The deliveries were to cities and towns within a hundred-mile radius. There was no information on what was delivered.

All but one of the deliveries had been made to the south, in the direction of Tikrit.

"The thing's range is what, a little better than fifty miles?" said Guns. "So they'd have to drop it off, then take it farther south."

"You're getting ahead of yourself," said Rankin. "From these books, the deliveries could be envelopes. Neither of those trucks was big enough for a Siren missile."

He glanced over at James as he said that. James shrugged. He'd already figured out what they were looking for, more or less. As far as he was concerned, knowing the name of the missile wasn't much of a big deal, unless he had to write about it.

Rankin called Corrigan and gave him the information. Corrigan told him they were already alerting the Iraqi authorities as well as U.S. forces about the possibility that the missile had been brought into the area.

"What about the Russian?" Rankin asked. "Can you check the hotels?"

"I doubt he'd stay in a hotel," said Corrigan. "Besides, we don't have unlimited manpower."

"What's Ferg think?" asked Rankin. "Did that Birk Ivanovich or whatever sell them the cruise missile for sure, or is this still a hunch?"

"I don't know. Ferg's out of communication right now."

"What do you mean, out of communication?"

"He was being chased last night near Latakia, offshore. Van Buren ordered a diversion, and he seems to have gotten away. He called in from the city a while later, but he got separated from his sat phone. We don't know what's going on."

Rankin stared at the phone. "He'll turn up," he told Corrigan finally.

SOUTH OF LATAKIA, SYRIA

Ferguson felt something brush against his leg.

Still half-sleeping, he thought it was a dog, and twisted his head to see what was going on. He couldn't see anything, and it was only when he curled around for a better view that he realized it was the Mediterranean, lapping against his body; the copse he'd found to hide in was on the sea, and at high tide the water covered what he'd thought was dry land. He rolled onto his haunches, rubbing the crust from his eyes and trying to get his bearings. It was past three o'clock in the afternoon; he'd slept for close to twelve hours.

Brushing the sand and dirt from his face, Ferguson pulled off his shoes and borrowed pants, stripping to his bathing trunks. Then he waded into the surf, splashing water on his face and hair, shaking his head like a St. Bernard clearing its water-logged coat. It was an overcast, muggy day; insects buzzed around him. He reached into his shirt pocket for his small pillbox and took his medicine, washing it down with seawater as he had the other day. Then he sat back in the bushes, trying to plot out his next move.

When he first heard the helicopter, he didn't think much of it. But as it gradually got closer Ferguson decided to move to a spot where he couldn't be seen. His bicycle lay fifty yards farther south, in a ditch by the dirt road he had taken here. It was too far to retrieve without being seen.

A clump of low trees sat ten feet away. They wouldn't provide a lot of cover, but they were better than sitting out on the rocks. He moved back and stood behind the trunks of two, flattening his body against them. He thought there was a possibility the helo had been sent by Van for him, but as it came closer he saw that it was an Aerospatiale Gazelle, an oldish general-purpose type used by the Syrian military and painted in the swirls of Syrian camouflage. And it was definitely looking for something, if not him; it moved at a deliberate pace down the shoreline.

The chopper flew south about a hundred yards then slowly circled back. It skittered slowly toward a small wedge of sand and rocks to Ferguson's left, looking very much like it intended to set down.

He decided he'd make a run for it when it did. If he could get to the highway he might find a place to hide or even a truck or something to hop onto. The helicopter took its time descending, however, and for a moment he thought, perhaps wishfully, that it was going to move on. It leaned ever so slightly to one side, shuddering as its pilot momentarily lost his touch five or six feet above the ground.

When he saw that, Ferguson bolted. The ground was hot against his bare feet, but he didn't stop, sliding into the ditch in front of the highway as the helicopter's engine revved. Ferg crawled on all fours for about ten yards, then dashed across the road. The helicopter moved along the water behind him. A truck appeared from the dip in the road ahead, moving slowly up a long grade. It was an old farm vehicle, struggling to make it up the long hill, and he thought he might be able to hop in the back fairly easily. The only question was whether the truck would get there before the helicopter pilot flew over the roadway and spotted him.

Ferguson squatted in the ditch, waiting. The chopper started over the land. As he waited for the truck, Ferg saw a car coming down from the north; it was tempting to wait for it, since it was going in the direction he eventually wanted to take and surely could go faster than the truck. But it might not stop for him, and he had no weapon to use to help persuade the driver. With a split second to decide, he stayed with his original plan, rocking forward and then leaping up as the truck passed. In two bounds, he had his hands on the wooden stakes at the rear; he swung up his feet and held on.

The rear was filled with crates of lettuce going to market in Latakia. As he pulled up and got into the bed, the helicopter passed overhead. Ferguson looked back toward the beach area and saw that it had dropped several soldiers, one of whom was running toward the road.

Except it wasn't a soldier. It was Thera.

NEAR AL FATTAH, IRAQ

"Remember that restaurant on the road leading to town, Stephen? They had great beer. Always cold. How do you think they got beer there?"

"They made it at a still. They just put it in some old bottles they had."

"No way."

Guns checked the map as he drove, listening to the two men describe how much Tikrit and the surrounding area had changed over the past year. It was as if they were speaking about a place they'd lived all their lives, not one they'd spent only a few weeks in. But they'd been glad enough to get out of there after the last place they checked proved to be nothing more than a fruit stand.

Neither man had said anything about what had actually happened when they'd been together two years before. Guns didn't figure there was much sense prying, especially where Rankin was concerned, and, besides, driving through this part of Iraq required every ounce of attention he could muster.

The attacks that were a regular feature of life during the first year of the occupation were well in the past, but animosity toward Americans still ran deep. Guns and Rankin had donned generic green fatigues as soon as they arrived in Iraq, and there was no question of fitting in. Even the children they passed gave them dirty looks.

The last delivery they had to check was in Al Fattah, which lay to the east of Tal Ashtah New, roughly forty miles by road north of Tikrit. As they had at all of the other stops, Guns took his M4 with him when he got out of the vehicle; even though the day had turned very warm, he pulled on the bulletproof vest. Rankin did the same. Only James left his in the car. He'd taken it with him but hadn't bothered to put it on.

They'd refined their story by now and presented themselves as inspectors trying to make sure that goods had been properly delivered. Armed men asking about packages might draw stares in other countries; in Iraq it seemed to be par for the course. Nobody seemed surprised by their questions, though getting them to cooperate was more than a little difficult.

The drop-off point had been a lumberyard. A man who said he was the manager led them around to the back and showed them two large pallets of two-by-fours the trucks had brought. He offered copies of the paperwork, but they declined. The yard covered roughly five acres with enough construction materials to build an entire city. There were piles of bricks and stone and sand, huge cement pipes, old timbers, even long I-beams of steel and a heap of scrap metal. Many of the items had been salvaged from wrecked buildings, but there were new materials as well, including PVC pipe and massive coils of electrical wire. Most of it was out in the open. A new building was going up at the far end of the yard, near a rusting railroad siding. It was only half completed, and in fact had been that way for a while, but the manager waxed eloquent about the booming business, talking excitedly about how great their opportunities were now that democracy had come. Security was an important concern, he added; they were always trying to get more and better guards, and worked with the American authorities to do so. He meant it as a hint; contractors were forever changing jobs here.

The manager was one of the few Iraqis they'd met who didn't openly sneer at them. His guards were armed with American M16s, and Guns guessed that they had been trained by one of the firms that had helped provide protection during the early days of the occupation.

Rankin looked at the men and thought any one of them could have been gunning for him two years before. He checked through the yard, then went out and looked at the train siding. There was a single car there, an old tanker with the word *kerosene* stenciled on the side in English. The thing smelled as if it were leaking: one joker with a cigarette and the whole damn place would go up. He walked down a ways, saw some old tires and discarded sewer pipes along with another pile of battered bricks.

When they got back in the car, Rankin stared at the fence.

"You ever do any construction work, Guns?"

"No."

"You, James?"

"Work with my hands?"

"I never heard of getting wood by airplane," said Rankin. "That's not the sort of thing you fly in."

"We looked around the place pretty good," said Guns. "I'm sure they could hide some guns and such but nothing as big as the missile we're looking for. I looked in all the wood piles. There were no crates that I saw."

"A lot of toilet seats," said James. "No missiles."

"We're out of range here anyway. Over a hundred miles."

"Maybe it was here and they moved it," said Rankin.

"Easy enough," said Guns. "Doesn't help us now."

"What do you think about that railroad track?" asked Rankin.

"Pretty rusty. Tanker car on it looks older than you."

"What do you think, James?"

"I think we should get something to eat. And then a whole lot of vodka."

Rankin considered that. "Where would you get vodka in Tikrit?"

"Tikrit? You don't want to go there."

"Wasn't my question."

"Couple of places. There's a Russian bar on the north side. They've got real stuff. Or they used to. Before the war."

"Let's check it out now."

"You really want to go there, Stephen?"

"No. But that's where we're going. Tell Guns the turns, all right? I have to call in."

Most of the people in the bar were involved in the oil industry in some manner, even though Tikrit itself was hardly an oil-producing center. Following the occupation, Russians had filled many of the middle-level management jobs in the oil industry, both in the field and in the offices. Company management—in general foreign—trusted them more than they trusted the Iraqis; the Iraqi workers didn't resent taking their orders quite as much as they would have an American's.

Guns's Russian worked well here. The bartender asked him where in

Russia he was from. Moscow was an easy and noncommittal answer; but he supplemented it with a mention of Chechnya, saying he'd served there until recently and peppered his conversation with geographical details he remembered from their last mission. Without mentioning Vassenka by name, he said he was looking for a friend who'd come to Iraq very recently and also knew Chechnya. The bartender didn't seem interested, and Guns simply took their drinks over to the table where James and Rankin had already sat down.

Ten minutes later, a man approached them, speaking volubly in Russian about atrocities in Chechnya. Guns thought it was a test and said nothing. Finally Rankin decided their best course was to leave. As they got up, the man became more vocal. They left money on the table and started for the door. As they reached it, the bartender came out from around the bar, tapped Guns on the arm, and suggested that he look for his friend in Balad, a town to the south a little less than fifty miles north of Baghdad.

"Jurg, right?" said the bartender.

Guns nodded.

"He was still looking to hire men yesterday. Perhaps he will have room for you on his crew."

"*Spasíba*," said Guns. "Thank you."

Saved by Van and Thera—the helicopter was actually a rental that Van Buren's men had painted a few days earlier in case it was needed—Ferguson returned to Cyprus. While waiting for some replacement clothes from town, he vanquished his hunger with a large steak and got an update from Corrigan.

The Defense Department analysts brought in as consultants were having a field day poking holes in the theory that the SS-N-9 would be used in Iraq. The fact that the missile was a naval weapon seemed to them to rule out any possibility of its use on land. Admittedly, it was designed to travel at low altitude over open terrain, where it would have an unobstructed flight path, but it could be used over land, and Vassenka was supposed to be enough of an expert to make sure it would work. If the missile had been fitted with a GPS guidance system, it stood an extremely good chance of hitting its target. Whether it was the optimum tool for the purpose wasn't the point. Vassenka himself would undoubtedly have preferred something along the lines of what NATO called the SS-12 Scaleboard, a large, liquid-fueled rocket with a range of roughly five hundred miles. Or for that matter a Scud, fitted with a similar guidance system.

Ferg thought that Vassenka might be able to fit the Scuds with GPS kits; along with alterations to the notoriously fickle steering fins and so-so engine, the improvements would make the missile considerably more effective than those Saddam had used during the first Gulf War. The location of these Scuds was admittedly a huge question. Most of the analysts doubted that the resistance could be hiding more than one or two, though they conceded that Vassenka might have been "retained" to supply some from Korea or elsewhere along with rocket fuel and his improvements.

In any event, with the rocket fuel confiscated and Khazaal dead, the Scuds no longer seemed to be a threat. Rankin and Guns were checking leads on who might be left in Khazaal's organization, making sure they didn't have the Scuds. It was a long shot, and this wasn't their sort of work, so it wasn't particularly surprising that they hadn't turned up anything.

Which brought them back to the Siren missile.

"I'm with the intel guys on that," said Corrigan. "You wouldn't use it against an urban target. It flies too low."

"For somebody like Vassenka, that's not going to be a problem," Ferguson told him. "If he can make a Scud accurate, he can make a Siren missile hit something in a city."

"You don't even know for sure that there was a missile."

"Don't start, Jack," said Ferg.

"I'm just pointing out—"

"Let me do the thinking, OK? Birk doesn't lie about what he's selling," Ferguson added, softening his voice a little. "Make sure Rankin knows I think the Siren might be a real threat. Tell him not to pay too much attention to the intelligence people. Not that he ever does."

"There'll be extensive coverage of the area where the missile could be launched from," Corrigan said. "Even though they don't think it's possible, they don't want to end up looking like fools. Predators, a Global Hawk, all sorts of aircraft will be overhead."

"All right."

"Airborne jammers will block the Glosnass and GPS satellites if there's a launch," added Corrigan. He was referring to devices designed to block the signals the guidance systems used to orient themselves. "A lot of systems are in place."

"Didn't the Air Force use a GPS bomb to destroy one of the Iraqi jammers during the war?" asked Ferguson.

As a matter of fact, the Air Force had, but jamming remained more art than science. Even if the GPS system was successfully blocked, the missile would carry a backup internal guidance system; the best defense was to find it before it launched.

"You going to Iraq?" Corrigan asked.

"I have some things to check out over here," said Ferguson. "I don't know at this point that I can come up with anything that Rankin or Cent-Com won't."

"I'll tell him you said that."

"You'll give him a heart attack. Have you found *Islamic Justice* yet?" Ferguson added, serious again.

"Come again?"

"Birk's yacht, the *Sharia*?"

"We told you, it's not in Syrian waters or anywhere nearby."

"Is that a no?"

"Yeah, that's a no."

"I have a new place to look: off Israel."

"Israel?"

"Fifty to sixty miles from Jerusalem."

"Ferg, we have every available photo expert looking around Baghdad for the missile launchers."

"Get me the satellite photos and I'll look."

"Ferg, to pick out a yacht that size . . . All right. It'll take a few hours."

"E-mail them as soon as you can. I'm not sure where I'll be."

Ferguson found Thera waiting outside the secure communications shack.

"Dinner?" he asked.

"A little early."

"Not by the time we get there."

"We're going to Iraq?"

"No. I think Rankin can handle that all right. I have another wild goose chase for us. Grab your gear. Pack some sensible shoes."

"Always."

"And a bathing suit."

"I have my diving suit."

"Bathing suit. It may come in handy."

18

BAGHDAD
LATER THAT NIGHT . . .

The security people had already heard about the Russian missile and Vassenka by the time Corrine spoke to them. They were skeptical, especially when they heard that the missile had supposedly been delivered to Tikrit.

"It's well out of range," an Air Force major told her. "I wouldn't worry about it."

"The idea was that they would move it," she said. Corrigan had arranged for Rankin to give her a briefing an hour before. They were following a lead on Vassenka, though she had gathered from Corrigan that it was a long shot.

"We'll have coverage around the clock," said the major. "If they come out to set it up, we'll see them. It won't be a problem, believe me."

"I'd like to," said Corrine.

The others looked at her, waiting for her to add something optimistic, but she didn't.

19

The marina where Thatch's credit card had been used catered to very well-off locals and a few extremely wealthy tourists, providing general services and specializing in week-long rentals of cabin cruisers. From the amount of the charge on Thatch's card, it appeared that the account had been used for one of the latter: a deposit equivalent to a thousand dollars had been charged, along with a fee close to five hundred entered separately.

Ferguson wanted more information than the simple line in the account would give. When he and Thera arrived, the marina's business office had just closed, which was perfect, actually.

"How do you figure that?" asked Thera as he walked back up the road toward their rental car.

"I am pretty hungry," he told her. "Let's go have some dinner and come back later."

"Later?"

"I prefer to do my breaking and entering at night."

A half hour later, having not only talked his way into the exclusive Ile de France restaurant several blocks away but also secured a table with a superb view of the Mediterranean, Ferguson ordered a bottle of Les Bressandes, a Burgundy red that was both obscure and *tr*é*s* expensive. He was not quite the wine snob that the choice implied; he chose the wine as well as the restaurant primarily because of the price. He watched Thera as she studied the menu, trying to gauge her reactions to the place, the prices, and the ambience. He was back to looking for context, though he remained aware that there were limits: a person might be comfortable with wealth or uncomfortable, envious or indifferent; none of those things made him or kept him from a being a thief. Or her, in this case.

"Here's mud in your eye," said Ferguson, clinking glasses with Thera after the wine was poured, scandalizing the overly pretentious wine steward who had hovered nearby.

"Wow, this is good," said Thera, taking a sip. She looked around the restaurant. "You eat in places like this all the time?"

"When the job calls for it."

"And it does here?"

"Absolutely." Ferguson picked up the menu. "I'm going to have a lot of food: soup, salad, the whole nine yards. Get a good feed bag going."

Thera saw the look of disdain on the waiter's face as he overheard Ferguson's American slang. But when he asked Ferguson in a rather forced French accent whether *Monsieur* was prepared to order, Ferg ripped off his order in French so rapid and fluent that the man—who came from the Ukraine, not France—was lost.

"You love doing that to people, don't you?" Thera asked. "You just love riding them."

"He was pretty pretentious."

"But you would have ridden him anyway."

"Probably." He reached into his pocket and took out the bracelet. "Look what I found on the beach."

Thera took it. "Wow."

"You can have it, if you want," Ferguson added.

"Where'd you get it?"

"Told you. I found it on the beach."

She took it in her hand, unsure exactly what to say. "Ferg . . . Listen, Bob, I don't want to be part of this."

"Part of which?"

"Part of whatever it is you're doing. You're skimming money, right?"

"What if I were?"

"God, you can't. That is so—" She folded her arms in front of her chest, surprised that he was so blatant about it. Then she worried what he might do.

"That's from the briefcase, isn't it?" she said. "And you didn't turn the money in from the car in the desert."

"Why would I take money?" he asked her.

"You tell me."

"Why would you do it?"

"I wouldn't."

She'd been a little too loud. From the corner of her eye she saw heads turning in their direction. Thera reached for her glass and took a slow sip.

"You think I held that money?" he asked her. The idea that someone might question *his* honesty had never occurred to him.

"Yes." Thera stared at his eyes, trying to decipher what was going on. Was he testing her?

"Why would I hang on to that? It was counterfeit."

"No."

"Yeah, it was."

"Really?"

"Check."

"Should I call Corrigan?"

"Corrigan wouldn't know counterfeit money if he printed it himself. Call Van Buren. We're due to check in anyway. Give him our location and say 'Oh, by the way, that fifty g's Ferguson found in the desert . . .'"

"But maybe you lied to him."

"I guess. And I swapped it out with counterfeit money I just happened to have with me."

"I will ask him."

"You should."

Their dinners came, and they ate in silence. If she was giving him a performance, Ferguson thought, it was a world-class one.

So who took the jewels?

Oh, thought Ferguson. *Sheesh.* "Talk about in front of my face," he muttered.

"Excuse me?" said Thera.

"A lot of food here," he said, picking through the vegetables.

When dinner was over, Thera went and called Van Buren. The colonel confirmed that Ferguson had turned in the counterfeit money.

"Why are you asking?"

Embarrassed but relieved, she said, "I'm getting nosy in my old age."

Even though it was well past sundown, the tiny lights lining the marina docks as well as the building made anyone at the front easily visible. The back of the building, however, was cast in shadow, and the window was open. Unfortunately, the building backed onto the water, which meant the only way in was to climb up out of the waves or a small boat. Ferguson picked one up from a row stacked on shore and plopped it into the water.

"You think there's a burglar alarm inside?" asked Thera.

"I'm kind of hoping they don't have anything worth stealing," said Ferguson, leaning down and paddling with his hands. "I wouldn't want to be tempted."

"Am I going to hear about this for the rest of my life?"

"Just a good portion of it."

Ferguson paddled the boat under the window and held it against the structure. The open window argued strongly that there wasn't an alarm, but Thera checked anyway, bringing up the infrared glasses and using them from the corner of the window to look first for a pyroelectric sensor and then a laser or similar device. Pyroelectric sensors, commonly found in cheap motion detectors, worked by scanning the air for a change in heat energy. While not difficult to defeat—Ferguson had a soapy substance that would blur the sensor's window, effectively dulling its vision—the sensor itself had to be spotted, and looking around the room carefully took some time.

"Ah, just stick your head in. If the alarm goes off, we'll know something's there," said Ferg.

"Maybe it'll be a silent alarm."

"The stuff they have that's worth stealing is out on the water," said Ferguson. "If they didn't chain the small boats, they're not going to go crazy with burglar alarms. The front door is probably open."

"Patience is a virtue," said Thera, pulling out the bug detector to look for a device that used sonar or radio waves.

"I thought it was one of the deadly sins."

"Oh, the nuns would be proud of you."

Satisfied that there were no alarms, Thera pulled herself up and into the building. By the time Ferguson followed, she had found the computer and was hunched over the keyboard, waiting for it to boot up. The machine wasn't password protected, but the point-of-sale program used to record rentals and credit card charges was.

"We can steal the drive," Thera suggested. "Have someone analyze the data."

"We don't have to do that," said Ferguson, staring at the wooden board where the boat keys were hung. Double sets sat on each peg, except for one: A3. The alphanumeric system referred to the mooring places. Worst case scenario: they could have figured out what the boat looked like by comparing the photo of the marina on the wall with the boats outside. But that wasn't necessary; the boats each had a little paper file with important information in the cabinets next to the desk, and Ferguson found that A3 was a fiberglass cabin cruiser that could sleep six. It was called the *Jericho*, and its engines had been serviced two months before.

"This is the boat," he told her, showing her the file.

"Who's using the card? His sister?"

"I'm not sure yet," said Ferguson. "Except that it's not Thatch."

"It has to be the sister," said Thera. "Or Mossad. They had access to his wallet and card."

"Could be us," said Ferguson.

"You can rule us out."

"Not yet. Come on. We need to get to the airport, and I have to check my e-mail."

BALAD

AFTER MIDNIGHT . . .

The security was so tight that Rankin, Guns, and James had trouble getting into the city. Troops had staked out all of the areas that Rankin and Guns had ID'd from satellite photos as possible launch sites and several others besides. Heavily armed Iraqi units crisscrossed the major roads and many of the minor ones, and there were already several helicopters and an AC-130 gunship orbiting overhead. An insurgent couldn't set off a firecracker in town, let alone set up a cruise missile.

More important, there were no Russian bars in the city, and even if there had been, they'd be closed; a nine p.m. curfew had been imposed.

They stopped at a temporary battalion headquarters near a checkpoint north of the city, catching some coffee and gossip. Word of the missile had been broadcast, and in fact a patrol had already investigated what turned out to be a false alarm.

The senior NCO on duty offered them a tent to sleep in. James wanted to take him up on the offer, but Rankin and Guns insisted they'd find their own place to stay. Which struck James as funny; the military guys were the ones who were supposed to be willing to rough it, not him.

James slid into the back of the Hummer, trying in vain to sleep as the truck bounced along the road. Rankin drove, the sound of the tires drilling into the side of his head, his body tense. His Beretta sat in his lap, and every so often he glanced toward his Uzi next to him.

"So you caught that guy up in Tikrit, huh?" said Guns, trying to talk to stay awake.

"Pretty far from there," said Rankin.

"Musta been tough, huh?"

"Catchin' him was easy."

Guns waited for more, but Rankin didn't volunteer anything else. After a minute or two, James slid forward. Guns thought—hoped—he'd supply more of the story but he didn't. Instead he asked what Guns did "in real life."

"This is real life," said Guns. "I'm a marine."

"For real?" asked James.

"Well, yeah. What do you think?"

"How'd you get hooked up with Stephen?" James asked.

"Lucky, I guess."

"Classified, huh?"

"It was an accident," said Guns.

"Everything in life's an accident," said James.

"You believe that?" asked Rankin.

"Pretty much."

"Lonely thing to think," said Rankin.

"You think God moves us around like pieces on a chessboard?" asked James.

"I didn't say that," answered Rankin. "You don't believe in God at all."

"That's not true. I told you, I don't believe in God in our image, as something we can understand. I think God's mysterious, beyond us. That's why I don't get hung up on religion."

"You can't just turn religion on and off," said Rankin.

"I didn't say you could." James leaned back in his seat. "What do you think, Sergeant?" he asked Guns. "You go to church?"

"When I can."

"Which one?"

"Next you're going to ask what kind of underwear he likes," Rankin said.

"I'm a boxer guy myself," said James.

"Methodist," offered Guns, but the other man had pushed back in his seat, watching the shadows along the road.

TEL AVIV

The security staff at the American embassy gave Ferguson an incredibly difficult time when he asked to use the secure communications facilities, so much so that at one point he was tempted to deck their supervisor. He didn't, but only because she looked like the type who might enjoy that sort of thing. She didn't know him and wasn't impressed when he offered to give her Parnelles's home phone number. Finally he managed to convince her that she should call Slott to see if he was legit. The woman didn't have the guts to come out and apologize herself, sending one of her red-faced peons out to show him to the room.

"You wouldn't want them to let just anyone in," said Lauren when he called the desk.

"Yeah, I hear Yāsser Arafāt was at the door just the other day," said Ferguson. "Listen, I need to feed you a picture of a boat for the satellite interpreters."

"Ferg, we're *really* stretched."

"No kidding. I thought you guys were goofing off. Tell you what, though, take the people you have looking for the Siren missile around Baghdad off the job. It's not there."

"Where is it?"

"The Red Sea, I think."

"The Red Sea?"

"Near Mecca," said Ferguson. "But I'll worry about that. I want them to look for a Scud within range of Baghdad."

"Huh?"

"That's why Vassenka went to Iraq. I don't know if the plane is a red herring or not. I have to talk to Rankin."

"What am I doing?"

"You're going to receive a photo of a boat that I send you and find someone who can tell me what it would look like in a satellite photo," said Ferguson. "Better would be to find someone who could figure that out for me, but I'll do it myself if I have to. Then you're going to send an alert out about a Scud missile in Iraq. Don't bother canceling the cruise missile; there's always a possibility I'm wrong. It's happened two or three times in my lifetime."

"Ferg."

"All right, once. But there's always a chance."

Rankin sounded as if he were sleeping when he answered his phone. "Rankin."

"Hey, Skippy, top of the morning to you."

"Ferguson."

"Listen, I've been doing a lot of thinking about Vassenka and what Khazaal had going."

"And?"

"Khazaal had to have had a Scud or at least parts for one. More, maybe. Vassenka's there. He must have brought fuel with him."

"I thought you said he brought a cruise missile."

"Never mind that."

"Ferguson—"

"The other thing that I'm thinking, I'm going to bet that Vassenka improved the range. Because at a hundred miles, we would have found it already, right?"

"They have a hundred-mile range," said Rankin.

"I think it's a little more. Check with Lauren. You know what? Tell her to get Thomas Ciello working on this. Get a rundown of all the mods Vassenka might try. The range has to be more. That was probably the key to the plan in the beginning."

"Ciello? Is that the UFO nut?"

"One and the same," said Ferguson. "I'll tell you, though, the way things have been going lately, I think I'm starting to believe in UFOs."

SOUTH OF THE SUEZ CANAL

The adrenaline shook Ravid so fiercely that he couldn't sleep. Finally he got up and began pacing around the small boat. The man at the helm nodded but said nothing.

They were beyond the Suez, the Egyptians paid off, and their paperwork taken care of. With every mile it became easier, but with every mile his heart seemed to beat faster. There were only hours left.

Once the missile was launched, Ravid would kill himself. He would not wait until it struck the target. What was the sense? He knew it would strike, and frankly if it didn't he would not want to taste the bitterness.

He had debated how exactly to do this—there was no question that he would do it—and finally decided to simply place a pistol in his mouth. It was a sure and simple solution, though it presented a problem: he didn't have a pistol.

He would have to borrow one but before the time for the launch. Well before. Otherwise they might try and stop him when the time came.

That was the strange thing, wasn't it? To stop someone from killing himself—what was the point?

Ravid curled his feet beneath him as he sat on the deck. Something itched at the very back of his throat.

He took a long, slow breath, thinking about the day he got married, remembering the moment when he looked at his new wife and felt incredible lust. And the day their son was born. He had nearly been stopped at a checkpoint the day before, disguised so he could come see her.

The ache remained. The men had brought beer with them; there were bottles in the cooler.

Ravid thought of Mecca and its destruction. He envisioned his revenge.

Not his only, nor that of the men who had come gladly to help him, an army of the wrathful, but revenge for everyone murdered by Muslims in the name of their God. For Jews, Christians, Israelites, Americans, Buddhists, Chinese—everyone. Let the Muslims taste what jihad truly was.

Ravid rose. The thirst had receded again. A light breeze blew; he felt it cool his face as he turned toward the dim lights of the shore in the distance.

Hours now. Just hours.

BAGHDAD
EARLY MORNING . . .

Unable to sleep, Corrine got out of bed at 4:30. She took a shower and got dressed, then left her room in the embassy annex to go over to the main building, where a command center had been set up to keep track of the president's progress. He was running late: no surprise there. Air Force One was now scheduled to touch down at 9:12 a.m.

The precision of the estimate would have amused him.

Corrine poured herself a cup of coffee, checking the overnight reports. While she'd been preoccupied with the First Team and the possible SSN-9 missile, the Secret Service, military security, and Iraqi interior ministry had been chasing down literally dozens of other rumors and possible plots. A suspected suicide-bomb factory had been raided overnight; rather than giving up, the five men inside had ignited their weapons store. Two of the soldiers involved in the raid had died. A truck filled with rocket-launched grenades had been stopped on the highway leading to the airport a few hours ago; its driver had been shot. A patrol of American soldiers had been sent into a town to the west of the airport after a report that a surface-to-air missile had been spotted; a firefight had followed.

Corrine imagined McCarthy looking at the reports. He'd nod, then say something about how much trouble it was to shoe a horse that hadn't been properly cared for. "Doesn't mean you give up," he'd say.

She'd heard him use that expression several times about Iraq and many more times about other problems in general. That was one of the things she liked most about him: he was always realistic and somehow optimistic at the same time. "Look far enough ahead," he'd say, "and you can't help but smile."

She was about to check in with Corrigan when one of the Secret Service people interrupted to tell her that the caravan for the airport was about to leave.

"Can you arrange for me to take a later one?" she asked.

"This is the last one, ma'am. They're going to shut down traffic at six."

Corrine managed to squeeze into one of the three vans that were heading over to the airport. The procession was sandwiched between a pair of armored Humvees. Two Delta plainclothes bodyguards sat in the front of each of the vans. Corrine barely had time to buckle her seat belt before the van started moving; by the time they left the compound the trucks were doing over fifty.

Speeding onto the highway, Corrine caught a glimpse of pink at the edge of the horizon, a brilliant band of predawn light greeting the day. *Jonathon has a good day for it*, she thought. He was the sort of man who liked to smile at the sunrise, saying good weather was in his genes.

"Faster!" yelled one of the men in the front of the van.

As Corrine started to look up to see what was going on, something exploded. Her body become weightless, even as her eyes remained fixed on the beautiful fringe between earth and heaven.

CIA BUILDING 24-442

Thomas Ciello sat in his office staring at the computer. On the left part of the screen was a summary report by one of the CIA's weapons teams about the possibilities of a missile being used in Iraq. Prepared six months before, the paper declared that *if* Scud missiles remained in Iraq, they were most likely stored as component parts scattered in hiding areas. Assembling the devices would require expertise and time. The analysts, being of a mathematical bent, had even put this into an equation, attempting to show that expertise might compensate for a lack of time and vice versa.

On the right part of the screen was a report from the Agency photo-interpretation team that had just finished examining the area around Baghdad at Ferguson's request, looking for a Scud missile or a prepared launch site. The report filled two pages, but the summary amounted to a single word: *nothing*.

Thomas had looked at the satellite and U-2 photos appended to the report and found nothing to suggest that the interpreters had missed something. A new series of infrared images would be available in a few minutes, and he was already near the top of the dissemination list.

Needing a break, he got up and went to his desk, retrieving a candy bar from the bottom drawer. As he unwrapped it, he started skimming through Professor Ragguzi's book again. He hadn't gotten very far the other day, thrown off by the Turkey reference. Now that he knew it wasn't a mistake, he could start reading again. It was as if he'd been blinded by that, as if all he could see were errors or potential errors. Now that he understood the professor's point, he could read it again with a clearer, fairer mind.

Oh, he realized. That's the problem. Everyone's looking for the missiles.

He pushed the candy bar into his mouth, threw the blanket over his desk, and ran to talk to Corrigan in the Cube.

25

NORTH OF TIKRIT
DAWN . . .

Rankin pulled the sat phone from his pocket as it began to vibrate. He pried the antenna out from the body of the phone awkwardly as he drove, both hands on the wheel. The others were dozing, and the truth was he felt like pulling over and joining them.

"You need to look for sewer pipes," said Corrigan.

"What are you talking about?"

"Hold on."

A new voice came on the line. It was Thomas Ciello. "They're hiding the missile somewhere."

"You think?" said Rankin.

"A sewer pipe or something like that. I have the interpreters on it. There are a couple of places in Tikrit. I think you should go there."

"Why would they hide it in a sewer pipe?" Rankin's experience with intelligence types had not been very good, and Thomas was crazier than the rest.

"Not in it; with it. From the air, it would look like it belonged. You'd really have to get up close to check it. I have them looking at old sites," added Thomas. "I think maybe it was in a pile for a long time and then recently moved. There are about forty sites within the hundred-mile range, and nearly double that if we got to a hundred and fifty miles. It would be nearby, I think. I mean, we could look through the whole country, but—"

"A hundred and *fifty*?" asked Rankin.

"Oh yeah. I was going to tell you that, too. That's the total range Vassenka can achieve. There are a few simple modifications. The rocket fuel has to be properly prepared, but once that's taken care of, everything else falls into place." The analyst spoke quickly, as if he were afraid that he would run out of breath before he got his entire idea out of his mouth. "It's probably going to be set up at the last minute, so maybe there's a place with an overhang or something they're counting on, even say a tarp or something. I wanted to look at every mosque that had a roof repair recently or ongoing, and—"

"Could you hide rocket fuel in a kerosene tank?" asked Rankin. "Not a tank; a tank car. Like a train."

"Kerosene?"

"It said kerosene."

"The Russians developed it from the V-2. There were experiments," said Thomas.

"What are you mumbling about?" asked Rankin.

"I have to get back to you."

"Do that." Rankin tossed the phone to Guns, sitting in the seat next to him, then pulled a U-turn across the two lanes of traffic.

26

BAGHDAD

Something about the way the van's momentum shifted reminded Corrine of an accident she'd been in as a six-year-old. She hadn't thought of that moment in years, but it came back to her now, and she pushed her neck down against gravity, hunkering in the van as she had in the sedan that had gone off a mountain road in a snowstorm two decades before. She felt the six-year-old's mixture of horror and fascination, the fear when her mother didn't answer right away. She heard the loud crack of the airbags and the long hush that followed, the incongruous silence as the car lay in the field, slowly being covered by snow.

And then she was back in the present, the van on its side, thrown off the pavement by the force of a two-hundred-and-fifty-pound bomb buried beyond the shoulder of the highway.

"Out! We have to get out!" said one of the bodyguards.

"Out, yes," Corrine said. She grabbed at her seat belt latch and undid it, then pushed up against the door. The door flew from her hand. One of the soldiers who'd been riding in the rear Humvee reached in and grabbed for her, helping her pull herself out. She jumped down to the ground, pushing against the chassis to steady herself. Remembering where she was, she ducked down and took out her small Smith & Wesson pistol, holding it in both hands as she scanned the side of the road.

"In the Hummer! Everybody in the Hummer! Let's go, let's go, let's go!" shouted the soldier who'd helped her out.

A helicopter whipped toward them.

The driver of the van had been lifted out and helped down to the pavement, moaning. The airbag had exploded in his face, and he was burned. Corrine grabbed his arm and led him toward the Humvee. She pushed him inside and then ran back to the van. The passenger on the far side of her had been cut by a piece of metal or glass in the door and was bleeding profusely.

Corrine grabbed the sleeve of her shirt and ripped it off, trying to stop the blood.

"Into the Humvee," said one of the soldiers. "Come on now. Out of here."

"We need a medical kit," she said.

"In the Hummer, ma'am. Come on."

Corrine kept her hand pressed to the man's neck as the soldier took him in his arms and carried him to the truck. She wedged herself into the back, where a medical kit lay open on the floor. She grabbed gauze and wrapped it over the sleeve and wound, pushing in tightly to try and staunch the flow of blood. She could feel the man's pulse ebb and flow beneath her fingers.

"Hospital," she said.

"We're in! Go!" yelled one of the soldiers, and the Hummer jerked forward.

"This is one screwed-up place," muttered someone. Corrine didn't know who said it, but she certainly agreed.

THE RED SEA

Getting to Yanbu on the coast of the Red Sea at the lip of the Saudi Arabian desert was only half as hard as finding a serviceable boat there. Finally Ferguson found a man who ran a diving business who agreed to rent them a vessel for the day, as long as they paid twice the normal rate in cash. Ferguson didn't have that much cash; it was Thera who suggested the bracelet.

The man said he would take a credit card.

Once they cast off, Ferguson had Thera take the wheel. He unpacked their weapons from the duffle bags and called Corrigan for an update.

"I have a lot of stuff going on here, Ferg."

"Gee, Jack. No kidding. I thought you were hanging out knocking down beers."

"Rankin thinks he knows where the Scud missile is."

"Good. Can you get me a Global Hawk down here? The satellite image is pretty old."

"Every available asset in the Middle East is over Iraq. There's a satellite coming over your area in twenty minutes. A team is standing by to analyze it. That's the best I can do."

"Where's Van?"

"They're en route to back up Rankin."

"All right," said Ferguson. "The photo guys know what the *Sharia* looks like?"

"They'll do their best."

"Call me back." He snapped off the phone.

Thera looked over from the wheel. "What did he say?"

"Not much. I figure we have about twenty miles before we have to really worry. Open the throttle up and let her rip."

"It could be a wild goose chase. The boats in the satellite photo aren't necessarily the ones we're looking for, and they might not have come this way."

"I hope so," said Ferguson. He was putting two and two together and coming up with forty-four: the most recent satellite photo showed a yacht like the *Sharia* in the Red Sea. He hadn't been able to find the speedboat, or, rather, he'd seen plenty similar. His theory was that the *Sharia* had gone south alone for some reason, with Coldwell or whoever had used Thatch's credit card joining up from Tel Aviv. He might be wrong, but being wrong would be easier to deal with than just missing them.

"Did you really think I stole the jewels?" asked Thera.

"I still do."

"That's not funny."

"Nah. You would have plugged me in the back by now if you had." Ferguson reached into his bag and took out a battered Boston Red Sox cap to shield his eyes from the sun. Then he took out his binoculars and began scanning the horizon in the direction of Mecca.

"That's good enough for me. We're going to do a reecee on the lumberyard. Have Van meet us there."

"He's twenty minutes away."

"We'll be inside. Tell him about the building."

"Do you really think—"

Rankin killed the phone and stuffed it into his pocket. Ferguson didn't get second-guessed like this. When he said something, people saluted.

"You think we should update the CentCom security people?" Guns asked.

"They're only going to tell us again to check it out and get back to them," said Rankin, opening his door. "We can get up there before CentCom gets back to us anyway. Gear up."

"I'll stay with the car," said James. "Somebody's got to, right?"

"No. We may need you," said Rankin. "If we come across someone who speaks only Arabic."

"Your Arabic's fine, Stephen."

"Yours is a lot better. I'm all right with a few phrases, but once they get going, I get lost."

"It's a long walk," said James.

"Don't be such a wimp."

"I am a wimp."

"Yeah, right."

Guns didn't think it would be that bad an idea if someone stayed back with the vehicle, but he didn't feel like arguing with Rankin. They put their weapons into civilian-style knapsacks—having guns out might panic the wrong people—and trotted across the road. They continued across a patch of scrubby land to the railroad tracks, then walked down them in the direction of the lumberyard. After about fifty yards, Guns spotted a ditch on the far side of the tracks. They had to pick their way over rubble at several spots, but it covered their approach. They walked to within fifty yards of the tanker car, where Rankin saw a guard slouched in the shade.

"Case closed," said James.

"Doesn't prove anything. We have to get inside."

"Just send the police out here."

"Man, James, you really are wimping today," said Rankin.

"I tell you, I'm a coward."

Guns looked over at the journalist. He thought he'd see him smile or wink, but the look on his face was very serious.

"You have your sat phone?" Rankin asked him.

"Yeah."

28

NEAR AL FATTAH, IRAQ

There were guards at the entrance to the lumberyard. Behind them, th
fence was locked and chained. James told the men that they had busines
with the manager. The men told him the manager wouldn't be in until ten o
eleven, and the yard wouldn't open until then.

"Tell them we'll wait inside," said Rankin.

James tried it, but the guards claimed not to have the keys.

"Have them call the manager."

"No phone," translated James. "I think they meant the manager. That
very possible. Half the country doesn't have working phones."

Rankin looked at the men. There were four of them. They were sepa
rated well, positioned in such a way that they could pummel the vehicle i
anyone inside opened fire. The fence to the yard opened on a set of barrie
and a stationary forklift; it was impossible to simply crash the gate and get ir

"Tell them we'll come back," said Rankin.

"Ask for a place to have breakfast," suggested Guns. "A good, lon
breakfast."

"You hungry?" asked Rankin.

"If they think we're having breakfast, they won't be watching for us."

"You got that from Ferg," said Rankin. He turned to James. "Ask for a
American-style breakfast."

They drove a mile down the highway to a spot where the road curve
and they could stop without being seen from the lumberyard. When the
stopped, Rankin called Corrigan in the Cube. "What did the space cadet fin
out about kerosene?"

"Kerosene was used for the very first set of rockets developed," sai
Corrigan, who was reading notes Thomas had prepared. "It would require
heavy modifications but is potentially usable, if an expert prepared the
rocket. Other possible fuels include—"

"I have a number for you to call if we get greased."

James took a small pad and pen from his pocket and wrote it down. "I don't know where we are."

"The guy you talk to will. You call that number and you duck. You got me?"

"Stephen—"

"You duck. Run the other way. No heroics. Because they will take out everything in their path. Everything."

James shook his head.

Rankin looked at Guns. "We flank this guy?"

"I think I can crawl up behind him if you attract his attention."

"Shoot him if you have to."

"Don't worry about that."

Guns crawled two car lengths beyond the tank car, then got out of the ditch and moved to the tracks. He thought of climbing up the car and attacking the guard from above but decided he'd have trouble if the Iraqi moved before he could attack.

When Rankin saw that Guns was in position, he moaned, softly first, then louder. The guard walked a few yards in his direction, gun pointed at the ground.

Guns began to follow, stepping as lightly as he could. When he was no more than twenty feet away the guard stopped. Guns froze, standing so silently he could hear a rasp in the man's chest as he breathed.

The Iraqi turned toward him anyway. Rankin took him down with a burst that caught him in the side of the head.

Guns cursed, then leapt toward the fence. Rankin ran and grabbed the gun the Iraqi had dropped, then joined Guns as the marine put his rifle to the lock on the twelve-foot-high gate where the train entered the yard and blew it off.

The gate didn't budge when they pushed. Rankin reared back and threw himself against it. When it still didn't move, he began to climb. He had just reached the top when a guard appeared from the area of the building. The man yelled something, then dropped to one knee and fired his M16.

Losing his grip, Rankin slid down the fence to the ground inside the lumberyard. He crumpled to the ground, safe behind a pile of lumber. Guns managed to pry enough of the gate away from the fence to get in without exposing himself to the gunfire.

Rankin pushed up and fired a burst from his Uzi. As he ducked back under a hail of bullets, he saw a long hose that ran from the building out toward the gate they had just climbed. "Guns, you remember that hose?"

Guns looked over. The hose, a little thicker than a standard garden hose and red, sat in the middle of the aisle he had walked down the day before.

"I don't think so. You smell that? There's kerosene all over the place. Worse than the other day."

Rankin wasn't sure about that, but he did know this had to be the place.

"Call in support," he told Guns. "Get an attack plane or an Apache up here to take out that building. The rocket has to be in there. Get them up here fast."

A heavy machine gun drowned out the last of his words.

THE RED SEA

Ravid checked his watch. The American satellite was just now passing overhead. They would begin to assemble the missile as soon as it was gone.

According to his calculations, it would take a bit over two hours to get the missile ready for launch. They would be vulnerable to detection during that time, of course, but it was unlikely anyone would be watching too closely. Certainly the Americans would have every available resource focused on Baghdad. And the Israelis would not bother to protect Islam.

Two hours, and revenge would be his.

Revenge and so much more.

BAGHDAD

By the time they got to the hospital, the man Corrine had tried to save had bled to death. She realized it a few blocks away, but refused to let go of him, as if admitting the obvious was some sort of sacrilege. Only when the doctor started to reach into the Humvee for him at the emergency entrance did she remove her hand and shake her head.

"You better look at the others," she said.

Inside the building, a nurse steered Corrine to a gurney.

"No, I have to get to the airport," Corrine told her. The woman started to argue, but Corrine just walked away. She saw a female doctor working on one of the men who had come in with her. His arm had caught some shrapnel, but the wounds weren't serious.

"Do you have a shirt I could borrow?" Corrine asked. "I'm not wounded; this isn't my blood."

The woman's shirt was a size too big, but it was clean. Corrine found a pair of fatigues in a nearby locker and pulled them on as well. Then she went over to the administration desk, where a major told her that the city was being locked down and all the roads were now closed.

"Well, Major, you'd better open them for me," Corrine told him. "I'm the president's counsel, and if I'm not there when Air Force One touches down, you and everybody you know will never get another promotion."

The major told her she could stuff her threats and turned to walk away.

She grabbed his shirtsleeve. "Look, I was out of line and I apologize. But I need to be there."

He still wasn't happy, but a few minutes later an AH-6 Little Bird helicopter put down in the parking area outside the building.

"Airport," Corrine yelled as she got inside.

"I know," yelled the pilot.

Corrine held on as the helo picked up its tail and skittered toward the airport. Two Blackhawk helicopters skimmed over the roadway nearby, running a patrol. An AC-130 Spectre gunship orbited over the outskirts of the airport, its black hulk prominent against the blue sky.

From the air, it looked as if there were a full division of American soldiers on the ground at and around the facility. Vehicles of all descriptions guarded the perimeters and surrounding roads. Even though their aircraft had been cleared in, and even though everyone on the field knew who its passenger was, a pair of armed guards met Corrine and escorted her to an area on the infield where her ID was checked. Corrine knew the Secret Service agent supervising the checkpoint, but the woman searched her anyway.

As she started to walk toward the terminal, one of the soldiers nearby craned his head up. The president's plane had just appeared overhead. The earlier reports that said it was behind schedule were part of a disinformation campaign to keep potential enemies off guard. The blue-and-white 747 turned tightly and nearly dropped straight down on the runway, the pilot using all of his skills as well as every ounce of the aircraft's aerodynamic qualities to lessen the chance of a surface-to-air strike. The plane raced to the end of the concrete before stopping. Then, rather than taking the ramp, it turned at the very edge of the runway and taxied back toward the middle of the strip. A military honor guard double-timed out of the terminal, and Corrine headed toward the reception area, where the ambassador was already waiting.

He did a double take when he saw her. "You all right?"

"I am now."

Four men rolled a ladder out to the plane. It was a bare metal model, not because of economy but because the Secret Service wanted to be absolutely sure there was no possibility of unseen explosives being planted on it.

Two helicopters hovered overhead as a Secret Serviceman popped his head out of the hatchway. President McCarthy emerged a moment later, strolling down the steps as casually as if they were back in Washington. Ambassador Bellows and several members of the CentCom command in Iraq stepped forward to meet him. Corrine felt her shoulders sag. She wanted to relax, but she knew it was far too early for that.

"Miss Alston, there you are," he told Corrine when he spotted her. "You lead an interesting life, young lady. Very interesting." He took her hand, squeezed it, and leaned close. "I am glad to see that you are all right."

"Thank you, Mr. President."

"Now tell me all about it," he said a little louder. "Stay at my side, *deah*. I must say, there is nothing that makes an ol' Georgia stallion look more handsome than to have a fresh young filly by his side."

Ambassador Bellows beamed at her from behind the president, then stepped up to introduce members of his staff. A Secret Service agent came up and gave Corrine a cap and pin similar to the president's and the chief of staff's so they'd know her at a glance. When the president finally finished shaking everyone's hand, they were shown to a line of limos that had just come up. The president, Corrine, and chief of staff got into the lead limo. The cars drove across the complex toward a hangar for a ceremony with the troops. As they approached, the president's limo turned off into a building next to the one where the ceremony was planned. Rather than walking there, the trio and the Secret Service bodyguards hopped into a pair of SUVs and drove to a second hangar. McCarthy strolled to the back of the building, where an AH-6 similar to the aircraft Corrine had taken here was waiting.

"We're getting into that?" Corrine asked.

"Don't fret, Miss Alston. These are fine aircraft," said McCarthy. "I flew one of these when I was in the National Guard and you were nothing but a gleam in your daddy's eye."

"I'm not fretting. I don't want you to fall out."

McCarthy gave her one of his best down-home grins and climbed into the bird. "If it'll make you feel any better. I'll set myself back here. Someone else can drive."

Within a minute, the helicopter took off, joining a formation flanking two larger, slower aircraft over Baghdad. Five minutes later, they set down outside the new Parliament building.

The Secret Service people tried to hurry McCarthy inside, but the president was not one to be rushed. He greeted the servicemen nearby, shaking each man's hand as calmly as if he were on a campaign swing back home.

"Now, Miss Alston," he said, taking her by the arm as they entered the building. "Y'all have been here and I'd appreciate a nice homey tour. First hand, as it were."

"Anything you say, sir."

When they were in the hall, the president stopped her and leaned his lanky frame toward her. "We won't get another chance to talk, so tell me, *deah*: Is Peter the man to carry water for me between the Israelis and the Palestinians, or should I find another horse for that plow?"

"You told me it wasn't up to me."

"It is not, Counselor. I am looking, however, for an unvarnished opinion. Yea or nay."

"It's not as simple as that," she protested.

"Would you trust him?"

Corrine took a breath. Her responsibility was to the president, not to Bellows, and the answer to his question was clear.

"I'm afraid he won't tell you what's really going on," she said. "I don't know that he would even realize he was lying. You said you wanted someone who would tell you what you didn't want to hear. If that's your criterion, I would say absolutely not."

McCarthy's eye narrowed ever so slightly. Then he smiled and continued walking.

31

NEAR AL FATTAH, IRAQ

The machine gun seemed to drain the air around him, as if it were a vacuum trying to suck all the life away. Rankin hugged the ground, the bullets so close he didn't even dare squeeze his hand beneath his body for one of his two grenades.

Whoever was working the gun began walking the bullets toward the railroad track. Rankin squirreled around, reaching for one of the grenades. He reared back and tossed it, but felt it go off his fingers awkwardly, flying to the left of where he intended. He cursed loudly and hit the dirt as the machine-gunner began firing in his direction again; the grenade exploded harmlessly behind a pile of cement bags.

Guns wasn't under direct fire and managed to move forward on his elbows and knees, trying to find an angle where he could see what was going on. He reached the end of the row and saw the machine gun in the distance, but not the gunman, who had found a spot between two large stacks of cement blocks. He pulled out one of the two small grenades he had and tossed it in a high arc; the grenade hit the ground a yard behind the man and exploded.

By then Guns had pulled out his sat phone. "Corrigan. We're in the lumberyard. We're taking heavy fire. This has to be the place."

"There's an AC-130 gunship en route, no more than ten minutes away," said the desk man. "Van's right behind them. Get out of there now!"

"Tell the president not to land."

"He's on the ground already and in the city. Get out of there!"

"Rankin!" yelled Guns. "We have to stall them. AC-130's on the way."

"Let's circle. You go wide right. Once that gunship shows up, get the hell away."

"No shit," mumbled Guns. He dashed between the rows of wood, expecting bullets to start spraying again. He could hear machinery working in the direction of the building and a truck or something headed in his direction. It was a forklift with a load of cement bricks at the front and four or five men behind it.

Guns ducked as they began to fire. He took his last grenade and threw it in their direction. As it blew up he dove across the open alley, rolling behind a pile of sand. He ran to the side, hoping to flank anyone who'd survived his grenade.

Meanwhile, Rankin worked his way to the fence on the opposite side of the yard. The building sat about fifty yards away, beyond a hodgepodge of lumber and building materials. He caught sight of three or four Iraqis hunkering down, going in Guns's direction. He hesitated but let them go; his first responsibility was preventing a launch before the gunship arrived.

Moving mostly on his hands and knees, he managed to work parallel to the rear of the building, where he could see through the open wall. The tractor of a large truck sat at the edge there, its motor running.

The missile sat on a trailer with a girderlike gantry, fully erect, behind it. The cylindrical finger sat below the blue tarp of the roof, a simple but effective menace.

He was fifty yards away. Two spotlights sat across from him inside the building, facing the ground beyond the rocket. Their beams were overpowered by the daylight. Rankin realized that they must have been turned on hours before; the Scud must be ready to fire.

Rankin rose to throw his grenade. As he did, a burst of gunfire caught his side and leg, sending him pirouetting to the ground. The grenade, its pin gone, flew up from his hand. He watched it hover there, unsure where it would go. He couldn't move.

He'd been paralyzed two years ago as well, but then not by a bullet but by fear. More than fear: by the certainty that he was going to die.

They all saw it. And they all felt the same thing, except James.

James, the guy who was just there to write about them, just along for the ride. He jumped up, bounded onto it, saved them all.

And it didn't explode.

This one did, but it fell on the other side of a huge pile of sand Rankin had fallen behind. As dirt flew everywhere, Rankin pulled up the Uzi and fired back in the direction of the man who'd shot at him. The man tumbled to the ground.

Rankin struggled to get up. His vest had protected him against the bullets that hit his side, but two bullets had hit his leg, both in his calf, and it collapsed under him. He rolled against the dirt, off balance and dazed.

On the other side of the yard, Guns worked to get behind the forklift. The driver was slumped against the wheel, and there were other bodies on the ground near it. Two Iraqis turned the corner behind it, moving cautiously forward, unaware that he was behind them. He waited until he had good shots on both, then fired, cutting them down. The marine climbed up on a stack of bricks, peering around to make sure no one was hiding in ambush. Not seeing anyone, he jumped and ran to it, throwing the dead driver to the side and jumping on. Climbing in behind the wheel he accidentally got his foot on the accelerator and the truck jerked forward. He let it go, steadying his speed—the engine didn't move very quickly—and wheeled down the next aisle. The wall of cement blocks on the front provided good cover, but it was impossible to see without peering to the side. He turned again, heading in the direction of the sideless building where the missile was being readied.

The front of the vehicle began to shake. Guns realized he was being fired at and jumped off the back as the fusillade intensified. A machine gun—an M60 set on a bipod—joined the four Iraqis firing M16s from near the building, chewing the bricks into dust.

Guns got to the next aisle, ducking behind a pile of bagged stone. As the gunfire continued, he climbed up and burned a box of bullets before the machine gunner managed to return fire. As he slid down to the ground he heard a rumble and thought it was the AC-130 approaching.

It wasn't: the missile had been ignited and was building pressure to launch.

THE RED SEA

Thera took a swig from the water bottle, letting the cold liquid run down the sides of her mouth. The heat was already building; it was going to be a hot, muggy day.

"How much farther?" she asked Ferguson. He was up at the bow, listening over the phone as an aide back in the Cube told him what they saw on the new satellite photos.

"Ten more minutes," he told her, taking his glasses and studying the horizon.

They'd passed two medium-sized oil tankers and a host of small dhows. The interpreter had spotted a boat that looked somewhat like the *Sharia*; he couldn't tell because it had a tarp covering the rear deck.

Not a good sign.

Ferguson was just about to put his phone back in his pocket when it began to ring. He saw an odd string of numbers on the face and opened it carefully, as if it might explode.

"Ferguson."

"Hey, Ferg."

"Michael. How'd you get the number?"

"I persuaded an old friend that it was important."

"OK." The only old friend it could be, Ferguson knew, was the general. "What's up?"

"Aaron Ravid's wife and son were killed by Islamic extremists eighteen months ago by a suicide bomber. He was taken out of service, but for some reason they called him back."

"Why?"

"I'm afraid that you would have to take that up with someone else."

Ferg could guess: it must have had to do with Meles. The Israelis didn't have too many agents with good access in Syria. New faces were one thing; a deeply planted, well-experienced agent was something else. They'd weighed the risks and called him back.

"Michael, thank you," said Ferg, ending the transmission.

NEAR AL FATTAH

Rankin began shooting at the building, pouring the rest of the Uzi's 9mm slugs at the steaming cylinder. He fired until the magazine was empty, fired even as the missile began to lift off the pad.

Then a sharp crack split the air, and he heard the sound of metal being torn apart. A ball of flames shot across the ground to his left. Before Rankin could do or think anything else, he felt himself being pushed backward as the building exploded. A fireball shot up from the truck that had been used as a launcher, the flames catching the tail of the modified Scud. Even as the missile pulled away from the ground through the hole in the roof, it had begun to veer off course.

Lying on his back, Rankin saw it twist to the right. A black finger curled around the side and then it keeled over, moving sideways through the air like a kid's balloon that had just gotten a pin it. The warhead exploded with a tremendous thunderclap. The framework of the building was on fire, ignited by the same flame that had run up the fuel line from the train car. Thick black smoke furled out across the yard.

"Guns! Guns!" yelled Rankin. "That was a great idea. Guns!"

"Over here," said Guns, opposite where Rankin expected him to be. The marine fired a fresh burst at the spot where the machine gun had been, but the Iraqis had retreated as soon as the missile launched and were now running to escape. The AC-130 droned in the distance, an angry bee late to the picnic.

"Guns?" Rankin, hobbled by his wounds, pushed in his direction.

"Down!" yelled Guns, spotting a figure with a pistol. He fired his M4 too late; the other man ducked as he fired.

Rankin went down. The bullet had missed, but the jerk to his knee was too much and he lost his balance. He dropped his gun as he fell. Before he could roll onto his stomach and retrieve it, the other man kicked it away.

It was Vassenka. The Russian extended his pistol slowly. "I hate Americans," he said, taking aim, "but I love watching them die. Slowly. With great pain. I do this for free."

A shot rang out from behind Rankin, then another. The bullets hit Vassenka in his chest. Staggering, he looked up, surprised.

James fired twice more. Vassenka sunk to his knees, then fired his own gun, striking James in the chest before collapsing.

Guns ran over and kicked the pistol from Vassenka's hand. All four of James's bullets had struck the Russian, but they were .32 caliber, small slugs in a big body. One had hit him close to the neck, and blood pumped steadily from the wound.

There was a chance he might live if someone stopped it from bleeding quickly. Guns took his weapons, stuffed them in his belt, then left him to die.

Rankin crawled over and cradled his friend's head in his arms. "James?"

"Hey, Stephen. I got tired of waiting, man. I hope you don't mind that I set the thing on fire. I figured you guys were in trouble."

Unlike James's gun, Vassenka's pistol fired a large, thick slug. Blood was surging from the wound into James's lungs and chest cavity.

"You saved my life," Rankin told him.

"You should have thought of that, Stephen. Just set the damn thing on fire. You're a bright guy. You should've thought of it. Not me."

"I should have thought of it, James. You're right."

"I thought it was going to explode."

"The rocket? It went off course."

"The grenade," said James, remembering. "I really thought it would go off."

"So'd we all."

"I wanted to die, man. That's why I went with you guys. I just wanted to be gone. And since that time, so many times, I might have done something worthwhile, but what am I?"

James began coughing.

"You're a hero. You saved my life," Rankin told him. "You saved a lot of people's lives."

James closed his eyes, slipping away. "I really thought the grenade was going to explode."

ACT VII

It is done.

—Revelation 16:17 (King James Version)

1

THE RED SEA

Ferguson could see the *Sharia* about a mile ahead. The yacht sat dead in the water, not moving. Nor was there anyone topside. A large tarpaulin flapped on the deck at the stern, covering several large crates. So maybe Birk hadn't sold the missile after all, or at least hadn't gotten around to delivering it.

"You sound disappointed," said Thera as Ferguson described what he saw.

"Not necessarily," he told her. "Come up slow. Remember, the guy who owns that tub is an arms dealer. He could have anything short of a nuke aboard. He might even have that."

"You sure we should go aboard ourselves? Why don't we just call in backup?"

"Who are we going to call?"

"The navy comes to mind."

"It'll be next week before they can spare someone."

Ferguson picked up his shotgun, deciding to stick with nonlethal bullets as his first choice. But he strapped on the waterproof backpack with the MP5N just in case.

They circled around the *Sharia* without seeing anyone. The anchor line was extended into the water.

"Let me get off, then you pull away," Ferguson said. "I'm worried about booby traps."

"If you're worried about booby traps, why don't we just wait for the navy?"

"If we wait and then this turns out to be nothing, how would I show my face at the next bar fight?"

Ferguson went over to the side, watching the yacht. He stepped, up then swung over the side, jumping across to the platform at the fantail. Once on the deck, he looked at the tiedowns to the tarp, trying to find booby traps. He couldn't see any, nor did the detector find any bugs or radio devices. Ferguson walked up to the bow, then went back along to the cabin area.

"Birk?" he yelled. "Yo, guess who."

No one answered.

"Hey, you dumb Polack, what are you doing?" Ferguson shouted. "Did you ever hear the joke about the Polish guy and the Irish guy and pig?"

Ferguson stepped down into the galley area and through the enclosed space to the ladder that led down to Birk's suite of living quarters.

"Birk!"

The door to Birk's cabin was ajar. Ferguson could see part of Birk's bed, its covers taut and neat.

He pushed the barrel of his shotgun into the crack and edged the door open. Mildly surprised not to find Birk's body on the bed, he slipped into the cabin. It looked pretty much exactly as he remembered from the other day.

Back topside, Ferguson took out a knife and hacked off the lines holding down the tarp. The two crates below the plastic were empty.

"How are we doing?" yelled Thera from the other boat. She'd cut her engine and was drifting toward him.

"Not so well," said Ferguson.

"Should I come aboard?"

"No, I'm just about done here. Come up alongside. I'll be right back."

Ferguson went up to the bridge area, looking for a logbook or some other records. None were visible, and the only chart he could find was a generic map that looked as if it came from a geographic atlas; it surely wasn't the sort of thing a sailor would use to plot a long trip. Birk, who thought he was a real sailor, would surely have used real charts.

Ferguson looked around for a gun locker, interested in a grenade launcher or something large enough to stop another boat. Birk had stowed a variety of weapons on his first yacht, partly for defense and mostly to wow visitors. Most likely, thought Ferguson, he would have done the same aboard the *Sharia*.

There were lockers in a storeroom next to the main lounge. In one there was a kit for an SA-7. Designed as an antiair weapon, the lightweight shoulder-launched missile would home in on any heat source, and Ferguson thought he could use it against a ship if necessary. His credit was good enough that the arms dealer wouldn't mind if he borrowed a few items.

He surely wouldn't; his body had been stuffed into the longest of the lockers, right over a cache of grenade launchers.

BAGHDAD

Corrine watched the president as the audience of Iraqi government representatives rose to applaud. His gaze mixed confidence with just a touch of bemused awe, as if he were wondering to himself why everyone rose in his honor. The suggestion of humility had stood him well in politics, but it was not part of the polished act of being a politician; Jonathon McCarthy really was a humble man, or in his words, "one who knows where he stands in God's eye." It was a perspective, he had told her during his presidential campaign, that helped give him strength during difficult times.

That hadn't made sense to her then, but now she saw part of what he meant. McCarthy could see himself as one small step in a long march toward a goal, a view that helped him persevere against great odds but a difficult one for a powerful man or woman to take. It must be nearly impossible if you were president.

"Thank you, Mr. Prime Minister, cabinet members, parliament," said the president, beginning his speech. "It has been a long, difficult journey here since the dictator was deposed and incarcerated three years ago. There has been a great deal of suffering in this country and more pain than words can say."

Corrine listened as he continued, talking about the hope of democracy and the need for Iraq and other countries in the Middle East to find their own path to the future. "Religion will play an important role, as it always has, throughout the world, not just in the Middle East but especially in the Middle East," he said. "Islam is built on strong traditions of justice, of kindness, of strength, which are essential to the future. It also, like many religions, has given rise to fanaticism from time to time. So has Christianity. So has Judaism. Islam is not the destructive, backward-looking religion that some—in the West as well as the East—have tried to pretend. And the countries whose people embrace it must shun that path and look to a hopeful, positive future."

The hall rose as one. Corrine watched the president savor the moment.

"The path will be a difficult and winding one, full of hard and bitter re-treats and reversals," he continued. "We must persevere. All of us—Iraqi and American, Muslim and Christian, Jew and nonbeliever—must persevere and put aside our differences, avoid the temptation to destroy, and instead build toward the shining future that lies ahead . . ."

THE RED SEA

"We missed it," Ferguson told Thera back aboard the diving boat. "Either it's in one of those tankers we passed, or it was delivered on shore some-where."

"Maybe Birk never had it. Maybe that's why he's dead."

"Nah. Birk doesn't lie. Especially about stuff like that."

Ferguson took out his sat phone and called the Cube to talk to Corri-gan. Rather than getting the photo interpreter to look at the satellite recon-naissance again, he asked for Thomas Ciello.

Corrigan gladly handed him off.

"Thomas, this is Ferg. I need you to pull out a series of satellite photos on the area where we are, going back say a week. Fifty miles one way or an-other. First I want to know if there are any ships that have been in more or less the same place over that time or at least during the last few days. Then I need you to look at the deck of the ship today; see if you see anything differ-ent."

It took the analyst about five minutes to bring the photos up on his screen. In the meantime, Thera pointed the boat northward and set the throttle to full.

"There is a ship," Thomas told Ferguson. "There's an old tanker about five miles north of you that's been anchored there for three or four days. There's something on the shore side of it, maybe a small boat, but it's hard to see because of the angle."

"Get me a GPS location. Then give me Corrigan."

Corrigan came on the line after Thomas passed along the reading.

"I want you to call the Saudi military and the government," Ferguson told him. "Tell them Mecca's being targeted by a missile on a tanker in the Red Sea. Use the open channel to make sure it goes through. No scramble. Do it right now."

"Are you sure, Ferg?"

"Do it, Jack. Now."

As the tanker came in sight, Ferguson coiled a long nylon rope around his arm, adjusted the mask and snorkel, then slipped off the edge of the diving boat. The line unfurled until he was about ten yards aft and to the starboard side of the craft, then tugged and began pulling him forward through the water. He waited until he could see the bow of the tanker, then untangled his hand and let go of the rope.

As the diving vessel continued northward, Ferguson swam toward the ship.

Neither Thomas nor the photo interpreter who'd looked at the satellite pictures earlier had said that the small boat near the tanker was the boat that had been rented with Thatch's credit card. Ferguson was actually just guessing, though when he saw the name painted at the stern was *Jericho* he figured his guess had been pretty good.

Ferguson had put on flippers, but he was also wearing a Kevlar vest beneath his wetsuit, and though it was considered relatively light for the protection it offered, it still slowed him down. As he swam toward the boat, he heard voices floating down from the tanker. The *Jericho* itself was empty. A metal ladder for swimmers was bolted at the stern. He climbed up over it and into the vessel, then unzipped the MP5N from the waterproof pack he'd lugged on his back. He clipped a pair of the smoke grenades in the belt from the pack at his chest and took out the Beretta pistol as a backup. He stuffed two extra magazines for the MP5 in his pockets and prepared to say hello to whoever was above on the tanker.

One line fore and another aft held the *Jericho* in place against the ship. Ferguson went to the line near the bow, tugged gently, then began hauling himself up the tanker's flank.

Out on the diving boat, Thera cut her speed and turned toward the channel, making a slow, lazy turn back south. She couldn't see much on the tanker from where she was, though she did see one sailor at the side watching her.

She had to do better than that. Letting the boat drift, she went to the forward deck and peeled off her outer clothes, revealing her bathing suit.

The rope holding the *Jericho* to the tanker came off the side through an oblong opening about a foot high and two feet wide. When Ferguson reached it, he craned his head toward the ship, trying to peer through, but the metal structure prevented any view of the deck. He had to go over blind.

Ferguson took a breath, then pulled himself up over the side.

Thirty feet to his right, a stubby, aircraftlike missile sat in the middle of the deck. Two men were working on one of the wings.

Ferguson lifted his MP5N and fired a brief burst into the air.

"Hello! What we want to do is move away from there," he shouted. "Back up! Now, boys."

The men threw up their hands. Ferguson glanced toward the superstructure of the ship. There were two or three people there, and at least one other sailor near the rail on the opposite side of the ship.

"Who are you?" yelled a man.

"That's my Siren missile," said Ferguson. "I want it back."

"Where exactly do you want it?" said Ravid, emerging from a hatchway on the deck to Ferguson's right.

"Raise the pistol at me, and I'll shoot the missile," Ferguson warned, guessing—correctly—that Ravid had a weapon in the hand he had down by his side.

Ravid held the gun up but not aimed at him. "You would die for Islam?"

"I don't quite look at it that way," said Ferguson. He kept the MP5N aimed at the missile. "You really think it would be a good idea to drop a Siren missile on Mecca?"

"It's a start. I only wish it were a nuke."

"Because some crazies killed your wife and son?"

"She was a Muslim," said Ravid. "It didn't save her."

"I'm sorry. This isn't good, though. You can't just kill people, right? The people there are as innocent as your wife and kid."

"No, they're not."

"God wouldn't want you to kill innocent people."

"There is no God," said Ravid. "So you've dogged me the whole way?"

"Not the whole way. Tell me you didn't blow up Thatch."

Ravid frowned.

"Just an accident?" Ferguson took another sidestep on the deck. He'd been working to try and get close enough to Ravid to roll and knock him off balance, but it wasn't going to be easy.

"There are no accidents."

"Oh, sure there are." Ferguson took another half step. "People die in bathtubs all the time."

"You won't." He raised his gun.

"This isn't going to make you feel better."

"Oh, yes, it will." He fired, striking Ferguson in the chest and side, the bullets piercing his wetsuit.

Ferguson, protected by his bulletproof vest, pitched himself downward and fired his gun. His bullets caught Ravid across the chest as well, twisting his aim wide and sending him back in a stagger.

Revenge would be so sweet, thought Ravid. All these years he had pretended to be one of them, and now he would have his revenge.

He fired his gun and gave the order to fire the missile. But his last shots were unaimed, and the words a bare whisper. Ferguson fired another burst, striking him in the head. Ravid tried to talk but choked, his last thought dying on his tongue: So sweet, revenge.

By the time Ferg got to his feet, the others had scrambled for cover. He ran past the missile launcher to the other side, looking first for them and then examining the launcher, trying to think of how he might disable it. A thick wire ran off one side of the metal base. As he reached into his pocket for his phone to call the weapons expert, the missile ignited. Surprised by the rumble, he turned and emptied his gun into the billowing smoke, but it had no visible effect; the missile shot off the ship.

"Use the SA-7," he yelled to Thera. "The SA-7!"

Then he dove headlong into the water below, arcing down to the waves.

Thera had already sighted the Siren with the weapon even as Ferguson dove. The surface-to-air missile leapt from the launcher, trailing the thick oval of flame and smoke heading toward land.

As an early cruise missile, the Siren had one great vulnerability: it was basically a slow and lumbering airplane, and presented a fat and juicy target to even a rudimentary air-to-air missile such as the SA-7. But Thera had given the siren too much of a head start. After a few hundred yards the SA-7 stopped gaining on its target; it began to steer right, then faltered and disappeared.

"Jesus," said Thera.

Something flashed in the distance. There was a loud thunderclap, and then a bright finger of flame and a plume of black smoke rose from the shoreline.

"It blew up! It blew up on its own," said Thera as Ferguson climbed aboard the boat.

"No," said Ferguson. "Listen."

It began as a whisper in the distance, but within a few moments the throaty roar of a pair of F-15s boomed high overhead. The missile had been shot down by an Israeli interceptor.

"Helicopters," said Ferguson, pointing behind him. A pair of Sikorsky Vas'ur 2000 (improved H-53s) and a quartet of Bell Tsefa gunships roared over the water from the north. "They're going to want us to lay flat with our hands out. Nice thong, by the way. Wicked Weasel?"

THE RED SEA

Tischler was with the troops who roped down to the tanker. He took his time coming to the diving boat. By then Ferguson had been searched by several Israelis—it was obvious Thera was unarmed—and allowed to get up off the deck. Ferguson went below and retrieved a beer from the ice chest. He was drinking one when the Mossad supervisor came aboard.

"Why'd you wait so long if you knew what was going on?" Ferguson asked him.

"I didn't know what was going on. We followed you."

"You couldn't have found Ravid on your own?"

Tischler didn't answer. They could have, certainly, though they might not have thought to if the Americans hadn't raised questions. Or at least that's what Ferguson thought. Tischler wasn't the type to say.

"The operation was always to get Meles," said Ferguson. "And you tipped us off about Khazaal as a matter of courtesy. Am I right?"

Tischler shrugged.

"But Ravid wanted more. He didn't tell you, but he'd probably been looking at getting more for quite a while. Did he stumble across Seven Angels, or did they come to him?" asked Ferguson.

"I assume he ran into them in Syria. There are all sorts of crazies there."

"The sister . . . is she on the boat?"

Tischler shook his head. "I would have told you if she was. There are no Americans. Probably Ravid killed her."

"So he used Thatch's credit card, not her," said Ferguson.

"I would believe so."

Ferguson thought so as well.

"Ravid took Khazaal's jewels and used Coldwell to buy the missile, because Birk might not have sold it to him. And you just watched?" said Ferguson.

"We would not have let that happen if we had been in a position to observe it."

"You expect me to believe it?"

"You missed it as well. You were there, Ferguson. It happened under your nose."

"True enough."

"I wish that the outcome were different. He was a valuable man."

Ferguson thought about the words Tischler chose: not a *good* man but a *valuable* man.

"Listen, Tisch. I have one question that I absolutely need an answer to," said Ferguson. "You give it to me, or you give it to Parnelles. Either way, we get an answer: The suicide bomber who took out Thatch . . . coincidence?"

"Coincidence. Unfortunate," added Tischler. "It would have been useful to see who he spoke to."

"And Ravid being in Tripoli when the attempt was made on Alston . . . was he there because of the rocket fuel? I know Meles was actually the one who set that up and that there have to be more Scuds than the one Rankin got, but I want to know about that attempt on Alston. Was it a coincidence? Or did he arrange that, too?"

"He was en route to Syria. He had to make contact with Meles in Lebanon. One believes in coincidences, or one doesn't. You're free to go." Tischler turned to go back to the small boat he'd used to come over from the tanker.

Ferguson went over to the side. "Hey."

Tischler turned around.

"I'm sorry about Ravid," said Ferguson. "I heard his wife and kid died. If that had happened to us, we would have pulled him. In the old days, you guys would've, too."

"What you would do is of no concern to me, Ferguson. I told your father that a long time ago, and I tell you that now."

"You figured you could ride Ravid one more time, right? To get Meles.

Because Meles was worth it." Ferguson smiled, because he could tell from the slight twitch in Tischler's face that he had hit the mark. "Would you have felt that way if he had destroyed Mecca and every Arab in the world descended on Israel?"

"You're wrong, Ferguson. What happened here is something completely different. American extremists wanted to cause Armageddon. They attacked Mecca, and he died stopping them."

"You think anyone's going to believe that?"

"It's the truth," said Tischler flatly. "Or perhaps it wasn't crazies. Perhaps it was a CIA plot from the very beginning."

"What are you going to do with the people on the tanker?"

"They're my prisoners," said Tischler. "They're Israelis. They're coming back to Israel."

"You have charges that will hold them?"

"We have a number of charges, beginning with currency transfers that were in violation of Israeli and international banking laws."

"You recover the jewels?"

"Not yet."

"You might want to look on Birk's boat, south of here," said Ferguson. "Those people are going to stand trial, right?"

"That's not my decision."

"I could arrest them and turn them over to Saudi authorities," said Ferguson. "They were targeting Saudi territory."

"You seem to lack authority to make an arrest stick."

"I could call the Saudis."

"By the time they get here, we will be gone. In any event, this will be a matter for the courts to consider . . . if it gets that far."

"The Saudis know what their target was."

"They're my prisoners, Ferguson. You're as obnoxious as your father was and twice as stubborn."

"I take that as a great compliment."

Do you think they'll put them on trial?" Thera asked after Tischler and his men left.

"They want to keep this quiet. They'll come up with some BS charge to keep them on ice, like we would do a plea bargain in the States. There's no way they'll risk any sort of serious leak."

"That's why you told Corrigan to call the Saudis on an open line," said Thera. "You thought the Israelis were listening in. You think they set this up, and they only intervened because they thought it would come out."

"I was just hedging my bets in case I was wrong," said Ferguson. "I figured they were tracking us, but I couldn't be sure. Probably they meant to take out the ship all along, and we just happened to be in the right place at the right time. We were in the wrong place with Meles and Khazaal. Things even out."

"If you believe in coincidences," said Thera.

"Look at it as God's work, if you want. Of course, then you have to decide whose God it was."

"God doesn't work that way."

"How would you know?"

Ferguson laughed at her frown, steering the boat back toward its home port.

EPILOGUE

I saw a new heaven and a new earth: for the first heaven and the first earth were passed away; and there was no more sea.

—Revelation 21:1 (King James Version)

SUBURBAN VIRGINIA
TWO WEEKS LATER

Just in from his morning rounds visiting the shut-in members of his parish, Father Tim Casey sat down at the kitchen table in the rectory. The pain today was a little more intense than the day before, which itself was more than the day before that. But it was the Lord's pain, he told himself, and he could manage it. He would push himself until the end: hardly a struggle at all, as long as he caught his breath.

How he would tell the children that the parish council had vetoed the winter basketball program—now that was a problem he couldn't resolve. It was the sort of secular matter that had to be left to the council, truly, but it would break the kids' hearts, and a few of their parents' as well. That pain he couldn't bear; he was too weak to see others' distress.

He'd put it off another day at least.

Casey picked through the mail. Most of it was junk, advertisements and the like. There was an electric bill and a belated card on his anniversary as a priest that he recognized from a former student, a conniving no-good liar, now a rich banker in Boston, God forgive him.

There was an envelope from the morning mail addressed to him and marked PERSONAL in large red letters, with a stamp he didn't recognize and no return address. He picked it up and tore open the end as his housekeeper came in.

"Isn't it wonderful, Father? An everyday miracle."

Mrs. Perez was in the habit of exaggerating, and she could very well have been talking about a new cleanser for the kitchen floor. Father Casey gave her only part of his attention, reserving the rest for the envelope. There was an odd book in it, the sort that the priest associated with raffles.

It was only as he flipped through them that he realized they were airline tickets. And a hotel. Transfers between them. And a bus tour.

All for Jerusalem.

Nonrefundable, according to the script.

"Anonymous," said Mrs. Perez.

He'd find a way to get these exchanged, he thought. They would fund a quarter of the basketball season, if not more.

Still, if he couldn't . . .

God was tempting him. He would do the right thing. The priest felt a twinge of guilt as he looked up.

"He spoke to the treasurer himself. The money was wired into the account," said Mrs. Perez.

"What are you talking about?" he asked the housekeeper. "Who spoke to the treasurer?"

"A parishioner who wishes to remain anonymous. He funded the basketball season—the entire season—And asked for not so much as a God bless you in return. He must be a saint, father. A true saint."

Casey blinked. "Aye," he said, looking back at the tickets. "A saint and a sinner. . . . The best of us are."